BASEBALL
When the Grass Was Real

BASEBALL
WHEN THE

GRASS WAS REAL

Baseball from the Twenties

to the Forties

Told by the Men

Who Played It

DONALD HONIG

COWARD, McCANN & GEOGHEGAN, INC.
NEW YORK

SBN: 698-10660-1
Library of Congress Catalog Card Number: 74-30610

Photographs not otherwise credited are used by permission of The National
Baseball Museum and Library and the Card Memorabilia Association.

Excerpts from the chapter on Pete Reiser have appeared in *Sports Illustrated*.
Excerpts from the chapter on Wes Ferrell have appeared in *Atlantic Monthly*.

Acknowledgment is gratefully made to the Who's Who in Baseball Magazine
Company, Inc. for permission to reproduce the cover of their 1940 edition.

PRINTED IN THE UNITED STATES OF AMERICA

For Larry Ritter

CONTENTS

ILLUSTRATIONS

9

Front endpaper:
    American League Team of 1933, the first All-Star game.

Top row (left to right): Lou Gehrig, Babe Ruth, Oral Hildebrand, Connie Mack, Joe Cronin, Lefty Grove, batboy, Bill Dickey, Al Simmons, Lefty Gomez, Wes Ferrell, Jimmy Dykes, clubhouse boy. Bottom row: Eddie Collins, Tony Lazzeri, Alvin Crowder, Jimmy Foxx, Art Fletcher, Earl Averill, Ed Rommel, Ben Chapman, Rick Ferrell, Sam West, Charlie Gehringer, batboy.

Back endpaper:
    National League Team of 1933, the first All-Star game.

Top row (left to right): Gabby Hartnett, Jimmie Wilson, Frankie Frisch, Carl Hubbell, Bill Walker, Paul Waner, Woody English, Hal Schumacher, Pie Traynor, Andy Lotshaw (trainer). Second row: Wild Bill Hallahan, Dick Bartell, Bill Terry, Bill McKechnie, John McGraw (manager), Max Carey, Chick Hafey, Wally Berger, Lefty O'Doul, Chuck Klein. Bottom row: batboy, Pepper Martin, Lon Warneke, Tony Cuccinello.

ACKNOWLEDGMENTS

Inevitably a book of this nature evolves into a collaborative effort. It cannot be done without the generosity, cooperation, advice, assistance, and encouragement of others. The author would like to express his gratitude to the following:

E. R. Saltwell and Barney Sterling of the Chicago Cubs.

John F. Beegan, news librarian of the Hartford *Courant.*

Eugene Ferrara, photo sales manager of the New York *Daily News.*

Harry E. Fear, of Chicago's Executive House.

The Card Memorabilia Associates, Ltd., Amawalk, New York, for assistance in photo research.

Also, grateful acknowledgment is made to the National Baseball Museum and Library and to Jack Redding, in particular, for assistance in photo research.

In addition, the author would like to note the contributions of his editor, Bill Henderson, Joan and Theron Raines, Stanley Honig, and the steady counsel of David Markson and Larry Ritter.

Above all, the author wishes to express his heart-felt thanks to the ballplayers who so generously and good-naturedly shared their memories with him, as well as allowed him to use pictures from their personal albums.

INTRODUCTION

Anyone familiar with Lawrence Ritter's classic *The Glory of Their Times* will recognize immediately the inspiration for the present book. As were thousands of others, I was both charmed and entertained by Larry's book and, like thousands of others I'm sure, wished he would do another, telling the stories of the players who followed those whose memories he had so superbly recorded.

Most of the players interviewed in *The Glory of Their Times* were born before the turn of the century; consequently, their stories reflected a game and a society, too, that have undergone vast changes. With the passage of time and the mellowing of memories, I felt another collection of baseball reminiscences was justified, recording the stories of players of a later era. For several years I urged Larry Ritter to do another book. For various reasons, he couldn't. I persisted. Finally he said to me, "Why don't you do it?" The suggestion was too tempting to ignore.

So in the spring of 1974 I set out across the country to meet and talk with former big-league ballplayers. Predictably, there was no pattern to where they lived and what they were doing. I found them in big cities and in small towns; some were retired, some employed outside baseball, and some still maintained their affiliation with baseball in one capacity or another. Spud Chandler, Billy Herman, and Clyde Sukeforth are scouts; Pete Reiser in 1974 was coaching for the Chicago Cubs. With all of them, however, baseball was never far from their thoughts. They follow the game today, and their memories of their own playing days are bright and vivid. And their willingness to share these memories made interviewing them a pleasurable experience.

Their careers extended from the early 1920's to, in a few cases, the 1950's. The greatest emphasis, however, is on the 1930's, an era bound on the one side by Babe Ruth and Lefty Grove and by Ted Williams and Bob Feller on the other. It was the time of the Depression and the approach of a world war, both of which baseball survived, a rock of stability and diversion in times of great turmoil and upheaval.

"You never see two games alike," says Ted Lyons. Others would agree. And since it is inexcusable to discuss baseball for more than a few minutes without a flavoring of statistics, it should be noted that the men herein interviewed in aggregate played in approximately 16,000 major-league games.

And so the talk and the memories flow, of men and games, of balls thrown and hit forty years ago, of ground balls and line drives, of hits and errors recorded in the scorebooks of antiquity, of triumph and disappointment, of the joy and drama inherent in the flight of that round white ball with the red stitching.

DONALD HONIG

1

WES FERRELL

WESLEY CHEEK FERRELL
Born: February 2, 1908, Greensboro, North Carolina
Major-league career: 1927–41, Cleveland Indians, Boston Red
    Sox, Washington Senators, New York Yankees, Brooklyn
    Dodgers, Boston Braves
Lifetime record: 193 wins, 128 losses

On the mound, Wes Ferrell was tough, competitive, and a
winner. Pitching for teams that were seldom in contention, he
nevertheless won more than 20 games six times, including two
seasons of 25 victories. A hard-hitting pitcher, Ferrell left
behind a lifetime .280 batting average and a total of 38 home
runs, a record for pitchers.

Ferrell teamed with his brother Rick at Boston and Washington for several years to form one of the great brother batteries of all time.

There were seven of us boys in the family, and we learned farming before we learned anything else. My father owned 150 of
the prettiest acres in North Carolina, or anywhere else for that
matter. Driving in here, you probably saw those old bulldozers
snortin' away. Well, that's our old farm they're bulldozing. They're
fixin' to put up apartments, right smack over that beautiful land.

We raised hay, wheat, corn, and tobacco, too, of course, and we
raised that old sorghum molasses, that we cook down here in this
part of the country. And we had livestock, too, about sixty or seventy cows.

But more than anything else we raised ballplayers on that farm.
We'd go out into the fields after harvesttime and hit for hours. Just
hit an old beat-up nickel ball far as it'd go and chase it down and
throw it around. Saturday and Sunday were our big days, of course.
That's when we played team ball, around the countryside here.

You know, back in those days baseball was the only sport you could make a living at. My folks didn't quite understand how I could make any money out of playing baseball. They thought I was sort of spending my time doing nothing. But me and Rick, we worked darn hard at it; we never let up. Brother Rick had a great career: caught more games than any catcher in American League history.

Rick was my catcher when we were growing up. We were always real close. Slept together, ate together, went rabbit hunting together. We always said we were going to make baseball players of ourselves. That was what we was wanting to do. It was just a dream back then, of course, but it turned out to come true. And it happened so doggone fast, too. It seemed that one day I was thinking about my boyhood hero Babe Ruth, and then almost overnight I was standing on the mound in Cleveland trying to strike him out. Overnight isn't far from the fact either. Spring of '27 I was still living on the farm, and in the fall I pitched a few innings for Cleveland. Eighteen years old.

After high school I went to a military school in Oak Ridge, not far from home. I was playing ball, too, of course, and looking pretty good. What happened was, some college boy down here saw me pitch and told me I ought to go up to East Douglas, Massachusetts, and pitch for that club in the Blackstone Valley League. Semipro ball. So I did that. I was getting $300 a month, plus free lodging and free food. That was in the summer of '27.

I did okay up there, because I got a letter from a Cleveland scout named Bill Rapp. He asked me if I would sign with Cleveland and how much I wanted. I wrote back telling him $800 a month and $3,000 to sign a contract. What the heck . . . why not lay it on real fancy. Pretty tall figures for those days, particularly for a kid who'd only pitched a few months of semipro ball. But he wrote back and told me to go to Cleveland and see Mr. E. S. Barnard, who was president of the club at that time, that he thought I could get the money.

So here I go, still a little old country boy with a drawl thick as molasses, getting on the train and heading out to Cleveland. When I got off the train I asked somebody how to get out to League Park.

Wes Ferrell.

They put me on a streetcar, and I told the conductor where I wanted to get off. It was quite a long ride, and finally he looked around at me and said, "This is it."

I get off the streetcar, and I'm looking for a ball park. Now the only ball parks I'd ever seen were back home and in East Douglas, and what those were were playing fields with little wooden fences around them. So I'm looking around, and I don't see a ball park. Some kids were playing in the street, and I asked them where League Park was. They pointed and said, "That's it." Well, I turned around and looked up, and there's this great stone structure. Biggest thing I ever saw in my life. They called this a ball park? I couldn't believe it. Then I heard a little noise in the back of my mind: *major leagues.* The sound of those two words was like instant education.

So I took a tighter hold on my suitcase and walked through the gates of that thing, staring up and around at everything like I was walking through a palace. I went past all those great stone pillars and got up onto a concrete runway and looked way down and there at the end was a beautiful green ball field and guys playing ball on it. There was a game going on. And all of a sudden the notion of baseball got as big as all get-out in my mind. Seeing it being played down there in that setting was just beautiful. It was inspiring.

Then I remembered why I was there, and asked directions to Mr. Barnard's office. When I walked in, I saw this sharp-eyed, half-bald guy. I introduced myself and we shook hands.

"I understand you want eight hundred a month and three thousand to sign a contract," he said.

"Yes, sir," I said. I was trying to keep my eyes off of all those pictures he had on the wall: Tris Speaker, Walter Johnson, Christy Mathewson, Ty Cobb, as if I felt funny asking for all that money in front of *those* guys.

E. S. Barnard was smiling at me.

"Son," he said, "look down there." He had a window, and looking through it, you could see the ball field. "See that center fielder?" he said. "He's a regular on this ball club, and *he's* not making eight hundred dollars a month. Now I don't know if you're good enough to make this club or that we even want you. I don't know. But I'll tell you what I'll do. I'll give you three thousand to sign a contract and five hundred a month, for two years. And if after that time we retain you, we'll give you an additional three-thousand-dollar bonus."

I mulled it over, took another glance at those pictures, and said, "I'll take it."

The next spring I went to spring training with Cleveland down in New Orleans. I pitched good ball. Hell, I was as good as anybody they had on that club. Then the season opens, and I can't get in there. They've got me throwing batting practice for two weeks. Finally I got sick of it. So the next day I went into the outfield and stood there. Next thing I know they're calling me.

"Get in there and throw some batting practice."

"The hell with you," I said. "I didn't come up here for that."

That startled them. Here's this kid telling them what he's not going to do.

So they sent me to Terre Haute, which was fine with me. I won myself 20 ball games. I came back to Cleveland the next year, 1929, and I stuck. First club I got in against was the Tigers. They had a great ball club. Harry Heilmann, Bob Fothergill, Dale Alexander, Charlie Gehringer. Hitters. I was sitting in the bullpen. Just a kid, still scared at seeing so many people in the stands, still feeling more like a fan than a player.

It was a cold April day, and I've got the horse blanket covering me. I figured I'd be the last guy in the world to be in that ball game. But then our pitcher started getting in trouble, and Roger Peckinpaugh, the manager, starts waving down to the pen. Glenn Myatt, the bullpen catcher, got up.

"Hey, Wes," he says. "Come on."

"What do you mean?"

"You're first relief pitcher."

"Me?" I said. "What are you talkin' about?"

I was scared. I didn't want to get out there in front of that big crowd. But I loosened up fast, cold or no cold. They finally got our pitcher out of there, and here I go, walking in across that green grass—I don't think I even touched it. I get out to the mound and look around, and there's all those people staring at me. "Hell, boy," I told myself, "here you are. Do the job or go home."

Harry Heilmann.

First guy I faced was Harry Heilmann, standing up there with that big bat like a tin soldier, feet close together. Four times American League batting champ. I threw that ball by him so fast he never did see it. Got him out, got them all out. Two innings of shutout ball. Throwing the ball harder than I ever dreamed I could. I guess I was so excited or something, or maybe I just grew into it all of a sudden.

They made me a starter after that. Had a good year, right along. But I'm still making only $500 a month, playing out the second year of that contract. That's around $3,000 a year. We had this pitcher with us, Johnny Miljus, used to be with the Pirates. He liked me. He told me, "If you don't get ten grand next year, I'm gonna beat your brains out."

They called me up into the office in the middle of August. I'd won about 16 by that time. Billy Evans was the general manager.

"Wes," he said, "I want to sign you up for next year. We want to give you a two-thousand-dollar bonus and five hundred a month."

"Mr. Evans," I said, "I don't care anything about a bonus. I'll tell you what you do. You give me eighty-five hundred for the year and I'll take it."

"You'll never get it," he said.

Then we went on a long road trip, and every day Miljus is saying to me, "You get that ten grand next year." Then it was near the end of the season, and I'm a 20-game winner. My rookie year this is.

I was shagging flies in the outfield before a game when Mr. Evans waved me in.

"Wes," he said, "we're gonna give it to you."

"Mr. Evans," I said, "I want more money now."

Doggone if I don't get my ten grand. Plus they had to give me an additional three thousand for retaining me for two years. So I had some money. And I'll tell you where I was real lucky. Wall Street had just gone busted, so I didn't have the opportunity to make bad investments, like so many of the fellows did. If I'd made that money the year before, it would've flown right out of my pocket.

The next year I won 25, and they gave me a two-year contract calling for $15,000 and $18,000. I won 91 games my first four years; four 20-game seasons—21, 25, 22, 23. Nobody's ever done that, before or since.

What would I be making today with that record? You name it. But I'll tell you something, $18,000 was a lot of money in those days. That was during the Depression. Those were bad days. Why, I think I had more money than Mr. Bradley did—and he was the president of the ball club then. I was sure as hell driving a finer automobile than he was. I'll say things were bad. After my fourth straight 20-game season I got *cut* $7,000. The ball club couldn't help themselves; they were barely surviving.

Being a big league star was exciting. I was going to the best hotels in the biggest cities and meeting the most famous people. You were always a star in somebody's eye; you were popular; you were known. You never waited on a line; you never wanted for service, wherever you went. You never looked for that sort of thing; it just naturally came your way. People *want* to do it. Makes them feel good, I guess.

It builds your pride; at least it did mine. I wanted to look better, to dress better, to be a better guy. You stop to think that here are people who have driven maybe 300 miles to see you pitch a ball game, and then they hang around and want your autograph. It's very flattering. And if you're lucky and take it in the right spirit, it makes you a better person.

You know, off the field I was shy. I'd just come up from the farm and wasn't used to seeing lots of people and surely wasn't used to having crowds cheering me and looking for my autograph. It was a struggle for me because I didn't want to seem conceited.

Now on the field I was different. I had to be. I gave the impression that I was mean. After all, this was my job, my livelihood. So I put an act on. I'd look wild warming up. I'd stomp and storm around out there like a bear cat, fight my way through a ball game, fight like the devil, do anything to win. And I got that reputation for being temperamental and mean, and it stuck, even with people who should have known better. I'll tell you something that struck me as so damned funny. In 1933 we had the first All-Star game, in Chicago. Connie Mack was managing the American League team, and he always liked me. Well, we were having our meeting at the hotel before going out to the ball park. Connie is telling us all what to do.

"Lefty Gomez," he says, "you're starting. Ruth, you're playing right field. Gehringer, you're playing second base. Gehrig, you're on first. Simmons, you're in center field." And so on, right down the lineup. All these great stars. Then he says, "Wes Ferrell."

"Yes, Mr. Mack?" I said.

"I want you to be in the bullpen for the first six innings. *Will that be all right with you?*"

Well, that was the funniest thing I ever heard. Here he is, telling all these great stars what to do and then asking me if that was all right with me. I guess Connie thought I was the meanest man in the world.

Of course the game was tougher then, in my opinion. When I first came up, just a kid, they'd tell me to throw at a hitter.

"What do you mean, 'throw at him'?" I asked.

"Throw at his head," they said.

"I'll kill him," I said.

"That's an order, Ferrell. You throw at him."

I'm in Philadelphia one time, and a fellow named Hale is playing third base for Connie Mack's club. Peckinpaugh tells me I've got to throw at Hale. So I powdered one at him, and his feet went up and his head went down. Damn near took the button off his cap. When he got up, he was white as a sheet. They took him out of the ball game—which is what Peckinpaugh wanted.

That's when they had the art of hitting, in those days. There were so many good hitters you just had to go out there and take command. A team had a string of guys in the lineup hitting .320, .330, .340. Like facing machine-gun fire. When a guy hit a home run in those days, the next two hitters went down. They knew it was coming. Once, in a game in Detroit, somebody hit a home run off of me, and up comes Fothergill. A real hitter. I lowered the boom on him, putting it right over his head. He gets up, dusts himself off, and I get him out. Next fellow comes up—I forget his name—and lies down flat on his back in the batter's box.

"Hey, Wes," he yells, "I'm already down. You don't have to throw at me."

I got to laughing so hard I just laid one right in there, and damn if he doesn't knock it back through my legs for a base hit.

I never threw at Ruth, though. You just didn't want to do that. He was baseball. What was it like pitching to him? Like looking into a lion's jaw, that's what. Hell, man, you're pitching to a *legend!* And you knew, too, that if he hits a home run, he's gonna get the cheers, and if he strikes out, he's still gonna get the cheers. You were *nothing* out there when Ruth came up.

You look around, and your infielders are way back and your outfielders have just about left town, they're so far back. And here you are, 60 feet away from him. You got great encouragement from your infielders, too. The first baseman says pitch him outside; the third baseman says pitch him inside. They're worried about having their legs cut off. "Take it easy, boys," I told them. "I'm closer to him than you are, and I'm not worryin'." The hell I wasn't. Ruth could swivel your head with a line drive.

But I always had pretty good luck with Babe. He was a guess hitter, you know. I'd watch that right leg; it told me what he was looking for. Sometimes he'd have his back almost to the pitcher, with that right leg pulled around toward the catcher. That's when he was looking for curves or slow stuff. When he was looking for a

Babe Ruth:
"He was baseball."

fastball, he'd place that right leg differently. So I'd pitch accord-
ingly to him. Ruth hit only three home runs off me in the seven
years I pitched to him. And he never beat me a ball game.

After the Babe died, I went to an old-timers' game in New York.
After the game we all went to Toots Shor's restaurant for the shin-
dig. Mrs. Ruth was there. I'd never met her, so I went up and
introduced myself.

"You're Wes Ferrell?" she said.

"That's right," I said.

"Babe said a lot of things about you."

"What do you mean?" I asked.

"He'd come home and say how tough it was to get a base hit off of you. It upset him quite a bit."

Well, that flattered me more than anything in the world.

I had my troubles with Roger Peckinpaugh, you know. But I always worked hard for him, same as any manager I ever pitched for. Starting, relieving, pinch-hitting; I was always on call, happy to do anything to help out the ball club. Hurts my arm today just to think about it.

There was this game against the Athletics, in 1931. It was supposed to be a home game for the Athletics, but there was no Sunday ball in Philadelphia at that time, so we caught the sleeper out of Philly on Saturday and went back to Cleveland. Connie Mack figured there was no sense bringing the whole team for just the one game, and he left some of his ballplayers home. So he was short of pitchers.

I forget who started for the A's, but we got him out of there in the first inning. Eddie Rommel came in and pitched the rest of the game—seventeen innings. We got about 30 hits off him. Johnny Burnett, our shortstop, set a record that game: he got 9 hits. Alva Bradley, the Cleveland owner, said later it was the most exciting ball game he ever saw. Well, I didn't think it was so damned exciting.

I relieved Willis Hudlin in the seventh and pitched right on into the eighteenth inning before they beat me with a bad-hop base hit. Jimmie Foxx got a single, and then Eric McNair hit a line drive to left that took a crazy hop over Joe Vosmik's head. Jimmie came tearing around, and I'm beat. I should've won it in the ninth, you know, but Eddie Morgan made an error at first on the easiest ground ball you ever saw and that tied it.

Now, that was just a little relief stint, those eleven innings. A few days later I'm taking my *regular* turn, against the Yankees in New York. I go out there, and I just don't have anything on the ball. They beat me. I'm sitting in the clubhouse after the game, and Peckin-

Roger Peckinpaugh: "The guy hardly ever spoke to me."

paugh comes over and says, "Hey, why didn't you bear down out there?"

"What the hell are you talking about?" I said. I was steamin'. "I've been winning twenty games a year for you and pitching out of turn whenever you needed me, and you ask me why I wasn't bearing down? I *always* bear down. I just didn't have anything to bear down *with* today."

Well, that didn't sit too good with him. Then we go up to Boston, and I start another ball game. They get one or two runs off me in the second inning, and he wants to take me out.

"Hell," I said. "I ain't coming out. I just got in here."

Finally I had to leave, and the next thing I know I'm suspended.

They called it insubordination or something like that. I went back to Cleveland and sat around doing nothing for fourteen days, in the middle of one of my finest years. What a waste of time.

Couldn't get along with Peckinpaugh, no matter what. The guy hardly ever spoke to me. He got fired in 1933, and Walter Johnson came over to manage. Here was a fine guy, nice as could be. Religious type of person, a real gentleman. He had some drawbacks as a manager, though. Had trouble expressing himself. He'd hold a meeting, and you'd hear him say, "Now, dadgummit, confound it, I want you boys, doggonnit, to get out there and get 'em." That's how he'd tell you. Never profane, though. A very kind person. Never had any trouble with his ballplayers. Not even with Fiery Wes Ferrell. Fiery Wes Ferrell. Boy, I've got to laugh at that. I guess I've still got the reputation, but reputations aren't always justified. Here, listen to this. I was with the Red Sox and pitching a game in Yankee Stadium against Monte Pearson. I had them beat going into about the fifth or sixth inning. The Yankees had two men on and DiMaggio is up. I walked over to Eric McNair, who's playing shortstop. Cronin, who was the manager and the regular shortstop, wasn't playing that day. I forget why.

I tell McNair, "Now, I'm gonna throw him a slider and try to make him hit it to you."

I go back to the mound and make my pitch, get it right where I want, and doggone if Joe doesn't hit it right straight to McNair. But the ball was hit right off the end of the bat and had such spin on it that when it hit the ground, it got away from McNair. Two runs scored. I figured I should have been out of the inning, and I got mad. Then a couple base hits followed on top of that.

I look over at Cronin. He's standing up in the dugout with his hands in the air. I thought he wanted to take me out. I look around, and my infielders are standing around with their hands on their hips, looking at the ground. I figured I'm gone, and I walked off the mound. In those days you had to go through the Yankee dugout to get to the clubhouse. I went right past brother Rick—he was with the Red Sox too then—and he didn't say anything to me. I was told later that Cronin started to yell at me not to leave, but I didn't hear anything. I thought I was out.

Next thing I know I'm sitting in my hotel room, and somebody calls me on the telephone to tell me I'm suspended, fined $1,000, and a lot of stuff like that. Boy, I nearly hit the ceiling! I couldn't believe what I was hearing. I would *never* walk out of a ball game. Ask Peckinpaugh—he needed a lasso to get me out of the game that other time.

They had a big meeting that night, and I told Cronin that it was all a misunderstanding, that he knew my record, how hard I worked, how willingly, and that I was the last one in the world to run out on a ball club.

Well, nobody said much. They send me back to Boston and I find the newspapers filled with the story: "Wes Ferrell Suspended. Walks Out of Ball Game." A lot of crap like that. Two days later I

Rick and Wes: "Brother or no brother, he ought to be in the Hall of Fame."

was out pitching again, in my regular turn. Wasn't fined, wasn't suspended. It was all a misunderstanding and was soon forgotten by all concerned. But that's how you get a reputation as being this or that sort of fellow.

Like I say, Rick was there with me on the Red Sox. When I got traded over to Boston in 1934, he was already there. We got along real fine. Usually thought alike. Brother or no brother, he was a great catcher and ought to be in the Hall of Fame. He was a real classy receiver. You never saw him lunge for the ball; he never took a strike away from you. He'd get more strikes for a pitcher than anybody I ever saw, because he made catching look easy.

Well . . . I say we got along real fine, and we did . . . but I'll always remember a game I was pitching against the Detroit Tigers. Brother Rick is giving me the signs, the little old one-two-three for fastball, curve, straight change-up. I kept shaking him off; I wanted to throw my change-up curve. Finally he got tired of squatting there and being shaken off, and he got up and walked around in front of the batter.

"Throw any damn thing you please," he said. "You can't fool me no way. I know you well enough."

Boy, that made me mad! That's all I wanted to know. I wanted to powder that ball by him so fast he wouldn't see it. "A great star like me?" I says to myself. Me winning all those games, and he thinks he's going to catch me without signs? I kicked the mound around a little bit, pulled my cap down tight on my head. Then I fired him a curveball—one of the best I'd ever thrown, I swear—and he just reached down across his body and caught it backhanded with that mitt of his. Showboating. I'd throw him my best fastballs and he'd catch them soft—you know, wouldn't let it pop.

Well, we went through the whole ball game that way. Just a-stormin', and a-throwin', and a-powderin' that ball. And here's Cronin, standing out at shortstop, wondering what in the world's going on up there—he's not seeing any signs!

I pitched a two-hitter. Beat the Tigers 3–0. One of my finest games. I was so happy I was tickled to death. After it's over, I go into the clubhouse and I'm sitting there. Everybody's coming over to shake my hand on the game. And there's brother Rick, sitting two stools away. He won't look at me. I keep glancing over, but he won't look. We're pulling our socks and our uniforms off. Finally I glance around again, and now he's looking at me.

"Well," he says, "you pitched a pretty good ball game. But damn you, if you'd listened to me, you'd of pitched a *no*-hitter!"

I'd already had a no-hitter, you know, in 1931, against the St. Louis Browns. And guess who almost beat me out of it? That's right. Brother Rick. He came up in the late innings and hit one to Bill Hunnefield at short. Hunnefield came up with it and threw a little high, and they called it an error. And I'll tell you, I never saw anybody run harder than Rick did going down that line—and that's the way it's supposed to be.

I held out the year I was traded to Boston. Missed most of spring training. I was just sitting tight, right down here on the farm. Rick told me to keep quiet, not make any noise, that he'd heard the Red Sox were trying to get me. I was keeping myself in shape as best I could, running, throwing.

Now, the Lucky Strike tobacco people over here in Reidsville had a ball club, and they wanted me to come out and pitch for them against some amateur club from Virginia. They said they'd give me $100. Well, I thought this was great. I'd get the chance to pitch a game, give myself a workout against a bunch of humpty-dumpties and make $100 in the bargain.

So I went over to Reidsville. A real country ball park. I had to dress in the boiler room of a factory, leaving my clothes in this filthy place that was dusty and smelly and full of cobwebs, and then go on out to the ball park. It was no Yankee Stadium, I can tell you. The fence was half broken down; the little bleacher section they had was rickety. But a lot of people showed. They came from miles around, some of them in horse and buggies. Come to see the great Wes Ferrell pitch. The man who had pitched to Ruth and Gehrig and Foxx and Simmons; come to see him dazzle a collection of country boys. They came crowding around me while I'm warming up, talking to me the whole time. "Hi ya, Wes." "How's it look, Wes?" And I'm smiling and nodding and saluting them off of the peak of my cap and telling them that it looks just fine.

Then the game starts. The first guy comes up. Left-handed hitter.

Wearing overalls and tennis shoes and a faded little cap. And smok-ing a cigarette! I get two strikes on him. He steps out and flips away the cigarette. Oh, I'm thinking, what a smooth way to earn $100. I wind up and give him my high hard one . . . and he hits it over the center-field fence. Well, that was the pattern. The great Wes Ferrell never pitched harder in his life, and those guys killed me. Line drives all over the place. I finished out the game in the outfield. Never been so embarrassed in my life.

After the game they paid me off in nickels and dimes and quarters and dollar bills. I wanted to turn my back when I took it, I was so embarrassed. I went back to the boiler room and dressed, and soon after that I came up with the biggest case of crabs you ever heard of, from leaving my clothes in that damn filthy boiler room. By God, what a day!

Of course, people always ask me who was the greatest hitter I ever faced. They expect I would say Gehrig or Ruth or Simmons or Foxx. But I don't. I say Gehringer. Charlie Gehringer was the toughest hitter I ever faced. The reason I say this is because he'd never offer to hit the first pitch. You could just lob it in there, throw it right down the middle of the plate, and he'd just stand there and follow it into the catcher's mitt. Sometimes he'd spot you *two* strikes. And you say to yourself, "Well, as good a pitcher as I am, I'm gonna get him out." But you couldn't do it. He'd hit that ball. And he'd beat you ball games. Yes, he would.

You threw it down the middle to Ruth, he'd knock you off the mound. Gehrig too, and Foxx and Simmons and Greenberg and Di-Maggio. They'd kill you, those fellows. You had to start pitching hard to them, first pitch. Why did Gehringer do that? I don't know. I never asked him.

I didn't have too much trouble with Simmons. He was a great hit-ter, though. Believe that. Foxx was another great one. I'd strike him out three times, and then he'd hit a home run so far out of Shibe Park that you just had to stand there and admire it. A man hit a ball that far? No way you could get mad at him. You had to admire it. Foxx was a wonderful guy, too. Always smiling, always looking to have a good time. Loved his golf, like so many ballplayers. In fact, he ran his own golf course down in St. Petersburg for a while.

Jimmie Foxx:
"He loved his golf."

Hey, all this talk about pitching, don't forget I was a pretty fair hitter, too. I hit nine home runs in 1931, and that's still a record for pitchers. In 1933, when Vosmik broke his wrist, and my arm was a little sore, they put me in the outfield, and I hit close to .300.

One time I was pitching against Hod Lisenbee of the Athletics. He had me beat 1–0 going into the eighth inning and I hit a home run to tie it. Then in the thirteenth inning I hit another home run to beat him, 2–1.

Another time, when I was with the Red Sox, Grove was pitching and he was getting beat by one run going into the last of the ninth. Now, you know Lefty; he was a great competitor and a hard loser. A *very* hard loser. He's sure he's lost his ball game and is madder'n hell over it. He goes into the clubhouse. We get a man on base, and Cronin sends me up to hit. Tommy Bridges is the pitcher. Well, I hit the first pitch I see and knock it over the left field fence, and we win the ball game.

So we all rush into the clubhouse, laughing and hollering, the way you do after a game like that. And here's Lefty, sitting there, still thinking he's lost his game. When he saw all the carrying-on, I tell you, the smoke started coming out of his ears.

"I don't see what's so funny," he says. "A man loses a ball game, and you're all carrying on."

Then somebody says, "Hell, Lefty, we won it. Wes hit a home run for you."

Well, I was sitting across the clubhouse from him, pulling my uniform off, and I notice he's staring at me, with just a trace of smile at the corners of his mouth. Just staring at me. He doesn't say anything. I give him a big grin and pull my sweat shirt up over my head. Then I hear him say, "Hey, Wes." I look over and he's rolling a bottle of wine across to me—he'd keep a bottle of one thing or another stashed up in his locker. So here it comes, rolling and bumping along the clubhouse floor. I picked it up and thanked him and put it in my locker. At the end of the season I brought it back to Carolina with me and let it sit up on the mantel. It sat up there for years and years. Every time I looked at it I thought of Old Left. He rolled it over to me.

He was my idol. Lefty Grove. Fastest pitcher I ever saw. The greatest. Why, I wasn't good enough to carry his glove across the field. Dizzy Dean was great, and so was Koufax. And Bob Feller was fast, of course. Bob had spectacular stuff. Didn't have to fool around on the corners; just get it over the plate. But Grove was faster. He'd throw that ball in there, and you'd wonder where it went to. It would just *zing!* and disappear. You can believe he was that fast because that's all he threw. He'd just keep fogging them in there. He didn't start throwing breaking stuff until late in his career.

I got to know Lefty when we were both with the Red Sox, from '34 to '37. He was just about the finest friend I ever had.

I'll give you another good pitcher—Bobo Newsom. And what a character he was! One time I started walking toward him during a game and everybody thought we were going to fight, but it wasn't that at all. You see, what happened was, when I was warming up before the game Bobo came walking by. He'd finished his warm-ups.

"Hey, Wes," he says, "the one that gives up the first hit to the other has got to come over and shake his hand." I don't know how he thought these things up.

"That's okay with me," I said. I figured I was a better hitter than he was, so there was no problem.

We went along until about the sixth inning, and neither of us has got a hit off of the other. Then Newsom comes up and the SOB ties into one and hits it up against the left-field stands for a double. The fans are all yelling and cheering, and I'm standing out on the mound, knowing what I've got to do. I didn't know whether to cuss or laugh. Finally I turn around and here I go, walking toward second base. The umpires thought I was going to fight, and they started coming over. I walked up to Bobo, and he's grinning a mile across his face, and I start laughing too, couldn't help myself.

"What are you doing, Ferrell?" the umpire asks.

"I've got to shake this SOB's hand," I said. "We made a deal."

I shook hands with old Bobo and turned around and walked back to the mound. The fans went crazy over it; they didn't know what it was all about, but they loved it.

Who was the toughest team to pitch against? Well, I'll tell you how to figure that. You've got to look at their pitching staff. If I'm pitching against the Yankees, it's not Ruth or Gehrig or DiMaggio I'm worrying about, because I know I can get those boys out often enough to win. It's Gomez, say, or Ruffing I've got to worry about— because they can shut my club out. Same with the A's. It's not Foxx or Simmons, great as they were—it's Grove or Earnshaw that's going to beat me. That's the way you look at it.

I'm with Washington in 1938, winning 13 and losing 8, and Clark Griffith turns me loose. I was getting a big salary, and I guess he figured he'd save some money. Joe McCarthy called me the next day and asked me to join the Yankees, which naturally I was happy to do. They had a great ball club, with the pennant just about sewed up. McCarthy always liked me. Some years before, when I was still with Cleveland, I'd made some favorable comments on his ability to handle his pitching staff, and Joe never forgot that.

I thought McCarthy was a great manager. Still do. He was all business running his ball club, very professional. You didn't see guys running around all night and then kicking your game away the next day, which experience I'd had.

When I got up to the stadium, he called me into his office.

Lou Gehrig: "The fellows would laugh and kid him. 'Hey, Lou, you're getting old.' That sort of thing. Nobody knew the truth."

"We've got one rule around here," he said. "We don't second-guess the manager."

And he meant it. He was very professional. You got up there, you saw why the Yankees were winning all those pennants. They were all business, all baseball.

You know what burned up old Griffith? When he let me go he had to give me ten days' pay. And then I sign up with the Yankees right away. So I'm getting paid double. Well, we went down to Washington a few days later, and McCarthy starts me. I beat them in eleven innings—and Griffith is still paying me out. Oh, that did him to a turn, paying money to the guy who's beating him.

You know, something happened in that game. I thought it was curious at the time, though now I can understand it. We should've won the game in nine innings, but Gehrig made a bad play on a ground ball and let the tying run in. Instead of going to the plate and throwing the man out, he went the easy way, to first base. It was the kind of play you'd never expect him to make. Nobody knew at the time, of course, that Gehrig was dying. All we knew was that he wasn't swinging the bat the way he could nor running the way he could.

The next year, in spring training, it got worse. I was in the clubhouse with him one day down in St. Petersburg. The rest of the team was out on the field. Lou got up on the bench to look out the window to see what was going on on the field. It was some little effort for him to do that, and he wasn't too steady. All of a sudden he fell over, right down to the floor. Just like that. He fell hard, too, and lay there for a second, frowning, like he couldn't understand what was happening.

"You hurt yourself, Lou?" the trainer asked.

"No, I'm okay," he said. He got up and didn't say anything more about it. I suppose he didn't know what was wrong, any more than the rest of us. He'd hit a ball into right-center, a sure double, and run and run as hard as he could—he *always* hustled—and get thrown out by a mile. In workouts you'd see him straining and huffing and puffing, running as hard as he could, and not getting anywhere. The fellows would laugh and kid him. "Hey, Lou, you're getting old." That sort of thing. Nobody knew the truth.

I remember one time out on the golf course, it was during the St. Petersburg Open. A lot of us went out to watch the pros. I was following the crowd, and I noticed Lou, walking all by himself along the edge of the woods. I watched him for a while and noticed something peculiar. Instead of wearing cleats, which normally he would have worn for walking across the grass, he was wearing tennis sneakers and was *sliding* his feet as he went along, instead of picking them up and putting them down. Looking back now, I realize why. His muscles were so deteriorated that just the effort of lifting his feet a few inches to walk had already become too much. God, it was sad to see—Lou Gehrig having to slide his feet along the grass to move himself.

Yep, there's a lot of things that stay with you as the years pile up. It's all been so long ago now that I find it hard to believe I ever did it, that I was ever there. For a while after you leave the game, you dream about it a lot. You dream you're going to pitch and that you can't get your uniform on. You dream you can't get to the park, that you've lost your way. Crazy dreams, huh? But maybe not so crazy after all.

All of a sudden you're out of the big time, out of reach of all the glory you had. You had everything, all the time. I met so many fine people, all the celebrities. Musicians, singers, actors, politicians. Was even made a Kentucky colonel. It's great when somebody comes along and tells you they saw you pitch, how good they thought you were, how much they enjoyed it. But little by little it dwindles down, until you're back where you started.

Like I said, we sold off the old farm a couple of years ago to some developers, and they're bustin' and churnin' that earth now. Putting up apartments on the fields and pastures where me and Rick and all the rest of us used to play ball.

But still I've got those memories. I played against a lot of great stars. You name 'em. Ruth, Gehrig, Greenberg, Gehringer, Simmons, Foxx, Grove, DiMaggio, Cochrane, Feller. I saw them all. And they saw me. You bet they did.

Wes Ferrell.

CHARLES L. GEHRINGER
SECOND BASEMAN WITH DETROIT A.L. FROM
1925 THROUGH 1941 AND COACH IN 1942.
COMPILED LIFETIME BATTING AVERAGE
OF .321. IN 2323 GAMES, COLLECTED 2839
HITS. NAMED MOST VALUABLE PLAYER IN
A.L. IN 1937. BATTED .321 IN WORLD SERIES
COMPETITION AND HAD A .500 AVERAGE
FOR SIX ALL-STAR GAMES.

2

CHARLIE GEHRINGER

This was back in 1923. Bobby Veach, who was in the Tiger outfield with Cobb and Heilmann in those days, used to come out to Fowlerville to hunt. Fowlerville was where I lived, not all that far from Detroit. One of Veach's hunting companions was a local man, a fellow who was a great baseball fan. He'd seen me play quite a bit. He suggested that Bobby take me down to Detroit for a tryout because he felt that I had a future in baseball. Veach had never seen me play, but he took this man's word for it, and it was through Veach that it was arranged.

So I went to the Tigers' ball park for a tryout. Was I nervous? What do you think? Walking out onto that ball field was something I'd never even dared to dream of. I thought I might get there someday by working my way up through the minors, but *suddenly* to be there was just unbelievable. And of course Ty Cobb was the manager, and to be on the same field with him was just overwhelming for a kid. A frightening experience.

They were all out there, Cobb, Heilmann, the whole bunch. I hit with the scrubs. Cobb was watching me, but I couldn't believe he was paying attention. After I hit, I went into the outfield. I just stood around, still nervous, maybe a little embarrassed about being there.

Then Cobb was calling me in. I figured he wanted me to get out of the way. But when I came in, he said, "Get in there and hit again."

By this time the regulars were taking batting practice, and they didn't like the idea of me getting in with them. They didn't like that one bit. But it was by Cobb's orders. I stepped in and started hitting again. This time Cobb wouldn't take his eyes off me; I could *feel* him staring at me. Then they were all watching me—Heilmann, Manush, Veach, the whole gang. I guess they liked what they saw

Ty Cobb: "I could feel him staring at me."

because they stopped grumbling about me being in there. It was eerie. The only sound in that big, empty ball park was me standing there hitting line drives, with the whole Tiger ball club watching me.

Then Cobb sent me out to second base, and I started picking up grounders. I guess I was always pretty good with the glove. It came to me quite naturally. I never thought much about what I was doing. I just went and picked them up.

What happened next really amazed me. Cobb left the field and in full uniform, spikes and all, went up to Mr. Navin's office—he owned the ball club—and told Mr. Navin to come down to the field and watch me.

I worked out that whole week, and then they signed me. No, no bonus. But I did get a lot of tips on the stock market from Cobb, which didn't do me any good; I didn't have the money to invest.

Sure I wanted to play for the Tigers. They were my team. I used to cut all the pictures of Detroit players out of the paper and keep a scrapbook, and then sit and stare at them. I guess I couldn't help but to be a Tiger fan; I was born so close to Detroit.

I was born on a farm in Michigan, near Lansing. The nearest town was Fowlerville, where I went to school. It was general farming. We had a lot of dairy cattle, raised practically all the crops. I had an older brother who ran all the equipment, and I had to do the hard work, like shocking the wheat and picking up the corn and hoeing the weeds and working in the garden, and things like that. I think that's what gave me the idea of turning to something that might be easier, where at least the hours might be shorter.

I guess I started playing ball as soon as I was able to handle a bat, probably when I was about seven years old. When I was a kid, baseball was about the only sport you had in the country. And there was no television in those days, fewer ways to amuse yourself. So you played baseball.

I wasn't always an infielder. I pitched all through high school. I had a big roundhouse curve and good control, and it got me through the high school competition. But then I pitched a couple of semipro ball games, and that roundhouse wasn't fooling too many guys, and I decided I'd better try something else. So I switched to second base, though I played third when I attended the University of Michigan for two semesters.

Cobb took me under his wing right away. He kept telling me I was going to be tremendous. He really took care of me the first year or two. Went out of his way to teach me, and he taught me an awful lot. He more or less told me how to hit, where to stand in the batter's box against certain pitchers, how to spray hit—which I got to be able to do pretty well.

He always said that after Eddie Collins I was the best second baseman he ever saw. That was nice to hear, coming from a man who knew the game as well as Cobb did and who was kind of sparing with his compliments. So I guess he was satisfied with the way I took his instructions.

But he was tough to play for. Very demanding. He was so great himself that he couldn't understand why if he told players how to do certain things, they couldn't do it as well as he did. He just didn't seem to realize that it wasn't possible, and he got very frustrated with a lot of guys. But if you had the talent, then he could really help you. I think he made a fine hitter out of Manush, who pretty much followed Cobb's advice and, of course, had the talent to take advantage of it.

One of the things he always told me was, "Now, if you go to bat four times in a game and don't get a hit, work harder on that fifth time. Try not to get out of a game without a hit." That's one of the things he tried to impress upon me: Never give up. No matter what the score is, no matter what the situation. Always try harder and harder to get that base hit. That's what he preached, and that's what he practiced. Every time at bat for him was a crusade, and that's why he's off in a circle by himself.

He taught himself to hate those pitchers. It was a real vendetta between him and them. Of course, while he's got all those records today, I think it took a lot out of him as far as being a human being was concerned. You can't turn that kind of competitive drive on and off. He was the same off the field as he was on; he was always fighting with somebody. He was a holy terror.

I became a regular with the Tigers in 1926. That was when I really got to know Cobb. He got tough. Oh, he got tough with me. I was supposed to start the season in '26, but somehow in spring training I said something, or didn't say something, that provoked him and he took me out of the lineup about a week before we came home, and I never got to start. He never explained it to me, and nobody else ever did. He wouldn't even talk to me. The only way I managed to get into the lineup was because our second baseman, Frank O'Rourke, got the measles. So Cobb had no other choice but to put me in. But even then he wouldn't tell me to bunt or to hit or to do this or do that. He'd tell the coaches to tell me what to do.

To this day I don't know why he got sore at me. The only thing I can think of is something that happened in spring training. You know, those games get so dull, and Cobb was always after you to shake it up out there, make a little noise. He said that to me one time when I was coming in off the field, and I said to him, "Well, I'm making most of the noise out there. I'm making more noise than anybody else." That might have done it. I can't remember anything else I ever said or did that might have turned him sour. He was awfully touchy. I don't think anybody really got along with him. Of course, he'd never pick on Heilmann, say; Heilmann was too big a star. He'd pick on guys he knew couldn't battle back with him.

I remember one time, in St. Louis, he kept me after school, like a teacher would. Just kept me sitting in the clubhouse for an hour after everybody had left the ball park. This was because I'd let Ken Williams, who Cobb disliked very much, beat out a bunt. Now Ken Williams was a very powerful hitter. How are you going to play him up on the grass so he can't beat out a bunt? He'll knock your teeth out. I thought that was ridiculous. But he kept me sitting there for an hour.

He sure was a peculiar man.

Cobb left during the '26 season, and George Moriarty took over. He was a former ballplayer and had been an umpire too. His main forte was stealing bases, and home plate in particular. He wrote a book once called *Don't Die on Third.* He had everybody stealing home, whether you could run or not. He'd even get you in a hotel lobby and demonstrate how it should be done. He would show you how to get a lead. Then he'd start jockeying around between the potted palms and the furniture, and people would look at him like he'd gone balmy. I'll bet we set a record that year for having guys thrown out trying to steal home.

We generally had a heavy-hitting ball club over the years I was with the Tigers. We had guys like Heilmann, Manush, Greenberg, Rudy York, Pete Fox, Gerald Walker, Goose Goslin, Bob Fothergill. Fothergill was a likable character. He was a fun-loving fellow, always had a weight problem. Navin was always raking him over the coals about it. There was a story that I heard about Fothergill coming into Navin's office one winter's day to talk contract. Fothergill as usual was way overweight, and to conceal it, he came to the office wearing this big, heavy overcoat. Navin spotted him in the outer office and sensed what Bob was up to. So Navin went into his office, turned the heat way up, and then told Fothergill to come in.

Bob was anxious to get in and out of there as quickly as he could. But Navin sat back and began talking about one thing and another, and the sweat began pouring off of poor Fothergill.

"Why don't you take that coat off, Bob?" Navin asked. "Make yourself comfortable."

"No, it's okay," Fothergill said. "I'm comfortable."

Well, Navin just kept him there, talking, and Fothergill must have felt like he was in a steam bath. But he wouldn't take that coat off.

Bob Fothergill.

Finally Bob said, "Let's get this over with." I don't know what he signed for that time, but I'm sure it wasn't for the figure he had in mind, he was so anxious to get out of there.

Walter Johnson was near the end of his career when I came into the league, but he could still throw hard. Del Baker, our coach, had seen Johnson in his prime, and said he threw the ball so hard you could hear it. Of course, in those days they didn't toss a ball out of the game as quickly as they do today, so if it had a little rough spot on it I imagine it did whir.

I think Grove was the fastest I ever saw, but guys who had hit against them both said Johnson was still faster. It's hard to believe that anyone could throw harder than Lefty Grove, though. Most of the time the right-handed batters couldn't pull him. I could always pull Feller—of course, he was right-handed—but I could never pull Grove until the tail end of his career. I'd go up there telling myself I was going to swing the minute he let it go. I'd do that and still hit a ground ball to the third baseman. And as good a pull hitter as Heilmann was, he'd always hit Grove to right field.

Grove's fastball wasn't all that alive. It carried a little but never did anything tricky. But it was so fast that by the time you'd made up your mind whether it was going to be a strike or a ball, it just wasn't there anymore. A lot of times he'd come in to relieve when it was near dark, and then it was hopeless.

Does Grove say I used to give him trouble? Well, that's hard for me to believe. Though once I did hit two home runs in succession off him. Just guessed right, I suppose. No, he didn't knock me down the next time. But I'll tell you, he once hit me as hard as I've ever been hit. This was when I'd first come in the league, one of the first few times I faced him. Everybody told me, "One thing you don't have to worry about—he's never wild inside." Well, he let this one get away and got me right on the elbow. I thought the ball stuck there, that's how hard it came in. I had to leave the game, and that was the only time I ever saw Mr. Navin come into the clubhouse. He thought for sure that my arm was broken.

Wes Ferrell was another topflight pitcher in those days, and a good hitter, too. He won a lot of his own games with his bat. I think both of those Ferrell boys deserve some recognition. Rick was a fine catcher, and he probably hit better than some of the guys you've got in the Hall of Fame. You could do worse than put both those boys in the Hall of Fame.

Wes was one of your great competitors. He just hated to lose. I remember one time we were in Washington, playing the Senators. Ferrell had us beat by about 6–0 in the fourth inning, and he's going great guns. Then it started to rain. The skies turned black, and I tell you it just poured. Naturally the game was held up. I was sitting in the dugout, looking across at Wes, and I could almost *see* what he was thinking: God, am I going to lose this easy victory? After about fifteen minutes the rain stopped and the sun came out, and even before they could get the canvas off the field, there's Wes out there loosening up. He's determined to get that one more inning in to make it an official game.

I happened to be the first man he faced after the delay, and I hit a home run. That started it off. We began hitting and didn't stop until we'd tied the score. Bucky Harris was managing Washington then, and for some reason he left Wes in. Well, the next inning we get two more runs. That finished Wes. He went over to the bench, sat down, threw his glove disgustedly to the dugout floor, clamped down on it

Charlie Gehringer.

with his spikes and gritted his teeth and reached over and just started pulling that glove all to pieces, tearing up the fingers, the webbing, the stuffing, the whole thing.

And you know, there was an aftermath to that game. Mr. Briggs, who was then owner of the team, was listening to the game on the radio, and he was so happy with the way we won that game, coming from behind and all, that he bought everybody a tailor-made suit of clothes—which was quite a thing to do for twenty-five men.

One day I read in the paper about this kid the Indians had, named Bob Feller. He'd pitched three innings in an exhibition game against the Cardinals and struck out eight men. On our next trip to Cleveland Earl Averill said to me, "Boy, wait till you see this kid we've got. He'll remind you you're in the big leagues."

"I read about him," I said. "He must be pretty good, huh?"

"No," Averill said. "He's better than that. In fact, he's even better than *that.*"

Well, he was. Feller had terrific speed, and what made him even harder to hit was that tremendous curve ball. And he'd throw it to you anytime. This made him tough. There were a lot of guys in those days who could throw awfully hard, but the fact that Feller could snap off that curve made him all the tougher to hit. And he was just wild enough so you had to be foot-free up there.

We had a fine pitcher with us in Detroit in those days. Schoolboy Rowe. In fact, when he first came up, he was a great pitcher. He had one of the finest fastballs I ever stood behind. Of course, he was so tall, and looking at that ball from second base, I swear it looked like it was going to hit the ground; but they were strikes. That ball would carry in there, and it had plenty of smoke on it. For about four years he was really throwing hard; then he hurt his arm.

I remember when Rowe was going for the record for consecutive wins, in 1934. He had 15, one under the record held by Joe Wood, Walter Johnson, and Grove. We were playing Washington and losing by one run, late in the game. We were really breaking our backs for him; we wanted to see him make it. Greenberg came up with two men on and drove them in with a double. That gave Rowe what he needed, and he beat them, I think it was 3–2. But the next time out, when he was trying to set a new record, he got bombed by the Athletics.

We had Tommy Bridges on our staff, too. One of the finest curve ball pitchers I ever saw. I always said I was glad I didn't have to bat against him.

The Gehringer cut.

With a little luck, we might have had Carl Hubbell pitching for us too. What a front three that would have been—Rowe, Bridges, Hubbell. Hubbell was with the Tigers for a while when I was a rookie. Cobb gave up on him finally, and the Tigers let him go. Then the Giants scouted him pitching somewhere down South and bought him. This was after he had developed that screwball—which he didn't have when he was with the Tigers. He was in the Detroit system for four or five years and just wasn't getting them out with what he had. He never had a great fastball or curve. It was the screwball that made him. Later on, of course, when he became a great pitcher, everybody wanted to know why we'd let him go. Well, it was nobody's fault; he was a completely different pitcher when we had him.

When we had him, he sure wasn't the pitcher he was in the '34 All-Star game, was he? I guess what he did in that game still ranks as one of the greatest pitching performances of all time. You know, I led off that game against him. Got a single to center. Then he walked Manush. So there we were, on first and second, with Ruth, Gehrig, and Foxx coming up. I figured we were good for at least a couple of runs, that there was no way he could get by our three best hitters.

But he struck out Ruth, and on the strikeout we pulled a double steal. So now I was on third, Manush was on second, there was still only one out, and Gehrig and Foxx were coming to bat. Still a pretty good situation for us. But he struck out Gehrig. And then he struck out Foxx. To start off the next inning he struck out Simmons. And then he struck out Cronin. Bill Dickey finally broke the string by getting a single. I'm glad he did. It was starting to get embarrassing.

A lot of us went on a trip to Japan that year, after the Series. It was quite a good ball club we took over there. We had Foxx, Ruth, Gehrig, Frank Hayes, Eric McNair, Bing Miller, Earl Averill, Lefty O'Doul. O'Doul arranged it. He'd been to Japan a few times and had been impressed with the Japanese love of baseball. He was instrumental in introducing professional baseball to Japan.

We went over by boat, and when we arrived, you never saw so many people as greeted us at the dock and then later on the streets when we drove to our hotel. It seemed like all of Tokyo was out, waving and yelling. We could hardly get our cars through, the streets were so jammed. What was interesting was that they knew who we all were. You'd think being so many miles away and being such a different culture, the whole thing would have been strange to them. But apparently they'd been following big-league baseball for years and gee, they knew us all. Especially Ruth, of course. They made a terrific fuss over him, and he loved it.

Those Japanese fans had never seen anything like those big guys —Ruth, Foxx, Gehrig. They just couldn't believe anybody could hit a ball so far. Of course, the Japanese were so much smaller than our guys. I remember a few games Ruth played first base—Gehrig was in the outfield—and whenever one of the Japanese got to first, Ruth would stand on the bag to make them look smaller. The fans loved it. They loved everything he did. His magic was unbelievable.

The stadium in Tokyo held about 60,000 people, and you know, it was the darnedest thing—even before we got on the field to work out, the place was jam-packed. It was that way every day; we'd go out to loosen up and there they were, every seat filled—to watch the pregame workout!

We did a lot of crazy things. Sometimes we'd take infield practice without a ball. We'd go through the motions, whipping our arms through the air and yelling and throwing nothing. And then wouldn't you know it? After about a week the Japanese started taking infield practice without a ball. Probably thought that was the way to do it.

I got to know Ruth fairly well. He was a big lovable kid. Always a laugh, always a joke. You know, with all his great power, he never hit a ball hard on the ground. Ruth had that uppercut swing, and if he hit the ball on the ground, he more or less topped it, and it would be a big bouncer. Now Gehrig, he could really lash ground balls at you; he'd knock your shins off. But if Ruth hit a ball hard, it was gone; either that or one of those nose-dive line drives.

I'll tell you who hit probably the most wicked ground ball to second base—Al Simmons. He had that long bat, and he stood quite a ways back from the plate, and they tried to pitch him outside to keep him from knocking it upstairs, so then he'd hit it to the right side. And he'd slice them. You'd think you were in front of it, but you kept moving to your left and finally wound up catching it one-handed. He could blister it. He hit a miserable ground ball.

Remember the G-men? That's what they called FBI men back in the thirties. It was short for government men. Well, that's what they called us in the Tiger lineup, the G-men: Greenberg, Goslin, Gehringer. Goslin came over in '34 and helped us win two pennants. And of course, Greenberg was a great one. Hank was a self-made ballplayer. He made himself a great hitter through hard work and determination. When he first came up, he couldn't hit that curve ball, but he learned to hang in there. When they took him off of first base and put him in the outfield, everybody thought he'd get killed out there, but he worked hard at it, and he became pretty good in the field.

Hank loved to drive those runs in. If there was a man on first, he'd always say to me, "Get him over to third, just get him over to third." He drove them in, too. Had over 180 one year.

In 1937 we had four men with over 200 hits—Greenberg, Gerald Walker, Pete Fox, and myself. That must be a record. And a few years earlier we had four men on the infield who together drove in 460 runs—Hank, Billy Rogell, Marv Owen, and myself. That's nice hitting to have in your infield.

The infield that drove in 460 runs: Marv Owen, Charlie Gehringer, Billy Rogell, Hank Greenberg.

The bleachers at Detroit's Navin Field, filling up for the beginning of the 1934 World Series.

Rudy York was with us, too, in those years. Another powerful slugger. I roomed with Rudy for a while. He used to lead the league in burned-up mattresses. He would always go to bed smoking a cigarette. And he would fall asleep. If the cigarette burned his fingers, he'd wake up and put it out. But if it didn't, then he was in trouble. And so was his roommate. He burned up quite a few mattresses that way. He had to pay for them, too. I roomed with him for a year or two until I decided that my chances were better in some other part of the hotel.

I had kind of a long wait for my first World Series. It didn't come until 1934. The year before, we finished fourth. But then Cochrane took over as player-manager, and we got Goose Goslin from Washington, and apparently that was all we needed.

There's nothing like a World Series, no matter how many of them you might get into. It's a situation where you're not just up for every game, you're up for every pitch.

We played the Cardinals in '34, and they beat us, even though we had them down, three games to two. We felt we should have won the sixth game, but we got a bad umpiring decision at third base from Brick Owens. We had a bunt play on, with men on first and second. Cochrane was going to third, and Owens called him out. The pictures showed later that he was safe. That was a turning point in the game. We did get one or two runs that inning, but we should have had the bases full and nobody out, and maybe we would have got Paul Dean out of the ball game, and who could tell what would have happened? We got beat, 4–3. That tied the Series at three games apiece, and Dizzy beat us the next day. But we always felt that call at third probably cost us the Series, that there should never have been a seventh game.

Dizzy shut us out that seventh game, and we got clobbered, 11–0. That was the game where we had the riot. I guess you've heard of that. In the sixth inning Joe Medwick hit one for extra bases. He went tearing around like all those Cardinals did—that was the Gas House Gang, and they were all do-or-die guys. Marv Owen was straddling the bag waiting for the relay, and Medwick came flying in there and took Owen with him. The fans didn't like it—this was in Detroit. The ball game was lost by that time—the score was something like 9–0—and our fans were pretty disheartened. So when Medwick took his position in left field at the bottom of the inning, they seemed to focus on that play and let all their frustrations out on Medwick. They started throwing things at him, mostly fruit and vegetables. I don't know where they got all that produce from—it was fairly late in the game and you'd have thought they would have eaten most of it by then—but it seemed like the supply was endless. You almost thought that trucks were pulling up to the gates making deliveries.

Judge Landis finally took Medwick out of the game, and everything calmed down after that.

We won it again in '35, and this time we played the Cubs. They had a good ball club, with some very strong pitching. Lon Warneke and Bill Lee pitched fine ball games against us, but we got some good pitching ourselves from Tommy Bridges and Alvin Crowder. We went into the sixth game leading them, three games to two.

At the 1934 World Series: Dean, Frisch, Ruth, Cochrane, Rowe.

Same situation as the year before. We'd come close in '34, losing in seven, and when you've come that close, well, you know what it is to *almost* win; that's a very itchy feeling.

We won it in the last of the ninth. The game was tied, 3–3. Larry French was pitching for them. Cochrane opened with a single, and I was the next batter. Well, I tied into one and thought for sure I'd got myself a two-base hit down the right field line. But Phil Cavarretta had never moved away from the bag. I've talked to him a dozen times since, and he always says, "I don't know why I didn't get off. I just stayed there." He should have gotten off the minute the ball was pitched, since I'm more apt to hit one to his right than to his left. But for some reason he stayed right there, and I hit it like a shot right at him, so hard that it handcuffed him and trickled away. If he had caught it, he would have had an easy double play, since Cochrane was off and running. So I was out, but Cochrane got to second.

Goose Goslin was the next hitter. He hit a looper into center field that was just out of everybody's reach, and Cochrane scored. That was the thrill of a lifetime. You don't realize what the world championship means until you've won it. It was the first championship ever for Detroit, and the town really went wild. So did we.

Cochrane was great, a great inspirational leader. Boy, he was a hard loser, the hardest loser I think I ever saw. He was a good manager, strict but fair. He wouldn't stand for any tomfoolery. He wanted everybody to put out as hard as they could, and he set the example himself. Always hustling, always battling. Cochrane was in charge out there, that's what you could say about him—he was in charge.

How would I compare him with Dickey? Well, it's hard. Dickey could throw a little better, I think. Cochrane was probably a better all-around guy; he could run faster, he could do more with the bat, he could do more things to beat you. He didn't have quite the power that Dickey did, though. It's a hard choice to make. You might be more inclined to pick Cochrane over Dickey because of Mickey's aggressiveness. But Dickey certainly made catching look easy.

You know, I was on deck when Cochrane got beaned. That was at Yankee Stadium in 1937. Bump Hadley was the pitcher, and he could throw hard. He let a high inside pitch get away, and Mickey never saw it. He didn't even flinch. The ball hit him so hard it bounced straight back to Hadley. Cochrane went down like he'd been hit with an ax. He had a terrible fracture, way back through his head. Some doctors said that if the ball had hit him an inch lower, he probably never would have awakened. I've never seen anybody hit harder than that. It about finished Cochrane's career, and it was a blow to the team. He was our quarterback.

He told me later that he'd lost track of the ball the moment Hadley let go of it. That happens a lot of times, and you just have to hope it's not coming at you. Yankee Stadium had a very bad background for hitting. The ball would get lost in all those white shirts out in the center field bleachers, and you just couldn't see it.

You get these nicknames in baseball, they're hard to shake off, they stay with you forever. The one they pinned on me was The Mechanical Man. I think it was Gomez who started that one. He was supposed to have said, "You wind him up in the spring, turn him loose, he hits .330 or .340, and you shut him off at the end of the season."

Well, as a matter of fact, I always did look at the fielding part of it as being very mechanical. You just get that part done so you can go back and hit. I think hitting is the thing people remember most vividly, the home run or the base hit that wins the ball game. You can make the greatest fielding play in the world, and they probably won't remember it the next day. Particularly in the infield. Of course we remember some great catches made by Willie Mays or Joe Di-Maggio, because an outfielder has the opportunity to run a long distance or leap against a wall. But a great infield play just happens too quickly for the imagination to seize upon it. You ask somebody what's the greatest infield play they ever saw, and they probably couldn't tell you.

Take the double play, for instance. I don't think people appreciate how difficult that really is, especially when you have two guys running in different directions. The timing has to be perfect. You're throwing the ball to the base, not to the man, and he's not only got to be there at the same time the ball is, but he's got to be able to handle the throw and at the same time get out of the base runner's way. It may look easy and automatic, but if your timing is off just a fraction, you've messed it up.

I can tell you a good one on the old "Mechanical Man." Once we were playing the St. Louis Browns. I hit a ground ball to somebody, and they threw me out. That made two out, but I thought it was three, so I kept running, on around first and out to my position. In those days you used to leave your glove out on the field between innings, and I ran over and picked it up and took my position. I didn't realize it, but I was standing right next to the Browns' second baseman, Oscar Melillo.

"Charlie," he says, "thanks all the same, but I don't need any help."

Talk about a long walk back to the dugout.

I had a reputation for taking the first pitch, and I guess I did do that a lot. Why? I thought I was a better hitter with a strike or two on me. Too many times you go up there with the attitude of "Well, this is the first pitch, I'll take a swing at it." You're apt to be a bit careless, try to go for distance, and the next thing you know you've popped up. But with one strike or even two strikes, you're not going to be careless. You really knuckle down. You're going to get a good pitch, and you're going to hit it.

Yes, I had a good, long career. No regrets about any of it. I guess I had my share of the fun and the base hits. Getting into the Hall of Fame in 1949 was another great thrill. You know, these days I'm on the Old Timers Committee that votes on candidates for the Hall of Fame. If you've been out of baseball twenty years or more, you come under our jurisdiction. Who are my top choices? Well, I think Earl Averill should be in, and I think Billy Herman should be in, definitely. One of the greatest second basemen that ever lived. And there are some other guys who I think are deserving, like Freddy Fitzsimmons and Arky Vaughan and Joe Sewell and Ernie Lombardi. Chuck Klein is another one I always vote for.

I went into the service after the 1942 season. I'd about had it as a player. It was getting to be work, getting harder and harder to prime myself for the games.

I was stationed in California for two years. Then they sent me to the naval air station in Jacksonville. Ted Williams was stationed there at the time. They had a league of service teams down there.

Ted Williams.

Upon arriving in Jacksonville, I went to see the CO. He was a great sports fan, and he told me how happy he was to see me.

"We're going to have a fine team here," he said.

"I hope so," I said. "But as for myself, I think I'll just coach and not play."

"No," he said. "You're going to play."

"I'd rather just coach," I said.

"You're going to play," he said.

"But—"

"Because if you don't play," he said, "I'll send you so far they won't know where to find you."

"Okay," I said. "I'll play. I'll be happy to."

Later I was talking to Williams. Ted was so hepped up about flying those night fighters he couldn't think about anything else. I asked him if he was going to come out for the team.

"Gee," he said, "I've got such a heavy schedule that I just can't."

"Have you spoken to the CO yet?" I asked.

"No," he said.

"Ted," I said, "I think you're going to play."

"No, Charlie."

"Ted," I said. "Yes."

He did. He sure did. Those commanding officers took the whole baseball thing pretty seriously. Once we had a game scheduled at Montgomery Air Base, in Alabama, and they came and picked us up and flew us to Montgomery for the game and then flew us back again. Talk about wasting the taxpayers' money.

You know, when I came out of the service, I was in great shape. I think I probably could have played another year or so. I should have, too, to have gone after 3,000 hits. I fell short by about 160 or so. It didn't seem important when I was playing, but looking back now, it would be nice to have.

3

ELBIE FLETCHER

Elburt Preston Fletcher
Born: March 18, 1916, Milton, Massachusetts
Major-league career: 1934–35, 1937–49, Boston Braves, Pittsburgh Pirates
Lifetime average: .271

A popular and highly respected ballplayer, Elbie Fletcher was a slick-fielding, sharp-hitting first baseman who starred for many years for the Braves and the Pirates. Appearing in a big league lineup for the first time in 1934 as an eighteen-year-old fresh from high school glory, Fletcher stayed in the big leagues until 1949 (with time out for two years in the Navy). An indication of the respect opposing pitchers had for him is the fact that four times Fletcher received more than 100 bases on balls in a season, twice leading the league.

Did you know that I'm in the Hall of Fame? I sure am. Whenever I tell that to anybody they look at me like I'm crazy. "We know your record, Fletcher," they say. "You were a pretty good first baseman, but not good enough for that." And I tell them, "Look, when you get to Cooperstown I want you to go over to where they have the records on Johnny Vander Meer. Look at the box scores of his two consecutive no-hitters. In one of those games—the one against the Braves—you'll see my name: Elbie Fletcher: 0 for 2."

Sure, I still kid around a lot. I was always that way. Life is too short not to have your laughs. Did I kid around when I was playing ball? Well, not in the sense that I didn't take the game seriously. I took it very seriously, but I also enjoyed it. Heck, it was still the same game I loved on the sandlots. And when you can play it in the big leagues—well, you're on top of the world.

I grew up in a little town outside Boston, not too far from both

Fenway Park and Braves Field. It was great having two big league teams nearby; it meant that there was always a ball game. When I was a kid, I worked in a vegetable market in town. I got twenty-five cents a day. And I would take that quarter and buy myself a seat at either Fenway Park or Braves Field; it didn't make any difference. I'd sit close as I could get to first base, and I'd rivet my eyes on the first baseman, watching every move he made. You know George Sisler finished up with the Braves in '29 and '30, and he was still something to see around that bag.

I don't know when it got fixed in my mind that I was going to be a big league first baseman; as a matter of fact, I can't remember a time when I *didn't* want to be a big league first baseman.

I got my opportunity to go into professional baseball by winning a newspaper contest. A newspaper in the Boston area asked the fans to write in and recommend a high school player and say why they thought he might possibly have the qualifications to eventually become a big leaguer. Well, I organized a campaign on behalf of Elbie Fletcher. I had all my uncles and aunts and cousins and friends and everybody else write in recommending me. And as fate would have it, I won the contest. The prize was a free trip to Florida and spring training with the Braves. Talk about a dream coming true! This was in 1934.

So I got on a train and headed south. First time ever away from home. I was so excited I couldn't sleep. I just sat there and kept my nose pressed against the train window all the way to Bradenton.

Bill McKechnie was the manager then. He was a very kindly man. One of the coaches, Hank Gowdy, sort of kept an eye on me and on some of the other younger players. I don't know if he had been asked to do it or whether he was doing it on his own. Hank was an old-timer—he was the catcher for the 1914 Miracle Braves—and he was kind of strict and stern with us, though he was also very generous and good-hearted.

Well, when I got down there, they said to me, "Now, when you go into the restaurant to eat, you order right off the menu and just sign the check."

I couldn't believe it. This was just great. Eat all you want and whatever you want, and just sign your name! So the first morning I went into the restaurant with another boy, and we picked up the menus. I saw "breakfast steak" printed there. Well, back home I'd be lucky to see steak once a month. And here it was, right on the menu—and just sign your name!

So the waitress came over and waited for us to order. To tell you the truth, I was a little scared about ordering steak for breakfast, even though it was on the menu.

"What'll it be, boys?" the waitress asked.

I kept staring at "breakfast steak," biting my lip. I could just hear McKechnie or Gowdy saying: "Steak for breakfast? Listen, kid, who do you think you are, Babe Ruth or somebody?" But finally I got my courage up and said, "What about the steak?"

"What about it?" she said.

"Maybe I'll have the steak," I said.

Nothing happened. By that I mean she just wrote it down and walked away.

So that started it. I had steak every morning, for five or six mornings in a row. The waitress even got to know me. I'd come in and sit down and she'd say, "Steak, kid?" Then I started feeling sick. I was all bound up inside and was getting sicker by the minute. I didn't say anything to anybody at first; I was afraid they'd send me home. Then I told one guy, and word started getting around. Finally it got around to McKechnie, and he heard what was happening every morning at the breakfast table. He came up to me on the field and said, "I want you in the clubhouse tomorrow morning at nine thirty."

"I'll be there," I said.

Now that was pretty early, before the ballplayers came in. So I showed up at nine thirty, and there he was. Just the two of us.

"I understand you're having a problem," he said.

"Sort of," I said.

"Not feeling too well."

"No, sir."

"Wait here," he said.

He went away, and when he came back, he was holding this big bag filled with liquid, with sort of a nozzle on it. I looked at it and wondered what he was up to. He handed me the bag. I didn't know what in the world this thing was. He saw the puzzlement on my face and explained how I was to work the thing.

It was the first time in my life I'd ever had an enema.

When I was ready to leave the clubhouse, he said to me, "Fletcher. One more thing. From now on you're having breakfast with Hank Gowdy."

So every morning after that I sat down with old Hank and he'd pick up the menu, study it very sternly, and then bark up to the waitress, "Prunes and All-Bran."

God, it was awful.

You know, I was still in high school when I went away with the Braves that spring. When I got down to Bradenton, the Braves sent me to school for a couple of hours a day—I guess they had to do that. That enabled me to keep up with my studies, and when I got back to Milton High School, I was able to graduate with my class.

The day after I graduated I was in Harrisburg, Pennsylvania, making $250 a month, which was darn good money in those days. That was during the Depression, remember, and a lot of men with families weren't making anywhere near as much as I was.

I'll tell you how I happened to be getting that much money. Judge Fuchs was the owner of the Braves, and his son Bobby came around to my house and left a contract for me to sign. It called for $150 a month. Because I was underage, my dad had to sign for me. But he was a salesman, and he was on the road at the time. So there I was, sitting with that contract and unable to sign it. I was going out of my mind—I figured the Braves would forget about me if I didn't get that contract right back to them.

After a few days went by, I got a letter from the Braves telling me to disregard that contract, that they were enclosing one that called for $250 a month. Now $150 a month was more money than I'd ever seen in my life, so you can imagine how I felt about $250. The crazy thing was—I found this out later—the Braves thought I was holding out! My father was still on the road. I was having fits; nobody could control me. I must've asked my mother every fifteen minutes for days when he was coming home. "I told you when he's coming home," she'd say. "Now be still." Be still? How could I be still?

Hank Gowdy: "From now on you're having breakfast with Hank Gowdy."

When finally my father came home, I didn't even give him a chance to say hello; I dragged him over to the table and made him sign that contract.

I think my father was tickled to death to get rid of me. I was in my senior year in high school at the time, and he was wondering where he was going to get the dough to send me to college. I had a brother who was a couple of years older, and he wanted to become a doctor. So we had to skimp and save for that, and I guess we were living pretty close to the mark. I was wishing I could do something to make it easier. So when the Braves came along with their offer, it was an answer to a lot of problems.

I liked it in the minors. Sure, living conditions weren't the best,

*Bill McKechnie: "He was
a very kindly man."*

but you just didn't take notice of that. We were allowed $1.50 a day
for meals. We rode the buses and stayed in the worst hotels in town.
We'd sleep eight in a room, just put the mattresses down on the floor
and go to sleep. In fact, we'd only take two rooms and that would
take care of the whole ball club. But it was fun. We'd have water
fights and pillow fights. Hell, we were all seventeen and eighteen
years old. It was a great experience, being away from home, having
people make a fuss over you because you were a ballplayer. You'd
be on the field and make a good play or get a base hit and everybody would cheer, and you'd be asked for your autograph and then
later go up to your room and hit somebody over the head with a
pillow. That was the minor leagues.

I came up to stay in 1937. Casey Stengel was managing the Braves then. Unfortunately, we had a bad ball club. But life was made tolerable by the pranksters we had, guys like Al Lopez, Tony Cuccinello, Danny MacFayden. Now Danny had been wearing the same pair of old white shoes for weeks, and they looked terrible. He always used to put those shoes very neatly right in front of his chair, and later he'd slip his feet into them and get up and walk away. One day Cuccinello and Lopez nailed the shoes to the floor. Then they took a razor blade and cut along the soles, right around the whole shoe. After the game MacFayden showered and dressed and then slipped his feet into the shoes and got up and took a few steps and stopped. He looked down and found himself wearing the tops of his shoes. The laughter went all around the clubhouse till Stengel finally came over to see what it was all about. There was MacFayden still standing there dumbstruck, wearing the tops of his shoes and looking back over his shoulder at the soles nailed to the floor. Stengel just shook his head.

Are there more laughs on a second divison club? I don't see why there should be. Unfortunately, I was never on a pennant winner. I was always on teams that were out of contention. But I'll tell you something—it doesn't affect the way you play. You still play hard; you want that base hit, that run batted in; you want to dig out that low throw, make that good play. You're a professional, a big leaguer, and you take pride in that. Getting the base hit that wins the ball game is one of the greatest thrills you can have, whether you're in first place or last.

I guess the tightest pennant race I ever saw was in 1938. That was the year when Gabby Hartnett hit his famous "home run in the dark" that just about knocked Pittsburgh out of the pennant and won it for the Cubs. That's very vivid in my mind because I was traded over to Pittsburgh the next year to replace Gus Suhr.

And you know, it was sad, because that's all they talked about on that Pirate club that year: Hartnett's home run. I knew we weren't going to win it. That home run was still on everybody's mind, haunting them like a ghost. Management knew it, and that's why they were trying to shake up the club. But it didn't help. They talked about Hartnett's shot all year and finished sixth.

Pie Traynor was the manager when I was sold to Pittsburgh. He was a very fine man, extremely soft-spoken. You never saw him kicking lockers or throwing things after a tough game. He kept it inside.

Now Frankie Frisch was as different from Traynor in that respect as you could possibly get. Frisch took over in 1940. He was aggressive and fiery and, God, teed off all the time. He'd fine you as quick as look at you. He fined me $250 once. That was during spring training one year, in San Bernardino. I was watching the floor show at a nightclub and sort of let the night slip by.

I don't know what time it was when I got back to the hotel, but when I looked into the lobby, there was Frisch, Honus Wagner—he was one of our coaches—and Mr. Benswanger, the owner of the club. I walked around the block a couple of times, but each time I came back they were still there. Hell, I thought, they must be waiting for me. So I figured why make bad enough worse, and walked in. I marched right by them, said, "Good evening, gentlemen," and went upstairs. When I got up to my room, Debs Garms, my roomie, said, "They've been looking for you." "I know," I said. "I found them."

The next morning I went down to get my mail, and here's the letter in my box, addressed to Mr. Elburt P. Fletcher, with the Pittsburgh Pirate insignia on the envelope. It said: "Dear Mr. Fletcher: Due to the fact that you broke training rules you are hereby fined the sum of—" and it started with $50, but that was crossed out, and so was $100, $150, $200. They were all crossed out. It ended with $250.

Then I got to thinking I'd better call my wife because I knew some of the players would be writing home that Fletcher was fined $250, and I knew it wouldn't be long before she heard about it. So I put in a long-distance call and told her the story.

"All right," she said. "I'll go to the bank and take out two hundred and fifty dollars, and we won't say anything more about it."

Later I got a bill for $28 for the phone call. So that episode cost me $278. To see a floor show. I went into the service not long after that, for two years. When I got out and returned to the ball club, there was Frisch, welcoming me back with a big smile on his face.

Pie Traynor and Elbie Fletcher in 1939.

"Elbie," he said, "do you know what we're going to do for you? We're going to give you back the two fifty we fined you a couple of years ago."

That was Frisch. Always unpredictable.

He always said he was never taught how to lose, and when he was with those great Gashouse Gang teams in St. Louis, he didn't lose very often. Then all of a sudden he gets with a ball club that's giving him an education in losing.

It was a pity we didn't do better in those years because we had some good ballplayers. We had Arky Vaughan, Johnny Rizzo, Bob Elliott, and of course the Waners. Paul was kind of along in years when I joined the club, but he could still hit. He was a master. You know how some players have their favorite bat, how they rub it and hone it and baby it along? Well, Paul maintained that the bat had nothing to do with it. One day, just to prove his point, he told us to pick out any bat we wanted and he'd use it in the game. Each time he went up to the plate we'd toss him a different bat. Well, he went four for five.

"It's not the bat that counts," he said after the game. "It's the guy who's wheeling it."

That Joe Medwick was something to watch in his great years, too. A great bad ball hitter. In fact, when we used to discuss how to pitch to him, the word was, "Don't get cute. Throw him strikes." Now that sounds crazy, but the truth was that the ball Joe could hit best was the one that was outside or practically over his head. He'd pound the stuffings out of them.

Medwick came up through that St. Louis organization, and all of those guys were bearcats. They were mean players, and hungry. Remember Pepper Martin? I used to hate to see that guy come to bat. He'd hit the ball and you could hear him leave home plate, stompin' and chuggin', coming down the line like his life depended on him beating that ball. I used to try to get the ball and lift my foot off the base as quick as I could. I remember one time he cut the heel right out of my shoe. And that was a brand-new expensive pair of spikes. He wouldn't cut you on purpose; he was just an aggressive player. When we'd get him in a rundown, it was like being in a cage with a tiger. He'd never give up, and you knew that when it finally

At the 1939 World's Fair: Vince DiMaggio, Spud Davis, Elbie Fletcher, Frankie Frisch, and admirers.

came to the tag, he'd be diving or kicking, doing anything he could to get that ball out of your hand.

I'll tell you about another guy—Pete Reiser. There was a sweet ballplayer. Aggressive too, like Martin. He led the league his first full year up, in 1941. What a future he had, but he crashed into those fences too often trying to catch flyballs. He would do anything to get a ball. You know, a lot of times a fellow would get a base hit, and we'd stand on first and shoot the breeze a little. I was a friendly sort of guy. But Reiser wouldn't talk. Never would say a word. He'd get on base, and he'd be all concentration. And you just *knew* what he was thinking about: How am I going to get to second? How am I going to get to third? How am I going to score? Oh, but he had speed. He was *fast*. The slightest mistake, and he was gone.

Jackie Robinson was the same way. I remember when he came into the league. He was on first one time, and there was a pickoff play, and the ball got away and rolled not more than six feet from me. He saw where that ball was a split second before I did, and that's all he needed. By the time I picked it up I didn't even have a play at second on him. That's how quick he was. Unbelievable reflexes. And alert, always alert.

Sure, there was some grumbling when Jackie came into the league. I guess some of the Southern ballplayers didn't like the idea. But I tell you, every day that Robinson played he made them eat every word they were saying. He took a lot, but he stuck. I heard him called some awful things, by a lot of guys who didn't have the guts to back up what they were saying. Lucky for him, Jackie was playing in the right place. Those Brooklyn fans loved him and appreciated him.

I'll never forget those Brooklyn fans. Most rabid in the league. Ebbets Field was the most fantastic place to play in; I think everybody in the league always enjoyed going to Brooklyn. Never a dull moment. You'd be standing around during batting practice, and you'd hear some guy with lungs like a cannon yell out, "Fletcher, ya bum ya!" Not with any hard feelings or anything like that; just to let you know he was there. But I'll say one thing: If you made a good play, they were the first to acknowledge it. And of course that right-field wall at Ebbets Field was always nice for a left-handed hitter to shoot at.

Now that old Braves Field up in Boston was another story. There was always this terrific wind blowing in from right field. You'd hit a scorcher out there, a shot that would go out of any other park—and you'd see the right fielder come trotting in for it. Al Lopez caught up there for a few years, and I asked him one time in spring training what he did over the winter. "Well," he said, "now and then I'd turn on the electric fan and sit in front of it and think of Braves Field."

One thing I'll never forget as long as I live. In 1938 we were playing a game there against Chicago. The wind was whipping up stronger than usual, and the sky was getting dark. But we kept playing. Then a big billboard behind the left field fence blew over. The infield dirt was whirling around like crazy, and now and then a guy's hat flew off. But we still kept playing. Finally somebody hit a high pop fly. I called for it behind the mound. Then the shortstop was calling for it. Then the left fielder was calling for it. And then the wind took it and blew it right out of the ball park. At that point the umpires said, "Okay, boys. That's all for today."

You know what that was? That was the day of the big hurricane of 1938, probably the worst ever to hit New England. I could barely drive home, it was so awful, with trees lying all over the street. But that's how bad the wind was in Braves Field—we were playing in a hurricane and didn't know the difference!

In 1935 I went back to spring training with the Braves. Still just a kid, eighteen years old. That was the spring Babe Ruth joined the team, right at the very end of his career. We were all awed by his presence. He still had that marvelous swing, and what a follow-through, just beautiful, like a great golfer.

But he was forty years old. He couldn't run, he could hardly bend down for a ball, and of course he couldn't hit the way he used to. It was sad watching those great skills fading away. One of the saddest things of all is when an athlete begins to lose it. A ball goes past you that you know you would have been on top of a few years before. And then, being a left-handed hitter, you begin to realize that most of your good shots are going to center and left-center, and you know you've lost just that fraction of a second and can't always pull the ball the way you used to. And to see it happening to Babe Ruth, to see Babe Ruth struggling on a ball field, well, then you realize we're all mortal and nothing lasts forever.

In those days none of us were going to make enough money to give us real security when we retired. When you were through playing, you went out to look for a job. But that didn't depress me. I'd had many years of doing the thing I'd always wanted to do, that I loved most, and not many men can say that. A lot of people said that I was too easygoing, that I loved to play too much to have been as serious about it as I should have been. But I got everything out of it that I wanted to, and I have no regrets.

I still live in the town where I grew up, and the old diamonds are still there. Once in a while I go out with my sons and have a catch on the fields where I played as a kid. I look out at right field where I used to hit them so many years ago and think to myself, Gee, that wasn't such a long clout after all.

GROVE, ROBERT MOSES (LEFTY)
Born, Lonaconing, Maryland, March 6, 1900
Bats Left. Throws Left. Height, 6 feet 2½ inches. Weight, 175 pounds.

Year	Club	League	G	IP	W	L	Pct	SO	BB	H	ERA
1920	Martinsburg	Blue Ridge	6	59	3	3	.500	60	24	30	....
1920	Baltimore	IL	19	123	12	2	.857	88	71	120	3.81
1921	Baltimore	IL	47	313	25	10	.714	254	179	237	2.56
1922	Baltimore	IL	41	209	18	8	.692	205	152	146	2.80
1923	Baltimore	IL	52	303	27	10	.730	330	186	223	3.11
1924	Baltimore [a]	IL	47	236	26	6	.813	231	108	196	3.01
1925	Philadelphia	AL	45	197	10	12	.455	*116	*131	207	4.75
1926	Philadelphia	AL	45	258	13	13	.500	*191	101	227	*2.51
1927	Philadelphia	AL	51	262	20	13	.606	*174	79	251	3.20
1928	Philadelphia	AL	39	262	*24	8	.750	*183	64	228	2.57
1929	Philadelphia	AL	42	275	20	6	*.769	*170	81	278	*2.82
1930	Philadelphia	AL	*50	291	*28	5	*.848	*214	60	273	*3.00
1931	Philadelphia [b]	AL	41	289	*31	4	*.886	*175	62	249	*2.05
1932	Philadelphia	AL	44	292	25	10	.714	188	79	269	*2.84
1933	Philadelphia [c]	AL	45	275	*24	8	*.750	114	83	280	3.21
1934	Boston	AL	22	109	8	8	.500	43	32	149	6.52
1935	Boston	AL	35	273	20	12	.625	121	65	269	*2.70
1936	Boston	AL	35	253	17	12	.586	130	65	237	*2.81
1937	Boston	AL	32	262	17	9	.654	153	83	269	3.02
1938	Boston	AL	24	164	14	4	*.778	99	52	169	*3.07
1939	Boston	AL	23	191	15	4	.789	81	58	180	*2.54
1940	Boston	AL	22	153	7	6	.538	62	50	159	4.00
1941	Boston [d]	AL	21	134	7	7	.500	54	42	155	4.37
Complete Major League Totals 17 Yrs.			616	3940	300	141	.680	2271	1187	3849	3.06

World's Series Record

Year	Club	League	G	IP	W	L	Pct	SO	BB	H	ERA
1929	Philadelphia	AL	2	6⅓	...	...	....	10	1	3	....
1930	Philadelphia	AL	3	19	2	1	.667	10	3	15	....
1931	Philadelphia	AL	3	26	2	1	.667	16	2	28	....
World's Series Total			8	51⅓	4	2	.667	36	6	46	....

[a] Purchased by Philadelphia for a reported price of $105,000.

[b] Voted the most valuable player in the American League for 1931.

[c] Traded to Boston, December 12 with Max F. Bishop and George E. Walberg for Harold Benton Warstler and Robert G. Kline and reported cash of $125,000.

[d] Unconditionally released at his own request, December 9.

Elected to the Hall of Fame, 1947.

LEFTY GROVE

Remember that time I was going for my seventeenth straight win, in 1931? I remember that all right. Boy, do I remember that! Would have set a new American League record if I'd have made it. Fellow named Dick Coffman with the St. Louis Browns beat me, 1–0. After I lost that game, I came back and won six or seven in a row. Would have had about 24 straight wins except for that 1–0 loss. After that game I went in and tore the clubhouse up. Wrecked the place. Tore those steel lockers off the wall and everything else. Ripped my uniform up. Threw everything I could get my hands on—bats, balls, shoes, gloves, benches, water buckets; whatever was handy. Giving Al Simmons hell all the while. Why Simmons? Because he was home in Milwaukee, that's why. Still gets me mad when I think about it.

See, Simmons should've been in left field, but he wasn't. He went home to Milwaukee, for some reason that I can't remember, and we had a fellow by name of Jim Moore playing in his place. Misjudged a fly ball. He ran in on the darn thing and it dropped over his head and that scored the run that beat me, with two men out in the seventh inning. I didn't say anything to Jim Moore, 'cause he was just a young guy just come to the team and he never played in St. Louis before. It was Simmons' fault. He's the one I blame for it.

So now I'm tied with Joe Wood and Walter Johnson and Schoolboy Rowe at 16 straight for the American League record. But I would have had 24 if Simmons had been out there where he belonged.

I never graduated from high school, you know. There were too many kids in the family—four boys and three girls—and I had to go to work. My dad was a coal miner. Didn't get much in those days for digging coal; about half a buck a ton. All my brothers were coal miners. Me too. For two weeks. That was in 1916. My brother had sprained his ankle, and I took his place for a couple of weeks. I helped load around fifteen ton of coal a day, and at half a dollar a ton you can figure out what I made. Not a heck of a lot. The last day, when I knew my brother was going to come back the next week, I said to my father, "Dad, I didn't put that coal in here, and I hope I don't have to take no more of her out."

I never went back. That was it.

Then I was working in the B&O railroad shops in Cumberland, Maryland. Mechanic's flunky. An apprentice. Working in the round-house, on the big steam engines. Tearing them down, fixing them, taking the heads off the big cylinders, cleaning them, putting them together again. That was in 1918 and '19.

I played ball that year, in 1919, with Midland. We had no team in Lonaconing, where I lived. Midland was three miles up the road. I pitched amateur ball there one season. Sort of amateur ball. We got $20 apiece at the end of the season. We put all the money together, see, what we'd made during the season passing the hat or at the places where we had closed parks. At Midland the park was fenced in, and we charged a quarter. Then at the end of the season we split the money among ourselves.

There was this fellow, Bill Lowden. He was the manager of the Martinsburg team. Blue Ridge League. Class C. He lived only eight miles from me, had a garage down there. He came around and asked me to sign up to pitch for Martinsburg.

So I went to my master mechanic in Cumberland and said, "I want a furlough for a month and a pass to Martinsburg."

"What are you going to do up there?" he asked.

"I'm going to play ball. Or try to, anyway."

So he gave me my thirty-day furlough from the job and a pass for the B&O train. That was the winter of 1919.

Neither of my parents had any objections. My father thought it was great, me becoming a ballplayer. As long as I was getting paid. And I was getting a lot more playing ball than they paid in the mines. My dad was a baseball fan, though he hardly ever got to see any baseball. Didn't have much time. Hardly ever saw daylight. In those days the miners went to work when it was dark and came back

Lefty Grove. Connie Mack called him Robert.

Al Simmons.

when it was dark. They worked ten, eleven hours a day in the mines. Not much chance to see ball games, except on Sundays.

I went to Martinsburg, and we started training in April, I think it was. I won three and lost three there, and then Jack Dunn of the Baltimore Orioles in the International League came up and saw me pitch and bought me, for $3,500 and a pitcher. The reason Martinsburg sold me was because their ball park was just a little one and they built a new grandstand and a fence all the way around the park and they needed some money to pay for it. So Martinsburg got a new grandstand and fence, and Baltimore got me. Five years later Dunn sold me to Connie Mack for $100,600, so you might say he made himself a pretty good deal.

I went to Baltimore around the end of June and was 12 and 2 for the rest of that season. That was 1920. Won all those games with fastballs. Didn't have a curve then. Didn't know what a curve was.

They tell you I was tough to get along with in those days? Well, maybe. I was doing my work—that's where I was tough. Out there on that field, that's where. You've got to remember that a lot of guys against me were tough, so why shouldn't I be too?

Heck, when I broke in, those old guys were tough on us youngsters who were trying to get a toehold. In Baltimore, I mean. We had Irvin Jenkins, Fritz Maisel, Otis Lary, Jack Bentley, Old Ben Egan, guys like that. They were tough to get along with. Criminy, they wouldn't even speak to you. They figured you were coming there to take away somebody's job. I was there about two weeks before they let on they knew I was around—and I'd already won three or four games by then. Oh, boy.

At Baltimore I won two or three in a row before I lost one. Just fastballs. Didn't start throwing the curve until a couple of years later. About 1923 I started working on it. I tried to throw a curveball as fast as the fastball, and it would only break a little ways. Maybe six inches. Just a wrinkle. Maybe they'd call it a slider today. I don't know. We didn't have sliders. We had spitballs, we had emery balls, we had mud balls, shine balls, fork balls, knuckleballs, but no sliders. Now they've got sliders and palm balls and I don't know what else.

George Earnshaw was with me in Baltimore. So was Al Thomas, who later pitched for the White Sox. Joe Boley was my shortstop, Max Bishop my second baseman. At Baltimore and then later on at Philadelphia. Our pitching staff was Harry Frank, Rube Parnham, Earnshaw, Johnny Ogden, Thomas, and myself. That was a pretty good pitching staff. They all came up to the big leagues except Harry Frank. Parnham was up and back. Parnham, he was a funny guy. He'd pitch today and then get on a train and go back home, and it was hard to tell just when he was going to come back. So when he did come back he'd pitch a doubleheader to make up for lost time. I saw him pitch a doubleheader a couple of times.

See, we had an easygoing club. Real loose. No rules. No clubhouse meetings. It was a good life. Dunnie was hardly ever in the clubhouse. After his son died, he wouldn't put a uniform on. Young Dunnie died in the winter of 1921. Before that the old man used to wear a uniform and manage and coach at third base. But after his son died, he didn't even come on the bench. Fritz Maisel and some of the others managed the club. It took a couple of years before he

The 1921 Baltimore Orioles. Grove (known as Groves then) is third from the end at the left. Third, fourth, and fifth from the right are future major leaguers Max Bishop, Tommy Thomas, and Joe Boley.

finally came back. But every once in a while, even then, he'd think about his son, and things wouldn't be right, and he wouldn't be there.

We had a ball club at Baltimore, boy, it was a ball club. I've seen that ball club sit up in the hotel playing cards all night . . . no night games then, see . . . and we'd have a Pierce-Arrow limousine hired waiting for us at the hotel at a certain time, and around one or two in the afternoon we'd go downstairs and pile into that son of a gun car and get to the ball park just in time to start the game. No practice or nothing. Fifteen minutes after we got there the game would start. And that team won seven straight International League pennants.

We caught the Little World Series that first year I was there, which was the first year they had the Little World Series. Interna-

tional League against the American Association. Old man Dunn
came into the clubhouse in Toronto and told us about it. The Toronto Maple Leafs were right behind us, and we were playing them
four games.

"Boys," he said, "if we win the pennant we're going to have a
Little World Series, and the money will be split sixty-forty."

We thought about that for a minute, and then somebody said,
"Well, what are we gonna do this winter—eat snowballs or steaks?"

And everyone yelled, "We're gonna eat steaks!"

We went out and beat Toronto four games, and they couldn't
catch us after that.

After we started the Little World Series, against St. Paul, Mr.
Dunn came into the clubhouse in Baltimore and said, "Now, boys, if
you win this gosh-hank Series, I'll give you my share of the money."

Oh, boy, that was something *more*. So boy, we just went out and
beat St. Paul, and coming back on the train from St. Paul, we got
both checks—the players' cut and the owner's too. I forget what the
amount was. Around $1,800 apiece, in total. That was a lot of dough
in those days, 1920.

I was in the Little World Series in 1920, '21, '22, '23, and '24. We
won the International League pennant every year I was there. Alto-
gether, Baltimore won seven straight pennants: 1919 through 1925.

Let me tell you, those were some teams. We had a lot of guys
good enough for the big leagues. See, there was no big-league draft
from the International League. They can draft them from anywhere
now. But not then. Anyway, we were satisfied to stay there. We
were getting bigger salaries down there in Baltimore in the International League than lots of clubs were paying in the big leagues. So
why leave? We couldn't get $750 to $1,000 a month in the big
leagues in those days. Not on lots of clubs. But that's what we were
getting in Baltimore. And Dunnie was good to us. We'd play exhibition games with the big league teams, and all the money was pooled
and we got a cut. Plus we got the Little World Series money every
year. I started off there at $250 a month, and by the time I got sold
to Connie I was up over $750. We did fine.

Did I ever have any doubts about making that Baltimore team?
No, sir. I always thought I could make any team I went with. I just

had my mind made up I'd make it. Never bothered me who was up there with the bat. I'd hit 'em in the middle of the back or hit 'em in the foot, it didn't make any difference to me. But I'd never throw at a man's head. In all my years I've thrown at guys, but never at their heads. Never believed in it.

I used to pitch batting practice. You know, take my turn at it in Philadelphia. Those guys, Doc Cramer and them, used to hit one back through the box, and they knew damn well when they did, they'd better get out of there, 'cause I'd be throwing at their pockets. They'd try to hit one through the box their last swing, those guys, just to rile me up. Yessir, boy, I was just as mean against them as I was against the others. You can count on two fingers the guys who wouldn't throw at anybody in those days. Walter Johnson was one, and Herb Pennock was the other.

The Giants offered $75,000 for me, you know. But Dunn wouldn't sell me for less than $100,000, and I'm glad for that. I wouldn't have wanted to play for Muggsy McGraw. We wouldn't have got along. That was the winter of '23. I went to Connie Mack and the Philadelphia Athletics in the winter of '24.

Connie always called me Robert. When I got there in 1925, he was sixty-three years old. He sat on the bench in civilian clothes and a derby hat, waving his scorecard when he wanted to position somebody. I got along fine with him. He was just like a father to everyone. He knew how to treat each man.

I didn't do too well that first year with the A's. I think that was the only year I ever was under .500. I was just wild that year, that's all. Didn't pitch enough, I guess. I opened the American League season in 1925, in Philadelphia. Pitched against Walter Johnson. He beat me, 4–2. Ol' Walter. I don't know why Connie picked on me, a rookie. Guess he figured Walter'd win anyway, so why waste a good pitcher? But I can tell you that I opened a few more seasons after that, and I didn't lose 'em.

Walter Johnson. I used to go from home to watch that bugger pitch. We'd take a train from Lonaconing down to Washington—three- or four-hour trip in those days—on Sundays to see him pitch. We idolized that guy. Just sat there and watched him pitch. Down around the knees—whoosh! One after the other. He had something

Connie Mack. "He was just like a father to everyone."

all right. I pitched against a lot of guys and saw a lot of guys throw, and I haven't seen one yet come close to as fast as he was.

Bob Feller? I ought to know about him—I pitched against him. Feller wasn't as fast as Walter. *Heck*, no. I'd say Earnshaw we had pitching for us in Philadelphia was as fast as Feller. Big George Earnshaw.

The league was chock-full of hitters in those days. You had guys like Goose Goslin, George Sisler, Baby Doll Jacobson, Cobb, Speaker, Heilmann, Joe Sewell, Ruth, Gehrig. Gee whiz. Those days if you didn't hit .300, they didn't think much of you.

With us, Al Simmons, Jimmie Foxx, and those guys. Simmons, he was great. Bucketfoot Al. Always pulled that left foot down the third base line when he swung at the ball. Like to spike the third baseman. Big long bat, long as the law'd allow. Could he ever hit that ball! Whew! One year he held out till the season started—finally signed for $100,000 for three years—and came into opening day, no spring training or nothing, and got three hits. And hey, he was a great outfielder. They didn't give him much credit for it. They always watched his hitting. Good fielder. Never threw to the wrong base. Like Ruth. He'd know the runner. Mule Haas, Doc Cramer, Bing Miller. Great outfielders—don't think they weren't.

And I'll tell you something—their gloves were just a piece of leather. Little pancakes. I bring my old glove along now when I go to Old Timers' Days, and these kids, these modern players, look at it in the clubhouse and can't believe it.

"Christ," they say, "you didn't use that glove, did you?"

"I sure did," I tell them. "Kind of glove you got there," I say, "I used to use on the Eastern Shore to get minnies and crabs. We called them crab nets."

Best catcher ever caught me was Mickey. Best I ever saw. Then Dickey's next. Greatest catcher of them all, Cochrane was. Great ballplayer, all around. Good hitter, good runner, good arm, smart. Hardly ever shook him off. If Mickey was living today, he'd tell you I only shook him off about five or six times all the years he caught me. Funny, before I'd even look at him, I had in my mind what I was going to pitch, and I'd look up and there'd be Mickey's signal, just what I was thinking. Like he was reading my mind. That's the kind of catcher he was.

Jimmie Foxx? Oh, boy, what a ballplayer. He could hit that ball! You ever been in the White Sox ball park? You know how far it is from home plate to the left-center-field fence? There was a tennis court back of the ball park there, and Foxx hit two into that tennis court. Over the double-deck stand and everything. Two in one day. At Yankee Stadium he hit one into the third deck off of Gomez. It was like a damn rocket. Gomez said, "Christ, if I was on that son of a bitch, I'd be back in California now." That was no bunt there, that wasn't.

Foxx would hit all those home runs and *still* hit .330. Nowadays home run hitters are considered great if they hit .270. When I was

Two left-handers rub shoulders at the 1933 All-Star game: Hubbell and Grove.

pitching, I used to love to see those guys come up to the plate who swung from the heels. I'd laugh to myself because I knew I had them. When they swing that hard, they're bound to take their eye off the ball. Tickled me pink to see those guys come up there. It's the guys who came up with their bats choked, like Joe Sewell and Charlie Gehringer, who would give you trouble.

Foxx didn't choke up; Simmons didn't. But they didn't cut like they do today. Neither did Ruth. The Babe. We called him the Big Monkey, the Big Baboon. Babe didn't care a hell of a lot for me, you know. The Yankees used to come through Baltimore to play exhibition games, and he knew I was wild and I didn't give a damn whether I hit him or not; didn't make any difference to me. He quit the game one day. I was wild, and I tore a couple buttons off his shirt. He didn't even go to first base. He just said, "I don't want any of that," and went in and dressed. Babe never had much to say to me after that.

Well, after pitching for more than fifteen years, I went and got myself a sore arm in '34. Got it in spring training first year I was with the Red Sox. Don't know how I got it. First one I ever had, and it stayed sore all that year. The muscles in my arm were torn, but I was okay the next season.

Then in '38 I lost the pulse in my left arm. Can you believe that? Pitched against Detroit one day, and Charlie Gehringer hit a swinging bunt down along the third base line, and I picked it up and threw. I must have thrown my arm along with the ball.

They took me in the clubhouse, and the doctor felt my pulse and said, "Hey, Mose, by God you're dead. You haven't got a pulse."

They took me to St. Elizabeth's Hospital, and boy, talk about a guy being a guinea pig. They had seven doctors there. They couldn't figure out what happened to my pulse! They finally put my arm in a glass boot. A glass container, and these rubber attachments moved it up and down. They'd put my arm in there in the morning for three hours, from nine to twelve, and again from six to nine at night. Six hours a day. Soon as my arm would come out of the "boot," they'd slap it on a machine to check the pulse. That went on for fifteen days. Then the needle started to move. Came back and won 15 games next year.

Remember that '29 Series against the Cubs? Lots of surprises in that one. Biggest surprise was Howard Ehmke starting the first game. That sure was something. Nobody ever guessed it. It was supposed to be me or Earnshaw to start that Series. Up until the meeting that morning in Chicago—and that's when we found out. Connie said I was going to be a bullpen pitcher for the Series; all the lefties were. He thought the Cubs would be murder on lefties—they had all those right-handed hitters—Rogers Hornsby, Kiki Cuyler, Riggs Stephenson, Hack Wilson.

I relieved in two of the games. I relieved Earnshaw in the second game in Chicago—we struck out 13 between us that day—and then I relieved in that ten-run seventh inning game. Went into the last of the seventh trailing 8–0, but that didn't mean anything. We never thought we were out of it. We had a team, it was hard to tell what we'd do. Once against Cleveland we were losing 15–4, and we scored thirteen runs and beat 'em 17–15.

So I was down in the bullpen when that seventh inning merry-go-round started. Simmons started it off with a home run, and before it

The run that won the '29 Series. Jimmy Dykes greeting Al Simmons at the plate. Reproduced with permission from the Chicago Daily News.

was over, fifteen men had batted and we'd scored 10 runs. 'Course three or four were due to misjudged fly balls. Poor Hack Wilson was blinded by the sun a few times. It was tough out there, what with the sun coming just over the edge of the stands.

I came in and pitched the last two innings. Saw six men and struck out four of them.

We closed it out the next day. Went into the bottom of the ninth trailing 2–0 and scored three runs. Boy, some ball club, huh? Haas hit one out with a man on to tie it. Then Simmons doubled and Foxx walked, and then Bing Miller got the hit that won the son of a gun. I tell you, the place went wild when Simmons crossed the plate.

My three hundredth win? Durn right I'd made up my mind to get it. I *wanted* that. When I got to 275, I said, "By gosh, I'm gonna win three hundred or bust." And when I got number 300 in Boston in 1941—I beat Cleveland 10–5 that day—then that was all. Never won another game.

I knew it was time to go. You know how your ol' body feels. I just couldn't do it anymore. I wouldn't even go to a ball game for a couple years after that. I didn't coach anywhere—had plenty of offers—just had nothing to do with baseball. Not a thing. I just stayed up in the mountains and went down to the river and fished. Stayed home in Lonaconing. That's an Indian name. Means "meeting of the waters." Streams come out of the mountains there and meet and make one body.

I enjoyed every damn year I was in baseball except the first year with the A's, when I was a rookie learning the ropes, and the first year in Boston, when I had a sore arm. Except for those two years, I enjoyed it all. I loved baseball.

If I had to do it all over, I'd do the same thing. If they said, "Come on, here's a steak dinner," and I had a chance to go out and play a game of ball, I'd go out and play the game and let the steak sit there. I would.

5

BUCKY WALTERS

WILLIAM HENRY WALTERS
Born: April 19, 1909, Philadelphia, Pennsylvania
Major-league career: 1934–48, 1950, Boston Red Sox, Phila-
 delphia Phillies, Cincinnati Reds, Boston Braves
Lifetime record: 198 wins, 160 losses

Coming to the major leagues originally as a third baseman,
Bucky Walters made the transition from infielder to pitcher
with astonishing ease and instant success (he led the league
in shutouts his second year). In 1939 Walters was voted the
National League's Most Valuable Player, after recording the
league's lowest earned run average and winning 27 games.
(Since 1918, only three National League pitchers have won
more games in a season than Walters—Dazzy Vance, Dizzy
Dean, and Robin Roberts.)

In 1934 I was twenty-five years old and figured I had just about
won myself a job in the big leagues as an infielder. Finally. I'd
bounced around with the Braves and the Red Sox for a few years,
trying to convince somebody I could play the infield in the big
leagues if only they'd give me the chance. I thought for sure I was
going to stick with the Red Sox in the spring of '34, but around
cut-down time they sold me to the Philadelphia Phillies. I finished
out that year at third base for the Phillies and did all right, I thought.

Near the end of the season Jimmie Wilson, the manager, said to
me, "Hey, the season's practically over, how about pitching a game
or two?"

"Listen," I said, "I'm a third baseman."

"Who said you weren't? Anyway, what has one thing got to do
with the other?"

So I pitched three innings in Brooklyn against the Dodgers and did pretty well—shut them out. Then I started another game, against Boston, in old Baker Bowl, the Phillies' park. Did pretty well again. Then the season was over, and I went home and spent the winter thinking about how to improve my play at third base and how I might do something to pick up that .260 batting average of mine.

You see, I'd never thought much about pitching during those early years, even though it was suggested to me many times by different players. They'd see that good arm and tell me I should be a pitcher. But I'd tell them that wasn't for me. I liked to play every day. I liked to be in there.

When I got to spring training in '35, the Phillies had made a deal. They'd traded Dick Bartell to the Giants for, among others, Johnny Vergez, the third baseman. So that left me in a battle for third base with Vergez, and I thought I could beat him out. But then one day at Orlando I had a pretty bad game at third. I made a couple errors and went hitless.

That night Wilson and a couple of the coaches, Hans Lobert and Dick Spalding, got me aside and began telling me what a great future I'd have as a pitcher if I'd make the switch.

"Bucky," they said, "you can learn all there is to learn about pitching. But what you've already got is something that nobody can ever teach you—that great arm and that great fastball."

So I tried it. I found that I didn't mind pitching. Maybe it was because in the back of my mind I still felt I'd be going back to third base. I wanted to play every day. That was the thing of it. But I must admit I felt right at home on the mound. And I think I even had a certain edge, having been in the league for a little while, because I had always paid attention to what the hitters liked, what their strengths and weaknesses were, so that it was mainly a matter of me getting the ball there.

I was mostly a fastball pitcher when I started. I learned the curveball later on, but in the beginning it was that fastball. It had a tendency to sink, which was a great advantage for me, because most hitters tend to uppercut a little. So with that bat coming up and that ball sinking, you've got an advantage—*if* you can keep the ball down.

Bucky Walters.

You won't be surprised if I tell you I was never keen about pitching in Baker Bowl. The place was a pitcher's nightmare. It was about 270 feet to the right field wall, and it ran straight across that way. It was high, with a big fence. What a target! No matter how well you went, it seemed you always had three on base and some big lefty was standing at the plate looking at that right field wall. Visiting pitchers used to get sore arms the minute the train pulled into Philly, and all the crippled hitters got better and ran over each other to get into the lineup.

Jimmie Wilson. "He suggested I pitch a game or two."

But with the good fastball and the hitters not being too sure of my control, I did all right. I was 9 and 9 around the first of August, then got a sore arm and went on the shelf.

The arm came around in spring training the next year and I was able to pitch. I won 11 and lost 21 that year. Now that may sound like a pretty poor year, but I tell people that was one of my best years, because I pitched a lot of good ball that season. Jimmie Wilson said to me, "Look, don't be feeling bad about that record. If you weren't a darned good pitcher, you wouldn't have got the chance to lose twenty-one ball games."

If you look back over the years, I guess you'll find that some pretty fair pitchers lost 20 games in a season. Red Ruffing is one; Paul Derringer's another. Derringer lost 27 one year, believe it or not. A couple of years later, when we were both with Cincinnati, we won 52 games between us. Neither one of us were doing anything we hadn't done before; it just shows you what a different ball club and a different ball park can do.

Did I always want to be a ballplayer? Well, I guess I did. I can't remember when I didn't play baseball. I mean, you don't just start playing when you're nineteen or twenty. I always had a ball, and I always had a glove, from the time I can remember.

In those days—the late twenties—it wasn't so easy to get into professional baseball. A lot of the clubs didn't have more than one or two scouts, and the farm systems hadn't really started up yet, most of the minor league clubs being independently owned. So very often it was word of mouth. If somebody was good, word got around.

In my case, I was playing on the sandlots around Philadelphia. One day a fellow who had a contact with a club in Montgomery, Alabama, saw me playing shortstop, and after the game he asked me if I'd like to play pro ball. I guess he heard the quickest "Yes, sir" anybody ever heard.

My family wasn't too crazy about the idea. I'd never been away from home before, never been on a train, and they thought Montgomery was a long way to go just for a tryout, with no return ticket —I'd have had to hitchhike back if I didn't make it. But you never think about not making it, do you? I would've gone to China if I'd had to. Didn't make any difference to me. As long as it was pro ball.

I was the oldest of seven, and there wasn't much money in the family; but my grandmother dug up $10 somewhere and bought me a suitcase. First suitcase I ever owned; in fact, I think it was the first suitcase *any* of us ever owned.

Well, I didn't make it in Montgomery, but I must've made some kind of an impression, because they sent me up to High Point, North Carolina, in the Piedmont League. That began my travels through the minor leagues. Played everywhere from Portland, Maine, to San Francisco. I was property of the Braves for a while, and in '32 they sold me outright to San Francisco in the Coast League. I went out there and was having a great year, hitting around .380. Eddie Collins, who was general manager for the Red Sox at that time, saw me and bought me, and back across the country I went. In '34 they sold me to the Phillies. Still an infielder then.

I guess I was pretty lucky. Things were tough back in those days. Not many people today remember how tough. There weren't so many of those old greenbacks around. People were hurtin'. There weren't jobs. There wasn't anything. You saw guys selling apples on street corners. People were hocking their possessions, selling their houses, doing whatever they could to keep some food on the table. The bleacher people and the box-seat people both. Everybody.

Minor leagues were disbanding all over. I was playing in Portland in 1930, and in the middle of the season the league folded. Just weren't drawing. But I was lucky. I caught on with another club, another league. I was able to hang on. You had no guarantees in those days; you couldn't be sure of anything. As far as baseball was concerned, you just had to be fortunate enough to hang on until you got a break.

It was rough going in the big leagues, too. I can remember going on Western trips with the Phillies when sometimes you wouldn't see 500 people in the stands. The Phillies would make a western trip just praying they wouldn't get rained out in Chicago on Saturday or Sunday, so they'd have enough money to get home. Why, very often they used to have to sell a player or two just to be able to take the club to spring training.

Life is a little different today for a ballplayer. They get so many opportunities thrown at them away from the field there's a lot more money to be made. These fellows have got things going for them now that we never used to think of. Some guys would take a job in the wintertime, but in most cases when the baseball season was over, they just went home and took their shoes off or went hunting or played golf or goofed around. Is that what I used to do? Yes, sir. I made a job out of bummin'. A good one. Maybe it wasn't the smartest thing to do, but it was pretty much the style back then.

In my first year as a pitcher with the Phillies, 1935, I had the pleasure of pitching to Babe Ruth. I used to see him in spring training when I was with the Braves, because we both trained in St. Petersburg. I played third base in some of those games against the Yankees. And just for the hell of it I used to move in on the grass when he'd come up, to try to get him to hit one at me—and don't think he couldn't whistle them down that line if he wanted to. Why did I do that? I don't know. Maybe just to get him to look at me, take notice of me.

Well, when I faced him as a pitcher, he was past his peak, but he was still Babe Ruth, this great guy that I'd admired all my life. All I had then was the fastball, and I said to myself, "Well, if he's gonna hit it, he's gonna get the best one I've got." I wasn't trying to walk him, but I was trying to nick that outside corner. Well, I kept missing and ended up walking him. That's the only time I ever faced him. And I'll tell you the truth—I wouldn't have minded being one of his victims. Not at all.

Now, in 1938, around the middle of June, I'd won 4 and lost 8, and it looked like another one of those years where you were going to end up losing twice as many as you won, no matter how well you pitched. Then Jimmie Wilson called me one day and said, "We just made a deal for you. You're going to Cincinnati."

You might say that was a big break for me, going from a tail ender to a team that was shaping up to take two pennants, but actually I didn't want to go. I'd have rather stayed in the East, with my family. But that's the way things work in baseball.

I joined the Cincinnati club at an interesting moment—right in between Vander Meer's two no-hitters. He'd already pitched his first one, in Cincinnati against Boston. I joined the club in Brooklyn. It was the first night game ever in Ebbets Field, and Vander Meer was starting.

Well, he starts off that game, and you can see he has real good stuff. He had a powerful fastball and an exceptionally sharp curve. But he was wild that night, and it seemed he had men on base nearly every inning. But no hits. Then the crowd started getting tense—you know how they get when they start to smell a no-hitter. And this wasn't going to be any old no-hitter, of course. But he was wild, and working hard, going to three and two on almost every hitter.

In about the sixth or seventh inning, Bill McKechnie looked at me and said, "Sneak down to the bullpen." That was one of his favorite expressions, "Sneak down."

So I "sneaked down." Meanwhile, Vander Meer's still got the no-hitter going. And we had about four or five runs. But I thought to myself, "By God, if I'm going to get into this game, I'm going to be ready," So I started to warm up. I began to hear some booing. I looked around, couldn't see anything going on, and continued to loosen up. And they continued to boo. The harder I threw, the

Johnny Vander Meer.

louder they booed, until I realized why they were doing it: It was *me* they were booing, the fact that I was warming up. There was no way they wanted to see Vander Meer come out of there as long as he had that no-hitter going.

John stayed wild; in fact, he walked the bases loaded in the ninth. But he got Durocher on an easy fly ball to Harry Craft in center, and that was it. The only double no-hitter in baseball history.

Like I said, Cincinnati was shaping up to take those two pennants in '39 and '40. I could tell from pitching against them that they were coming along. Their farm system had produced some good ballplayers, and on top of that they made the right trades.

We had pretty good hitting, plenty of speed, and a great defense. We played a lot of tight, low-scoring ball games, and in the good years we won those games. We had Frank McCormick at first base, a very strong hitter; and Lonny Frey, Billy Myers, and Bill Werber at second, short, and third—all good, fast, smart ballplayers. In the outfield we had Wally Berger, Harry Craft—what a center fielder he was—and a good all-around ballplayer in right, Ival Goodman.

And big Ernie Lombardi catching. Everybody loved that guy. A sweet, quiet man. One of the most powerful hitters in baseball. He might have been slow afoot, but I'll tell you something you might think sounds strange—he was a good base runner. By that I mean when Lombardi went for a base, he always just made it, he was never just thrown out. I've seen plenty of these speedsters who can run like the wind getting thrown out on close plays. But not Lombardi—he was always just in there. And how he could hit! He used to have infielders playing 20 and 30 feet back on the outfield grass for him.

Cincinnati hadn't won a pennant in twenty years when we brought it in for them in 1939. Going into the Series, the Yankees

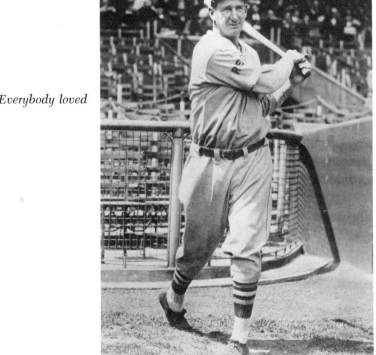

Ernie Lombardi. "Everybody loved that guy."

were the favorites, naturally. They'd won the championship three years running, and they had those great teams, with DiMaggio, Keller, Dickey, Gordon, and fellows like that.

Derringer pitched the first game, at Yankee Stadium, and it was a shame the way he lost it. It was 1–1 going into the bottom of the ninth. Keller hit a long fly that Goodman just couldn't hold onto, and it went for a triple. We walked DiMaggio, but Dickey looped one over short, and that was the ball game. A real heartbreaker.

I lost the next game, 4–0. Monte Pearson pitched a two-hitter against us. In fact, he had a no-hitter going into the eighth, when Lombardi got a single. We moved to Cincinnati for the third game, and they clobbered us. I remember Keller hit a couple out. He had a great Series.

Derringer started the fourth game. I came in in the eighth to hold a 4–2 lead. I didn't relieve very much, but in the spot we were in, down three games to none, there was no tomorrow. You've got all winter to either count your money or count your mistakes, depending on how it goes. Well, we messed up a double-play ball in the ninth, and the Yankees tied it.

It all came apart in the tenth. You wouldn't believe it, but we made three errors in that inning. We just never played that kind of ball. DiMaggio got the key hit, a single to right with two men on. Goodman bobbled the ball and the base runners were flying. Then that play occurred that they still talk about—"Lombardi's swoon." Swoon, my neck. The throw came home, and Lombardi took it just as Charlie Keller was coming across. Well, Keller ran into him hard and knocked him down, and the ball kicked away. Lombardi was stunned, he was hurt. If you want to criticize somebody, you can start with yours truly—I should have been there backing up, because that ball was just lying there. DiMaggio saw the situation, and he came home too.

They made that the big story of the Series. But it was a big story about nothing, because that run didn't mean anything. They beat us 7–4.

We got another crack at it in 1940. This time it was the Detroit Tigers. They came in with a good strong ball club—Hank Greenberg, Charlie Gehringer, Rudy York, Pinky Higgins, Barney Mc-

Cosky, fellows of that caliber. And good pitching—Bobo Newsom, Tommy Bridges, Schoolboy Rowe. This wasn't going to be any picnic either.

We went into that Series without Lombardi. He'd hurt his foot and couldn't do much more than pinch-hit. My old Philadelphia manager, Jimmie Wilson, who had become one of our coaches, had to be pressed into service and he caught most of the Series for us. He was forty years old and hadn't caught in a couple of years, but he did a great job.

Derringer started the first game, and they got to him early. The final score was 7–2, Tigers. It looked like here we go again. The National League hadn't won a Series game since 1937—ten straight losses.

I started the second game, and the first eight pitches I threw were balls. Walked two men right off the bat. Boy, it looked like that rut we'd fallen into was getting deeper and deeper. Wilson walked out to me, very slowly; I swear it seemed like it took him five minutes.

"Now look," he said, "just calm down. You're throwing too hard. Just be yourself. Let them hit the ball."

He was right, I *was* throwing the ball too hard; I was trying to strike everybody out.

Let them hit it. Well, Gehringer obliged me very nicely. He

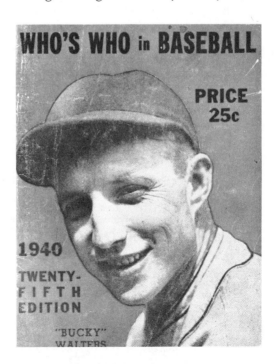

WHO'S WHO in BASEBALL

PRICE 25c

1940

TWENTY-FIFTH EDITION

"BUCKY" WALTERS

rapped it into right field, and that brought in one run and left men on first and third. And up steps Greenberg. Well, here's where I got one of the biggest breaks of my life. He went for a bad ball, a curve, and grounded into a double play. The run came in, but we were able to get out of the inning not hurting too badly. So we got the break we needed. You've got to get a few breaks in the game, or you can't win. Right?

Then we started coming back. Jimmy Ripple hit a home run for us, we got some other hits, and went on to win, 5–3.

Tommy Bridges beat us the next game, but then Derringer came back to tie it at two games. Newsom shut us out on three hits in the fifth game, and we were in trouble.

We came back to Cincinnati for the sixth game (and, we hoped, the seventh). I pitched that game, and I was up for it. I shut them out, 4–0. I even hit a home run—hey, don't forget that now; make sure you get that in the book. Hit it off Freddy Hutchinson. He made a mistake, and it went out. That's what usually do go out of the park—the mistakes.

Somebody said to me later, "Hey, why didn't you trot around?"

"I was," I said.

"No, you weren't. You tore around those bases like you were trying to catch a train."

The truth is I was floating. What a nice feeling.

Derringer came back in the seventh game against Newsom. It was the third game for both of them, but boy, they were sharp. It was a real duel. Newsom had us 1–0 going into the bottom of the seventh, but then we got two runs. Jimmy Ripple got a key hit in there, a double. Derringer held them off and we won it, 2–1. Won the world championship. And we felt pretty good about it, believe me. We'd beaten a good team, and it was about time the National League had won one of those things.

You know, I used to read the box scores all the time and watch the lineups. In 1942 I began seeing this guy Musial in the Cardinal lineup. A new face, you know. We hadn't played St. Louis for a while, so I'd never seen him. Next time we went into Chicago I went over to Jimmie Wilson. He was managing the Cubs then—he got around, didn't he?

"Who's this guy Musial down there at St. Louis?" I asked him. "He hit you guys pretty good."

"Yeah," he said. "He sure did. But you know, Bucky, I think you can get him inside. Good and tight."

Well, the next time I pitched against the Cardinals I waited for Musial to come up. Then he stepped into the batter's box, with that funny little stance he had—remember it? I said to myself, "Well, here I go. Might as well find out something right now." I put one inside. I thought I'd got it in there pretty good and tight. Boy, he hit a screaming line drive down the right-field line, I'll bet he put blisters on that ball. Well, I thought, there goes that theory. You could see that this fellow was going to make a lot of money in the big leagues, and that it wasn't going to be for stealing bases.

The most money I ever made? Well, after winning 27 games in 1939 and being voted the National League's Most Valuable Player —about $22,000. But that was my own fault. I should've made more. I thought I'd be around forever, and money really didn't mean that much. But I'm not complaining. There's more to baseball than a payday. Baseball got me a lot of nice things. I'd go back and do it again for the same price. As a matter of fact, I'd do it for half as much.

Stan Musial. "Who's this guy Musial down there at St. Louis?" I asked.

⑥

JOHNNY MIZE

John Robert Mize
Born: January 7, 1913, Demorest, Georgia
Major-league career: 1936–1953, St. Louis Cardinals, New York
   Giants, New York Yankees
Lifetime average: .312

A big quiet man, with a strong, graceful swing, Johnny
Mize is one of the great sluggers in National League history.
He hit .300 or better his first nine years in the majors, leading
the league with .349 in 1939. Four times he led the league in
home runs (twice tying with Ralph Kiner) and in 1947 became
one of the very few ever to hit 50 or more home runs in a
season, when he hit 51. Six times Mize hit three home runs in
a game, still a major league record.

In mid-season 1949, Mize was traded to the Yankees, where
he remained as a part-time player and devastating pinch-
hitter for five years, five pennants, and five world champion-
ships.

I grew up in Demorest, Georgia, in the northeastern part of the
state. Was it a small town? Well, I played more basketball than
anything else in those days because it was easier to get up a basketball team than a baseball team. In fact, I played more tennis as a
kid than either baseball or basketball because it took even fewer
people.

I never thought too much about being a ballplayer back then. You
know how it is when you're a kid; you just go from day to day,
growing up, not giving much thought to tomorrow. Tell you the
truth, when I was attending Piedmont College in Demorest, the
coach had to beg me to get me to go out for baseball.

After college, I started playing with different town teams every
Saturday. I hooked on for a while with a lumber company team
from Helen, Georgia. I got $5 or $10 a game. They might be playing

some team out of Atlanta or from Gainesville or Chicopee, which were cotton mill towns. The manager of the lumber company team would call me up and say, "We've got a rough game Saturday and want you to come down and play with us." I played first base some and the outfield some; when you're playing semipro ball with town teams, you're liable to play any position.

I guess I was busting the ball pretty good, and Frank Rickey, Branch's brother, heard about me and came down for a look. The Morris Lumber Company out of Rochester, New York, had this mill in Helen, where I was playing. The way I heard the story, somebody kept telling Warren Giles, who was connected with the Rochester club then, about me. He sent Frank Rickey down to take a look. He had his look and offered me a contract.

I guess I was pleased with the idea of going into pro ball. Things were pretty rough around home then—this was 1930—and playing ball meant you'd have a little money to spend. The Depression hit hard down in Demorest, though I suppose no harder than anywhere else. Some people worked; some didn't. You had your own gardens and raised what you could. And you had relatives around, and they all had some type of farm, so there was always food, nobody was going to starve. Whenever somebody came to visit, they'd bring vegetables and lay them on the table. We got by.

Let me tell you about that contract I signed. It wasn't legal. The Cardinals never knew that. I was only seventeen then—underage—so Frank Rickey went to Atlanta and got my mother to sign the contract. You see, my father and mother separated when I was very young and I lived most of the time with my grandmother. It was my grandmother who actually was my legal guardian. So I was never legally signed.

I always had that in back of my mind, but I never did anything about it. I've often thought that when I was twenty years old, I should have got my release from the Cardinals and signed with somebody else for a good bonus. By then I was playing for Rochester in the International League, one step below the majors, and hitting around .350. But I didn't, and I've regretted it ever since, the way things turned out. I've found out that in baseball they don't care a darn thing about you. Once you've stopped producing, you're

Johnny Mize, first base-man, Rochester Redwings.

gone. I went through this with the Cardinals. "You go along with us," they told me. "You'll always be with us, and we'll take care of you." The next year I was sold. So you take them at their word, you go along, and you find out where you end up.

In 1934 I was running out a double and tore the large muscle loose from the pelvic bone. That slowed me up a bit, I guess. So in the spring of '35 Branch Rickey offered me to Cincinnati, on a trial basis. I went to spring training with the Reds, but they didn't keep me. The way I heard it, Larry MacPhail, who was running the Reds at that time, wanted to buy me on condition my leg was all right, but if it wasn't, they'd return me to St. Louis and get their money back. But Rickey said no. "You either buy him or you don't. No conditions." Well, the Reds had just spent a lot of money buying ballplayers from the Cardinals. They'd bought Ival Goodman, Lew Riggs, and Billy Myers, and MacPhail felt he couldn't afford to gamble on me. So they turned me back, and the Cardinals sent me to Rochester.

Then I hurt my other leg, in a game at Montreal. I was running down the line after a foul ball, looking up in the air, and stepped in a hole. Same injury. That finished me for the season, and I went home. The injury was so bad that the club doctor recommended I retire from baseball. That didn't sound so good to me, so I got another opinion. I ended up having both legs operated on and came back okay after that.

I joined the Cardinals in '36. Rip Collins was the first baseman. I started out just as a pinch hitter, but when the year was over, I'd played in about 125 ball games. After the season they traded Collins to the Cubs.

The newspapers had pinned a name on that Cardinal team: "The Gas House Gang." That came from Pepper Martin sliding headfirst, and the dirty uniforms, and a general style of play. It was a good name to give them. Martin was the main one, I guess, when you come right down to it. He was the chief wild man and joker.

One time we were rained out in Philadelphia, and Pepper didn't have anything to do, and when Pepper was idle, you just knew that a situation was going to load up. So Pepper and Dizzy Dean and somebody else got hold of some overalls and workmen's caps and all kinds of tools and went downstairs to remodel the hotel. They went into the barbershop and told the barber they had to take his sink out. He chased them out, and they went into the dining room. They started crawling under the tables where people were eating and began hammering and moving things around. This went on until the complaints started reaching the front desk. The hotel manager came around to see what was going on, but by that time the boys had gone. They would do things like that. Anytime, anyplace.

Dean enjoyed the clowning and cutting up as much as anybody. But when he wanted to pitch, he could pitch. If he said he was going to shut them out today, why, he'd come pretty close to doing it. He was one guy who could pop off and back it up. Was he the best pitcher I ever saw? Well, when you've faced guys like Feller and Hubbell, too, it's hard to tell which one is the best. I faced Feller a lot in spring training when I was with the Giants. He was fast all right, but probably not as fast as Rex Barney. What made Feller tough was he had a real fast curve. A lot of pitchers do you a favor when they throw you a curve ball, but his was wicked. You couldn't lay back for it.

In 1939 I led the league in hitting with .349. Naturally after a year like that you look forward to talking contract. But when I sat down with Rickey, he said, "Well, your home run production stayed pretty much the same." No mention of my batting average. So the next year I hit 43 home runs, which is still the Cardinal club record, and led the league in runs batted in. But my batting average went down. When I went in to talk contract this time, he said, "Well, your batting average wasn't so good. Would you be willing to take a cut?" I led the league in hitting, then I led the league in home runs and runs batted in, and he wanted to know if I'd take a cut!

We always had good ball clubs in St. Louis, but most of the time we needed just a little bit more help. They had plenty of good ballplayers in the minor leagues in those years, but they kept selling them off. Guys like Bob Klinger, Bill Lee, Fritz Ostermueller, Cy Blanton. Those guys were good pitchers, Bill Lee especially. He was a great one for the Cubs. If the Cardinals had brought them up, we

"The newspapers had pinned a name on that Cardinal team: 'The Gas House Gang.' That came from Pepper Martin sliding head first . . . and a general style of play."

might have won a few pennants during those years. I heard later that Rickey got 25 percent of whatever he sold a player for. That's why every year he was selling these players. He sold Johnny Rizzo, too, and those other fellows I mentioned, Riggs, Goodman, Myers.

In '41 Slaughter collided with Terry Moore, and Slaughter broke his shoulder. Here we're fighting the Dodgers for a pennant. Rickey said we didn't have anybody in the minor leagues to help us. Then in September he brings up Musial. Why didn't he bring Musial up earlier? That's what all the players wanted to know. We might have gone ahead and won the pennant.

I'll tell you what the talk used to be about Rickey: Stay in the

pennant race until the last week of the season, and then get beat. I heard some talk to the effect that that was what he preferred. That way he drew the crowds all year, and then later on the players couldn't come in for the big raise for winning the pennant and maybe the World Series. I don't know if it's true or not, but that was the talk.

I got married to a St. Louis girl. Her father was a good friend of Sam Breadon, who owned the ball club. Breadon gave me $500 as a wedding gift. The next year when I was talking contract to Rickey, he said, "Well, you made seventy-five hundred last year." "No," I said, "I only made seven thousand." He said, "Really? Where's that five hundred that Breadon gave you?" That was Rickey.

You know, back when I broke in, throwing at hitters was part of the game. It was expected. If you couldn't take it, you were better off going home, because once they found out you couldn't take it then they would really let you have it. It never worried me. I always figured any guy that threw at me knew I could hit him, because the only reason you throw at a guy is to try and scare him. You let a pitcher scare you, and you might as well go up there without a bat in your hands. I always bore down harder against any man that threw at me.

Sure, I got hit in the head a few times. Those things will happen. Harry Gumbert hit me once; Brecheen hit me once. Were they throwing at me? I don't know. But one of them was a sinkerball pitcher; the other one was a control pitcher. And on each occasion I'd hit a home run the time before. Take it from there.

I was with the Giants when Brecheen hit me. We had a left-hander pitching for us that game named Monte Kennedy. He was wilder than a March hare. Fast and wild. Well, after I was hit, Mel Ott, who was managing, told Kennedy, "When Brecheen comes to bat, throw at him. Not at his head; hit him in the knee." He's telling this to a fellow who generally had a hard time just keeping his pitches in the ball park. But, son of a gun, when Brecheen came up, first pitch Kennedy hit him right in the knee. Brecheen was out for ten days. That's probably one of the mysteries of baseball, that Kennedy, wild as he was, could hit a guy on the knee with his first pitch.

Johnny Mize.

Before I was traded to the Giants, I thought I was going to Brook-lyn. Durocher called me in the winter of '41 and asked me what I thought about playing in Brooklyn. In fact, the day he got in touch with me was Pearl Harbor Day, December 7. I was down in the Ozarks, bird hunting. A guy told me I was wanted on the telephone. As I was walking to the phone, he said to me, "By the way, the Japanese have bombed Pearl Harbor." I thought he was nuts. Didn't pay him any attention. I got on the phone and my father-in-law told me there was a message to get in touch with Durocher. I called Leo, and he asked me if I wanted to play with the Dodgers. He said they were trying to make a deal for me. I told him it didn't mean a damn to me where I played. Then I got into the car and turned on the radio and found out that fellow was right about Pearl Harbor. That was a hell of a piece of news, and I didn't know what to think about it. When something like that happens, you don't know what's coming next until it comes.

Four days later I was traded to the Giants. I wasn't too crazy about playing in the Polo Grounds, because I wasn't that much of a pull hitter. Maybe if I'd have got there earlier in my career, I might have become a pull hitter, to take advantage of that short right field, but after hitting straightaway for so many years, I didn't want to start changing around.

In the middle of 1949 we were playing the Yankees an exhibition game. Before the game Stengel said to me, "How do you feel?"

"All right," I said. "But I'm not playing much."

"If you were over here, you'd play," he said.

"Well," I said, "make the deal."

I was only kidding, but then late in August they did just that. They were up against the Red Sox for the pennant that year, and it seems the Red Sox were after me, too; in fact, the Red Sox had one of their scouts following me around. Well, the Yankees got wind of that, and they made the deal first.

It was a good trade for me, going from the Giants to the Yankees. I got into a string of World Series. Five straight, starting in '49. I hurt my shoulder before the '49 Series and couldn't throw, but I pinch-hit twice and got two hits. One of them helped beat the Dodgers in the third game, at Ebbets Field. I got a single off of Ralph Branca in the ninth inning with the bases loaded, and that helped win that game.

After all those years in the National League I finally get into a World Series and find myself getting the base hit that helps win for the American League. So you don't want to get too sentimental about things, do you?

7

TED LYONS

THEODORE AMAR LYONS
Born: December 28, 1900, Lake Charles, Louisiana
Major-league career: 1923–46, Chicago White Sox
Lifetime record: 260 wins, 230 losses

In a curious way, Ted Lyons embodies baseball history in this century. He pitched to Ty Cobb, who came to the big leagues in 1905, and he pitched to Ted Williams, who left the big leagues in 1960. Lyons himself came to the Chicago White Sox straight from the campus of Baylor University and remained in the American League for twenty-one years, not counting three years out for service in the Marine Corps, in which he enlisted in 1942 at the age of forty-two.

Lyons was elected to the Hall of Fame in 1955.

It's true that I spent a long career with a team that was in the second division most of the time. But I didn't find it frustrating. I would have liked to have won more, but I'll say this: My ball club always hustled for me. I never could find fault with a ball club that put out. As long as I lived, I never complained about an error. We had a young shortstop who became one of the greatest, Luke Appling. He had a great arm, and once in a while he'd uncork one, and it would go up in the third row of seats. I'd say to him, "That's the way to throw it, Luke. Don't let up on the ball. Put something on it." You've got to encourage a guy after he's made an error. If you get on him for booting one, he's going to boot two more before it's over.

But I never resented the fact that we usually finished down in the standings. Sure, you'd have liked to finish higher; it would have been more pleasant once in a while. And if we could have won a pennant, just one, to see what it was like, it would have been nice.

But I never regretted being with Chicago all those years. It's a wonderful town, with wonderful fans, and I can't say enough for them.

Each day you start anew. Every day you start you think you can win. And something different happens every day. You never see two games alike. At least I never have, and I've been paying attention for a long time.

I started playing ball when I was eight years old. With a sock ball. Do you know what that is? That's an old sock that you fold up tight as you can and then get your mother to sew up. We used a broomstick for a bat. That was down in southeastern Louisiana, a long time ago.

Ted Lyons in 1925.

I occupied myself as a boy by playing baseball. All summer long, and then every other chance I could, between school time. I was a 90-pound second baseman in high school. I used a big Joe Jackson bat—I don't know whether you remember Shoeless Joe Jackson's name; he was one of the greatest hitters that ever lived—and I had to choke it up maybe two-thirds of the way and kind of push at the ball. A few years later I got up to 135 pounds, and I started pitching. I was sixteen years old then.

I always had my mind set on being a ballplayer. But I wanted to be a lawyer, too. I studied one term of law and then came to realize I had a little better fast ball and curve than I did a vocabulary. So I went to baseball. My family was wonderful about it. They said, "Well, you've played baseball all your life, from the time you were eight years old, through high school, through college." They told me to make my own choice. Their feeling was that if they talked me out of it and I went into something else and wasn't happy with it, they would feel responsible. I think they showed some wisdom there, and I think I made the right decision.

The scouting systems weren't so extensive then. But there had been several people down in that neighborhood. As a matter of fact, Connie Mack's Athletics trained in Lake Charles, about 20 miles from where I lived. Connie offered to pay my way through college if I signed with him. (For all he knew he might have been paying for an eight-year course—he didn't know if I was dumb or smart.) But I turned him down. Connie was a wonderful old fellow with a great memory, because in '29, when he won the pennant, he said to me, "You see, young fellow, if you would have taken my offer, you'd be pitching on a pennant winner." I said, "That's right. Or maybe I'd be at Oscaloosa trying to make it to the big leagues." You never can tell, can you?

I signed with the White Sox in 1923. I was in my senior year at Baylor University, in Waco, Texas. The White Sox were training nearby, and they decided to come over to Baylor and breeze around and watch the college workout. One of the newspapermen said to the coach, "Say, how about letting Ray Schalk catch one of your pitchers?" He was trying to work up some kind of an angle for a story, see.

The coach said that would be all right, and he called out my name—my middle name, which is Amar, a very unusual name, and I never did like it much. Ray Schalk got a kick out of it, and he called me Amar from then on.

Anyway, the coach said, "Amar, come over here and throw a few for Ray Schalk." So I went over and threw to Schalk for about two or three minutes. I had a pretty good fast ball back then, and I let him know it.

After the workout Schalk and some of the other fellows came over and said there was a possibility they might contact me. That pleased me because the White Sox were one of my favorite teams when I was a kid. At the end of the school year in June, after I'd graduated, I signed up. I got a $1,000 bonus. I took it and bought myself a Ford car. A brand-new 1923 Model T. That was my first car. Cost me $428. What would you say a new Ford would cost today?

Luke Appling.

I joined the ball club in St. Louis. Actually, I got there a day ahead of them; they were in Cleveland. Detroit was in town, and I stayed at the same hotel they did, the Buckingham. After I had my dinner that night, I went outside. There was a little place out front where the ballplayers used to sit and talk. I saw all the stars there— Ty Cobb, Harry Heilmann, Bob Fothergill, Hookie Dauss. I sat around for an hour and a half, listening to them talk baseball. I got a big kick out of it. I thought that was a pretty good start for a fellow his first night in town.

The next day the White Sox came in from Cleveland, and I was assigned to room with Hollis Thurston, who they called Sloppy, even though he was very neat. I never could figure that nickname. He walked into the room—we were perfect strangers—and he said, "Oh, so you're the college kid, eh?" He was one year older than I was.

So I joined the White Sox that day at the hotel, went out to the ball park with them, and pitched an inning in the first major-league game I ever saw. I was sitting on the bench enjoying the ball game, even though we were behind by five or six runs. Eddie Collins was filling in as manager—Kid Gleason had to go back to Chicago, for some reason—and Eddie looked back at me. In those days, in the old Browns ball park, you had two benches, one in front of the other. Naturally I was sitting on the back bench. Collins looked at me and said, "Hey, go down and warm up. I'll let you pitch an inning." I turned around to see who he was talking to, but there was nobody behind me. I kind of swallowed a little bit. "Do you mean me?" I asked. He said, "Yeah."

So I went down and warmed up. This was my debut, and I was beginning to wonder how I was going to do. When I walked out on the mound, I felt enclosed. You see, I'd been used to playing on pastures, where when somebody hit a ball you had to stop it from rolling. Well, this field had fences around it. And of course in those days the Browns had big crowds, because they were usually con- tenders, so there was a lot of noise.

I can remember the guys I faced: Urban Shocker, a spitball pitcher; Johnny Tobin, the leadoff hitter; and Baby Doll Jacobson. I got them out in order. I don't remember exactly how they went out, but I'd got off on the right foot and was tickled to death.

I received wonderful treatment from everybody when I was breaking in. They couldn't have been nicer. Great fellows. The White Sox at that time had Harry Hooper, Eddie Collins, Ray Schalk, Red Faber. All four of those fellows are Hall of Famers today. And they had Bibb Falk in the outfield, and Johnny Mostil, who was a great center fielder, one of the greatest. He could go get 'em. It was like turning a rabbit loose when the ball was hit out to center field. And they had Willie Kamm at third base. That was Willie's first year in the major leagues, and what a fine career he had ahead of him.

I guess I'm one of the few who have had long big league careers without ever having played in the minors. Frankie Frisch never played in the minors; neither did Eppa Rixey or Mel Ott. Bob Feller is another one; he came right out of high school. You can name some others, but not too many.

I think if you've played four years of college ball and you had good coaching, you've learned a lot of fundamentals. Of course, on top of that you have to have a little intelligence, to help yourself. And on top of that, you've got to have a pretty good arm. That's the biggest thing. I'll tell you a little story that happened around 1927. Walter Johnson was near the end of his career, and he came up with a sore arm. Well, so did I. One day I was walking down the clubhouse steps, working my shoulder with my hand. And here comes Walter, walking up the clubhouse steps, doing the same thing to his shoulder. We both stopped and looked at each other and grinned sort of selfconsciously.

"How's your arm, Walter?" I asked.

"It's terrible," he said. "How's yours?"

"The same thing," I said.

"That old stuff about pitching with your head doesn't go, does it?" he said.

That's what I mean, you see. You've got to have your arm in good shape. And in the big leagues it's got to be in good shape all the time. You couldn't go out there with a bad arm.

Well, I mentioned Walter Johnson. You have to mention Walter, don't you? He was just terrific. He was another one who never played in the minor leagues. He came up to the big leagues around

1907, just a green kid out of the West, and stepped right in, and nobody had ever seen anything like him. The thing that I think was so much in his favor was his delivery. He had long arms, and he came from down under, and his ball sank in onto a right-hand hitter. It was tough to hit. A left-hand hitter had the ball going away from him. I can't say Walter was the speediest I ever saw because he was past his prime when I came into the league. When I saw him, he wasn't quite as fast as Grove or as Feller. But Walter's ball did so much. And some of the other fellows who had batted against him six or eight years before told me that he just threw the ball by you, right over the plate.

I pitched against Grove quite a bit. I was in the league just a few years ahead of him, and I saw him come up. Of course I knew who he was even before he came into the league. He was with Baltimore of the International League, and we played them an exhibition game one time. He struck out fifteen of our batters. Here's this minor-league pitcher throwing nothing but fastballs and blowing them right past everybody. They knew what they were going to get, but it didn't make any difference. Somebody said, "Well, he'll never make it in the big leagues. All he can do is throw a fastball." And somebody else said, "Yeah, and all Galli-Curci can do is sing."

Oh, he was fast. He was terrific. I remember one time we sent Butch Henline up to pinch-hit against Lefty. Butch had just come over from the National League and had never hit against Lefty. It was in the ninth inning, and we had men on second and third. I don't know how they got there, unless we cheated. So Butch steps up, and Lefty pours in two strikes, throwing so hard you wondered the cover didn't fly off the ball. Then he threw the third one, and he had more on that than he did on the other two. Back comes Butch. He's absolutely demoralized. When he sat down on the bench, I said, "Butch, do you know that's the first time I ever saw him let up on oh and two? I'm surprised you didn't whale it." Well, he looked at me and his eyes got as big as silver dollars. "Let up?" he said. "Whale it? What are you talking about? I couldn't even *see* that thing!"

Bob Feller was another swifty. We'd all heard about him, about how fast he was and everything. But it wasn't until you hit against

Eddie Collins: "Eddie Collins was a guy like Ty with the bat— he could do anything with it."

Walter Johnson: "He came up to the big leagues in 1907, just a green kid out of the West. . . ."

him that you knew how fast he really was, until you saw with your own eyes that ball jumping at you. You've heard about a fastball being alive. Well, with Feller that wasn't just a figure of speech—his ball really moved. Do you remember Eric McNair? He'd be right on top of the plate, all the time. Well, one day in Cleveland Feller threw one right under McNair's chin. Almost got him. Then Feller struck him out, and when he came back to the bench, McNair said, "Fellas, you know I never give anybody an inch up at that plate. But I'm giving old Rapid Robert about a foot and a half from now on, because I don't mind being killed outright, but I don't want to be maimed the rest of my life."

I saw quite a bit of Cobb. I'd say he was probably the greatest all-around batter. He could hit the ball anywhere he wanted to, and he'd hit it wherever you pitched it. And he had so many gimmicks. In the spring he'd wear a long-sleeve shirt down to his wrists, and if you pitched a ball inside to him, he'd contrive to have it hit that baggy sleeve and he'd get on first base. In a close ball game I tried to keep it away from him, not give him a chance to do that to me, because he was a streak on those bases. He could upset a whole ball club.

Eddie Collins was a guy like Ty with the bat—he could do anything with it. He very seldom struck out. Eddie was just plain great, all-around. He could do everything. And he was a very intelligent guy. It was a pleasure to listen to him talk baseball. He'd never ramble, always came right to the point, and he was seldom wrong. If he told you how to pitch to a batter, well, you'd better do it. I'm pitching against Washington one time. Do you remember Goose Goslin? He could hit the ball a mile. Especially fastballs. Well, I kept trying to throw a fastball by him. I said I was going to throw a fastball by that Goslin if I had to try a hundred times. I really got stubborn about it. And Collins kept warning me about it. "Don't give that fella any fast balls," he said.

It comes down to the eighth or ninth inning, and the infield is in. Collins is our manager and is calling the signals for the catcher from second base. Goslin comes up, and Collins keeps calling curveball signs. I threw Goose two or three curves, and he fouled them off. I decided I was going to throw him a fastball. Buck Crouse was catching, and he gave me a curveball sign. I shook him off. He kept doing that, and I kept saying no. Finally he gave me a fastball. I threw it in, and Goslin hit it like a bullet. It hit Collins right on the shin and bounced out into left center field. Collins didn't go after the ball; he came after me. "I told you not to throw him a fastball!" he yelled.

After the game he rolled up his trouser leg to show me a big black and blue mark on his leg.

"Look what you did," he said.

"It's all right, Eddie," I said. "We won the game, didn't we?"

Then he started to laugh. "I guess we did," he said. Then he said, "But listen to me, Ted, you'd better let me call the signs after this, or you're liable to get somebody crippled out there."

You know, it's like I was telling someone not long ago. There are great stars in every era. You can go back to 1900, there were stars. And there are great stars today. But I would have to say that in the twenties we probably saw more great hitters than in any other era. Just think of some of those fellows: Cobb, Speaker, Gehrig, Sisler, Ruth, Simmons, Goslin, Heilmann, Foxx, and plenty of others. The only way you could pitch to them was by changing speeds. I always tried to keep the ball outside to them, but of course, when you do that, you're taking a chance on getting hit with a line drive because some of those big hitters would send that ball through the middle and pick you right off the hill. The only way you could get a fastball by was when you caught one of them guessing. If you'd been feeding him a lot of slow stuff, you might take a little chance . . . on untying the ball game.

I mean, it could be unnerving pitching to fellows like Ruth and Gehrig and Foxx. Foxx was something to look at up at the plate. He had great powerful arms, and he used to wear his sleeves cut off way up, and when he dug in and raised that bat, those muscles would bulge and ripple. One day I was pitching to him, and he swung and topped the ball around home plate. I came running in for it, but the ball kicked foul. I stood there looking at him.

"How much air you carrying in those arms, Jimmie?" I asked.

"Thirty-five pounds," he said.

"Looks it," I said. And it did. His biceps looked like tires carrying thirty-five pounds. He could hit a ball as far as anybody. You say you've heard stories about Jimmie's long-distance hitting? Well, I don't know which stories in particular you've heard, but I'd say you wouldn't go far wrong if you believed them all.

Harry Heilmann was one of the most marvelous men I ever met in baseball and one of the greatest right-hand hitters. He was a different type of hitter than, say, Hornsby; Hornsby had a smooth stroke with a beautiful follow-through; Harry had a choppy stroke, but powerful. He was a tough man to pitch to. That whole Tiger ball club was tough to pitch to in those years. I remember one year, until about June, they had three .400 hitters in the lineup. Heilmann, Manush, and Fothergill. Cobb couldn't even get into the lineup. I'd call that hitting, wouldn't you? Keeping Cobb on the bench! Fothergill came over to the White Sox a few years later, and he'd love to tell about that. "Remember the time Cobb couldn't get in the lineup?" he'd say, and he'd laugh and laugh.

Ted Williams was a Ty Cobb, as far as being an intelligent batter. He wouldn't hit at a bad ball. I got to know Ted fairly well; I pitched against him a lot, and I was in the service with him, out in Hawaii. We rode together in a jeep every day, in and out of Honolulu. All he'd want to talk about was hitting. One day we were

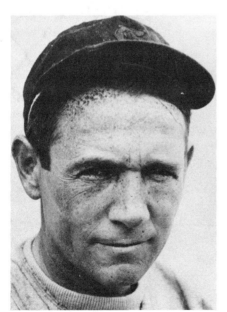

Harry Heilmann.

riding back from Honolulu, and all of a sudden from out of the blue he says to me, "Ted, do you think I'm as good a hitter as Babe Ruth?"

I said, "Well, wait till you get dry behind the ears. You've only been in the league a few years." I was just kidding him.

You know, he wouldn't talk to me all the way home. He just sat there brooding. I had to laugh; I knew what was eating him.

When we got back to the base, I said, "Now, let's get back to the subject. Listen, Ted, you're a little different from Ruth. Babe would hit at balls up around his cap—and those are the ones he'd hit nine miles. You wouldn't swing at one above your letters. Babe didn't mind going after a bad ball. You won't go a half inch out of the strike zone. You're two completely different hitters." And then I told him, "Of course you're as good a hitter as he was."

Then he was all right again.

I pitched a no-hitter, back in 1926, against the Red Sox. Do I remember much about it? Listen, I remember everything about it. You ever want to clear up a pitcher's memory, just ask him about his no-hitter. I'll tell you what I remember about it more than anything else. I'd been under the weather for a couple of days before that. I started the ball game by walking the first batter on four pitches. The next batter comes up, and the first two pitches to him are way off. So it looked like a bad day for old Mudville. The next pitch the batter hit, a line drive out to center field. It looked like a base hit, but our jackrabbit out there, Johnny Mostil, charged in and made a shoe-string catch and doubled the runner off first base. From then on there wasn't but one base on balls. And no hits, of course. A fellow said to me later, "It's a good thing Bill Barrett was in right field." And I said, "Well, yeah, I'd never been able to pitch it without a right fielder." But I knew what he meant. Bill Barrett did make some nice catches. The wind was blowing in that day, and he played extra short, and he caught a few balls that might have been hits.

The last play of the game I remember very well. The batter was an old Texas A&M boy named Topper Rigney. I got two fast strikes on him with curve balls. Then I didn't know what to throw him. I wasn't sure whether I wanted to waste one or not. Johnny Grabow-ski, my catcher, called for another curve ball. I decided to throw as

Jimmie Foxx: "How much air you carrying in those arms, Jimmie?" I asked. "Thirty-five pounds," he said.

good a curve as I could, but break it outside for a ball. Well, I got it outside, but it hit the corner of the plate, and he smacked it. It went to the right of Earl Sheely, our first baseman. He made a good backhand stop, and I ran over to cover first. When I took the throw, I just kept on running because the kids were already pouring out of the stands, coming to try and get that ball away from me.

I guess I had my little superstitions. Most ballplayers do. When I was going good on the mound, I liked to keep using the same ball. I didn't want the infielders throwing it around for fear it would get away and some fan pick it up. But talking about superstitions, I'll tell you a story about Wes Ferrell. There was a real fine pitcher. He'd battle you all the way. He kept you busy all right. Well, one time Wes and I had each won 10 straight games. He came into Chicago, and we were going to pitch against one another. Now, Wes was superstitious about having his picture taken on the day he was going to pitch, and I knew that. I knew, too, that if there was one way to upset a ballplayer, it was to monkey around with his superstitions.

We had this photographer who used to sit on our bench, named Brown.

"Hey, Brownie," I said, "how about getting a picture of Ferrell and me when he comes out, shaking hands and wishing each other bad luck?"

"He won't let me," he said. "You know how he feels about that."

"I know," I said. "But you just insist. Tell him we've both won ten games in a row, and this is a picture you really want. You seldom get two pitchers starting against each other who've won ten games in a row." And I gave him some more baloney.

"Okay," he said. "I'll try."

So Ferrell comes out. Temperamental, but a wonderful guy. Brown walks up to him.

"Wes," he says, "how about stepping over here and having a picture taken with Ted?"

"I don't like to have a picture taken before I pitch," Wes says.

So at about that time I walked over.

"Here's Ted right now," Brown says. "How about letting me get a little shot? It's a real occasion, with both of you having won ten straight. It'll be a great picture."

Wes shrugged. "Oh, all right," he says.

So Brown took a picture of us shaking hands, and while we were doing that, I said to Wes, "He's taking a picture of us shaking hands and wishing each other bad luck."

He laughed, but he gave me a funny look. I'm sure that was on his mind the whole game. I beat him, 2–1. Well, there was a big pot-bellied stove in the clubhouse, and he went in and pretty near tore that thing up. He stomped around in there for about an hour, steaming and snorting.

I saw Wes in Florida a few years ago, and I reminded him of that game. Did he remember it? Need you ask?

"I knew you guys were up to something the minute you started," he said.

"That's the only way we could have beat you," I said. "With that picture."

I played a number of years for Jimmy Dykes. He was a great manager. And he was a witty man, with a wonderful sense of humor. That came in handy during those years.

One time I was pitching a game against Feller, in Cleveland.

Wes Ferrell.

Feller was really rough to beat. If you beat him, it was 1–0 or 2–1.
This particular game was close, 1–1, in the ninth inning. They get a
man on second base, and Ray Mack was the hitter. There was one
out, and Feller was up next.

Dykes calls time and comes walking out to the mound.

"Let's walk this guy and get to Feller," he says.

"No, Jim," I said. "Let's not walk him. I'll make him hit something." In baseball parlance that means you're not going to give him
anything too good to swing at, hope he'll go for a bad pitch.

Jimmy wasn't too sure.

"If we get Mack," I said, "it'll be two out, and they might put in a
hitter for Feller." If they did that, we'd be rid of Bobby.

"All right," Jimmy said. "Okay."

I don't think he'd got back to the dugout when he heard something go *whack!* This fellow Mack hit a line drive into left center for a double, and there went the ball game.

So I walk off the mound, and Jimmy is waiting for me in the dugout. You know, most managers would have been a little sore about that. But Jimmy said, "Well, I'll say one thing. You did what you said you were going to do—you made him hit something."

You know, Jocko Conlon has just now gone into the Hall of Fame as one of the great umpires of all time. Well, there's a little story behind how Jocko became an umpire. He was with the White Sox for a while in the thirties, as a utility outfielder. Jocko was always a good-natured guy, and playful. We were in the shower one day, and we started boxing. That was dumb because there was soap all over the floor and it was slick in there. I put up my elbow; he hit me there and broke his thumb. He called me Elbows McFadden after that.

The next day Jocko comes to the ball park with his thumb in a cast. He gives Dykes some cock-and-bull story how it happened, and that's that.

A few days later we were playing in St. Louis. It was the middle of the summer, and the heat was murderous. Umpires were always passing out in St. Louis. I happened to be looking at Red Ormsby, and all of a sudden he just keeled over, knocked out by the heat. In those days you only had two umpires. So what they did was get a player from our club and a player from the Browns to umpire the bases. Jocko had that broken thumb, so Dykes told him to get out there. Well, he umpired at third base, and he called some of the best plays you ever saw. I told him later, "Jocko, you might have found your career." You see, he was just hanging on in the big leagues at that time. So he went into umpiring and became one of the best, and today he's in the Hall of Fame. Thanks to old "Elbows McFadden."

Toward the end of my career I became known as the Sunday pitcher. They figured I could only pitch once a week. I could have pitched more often than that, I think, but they put me on that schedule. Every Sunday I went out and pitched my ball game. And you want to know the funny thing about that? When I was a kid, my mother wouldn't let me play ball on Sunday. Then for three or four years that's the *only* day I played.

I try to keep up with baseball today as much as I can. I watch it on television, and I read *The Sporting News*. Sure I still read *The Sporting News*. I want to tell you how I first got to reading that paper. When we were kids down in Vinton, Louisiana, my best friend and I, we read everything about baseball we could get our hands on. Now my friend's brother worked at the Southern Pacific depot in town. Well, one day a train was going through town, and a fellow threw a newspaper out of the window. My friend's brother picked it up and gave it to us that afternoon.

"Here's something for you fellows," he said.

We looked at it and couldn't believe it. Page one was all baseball. We looked at the second page: all baseball. We looked at the third page: all baseball. Why, the whole paper was baseball! You never saw kids so elated. We subscribed right away. This was about 1914 or so. And I haven't missed an issue of *The Sporting News* since.

Ted Lyons: The Sunday pitcher.

8

GEORGE PIPGRAS

GEORGE WILLIAM PIPGRAS
Born: December 20, 1899, Ida Grove, Iowa
Major-league career: 1923–24, 1927–35, New York Yankees,
    Boston Red Sox
Lifetime record: 102 wins, 73 losses

A member of the 1927 Yankees, George Pipgras was an ace
pitcher on the great teams of the late twenties and early
thirties. Pipgras' best year was 1928, when he won 24 games.
After his playing days were prematurely ended by a freak
accident, Pipgras returned to the minor leagues as an umpire
and worked his way back to the American League in that
capacity.

When I came out of the Army in 1918, I went up to Fulda,
Minnesota, a little old country town, to pitch semipro ball.
There was a train that ran right behind center field, and every so
often when I was pitching, I'd notice the train would stop and just
stand still out there in deep center field. I didn't know it at the time,
but I was being scouted by the train conductor. He was a fellow
that was interested in baseball, and he recommended me to the
White Sox.

Can you imagine that fellow stopping the train to watch a ball
game? I hope his passengers were baseball fans.

The White Sox signed me and sent me to Saginaw, Michigan. But
I couldn't get the ball over the plate, and they released me. I had a
good fast ball, but I was wild, and I stayed wild, right through my
big league career. Always walked a lot of men.

In 1922 I was pitching for Charleston, South Carolina, had a good
year, and the Yankees brought me up. I went to spring training with
them in 1923, had one look at that pitching staff, and wondered how

in the world I was going to win myself a job. They had Herb Pennock, Bob Shawkey, Waite Hoyt, Sam Jones, Bullet Joe Bush. As a matter of fact, I didn't start pitching regularly until 1927. Dutch Ruether was with us then, and he was supposed to pitch one day. But he wasn't feeling well. So Miller Huggins told me I was going to start.

Well, I won the ball game, and after that I took Ruether's place. Shows you how chancy baseball is—if Ruether hadn't turned up sick that day, who knows when I might have got my opportunity and what would have happened?

Those '27 Yankees had everything. I don't think any ball club in history could beat them. They were tops. Any team that has Ruth and Gehrig has a head start, doesn't it? They gave a pitcher confidence. You knew that if you were behind a run or two late in the game, it didn't matter; Ruth would hit one, or Gehrig would, or they both would. Then we had Earle Combs, Tony Lazzeri, Joe Dugan, Bob Meusel. Every one a great ballplayer.

Bob Meusel had the best arm I ever saw. You know, even Cobb wouldn't run on him. I remember once, Cobb was on third with one out and somebody lifted a fly ball to Meusel. Ordinarily on a ball like that Ty would have come in. Wally Schang was the catcher, and when that ball went out to Meusel, Walley took off his mask and stood at the plate and yelled down to Cobb, "Come on in, Ty. Come on in." Taunting him. Cobb just stood there. Meusel caught the ball and held onto it. Schang waved to Cobb: Come on in. But Ty just stood there with his hands on his hips, scowling at Schang. Cobb was aggressive, but not foolish. He knew Meusel's arm, and he wasn't about to challenge it.

We won 110 games that year, 1927, plus four straight in the Series against Pittsburgh. I wasn't supposed to start in that Series. At least not as far as I knew. Urban Shocker was supposed to start the second game. Well, in about the seventh or eighth inning of the first game, right out of the blue, Miller Huggins looks over at me.

"George," he says, "can you pitch tomorrow?"

"Well, sure I can."

"Okay," he says. "Get a good night's rest."

A good night's rest! I'll tell you what I did. I went back to the hotel and began studying that Pirate lineup until my eyes started to hurt. How was I going to pitch to them? They had some good hitters—the Waner brothers, Pie Traynor, Joe Harris, Glenn Wright.

I guess I was a bit nervous when I got to the ball park the next day. Heck, I was pitching for a team that had won 110 games. I was *expected* to win. I got some great encouragement from Urban Shocker in the clubhouse—he was going to be first out of the bull-pen if I got into trouble.

"Listen," he said, "when you leave the game, leave the ball rough." He was a spitball artist, you see.

"Sure," I said. "I'll do that."

But I had no intention of getting out of there. I started off kind of shaky. Lloyd Waner led off and hit me for a triple, and he scored. But we came back with three in the third and three more in the eighth and beat them, 6–2. I was fast that day. Didn't throw but three curves. They kept coming up there looking for the curve but never got it.

We took the next two games for a clean sweep. As a matter of fact, I played in three World Series, and we swept each one in four games, in '27 against the Pirates, '28 against the Cardinals, and '32 against the Cubs.

I had a nice year in '28—24 wins. Huggins started me in the second game of the Series, against St. Louis. I drew an interesting opponent, Grover Cleveland Alexander. He was past his prime, of course, but that fellow still knew how to pitch. One thing I'll never forget. Alex had this reputation as being a pretty good man with the bottle. You've heard that. Anyway, you know how they always ask the starting pitchers to pose for pictures before a World Series game? Well, when I got together with Alex, I put out my hand for him to shake and he reached for it and I swear missed it by a foot, he was so drunk; either that or he had a wicked hangover. He just waved his hand around in the air until we made contact.

You knew that Alex wasn't right. He could throw the ball through the eye of a needle, but in that particular game he walked four or five men and gave up a lot of hits, and by the third inning we had him out of there. Lou Gehrig hit a tremendous home run off him. It

Grover Cleveland Alexander and George Pipgras, starting pitchers for the second game of the 1928 World Series. ". . . he was so drunk; either that or he had a wicked hangover."

was a ball that the center fielder broke in on, but it just kept rising and rising and finally hit the scoreboard. If you know where that scoreboard was in Yankee Stadium, you know what a clout that was. We won that game, 9–3.

Ruth and Gehrig hit home runs all over the place in that Series. What a Series those fellows had! Between them they hit seven home runs and averaged something like .600. There never was a one-two punch in any lineup like those two. At least I can't think of any. Can you?

In 1933 I was traded over to the Red Sox. I didn't like the idea, of course, but there's nothing you can do about it. Here I was leaving a winning ball club and going to a losing one.

We had Bucky Walters playing third base in Boston. What an arm! When he fired that ball across from third, it really moved. In fact, the first baseman sometimes had trouble handling it. They weren't thinking about making him into a pitcher then. Seems to me I heard some talk about his ball being too alive, but that would be nonsense since I can't believe a pitcher can have a ball that's too alive. Well, you know what happened. A few years later they did make him into a pitcher, in the National League, and he became one of the great ones.

You know, I broke my arm throwing a ball. Sounds incredible, doesn't it? It happened soon after I'd joined the Red Sox. I was pitching against Detroit. The batter was a fellow named Doljack. I had him oh and two and figured I'd waste a pitch. The moment I let go of the ball I felt my arm pop.

They sent me to a bone specialist in Chicago. He said that because of the amount of pitching I'd done through the years, the muscles in that arm had become stronger than the bone, and when I'd snapped off that pitch, well, the bone just wouldn't take it anymore. It's not a common thing; as far as I know, it's only happened a few times.

That finished me as a pitcher. I was only thirty-three years old and hadn't given much thought to the future, and frankly I didn't know what to do. So I talked to Tom Yawkey about it. Now there's a good man. He's a man who cares about his players and cares about baseball. He's a millionaire many times over and just as regular a guy as you'd want to find. I remember I was hunting with him at his plantation in South Carolina. This was right after I'd finished as a pitcher.

"I don't know what I'm going to do," I said to him. "Baseball has been my whole life. I just don't know anything else."

"Look," he said, "you know the game, you know the rules. Why don't you think about umpiring? If you want, I'll sponsor you."

Well, I went home and talked to my wife about it, thought it over for a month or so, and decided to take a shot at it. I called Yawkey and told him I'd do it. He got the American League to give me a job, in the Eastern League.

Well, I liked it fine, and I got along pretty well. I came into the American League in 1939. I was in baseball for seventeen years and was never put out of a game. I always remembered something Herb Pennock told me when I was just breaking in: "You're going to make a lot more mistakes than the umpire." So when the players used to get on me, I'd run them. I just wouldn't take it.

One time in Chicago, in a game between the White Sox and the Browns, I ran seventeen men out of there. They kept jumping on me, and I kept bouncing them out, off of both benches. That night Will Harridge called me—he was the league president.

"George," he said, "have you gone crazy?"

"No, I haven't gone crazy," I said. "They're going to let me alone out there, or I'm not going to be there."

"Don't you think you were a little bit rough on them?" he asked.

"Not at all."

"But *seventeen* men, George."

"All that yelling from the bench isn't necessary," I said. "I never read anything that said you had to yell at the umpire in order to play ball."

So the players knew I wasn't going to take it. And I worked a number of years with another fellow who wasn't going to take it— Bill Summers. When we walked out on that field, we were in charge, and everybody knew it.

Sure, we made mistakes. And when we did, we'd admit it. And once we'd admitted it, most of the players and managers would understand. Bill Dickey was a great one for that. He'd say, "What was wrong with that pitch?" And I'd say, "Nothing. I missed it." And he wouldn't say another word. Jimmy Dykes was another one like that. You've heard about Jimmy being rough on umpires, but I never found that so. He'd come storming out and I'd say, "Jimmy, I kicked it. Now let's get on with the game."

You know, most of the time when you see the manager out there, it's to protect his players. After all, the manager is sitting in the dugout, and say there's a close play at second base. There's no way

Umpire Pipgras, with former teammate Earle Combs.

he can see it. But he sees his player on the edge of getting the thumb, and he comes out there to break it up, to keep his player in the game. He's also got to let his players know he'll back them up in an argument. He's got to do that.

I was umpiring when Ted Williams broke in. There was a hitter. I never saw him swing at a bad ball. He had the greatest pair of eyes I ever saw. He'd take a ball an inch or two off the plate and never flinch. I'll tell you, he kept you on your toes, the way he took pitches. And when he took a pitch and you called it a strike, you couldn't help but to think you'd missed it. But Ted was great. He'd never look around at you. All the great ballplayers were that way— they'd never try to show you up.

People always ask me who was the fastest pitcher I ever saw. Well, I saw Grove and Feller in their prime, and you can't believe anybody could be quicker than those two fellows. But I'll tell you something. When I broke into the league, I batted against Walter Johnson. He'd been around a long time at that point, seventeen years or so. Well, I stepped into the batter's box, took two called strikes, and stepped out of the batter's box. I turned around and looked at Muddy Ruel, who was catching. I could see he had a little smile on his face, behind his mask. He knew what I was going to say.

"Muddy," I said, "I never saw those pitches."

"Don't let it worry you," he said. "He's thrown a few that Cobb and Speaker are still looking for."

And Johnson was past his prime then, remember. They told me that he'd slowed down a bit by then. So if that was Walter Johnson past his prime . . . well, who was the fastest pitcher of all time? I don't know. . . but I have a sneaking suspicion.

I like to play golf these days, you know. Well, the other day I was getting ready to putt the ball and some people were making noise. My partner asked me if that didn't bother me. "Look," I said, "if you've ever had the experience of standing out on a pitching mound, with seventy thousand people yelling their lungs out, with the bases loaded, the count three and two, and Jimmie Foxx at bat, why, you're not going to be bothered by a couple of people talking on a golf course."

9

BILLY HERMAN

WILLIAM JENNINGS BRYAN HERMAN
Born: July 7, 1909, New Albany, Indiana
Major-league career: 1931–47, Chicago Cubs, Brooklyn Dodgers, Boston Braves, Pittsburgh Pirates
Lifetime average: .304

Billy Herman had the reputation for being one of the most intelligent, as well as ablest, players of his day. In 1935 his 227 base hits led the league, and in 1935–36 he put together back-to-back seasons of 57 doubles. Herman was a winning player, superlative in the field, an incomparable hit-and-run man, a driving force on four pennant winners.

In February, 1975, Herman was voted into the Hall of Fame.

I came up to the Cubs from Louisville of the American Association in August, 1931. It was a bad ball club to be breaking in with because of that pitching staff. Biggest bunch of headhunters you ever saw. Charlie Root. Off the field, a very quiet man. Out on that mound, he was mean. So was Pat Malone. And so was Lon Warneke. Guy Bush, too. That was a mean staff. Every time they'd throw at a hitter naturally somebody on our club would get it right back. I think I must've had my tail in the batter's box as often as my feet. But I was young and agile then, and it didn't bother me. Not much.

But of course, you had a lot of that back in those days. It was bad. The rules they have today are better in that respect. The umpires will stop that sort of thing. But back then, say you had a little trouble with a ball club on opening day. Well, now you're playing them twenty-one more games. That trouble would pop up every one of those games. Maybe even carry over into the next year. You had some really bad throwing contests. And I mean bad ones. It's a wonder a lot more players didn't get hurt.

I remember a game we were playing in Chicago against the Giants, when Billy Terry was managing them. We went into the bottom of the tenth, the game tied. There's two out and a man on first. Hal Schumacher is pitching for them, and Chuck Klein is the batter. Klein ties into one, hits it for a double, and we win the game.

The next day Charlie Root is pitching for us against Hubbell. Charlie puts them down in order in the first inning, getting Terry for the third out. Klein is our third hitter, and when he comes up, Hubbell throws two pitches right behind his head. Getting even for the day before, see. Well, we knew Hubbell's control. He could throw strikes at midnight. He's not going to miss that far unless he's told to. So we're pretty mad. We're yelling and cursing on the bench. Everybody but Root. Charlie just sits there like a mummy, not saying a thing. He goes out and pitches the next inning and doesn't come close to anybody. We wondered about that, but nobody said anything.

Then in the third inning up comes Mr. Terry again. He steps in and cocks that bat; Root winds up and with his first pitch hits him right in the neck. Terry staggered around but didn't go down. Then he starts for the mound, and Root, being a gentleman, doesn't want to make Terry walk that far. He comes right out to meet him.

"What the hell did you do that for?" Terry yells.

"Why'd you make Hubbell throw at Klein?" Charlie yells back.

Well, we broke it up before they got together. But that's the way it was then.

You know, when I was a kid, baseball was about the only sport around. There wasn't much basketball or football to speak of. So I started to play ball. That was back in Indiana, in a little town called New Albany. I played on the high school team and then in an amateur league in Louisville, which wasn't too far away. I wasn't thinking of pro ball in those days, but when I got a chance, I jumped at it. Once I signed that first contract, well, then I had visions of going to the big leagues. That became my ambition.

Baseball was a good job in those years, after the Depression began. I was damn lucky to be playing ball. In 1932 I made $7,000, which was a ton of money then. I came from a big family, and some of my brothers were struggling just to earn eating money.

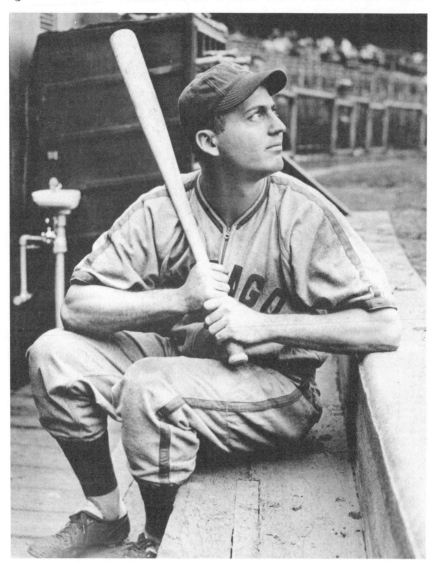

Billy Herman.

Rogers Hornsby was the manager when I joined the Chicago club in 1931. He was all business. You couldn't smoke or even drink a soda in the clubhouse or read a paper or anything like that. Sort of an odd guy, too. If you were a rookie, he wouldn't talk to you. Never say hello. You might get a grunt out of him, but that was about all. The only time you'd hear his voice with your name in it was when you did something wrong, and then you heard it loud and clear. If he ignored you, then you knew you were doing all right.

Hornsby wasn't popular with the players, which didn't bother him a damn. We had some good ballplayers, too. Gabby Hartnett was on that club, and Charlie Grimm, Kiki Cuyler, Woody English, Riggs Stephenson, Hack Wilson, plus all those hard-nosed pitchers.

Breaking in was kind of rough back in those days. Much rougher than it is now. A kid comes to a major-league club today, everybody talks to him and tries to help him along. But back then they more or less resented a young kid coming to the team; they knew he was going to take some older guy's job, and that older guy was their friend. So you were pretty much on your own.

I was a serious-minded player, and I didn't go out of my way to try and make friends with the older players. I figured that if I could show them I could play and that I meant to stay, they'd warm up. And that's just what happened. I played in twenty-five games that September and hit .327. Then I went to spring training in 1932 and won the job.

That was quite a year for a first-year man. We were rolling along just great, fighting Pittsburgh for the pennant. And then all of a sudden, in August, Hornsby gets fired. He'd been having some trouble with the general manager, Mr. Veeck—that's Bill Veeck's father. Veeck was questioning Hornsby's handling of the pitchers, and one thing or another. Hornsby, of course, wasn't the type who took criticism gracefully, and it finally got to the point where he had to go.

Most of the players were pretty happy about the change, especially since it was Charlie Grimm who took over. Grimm was as popular with the players as Hornsby was unpopular. Sometimes that kind of shake-up can demoralize a team, but it seemed to perk us up, and we went on to win the pennant. Root, Warneke, Bush, and Malone did most of the pitching for us coming down the stretch, and they were just great. But we should have gone home after winning the pennant; the World Series was a disaster.

We played the Yankees that year, and they clobbered us in four straight. You know, you hate to say it, but we were overmatched, strictly overmatched, and we were a damn *good* ball club. But they just had too much, in every department. We matched them in speed and defense and pitching, but they had that extra good power.

They had kind of a fat guy, with little skinny ankles, playing right field named Babe Ruth, and Lou Gehrig, Tony Lazzeri, Earle Combs, Bill Dickey, Frankie Crosetti, Ben Chapman. To give you an example of what we were facing, the Cubs as a team that year hit around 70 home runs; Ruth and Gehrig between *themselves* hit 75.

We had a lot of fire and spirit on the Cubs, but when we went out that first day and watched the Yankees take batting practice, our hearts just sank. They were knocking those balls out of sight. We were awestruck.

That was the Series in which Ruth supposedly called his shot. I say "supposedly." He didn't really do it, you know. I hate to explode one of baseball's great legends, but I was there and saw what happened. Sure, he made a gesture, he pointed—but it wasn't to call his shot. Listen, he was a great hitter and a great character, but do you think he would have put himself on the spot like that? I can tell you what happened and why it happened.

Gabby Hartnett and Charley Root. Reproduced with permission from the Chicago Daily News.

We were a young team and a fresh team. We had some guys on the bench that got on Ruth as soon as the Series started. And I mean they were rough. Once all that yelling starts back and forth it's hard to stop it, and of course, the longer it goes on, the nastier it gets. What were jokes in the first game became personal insults by the third game. By the middle of that third game things were really hot.

I think it was around the fifth inning when Ruth came up. Of course, it was always an occasion when that guy stepped up to the plate, but this time it seemed even more so. He'd already hit a home run, in the first inning with two on, and the Chicago fans were letting him have it, and so was our bench. I was standing out at second base, and I could hear it pouring out of the bench. Charlie Root was pitching. He threw the first one over, and Ruth took it for a strike. The noise got louder. Then Root threw another one across, and Ruth took that, for strike two. The bench came even more alive with that. What Ruth did then was hold up his hand, telling them that was only two strikes, that he still had another one coming and that he wasn't out yet. When he held up his hand, that's where the pointing came in. But he was pointing out toward Charlie Root when he did that, not toward the center-field bleachers. And then, of course, he hit the next pitch out of the ball park. Then the legend started that he had called his shot, and Babe went along with it. Why not?

But he didn't point. Don't kid yourself. I can tell you just what would have happened if Ruth had tried that—he would never have got a pitch to hit. Root would have had him with his feet up in the air. I told you, Charlie Root was a mean man out on that mound.

But, like I say, it's still a great story, and those who want to believe it will go on believing it, regardless of what anybody says.

You know, we had a great showman over in the National League, too. Dizzy Dean. What a sweet pitcher he was. He had all the equipment—good fastball, a great curve, and a good slow curve. But I wouldn't say he was the fastest pitcher in the league when I was there. I think Van Lingle Mungo was possibly the fastest pitcher I ever saw.

Dean was hardheaded out on the mound. He wanted to throw the

Lon Warneke. Reproduced with permission from the Chicago *Daily News.*

ball past everybody. If he'd thrown more curves and changes, he wouldn't have had to work so hard. He could be smart and cagey out there when he wanted to—he proved that later, when he was pitching for us in Chicago after he'd lost his great fastball. But when he had it, he loved to show it off.

But I always had very good luck with him, better luck than I had with his brother Paul, even though Dizzy was a lot better pitcher. I always used to kid Diz about how well I hit him. I'll tell you a story about that. In 1960 Billy Jurges was managing the Red Sox, and I signed on as one of his coaches. We were training out in Arizona, and Diz was living nearby in Phoenix.

Dean invited us out to his house one night. He showed us around and then took us into the den. The walls were decorated with pictures and trophies and all the mementos of his career. He also had a lot of box scores framed and hung up there. We got to kidding him about the year he won 30 games. He was proud as hell of that, and with good reason. But he always had a hard time beating the Cubs, and we let him know about that. So Diz pointed to one of the box scores.

"There," he said. "There's one I beat you."

Well, for some reason I went over and looked at the box score.

"No wonder," I said.

"What do you mean?" he asked.

"There's a reason why you won that game, Diz," I said.

"What are you talking about?" he asked.

"I didn't play that day," I said.

Diz gave me an indignant look and squinted at the box score. Sure enough, I wasn't in the lineup that game. It was the first time I ever saw Dean where he couldn't say a word.

I guess the only match in the league for Dean in those years was Carl Hubbell. What a great pitcher and fine competitor he was. I'll tell you something about Hubbell. When he was pitching, you hardly ever saw the opposing team sitting back in the dugout; they were all up on the top step, watching him operate. He was a marvel to watch, with that screwball, fastball, curve, screwball again, changes of speed, control. He didn't have really overpowering stuff, but he was an absolute master of what he did have, and he got every last ounce out of his abilities. I never saw another pitcher who could so fascinate the opposition the way Hubbell did.

But I had great luck with Hubbell. I was the type of hitter that he didn't like to pitch to. He liked those guys who swung hard and soon; he'd throw that little screwball, and they'd be out in front of it, hitting it off the end of the bat. But I was a right field hitter anyway, and a late swinger, so when that screwball was turning off, I'd go right along with it. But that Hal Schumacher—I couldn't hit him at all. He had a sinker, and I couldn't hit those guys. Bucky Walters, too. Same kind of pitcher. Sinking fast balls. Gave me fits.

I saw quite a bit of Pie Traynor, though he'd been around for a

Dizzy Dean: "What a sweet pitcher he was."

while by the time I came into the league. Son of a gun, he was a great player. Most marvelous pair of hands you'd ever want to see. The only problem he had was throwing. He was wild. They told me he was always wild. But the thing that helped Traynor was his quick release. You'd hit a shot at him, a play that he could take his time on, and he'd catch it and throw it right quick, so that if his peg was wild, the first baseman had time to get off the bag, take the throw and get back on again. It was the only way Traynor could throw; if he took his time, he was *really* wild.

But the best third baseman I ever saw, for a couple of years, was Billy Cox. He made the most outstanding plays I've ever seen. Brooks Robinson is great, and so was Clete Boyer; but Cox was amazing. He just made your eyes pop. Ballplayers have their own special lingo, you know, and what they said about Cox was that he had plenty of "cat." You couldn't believe how quick he was, going in any direction. And an arm like a rifle.

I'll tell you about another guy who awed me: Ernie Lombardi. For raw ability with a bat, I don't think anybody could top him. But he was so slow afoot that those infielders could play him so deep that he just didn't have any place to hit the ball. He had to hit it over the fence or against the fence or just too hard for anybody to be able to make a play on. If he was playing today, on this artificial surface, I don't know where the infielders would play him. The ball comes off there like a rocket, and the way Lombardi hit it he might kill an infielder today. He could hit a ball as hard as anybody I ever saw, and that includes Ruth and Foxx.

Nineteen thirty-five was a hell of a year. All season we were in third place watching the Cardinals and Giants battle it out. And then in September we suddenly got hot. I don't mean just hot—we sizzled. We took off and won twenty-one straight games. We played an eighteen-game home stand and won every one. Talk about the virtues of home cooking, huh? Then we went into St. Louis for a five-game series, needing only two to clinch. In the opener Lon Warneke beat Paul Dean, 1–0, and the next day Bill Lee beat Dizzy for the clincher. Lee was almost unbeatable that year. What an overhand curve that guy had!

How do you explain a ball club getting that hot? I don't know.

Maybe it's the power of positive thinking. All of a sudden we got the notion that we couldn't lose; there was no way we could lose. Winning can become an infection, just like losing can. We rode that streak right into the World Series.

We played Detroit that fall. It was a fine World Series, and an exciting one, even though, dammit, we lost. Three of the games were decided by one run. We were down three games to two and got beat a real tough ball game in Detroit. That Series should've gone seven games. We got some great pitching from Warneke and Lee, and a timely hit or two here and there would have made all the difference. But you've heard that story before, haven't you?

Detroit had a solid club. Some real hitters. Mickey Cochrane, Pete Fox, and those G-men: Gehringer, Greenberg, and Goslin. Tommy Bridges beat us two games.

Bridges started the last game, in Detroit, and that's a ball game I don't think I'll ever forget. Detroit up to that time had never won a World Series, and the fans were screaming from the first pitch. We went into the top of the ninth tied, 3–3. I got lucky against Bridges that day and had knocked in all our runs; even got myself a World Series home run. Larry French was pitching for us.

Carl Hubbell: "He was a marvel to watch."

Stan Hack led off the top of the ninth with a triple. So there he was, the tie-breaking run, standing on third base and nobody out. How many ways to get him in? Count 'em: base hit, fly ball, ground ball, balk, wild pitch, passed ball, error. Jurges came up. Bridges struck him out. Then came something they're still second-guessing Charlie Grimm for. He let Larry French hit for himself. Why did he do that? Well, Larry wasn't a bad hitter, for one thing, and for another, he was pitching pretty well and Grimm wanted to keep him in there. I didn't give it much thought at the time. When you're sitting on the bench, in the middle of all the action, you tend to go along with the manager's moves. The second-guessing comes later. That's what second-guessing is all about, isn't it?

Anyway, French tapped back to the mound. So now there were two out, and Hack is still standing on third, and he's looking lonelier and lonelier out there. Augie Galan was the batter. He got hold of one and hit a long fly ball, but it was caught. That fly ball had come too late.

When I think back to the 1935 World Series, all I can see is Hack standing on third base, waiting for somebody to drive him in. Seems to me now he stood there for hours and hours.

In the bottom of the ninth Cochrane got a hit. Then Gehringer hit a line shot that Cavarretta knocked down and got one out on. But Cochrane got to second. Goslin came up. And he got the hit that beat us. It was one of those hits that begins dying the moment it leaves the bat. I ran out for it, Billy Jurges ran out for it, Frank Demaree came in from center for it, but nobody could quite catch up to it and it just dropped onto the grass in center field, and Cochrane scored. Damn, that was so frustrating, running after the ball that's got the World Series riding on it, knowing that you're not going to catch it and knowing that you're not going to miss it by much. It just drops onto the grass and breaks your heart.

That 1935 team, damn it all, we had everything. It was one of the two best I ever played on—the '41 Dodgers was the other. The '35 Cubs were chock-full of good ballplayers. Some people said Chicago had the best infield that year that they ever had—even better than the Tinker-Evers-Chance infield. Well, it's not for me to say which was better, but besides myself we had Phil Cavarretta, Billy Jurges,

and Stan Hack. Then we had Hartnett catching, and Chuck Klein, Frank Demaree, and Augie Galan in the outfield.

We'd gotten Klein from the Phillies. He'd had a half dozen really sensational years over there. He got off to a great start with us and then pulled a hamstring muscle. He tried to play with it and it got worse. He was a hell of a competitor, but he was just tearing up that leg. The blood started to clot in it, and I swear, that leg turned black, from his thigh all the way down to his ankle. I think it just about ruined his career. He couldn't run anymore; he couldn't swing the bat so well anymore. I think it all stemmed from that injured leg.

Chuck was a real nice guy, and strong, very, very strong. They said he could rip a telephone directory in half with his bare hands, and I can believe it. But he was extremely good-natured, and serious, all business. Now we had Augie Galan. Augie was one of my best friends on the ball club. He loved to laugh and fool around, and he had a great imagination for practical jokes. His favorite victim was Klein. Say, why is it that the little guys—Augie wasn't too big—always like to pull pranks on the big strong guys? Is it because they know the big guy won't belt them? Well, whatever the reason, Augie had Klein figured pretty well, because even though Chuck would sometimes get furious at Augie, he never stayed mad—he wasn't that kind of a guy. But one time in New York, Augie almost got it. Boy, I'll tell you, he never came closer to having his head handed to him than that day.

Chuck invited Augie and me up to his room for a beer after the game. This was at the Commodore Hotel, right near Grand Central Station. Chuck was in a real happy mood—his fiancée was coming in on the train from Philadelphia, and he was looking forward to taking her out for a night on the town. So we went up to his room, and Chuck called room service, and they came around with a tray of beer and a couple of bowls of peanuts.

We were sitting and drinking beer and eating the peanuts for a while, and then there's a knock on the door, and the valet comes in. He's got Chuck's suit on a hanger, all cleaned and pressed. Chuck's face lit up when he saw how nice the suit looked. You know how a fellow wants to look good when he's taking his best girl out. He tipped the valet and hung the suit up in the closet. Then he looked at his watch—it was getting near time for that train from Philly to come in.

"Listen," he said, "you guys sit around and finish your beer. I've got to go and meet the train. I'll be back in a little while."

So Augie and me are sitting there. He's pretty quiet for a while, staring at the bowl of peanuts on the table next to him. And then he gets a brilliant idea. He goes over to the window and opens it about eight or ten inches or so and then pulls the blind down to that level. He sprinkles some peanuts onto the windowsill, then steps around and hides behind the blind. Well, there were always a lot of pigeons around that area, and sure enough they start coming to peck at the peanuts. As soon as one of them lands, Augie shoots his hand out and captures it. He takes the pigeon over to the closet, opens the door, throws the pigeon in, and closes the door. He does this about three or four times and then sits down and has another beer.

About a half hour later Chuck comes back. He's checked his fiancée into the hotel, and now he's going to change and get ready for his big night out. He opens the closet to get his suit and the pigeons come roaring out, right in his face. Chuck was so startled he stumbled back and sat down on the edge of the bed, and just sat there watching the pigeons circle around and around the room until they found the open window and got the hell out.

Chuck looked at Galan—he knew who'd done it—and just shook his head. That was okay. But when he took his suit out and looked at it I thought he'd explode: the pigeons had shit all over it. I'll never forget him standing there holding that suit up on the hanger, his eyes getting bigger and bigger. Oh, he was mad. I thought he was going to throw Augie out of the window. I really thought he was going to do it, he was so goddamned mad. Augie was lucky to get out of that room alive.

You know, the other night I heard a sportscaster commenting on how tough the schedule is today for the ballplayer. Well, I had to laugh. The players today don't know how easy they have it. Say

Chuck Klein.

you're leaving Chicago to go play a series in St. Louis and a series in Cincinnati. You know how they make that trip today? Buses to and from the ball park. Short plane rides. And everything air-conditioned, of course: buses, planes, hotels, clubhouses.

Now, back when I played, here's how you went from Chicago to St. Louis to Cincinnati—and I'm talking about July and August, when it's always 90 or more degrees in those towns. You got on a train at midnight, and maybe that train has been sitting in the yards all day long, under a broiling sun. It feels like 150 degrees in that steel car. Sometimes they'd have these blowers on either end of the car to circulate the air, and sometimes they wouldn't. You get into St. Louis at six thirty in the morning, grab your own bag, fight to get a cab, and go to the hotel. By the time you get to the hotel it's seven thirty, and you have an afternoon ball game to play. So you hurry into the dining room—and it's hot in there, no air conditioning—and you eat and run upstairs to try and get a few hours' rest. Then you go to the ball park, where it's about 110 degrees. You finish the ball game around five or five thirty and go into the clubhouse. It's around 120 degrees in there. You take your shower, but there's no way you can dry off; the sweat just keeps running off of you. You go out to the street and try and find a cab back to the hotel. You get back to the hotel and go up to your room, and you lose your breath, it's so hot in there. But the dining room isn't much better, so you order room service and stay right there and eat. Then you go to bed and try to sleep, but you can't, you're sweating so much. So you get up and pull the sheet off the bed and soak it with cold water and go back and roll up in a wet sheet; but it dries out after an hour or two, and you have to get up and soak it again. This goes on for four days in St. Louis, and you go on to Cincinnati and it's the same thing. For eight days you haven't had a decent night's sleep. And they talk about tough conditions today!

But hell, if you wanted to play ball, you played ball, no matter what conditions were like. And I guess you can tolerate almost anything as long as you don't know how much better it can be.

That 1938 pennant race was a pip. We were battling it out with the Pirates. It was brutally close, the kind of race where you knew somebody was going to go home after the season and think all winter about that one bad break or that one good break, depending on which side you were on. And, boy, that's just what happened.

There were just a few games left to play, and the Pirates came into Chicago for a three-game series, leading us by a game and a half. This was do or die, no question about it.

Gabby Hartnett was our manager, and he took a gamble in the first game. He started Dean. Dizzy's arm was gone; all he could throw were curves and changes. But he had guts. And he pitched one hell of a ball game for us. He had them shut out until the ninth, 2–0. Then they got a man on, and Lee Handley doubled with two out, putting the tying runs on. Al Todd was the batter. Hartnett had a tough decision to make right then and there: Leave Diz in or take him out? Well, he took him out and brought in Bill Lee. Bill had been just marvelous for us coming down the stretch. But Lee's first pitch was wild, and a run came in. You could almost hear the second-guessers cranking up. But Lee bore down and struck Todd out. One of the most beautiful strikeouts I've ever seen. That left us just a half game out, and set the stage for the next day. They're still talking about what happened that next day. Whenever you're talking about baseball's great moments, you've got to include what happened in that game.

We came into the bottom of the ninth tied, 3–3. Mace Brown was on the mound for the Pirates. He was their ace relief pitcher, and a real good one. It had been a drawn-out game, and by the time we came into the last of the ninth it was pretty dark, and it was obvious this was going to be the last inning. The Pirates were, in effect, playing for a tie at that point.

Brown got the first two men out, and then Hartnett was the batter. It was getting darker by the minute, and it looked for sure like we were going to have to play a doubleheader the next day, which would have put us in a bind, because we were short on pitchers.

Brown got two strikes on Hartnett, and we were getting ready to go to the clubhouse. Then Brown threw the next pitch, and he came right in with it. I don't know why he didn't waste one; maybe he figured it was so dark Hartnett couldn't see it anyway. But Gabby swung and rode it right out of there. You never saw such excitement in a ball park! The fans came pouring out onto the field, and it seemed to take Hartnett forever to get around the bases. He had to fight his way through to touch third and then fight his way through to touch home plate.

Well, that broke Pittsburgh's back. We went out the next day, and we could've beaten nine Babe Ruths. We beat them by something like 10–1. They were totally demoralized, even though technically they were still in the race. If they'd won that last game, they would have left town a half game ahead. But their backs were broken. That sort of thing can happen to a team, any team, big league or not. What it does, most of the time, is upset you badly for two or three days, and when it happens late in the season, you just don't have the time to recover.

You know, the Cubs had this odd pattern of winning pennants every three years. They won it in 1929—I wasn't there then—1932, 1935, and 1938. Well, they didn't win it in 1941, but I got into the World Series just the same. I was traded over to the Dodgers soon after the season opened in 1941.

I was surprised by the deal, but maybe I shouldn't have been. I wasn't a kid anymore, and at that particular time the Cubs had a young second baseman they'd brought up from the Coast League, named Lou Stringer. He'd had a great spring training, and they thought he was going to be a fine ballplayer. So they figured I was expendable.

We were in New York at the time, at the Commodore Hotel. I remember Larry MacPhail called me at two thirty in the morning.

"I've just made a deal for you," he said.

"At two thirty in the morning?" I asked.

"What's the difference?" he said.

The Cubs were playing the Giants, and the Pirates were playing the Dodgers. So I got my gear out of the Polo Grounds and went over to Ebbets Field. I got four for four my first game.

I walked right into a real hot pennant race with the Dodgers. We fought the Cardinals all summer. I remember we went into St. Louis late in the year—every damned game that year seemed crucial—and we just had to beat them. Another one of those head-on collisions, when it's all on the table. The opening game of that series was just unforgettable. One of the greatest ball games I ever played in.

Whitlow Wyatt was pitching for us against Mort Cooper. There was no score going into the eighth inning, and on top of it Cooper was pitching a no-hitter. Then, with two out, Dixie Walker hit a double, and I came up. Boy, you really want a base hit in a spot like that! We needed that game, and I hated to see Wyatt lose after the way he'd pitched. Well, Cooper gave me a pitch to hit, and I busted it for a double to score Dixie. That was the only run of the game. I'll remember that game as long as I live.

But I guess I didn't have much luck in World Series. Three with the Cubs, and three losers; and then another loser with the Dodgers, in '41. I'll tell you what happened to me in that Series. It was a very odd thing, something I'd never had happen to me before. We were

Billy Herman, Pete Reiser, Dolph Camilli, Dixie Walker, of the '41 Dodgers.

taking batting practice before the third game, in Brooklyn. I was practicing hitting the ball to right field, and on my last cut I swung kind of awkwardly and pulled a rib cage muscle. The pain just rushed into me; I could hardly breathe. I went into the clubhouse, and they taped me up, but I was in a lot of pain. Still, I was determined to play. The last thing in the world you want to do is sit out a World Series. I came up to bat in the bottom of the first inning and hit the ball well, but I almost collapsed from the pain. I had to leave the game, and I was pretty much finished for the Series.

That was the game where Fred Fitzsimmons had the Yankees shut out into the seventh. Then Marius Russo hit one back off Fred's knee and made him leave the game. Hugh Casey came in, got nicked for a couple, and we lost, 2–1. The fourth game was the one where Mickey Owen let the third strike get away from him.

You've probably heard all kinds of stories about what happened there. Was it a spitter? Did Casey cross Mickey up? Well, Casey swore it was a curveball. I think Owen might have "nonchalanted" the ball, putting his glove out for it instead of shifting his whole body to make the catch. Owen had a habit of doing that, and maybe that's what happened there. And the ball got away. But let's give the Yankees some credit, too. They jumped right in and took advantage of the break. They had the type of club in those days that wouldn't let you up once you were down. And we stayed down, too. We were licked before we went out on the field the next day. We couldn't have beaten a girls' team.

Say, listen, can we skip 1942? People ask me what went wrong in 1942, and I say to them: "What went wrong? We won a hundred and four games, didn't we? That's pretty damned good, isn't it?" You bet your life that was pretty damned good. The only problem was, the Cardinals won 106.

That was some season, beginning with spring training. We took spring training in Havana that year. We had a lot of hell raisers on that club. It was a wild time. Why, MacPhail had detectives trailing some of the guys.

You know, Ernest Hemingway lived in Havana at that time, and I spent a night with him I'll never forget. Hemingway liked to hang around with ballplayers, and one day he invited a few of us out to this gun club where he and his wife were members. Hemingway took a lot of pride in all this manly stuff, guns and boozing and fighting, things like that. He was a big, brawny man, and when he'd had a few drinks, he got mean, real mean.

So he invited Hugh Casey, Larry French, Augie Galan, and myself out to the gun club. Believe me, this was no Coney Island shooting gallery. It was a real fancy place. You had a guy with a portable bar following you around. You'd get up, take your shots, and there'd be a drink ready for you. This went on from three o'clock in the afternoon until dark. At that point Hemingway said, "Ah, the hell with this. Come on up to the house, and let's have a few drinks."

So we all went up to his house. He had a big beautiful home. He took us into a huge dining room-living room combination, with all terrazzo floors, and told us to make ourselves comfortable while he went and got the drinks.

He came back with an enormous silver tray, with all the bottles, the mixers, the glasses, the ice—the whole works. He set it up on this little bookstand in the middle of the floor. And we started drinking. Hemingway was a real great host. He couldn't do enough for you. He gave us each an autographed copy of *For Whom the Bell Tolls*, his book about the Spanish Civil War.

We talked a lot about the war. The war had just started, in December, and this was in March. Hemingway started talking about the Japanese and how far they were going to go. And you know, events proved him right. He said they were going to go down the Malay Peninsula, that they were going to take Burma, and this island and that island. He'd been a foreign correspondent in different parts of the world and knew a hell of a lot about a lot of things, and it was fascinating.

We had quite a bit to drink; then he laid out some food. After we ate, we had a few more drinks. It was getting pretty late now, and Mrs. Hemingway excused herself and went to bed. Hemingway was good and loaded by this time.

Now Hugh Casey was a very quiet man, and he wasn't saying much. Hugh never said much. But he was a drinker. I'd say that of everybody in the room, Hugh and Hemingway were feeling the best. But everything was still serious, with talk about the war and one thing and another. Then out of a clear blue sky Hemingway looked over at Casey, sort of sizing him up. Hemingway had this funny little grin; I assumed it was friendly, but then it might not have been.

"You know, Hugh," he said, "you and I are about the same size. We'd make a good match."

Casey just grinned.

"Come on," Hemingway said. "I've got some boxing gloves. Let's just spar. Fool around a little bit."

Casey grinned and shrugged his shoulders. Hemingway went and got the boxing gloves. He came back and slipped on a pair of gloves and handed Casey the other pair. As Hugh was pulling his gloves on, Hemingway suddenly hauled off and belted him. He hit him hard, too. He knocked Casey into that bookstand and there goes the tray with all the booze and glasses smashing over the terrazzo floor. It must have echoed all through the house because Hemingway's wife came running out.

"What happened?" she asked.

"Oh, it's all right, honey," he said. "Hughie and I are just having a little fun. You go on back to bed."

She looked at him, looked at Casey, looked at the mess on the floor, and then went back to bed.

Casey didn't say anything about the sneak punch. He just got up and finished putting his gloves on. Then they started sparring. Hemingway didn't bother to pick up the tray or anything, and they were moving back and forth across the broken glass and you could hear it cracking and crunching on that terrazzo floor whenever they stepped on it.

Boom, Casey starts hitting him. And hitting him. Then Casey started knocking him down. Hemingway didn't like that at all. Then Casey belted him across some furniture, and there was another crash as Hemingway took a lamp and table down with him. The wife came running out again, and Hemingway told her it was all right, to go back to bed, that it was all in fun. She went away, but this time she was looking a little bit doubtful about the whole thing.

Hemingway was getting sore. He'd no sooner get up than Hugh

would put him down again. Finally he got up this one time, made a feint with his left hand, and kicked Casey in the balls.

That's when we figured it had gone far enough. We made them take the gloves off. Then everything was all right.

"Let's have another drink," Hemingway said.

But it was getting very late now; we had to be back at the hotel at twelve o'clock. We told him that.

"Well," he said, "I'm too drunk to drive you back to Havana. I'll have my chauffeur drive you."

As we were going to the door, he grabbed Casey by the arm.

"Look," Hemingway said, "you stay here. The chauffeur'll take them. You stay here. Spend the night. Tonight we're both drunk. But tomorrow morning we'll wake up, we'll both be sober. Then you and me will have a duel. We'll use swords, pistols, whatever you want. You pick it." And he's dead serious about it. He wanted to kill Casey. Hughie'd got the better of him, and Hemingway wanted to kill him.

"Unh-unh," Casey said, shaking his head. He didn't want any part of it. So we left.

The next day Hemingway's wife brought him down to the ball park. You never saw a man so embarrassed, so ashamed. He apologized to everybody. "Don't know what got into me," he said. Well, I can tell you what got into him. About a quart.

Yeah, that was one hell of a spring we had in Havana in '42. When we got back to Daytona Beach to finish training, MacPhail called us together in the clubhouse for a meeting. He's got a sheaf of papers in his hand.

"Gentlemen," he said in an icy tone of voice, "I'd like to read you something."

What he had there were the reports from the detectives. You never saw so many faces turn red. Oh, that was quite a crew. Johnny Allen was with us then. There was a wild man. And mean. Hemingway was lucky he didn't ask Allen to stay for a duel. Johnny would have hung around for it.

Later that year, MacPhail called another meeting, around the middle of August. We had about an eight- or ten-game lead over the

Hugh Casey: "Hemingway wanted to kill him."

Cardinals, and I guess we were feeling pretty good about ourselves. But MacPhail called this meeting in the Dodger clubhouse one night.

"You guys are not going to win this," he said.

We could hardly believe what he was saying. I think it was Dixie Walker who spoke up.

"What the hell are you talking about, Larry?" he said. "We've got an eight-game lead."

"I know," MacPhail said. "But you're not going to win it. You're just going to have to play outstanding ball, or else the Cardinals are going to catch you and beat you."

Well, we didn't know whether MacPhail had had a few drinks or was just trying to needle us or what. But by God, he was right. Of course, we won 104 games, but the Cardinals won 106. You couldn't stop them. They just kept on coming. There was one point, late in the season, when we won six or seven in a row and *lost* ground. The Cardinals took eight or nine in a row over the same stretch.

It was a wild year all around. We had some wicked throwing contests. I remember one particular time. See, when I was traded from Chicago to Brooklyn, Jimmie Wilson, who was managing the Cubs at the time, made some remarks about me. He said that I was all through and that I wouldn't help the Dodgers. But I had a good year, and I guess he felt that made him look bad.

We were in Chicago one day, and Wilson had a fellow named Bithorn pitching and a fellow named Hernandez catching. Two Latins. That was the battery. I came up to the plate, and Wilson starts hollering from the dugout for them to knock me down. But they wouldn't do it. Bithorn throws one pitch to me, which is outside, and Wilson stops the game. He walks to the mound and takes Bithorn out and brings in this big Paul Erickson, who threw bullets. And then he puts in Clyde McCullough to catch. I mean, he's really determined to get me knocked down.

The game starts up again, and I step in.

"Well, Willie boy," McCullough says to me, "you know what they made this change for, don't you?"

"Sure, I know," I said.

So that goddamned Erickson, the first pitch he throws is right at my head. I don't know which way to go. Finally I go out across the plate and the ball whistles behind me. The next pitch is the same identical thing, and out over the plate I go again. So now it's three and nothing. I look down at Dressen, who's coaching third base, and they're going to let me hit three and nothing. Now, that seldom happened to me—I wasn't a power hitter. I guess they knew how goddamned mad I was.

So now he's got to throw a strike, and he does—and I hit it right out of the ball park. Three and nothing, and I hit a home run after they threw at me twice. That was one of the sweetest hits I ever got.

Talk about sweet hits, though, I was directly involved in one that somebody else got. Ted Williams has said a number of times that one of the greatest thrills he ever had in baseball was hitting the home run that won the 1941 All-Star game. Well, I can remember that home run as vividly as Ted, but for a different reason.

That game was played in Detroit, in Briggs Stadium, and we were

leading, 5–3, going into the last of the ninth. I was playing second
base for the National League. The first batter went out. Then Ken
Keltner got a hit, and Joe Gordon got a hit. Cecil Travis drew a
walk, filling the bases. The next two batters were Joe DiMaggio and
Ted Williams. Interesting situation, huh? Claude Passeau was pitching, and he was a good one, and a tough competitor. Well, he got
DiMaggio to hit it on the ground to Eddie Miller at short. It should
have been a double play, ending the game. Miller played the ball
cleanly over to me, but I made a poor throw, pulling the first baseman off the bag. Now a lot of people said that Travis slid in there
hard and made me hurry my throw. But that's not true. I simply
made a bad throw. So instead of the double play and the game
being over, Williams got the chance to hit. And he hit that home
run. You know, if you talk about the most famous home runs in
baseball history, I was there for three of them: the one Ruth supposedly called in the '32 Series, Hartnett's home run in the twilight,
and Williams'. I guess the only one I missed was Bobby Thomson's.

What's the funniest thing I ever saw on a baseball field? Well, I've
been in baseball for forty-five years, so that's a tough one. Funny
things aren't supposed to happen on a ball field, are they? But they
do, of course. I can tell you what happened in St. Louis one day. I
was with Brooklyn then. It was in either '41 or '42. We were playing
the Cardinals and getting the hell beat out of us, by something like
14–2. We're looking terrible. Durocher is so goddamned mad he
can't see. He's sitting in the corner of the dugout, right up against
the stone wall. That wall jutted out a few feet and behind it were
the box seats. I happened to be sitting next to him.

Well, a photographer comes over and wants to take Leo's picture.
Leo's hardly in the mood and waves him off. But the guy stays there.

"Get away," Leo says. "Get the hell away."

But the guy doesn't move. He wants to get his picture. So Leo
mutters something and reaches up into the bat rack and pulls out
one of those Louisville Sluggers, and the minute he does that, the
photographer ducks behind that stone wall, out of sight.

Well, why Durocher didn't put the bat back I don't know. But he
held onto it. He's sitting there, gripping the bat handle in his hands.
The next thing I know, out of the corner of my eye I see the lens of

this camera coming around the wall. The guy is going to try and sneak a picture. Leo sees it too. He looked at me, and he was just speechless he was so mad. The guy kept edging the camera out further and further. Suddenly Leo jumps up and swings the bat right into the camera, breaking the damn thing into pieces. The guy took off running, and Leo throws the bat after him, cursing and yelling.

Leo was a character. He was all business on that field, though. He was a good baseball man, a fine baseball man. But, like I say, a character, a real individualist. You just *knew* he wasn't going to get along with Bobo Newsom. Bobo was with us for a while in '42 and '43. He was a colorful guy in his own right.

Around midseason in '43 we were playing a ball game and Bobby Bragan was catching. Now Bobby had just recently made the switch from infielder and wasn't too adept behind the plate. There was a real tough situation, and Bobo throws a good pitch, a strike, and it gets by Bragan and we lose the ball game. Now, here's the thing about Newsom. Durocher had a real sharp tongue. Well, so did Newsom. He was quick and witty, and he always had an answer. (I guess it wasn't always the right answer—he was traded about fifteen times in his career.) After the game Durocher said something to him—I don't know exactly what it was—and Bobo answered him back. They got into a big argument, and Durocher fined and suspended him.

The next morning I was having breakfast together with Galan and Arky Vaughan at the New Yorker Hotel, where we were staying. Vaughan, you know, was a guy who always had everybody's respect, as a ballplayer and as a man. He never said too much, but everybody admired and respected him.

Arky's reading the paper. Durocher had given an interview saying that Newsom had crossed Bragan up, giving him a spitball, and that was why Bobo was suspended. But it had been building up, you see. Newsom had been getting to Durocher for weeks, throwing cutting little remarks at him. Bobo didn't mean any harm, but Leo was getting madder and madder. So finally he had a chance to stick it to Bobo, and he did.

So Vaughan's reading this, and he's very quiet, not saying anything to anybody. But something's bothering him, we could tell. So we go to the ball park. Durocher isn't there yet. We put on our uniforms and went out and loosened up. After batting practice we all went back to the clubhouse. By this time Durocher is in his office.

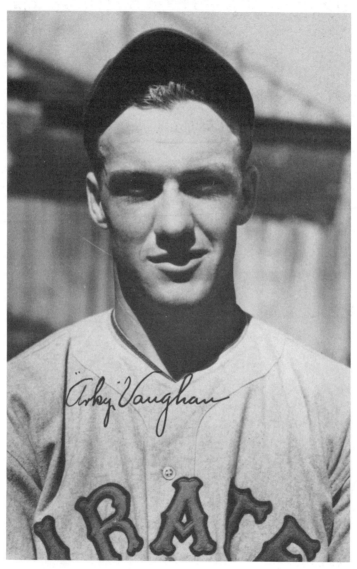

Arky Vaughan.

Well, Arky had been waiting all this time to ask Durocher if he'd been quoted correctly. He goes into the office, with a newspaper in his hand.

"Leo," he said, "did you tell this to the writers?"

"Yeah," Durocher said, "I told them that."

Arky didn't say another word. He went back to his locker and took off his uniform—pants, blouse, socks, cap—made a big bundle out of it and went back to the office.

"Take this uniform," he said, "and shove it right up your ass." And he threw it in Durocher's face. "If you would lie about Bobo," he said, "then you would lie about me and everybody else. I'm not playing for you."

Well, then everybody decides not to play. All of a sudden we're on strike. Finally, about ten minutes before game time Durocher is running around telling everybody it's going to be straightened out and asking them if they would play. A few of the guys started to relent, and he finally got nine men. But no Vaughan. Arky wouldn't play.

Around the seventh inning Branch Rickey—he was running the club then—came down to the clubhouse. Vaughan was still sitting there. Rickey started to work on him. He told Arky that he understood the situation, that he could sympathize, and one thing and another. Rickey could be very persuasive when he wanted to. But Vaughan wouldn't budge. Then Rickey said, "All I want you to do is put on your uniform, go out and sit on the bench for a few minutes and then come back. If you don't at least make an appearance, we'll have to discipline you. We'll have no alternative." Finally Vaughan agreed. He put on his uniform, walked into the dugout, and then turned around and walked right back out again.

Well, they straightened it out as best they could. I think they rescinded the action against Bobo. But it seemed to me like they got rid of Newsom pretty quick after that.

Leo was always fiery. A great baseball man, and he kept you on your toes. But sometimes he could really irritate you. One day we were playing the Giants in Brooklyn. This was in 1943. Some of our better players had gone into service, and I had become our fourth place hitter, which I'd never been. We got down to about the sixth inning, and we loaded the bases with one out, trailing by a run or two. I come up. The cleanup hitter now. The count goes to two and nothing. I look down to Charley Dressen, and he's giving me the take sign. Well, you don't take in a situation like that. But the sign was out, and I had to take. It was a strike. The next pitch is outside, and now it's three and one. I look down at Dressen again, and again it's the take sign. Boy, by this time I'm boiling. Hell, I was hitting around .330, and he's got me batting fourth. So I take again, and it's a strike. Full count now. The next pitch comes in, and I whale it—a line shot right at the third baseman, and boom, it's a double play. The inning's over, and now I'm really mad. I'm steaming.

I went out to my position, and Camilli is rolling the ball around the infield to us. He throws it to me, and I pick it up, and as I do, I see Durocher sitting on the bench with his chin in his hand, looking down. Well, I don't know what possessed me, but instead of throwing to Camilli, I fired it toward the dugout as hard as I could. It skipped off the grass in front of the dugout and hit Durocher square in the forehead. Down he goes, headfirst, right out on the floor of the dugout.

Albie Glossop, who was playing shortstop, yells over to me, "God-damn, you hit Durocher. Right between the eyes."

"That's exactly where I was aiming," I said.

Well, I figured I'm in for a good healthy fine. Leo gets up and goes to the ice bucket, takes out a big piece of ice, wraps it in a towel, and for the rest of that inning he's sitting there holding that ice up against his head. When the inning's over, I come in and sit down, not next to him, but not too far away either. I figured I'm going to get it now. But he didn't say anything. Not a word. He never said a word about it. So I got to thinking he believed it was an accident, that he didn't even know who had thrown it.

I went into the service after that season and didn't come back until spring training of 1946. Three years later. We were all in the clubhouse one morning, suiting up, getting ready to go out on the field. Durocher and Herman Franks, who were good friends, were clowning around down at the other end of the clubhouse, and all of a sudden Franks says, "Hey, Leo, do you remember the time you got hit between the eyes sitting on the bench in Brooklyn?" I was buttoning up my shirt, and I had to pause and smile; I hadn't thought of that in years. And then I hear Leo say, "Yeah. That goddamned Herman."

That was the first time I realized that Leo had known where that ball came from. But, goddamn, he'd never said a word about it. How do you figure a guy like that?

10

JAMES "COOL PAPA" BELL

JAMES BELL
Born: 1903, Starkville, Mississippi

James "Cool Papa" Bell was for more than two decades a star of the Negro Leagues. Considered by many one of the game's all-time ranking center fielders, a peer of Speaker, Mays, and DiMaggio, Bell's speed and baserunning feats were legendary. It was commonplace for him to score from second base on fly balls and groundouts. Kept from his true place as a major league star because of the color barrier, Bell played baseball all over the United States, as well as in Mexico, Cuba, Dominican Republic, Puerto Rico, for nearly thirty years.

In 1974 Bell's extraordinary talents were given belated recognition by organized baseball when he was inducted into the Hall of Fame at Cooperstown.

Of course, most of the time nobody kept any records, so I don't know what my lifetime batting average is. Nobody knows. If I had to guess, I'd say around .340 or .350. I batted .437 one year, in the Mexican League. I batted .407 in 1944, .411 in 1946. I played twenty-nine years of baseball, and the lowest I ever batted was .308, in 1945. Other than that it was .340 on up to .400. That's twenty-nine seasons, 1922 through 1950. Plus twenty-one winter seasons. That makes a total of fifty seasons. That's the way you have to count it, by seasons.

I was born in Starkville, Mississippi, in 1903; at least that's what I always figured, because that's what I was told. See, in Jackson, Mississippi, they've got two different ages for me. They didn't keep good age records back then. I went by what my mother told me, and she said it was 1903.

I started playing ball as soon as I could, just like the average kid. Everybody played baseball; there were neighborhood teams, but no uniforms or anything like that.

My mother always said that when we got old enough to work, she would send us away from Starkville because she didn't want us to come up the way she came up. She wanted us to try to get the best education we could. We didn't have a high school in Starkville, which meant I wasn't going to get much education there. So she sent me to St. Louis, in 1920.

I had brothers already living in St. Louis, you see, which is why she sent me there. I told my mother I'd go to school, but once I got to the big city, there was so much going on I didn't have time for school. So I hired on at the packinghouse, at fifty-three cents an hour. It was my first job in St. Louis.

I had five brothers, all good athletes. When I got to St. Louis, four of them were playing with a semipro team, the Compton Hill Cubs. I joined up with them, as a left-hand pitcher. I didn't have any trouble making the team; I'd been playing ball with grown men since I was thirteen. I never had trouble making any team, as a matter of fact.

I was a pretty good pitcher, but I wanted to play every day. I was with the Cubs about a year and a half, playing Sundays and holidays and during the week working in the packinghouse.

Then one day I pitched a good game against the St. Louis Stars, a professional team with a lot of first-rate ballplayers. A few nights later my brother, who owned a restaurant, said to me, "The manager of the St. Louis Stars was over here. Wants you to play ball."

Well, that sounded pretty good to me. But my mother and my sister didn't want me to play professional baseball. My sister wrote home to my mother and said I was going to play ball and leave St. Louis and they wouldn't see me anymore. But my brother said, "Now look, you go ahead on and play. It doesn't matter if you make a whole lot of money or not. You can live here when you're in St. Louis and don't worry about the rent, and you can eat here, too. Just so you can say you played pro ball."

James "Cool Papa" Bell in 1928.

So I went with the Stars and pitched for them for two years, making $90 a month. Then they switched me to the outfield. See, every time I pitched I'd get two or three hits. Some of the older fellows on the team told me I should be playing every day, and then the manager got the same idea. That was in 1924.

We played five days a week. We were in what they called the Western League, and we played against Chicago, Indianapolis, Detroit, Kansas City, Cleveland, Dayton, and Toledo. Then there was an Eastern League, with teams in the East. It was on the same basis as the white major leagues, only it was a lower scale. But the fields were pretty good, and in 1928 or '29 we installed lights, years before the major leagues did. We drew crowds of 3,000 to 5,000, and more than that once we got the lights.

When I started, they thought I was going to be afraid playing in front of big crowds, because I was a country boy. When I joined the team, Gatewood, the manager, said to me, "We're going on the road for a month. Now you just watch everything. You got a lot to learn."

Our first stop was Indianapolis. They beat us three games. So Gatewood said, "What the heck, I'd just as soon put you in there. But don't be afraid. Don't pay any attention to the crowd."

We got a big lead in the fourth game, and he put me in to pitch the last two innings. I struck a couple of them out, and some of the fellows said, "Hey, that kid's mighty cool. He takes everything cool."

So they started calling me Cool. When I'd go in, they'd yell, "C'mon, Cool," like that. But that didn't sound right. That's not enough of a name, they said, got to put something else on it. They added Papa to it and started calling me Cool Papa. That's where it came from. In 1922.

I was with the Stars from 1922 through 1931. Then the league broke up and I went with the Homestead Grays in Pittsburgh. I played with them in part of 1932, but then they stopped paying us. That was the worst of the Depression then, 1932. So I moved from there to the Kansas City Monarchs and finished the season with them. No salary there either. We were on percentage, barnstorming around. We wound up playing in Mexico City that winter, but still hardly making any money.

'Cool Papa' Bell's Foot Ease

(Remedy By A Famous Ball
Player)
QUICK RELIEF
DIRECTIONS: — Apply on
corn for three nights (for
hard corn bandage). Remove
with knife.
Price 25c

I used to have a soft corn between my toes, and I'd mix up a salve
to put on it. I made it up myself. It contained plain ol' wash soap,
turpentine, and lots of other stuff. Just mixed it all up. A newspaper
reporter heard about what I put on and asked me to give him some.
He must've liked it, because he suggested I start making the salve
for sale and get a patent on it. He said he'd write it up for me. So he
wrote an ad. I saw the ad and didn't like it. It didn't sound so good:
"Remove with knife. . . ." He said he'd straighten it out, but he never
did. I had a lot of the stuff but didn't sell much. Ended up giving
most of it away.

In the Negro Leagues the audience was mixed but mostly colored.
Even down South there were some white people at the games.
When we played the Birmingham Black Barons in their park, there
were always lots of whites in the crowd, but they were separated by
a rope. You could be sitting right next to a white man, but that rope
was always there. That was the system they had in those days.
That's what they called states' rights. States' rights doesn't mean
much to the Negro. You don't get justice with states' rights. Which
is a bad thing to happen.

In 1933 I joined the Pittsburgh Crawfords and stayed with them
four years. Left there in 1937 to go to the Dominican Republic.
Remember Trujillo, the dictator? He was killed a few years ago, you
know. Well, they were fixin' to do that back in 1937. But they like
baseball down there and they were having championship games,
and they said if he would win, they would keep him in office.

So Trujillo got a lot of boys from the States, as well as from Cuba
and Panama and Puerto Rico. Mostly he wanted Satchel Paige. We

were down in New Orleans in spring training in 1937 and Trujillo's men came there to get Satchel. But he didn't want to go. He kept ducking them for three or four days, but finally one day they trailed him to the hotel and came in looking for him—leaving their chauffeur out in the car. Paige slipped out the side door and jumped in his car to try to get away, but they crossed their car over the street and blocked it.

They told him they wanted him to go down there, and he said he didn't want to go. See, he'd just jumped his team in North Dakota the year before, and everybody was still mad at him, and he didn't want to jump again. That's why he was ducking them. But they showed him a lot of money, offered him a big salary, and he jumped again and went to the Dominican Republic.

But even with Satchel they needed some more ballplayers, because they were losing. So they asked him to send back and get some players from the Negro Leagues. He called Pittsburgh, where I was with the Crawfords. Now, I never did jump nowhere unless something was going bad, and that year it was going bad. The owner of the Crawfords was losing money, and he was giving us ballplayers a tough time, not paying us. Matter of fact, the whole league was going bad at that time. So I was *looking* for somewhere to go when Satchel called.

"We're in trouble down here," he said. "We're supposed to win this championship. I want you and some of the boys to come down. They'll give you eight hundred dollars, your transportation, and all your expenses for six weeks. Will you do it?"

"No," I said. "But make it a thousand and I'll say yes."

Satchel put the head man on the phone, and he said okay, he'd give us each $1,000. Then I said how about us getting some of the money before we get there.

"No," he said, "we can't do that."

"I have to have *something* before I leave," I said.

He said he would talk to his people about it and call us back. When he called back, he said, "Okay, we'll give you half of it in Miami, before you get here. We'll have the consul in Miami meet your plane on your way down, and he'll give each of you five hundred dollars."

They sent us the tickets, and we went to Miami. This man met us at the airport, and he took us to a restaurant. He never mentioned money, and he sure didn't look like he had any on him. But after we ate, he finally gave each of us the $500.

When we got to the Dominican Republic, we went to San Pedro de Macorís—about 40 miles from Santo Domingo—which is the little town they kept the ball club in. And there was Satchel. Boy, was he happy to see us.

They kept us under guard at a private club. Had a head man there with us all the time, with a .45 pistol. We were allowed out on only two days of the week. They said they were going to kill Trujillo if we didn't win.

The best team there was Santiago, and we beat them, finally, and we won the championship. We won it the last day of the season. I guess we saved Trujillo's life, but the people finally got rid of him later.

Then from 1938 through 1941 I played in Mexico, first with Tampico, then with Torreón. In 1942 I came back to the United States and played with the Chicago American Giants.

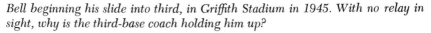

Bell beginning his slide into third, in Griffith Stadium in 1945. With no relay in sight, why is the third-base coach holding him up?

In 1943 the Giants wouldn't give me the money they'd promised me the year before, and at the same time the Memphis team wanted me. The owner of the Memphis team told me to come there; he promised to pay my way down. But when I got there, he said, "No, I never pay transportation for no ballplayers." And then he said, "Also, I have to fix your teeth. All my ballplayers have got to have their teeth fixed."

"There's nothing wrong with my teeth," I said.

"Yes, there is," he said.

See, besides owning the ball club, he was a dentist. All his players had to have their teeth fixed by him. Then he'd take his pay out of their salary.

"Look," I said, "it don't seem like we're gonna get along here. If this is the way you run your team, then I'm going home."

The Homestead Grays had been trying to get me, and I got in touch with them. So they started fighting over my contract. But that didn't mean anything. We always had contracts, but they didn't mean much. They wouldn't pay you your money, and that was that. You'd just go somewhere else.

In those days, the thirties, after the big-league season was over, the major leaguers would go barnstorming. We played against all of them. In 1931 Max Carey brought a team to St. Louis to play us. Bill Walker—he'd had a great year with the Giants—was scheduled to pitch the first game. We knocked him out in the very first inning. We beat 'em about 18–3. They had a good team, too: O'Neill catching, Bill Terry at first, Durocher at short, Wally Berger and the two Waner boys in the outfield, and some others I can't remember.

We played a team of big leaguers in 1929, with Charlie Gehringer on it. He was one of the best ballplayers I ever saw. That was a good team we played against. They had O'Neill and Wally Schang catching, Art Shires playing first base, Gehringer at second, Red Kress at short, Manush, Simmons, and Bing Miller in the outfield, Willis Hudlin, Bob Quinn, Earl Whitehill, and George Uhle pitching. We won six out of eight. Gehringer was the only one who looked good. He was some ballplayer.

Here's the thing. In a short series we could beat those guys. In a whole summer, with the team we had, we couldn't. We only had fourteen or fifteen men to a team. We'd play about 130 league games, and *another* 130 exhibition games. Anywhere from 250 to 300 games a season.

Later on there were those famous games where Satchel pitched against Dizzy Dean. I was in center field most all of those games. Dean was a good pitcher, no mistake about that. The feature for those games was always Paige and Dean. Nobody else got any publicity.

Dean beat us a game in New York broke our heart. We had beaten them four in a row, and we went to New York, and everybody said we couldn't do it again. Dean shut us out, 3–0, at Yankee Stadium.

There was a play that day I still remember. I was on second, and Josh Gibson was up. He hit one on a line way back in deep center field. Jimmy Ripple caught it, and I tagged up and rounded third and came all the way home. The ball came in to the catcher—Mike Ryba—the same time I did, but high, and I slid in under it before he came down with the tag. And the umpire said, "Out!" I said I was safe, but the umpire laughed, and said, "I'm not gonna let you do that on major leaguers. Maybe you can do that in *your* league, but not against major leaguers."

Heck, I often scored from second on a long outfield fly.

We went from there to York, Pennsylvania. Dizzy was supposed to pitch. They had guaranteed him $350, but the people were kind of slow coming in, so the man in charge decided to hold the game up a while till the crowd got bigger. Dizzy said he wouldn't pitch a ball until he got his $350. I was told he was afraid the receipts wouldn't cover his guarantee.

Finally the crowd got a little bigger, though not by much. The promoter came to us and said, "Look, you boys play here several times a year. All we've taken in is a little more than I've already promised Dean. Would you play anyway?"

So we said, "Okay, we're here, so we might as well."

Then Dizzy came into the clubhouse and said, "Listen, don't you all hit me. I just pitched Sunday, and my arm is still tired. So don't hit me, y'hear." He wanted to look good, you know.

Sure, Diz, we told him. Then we went out and got four runs the

Charlie Gehringer: "He was one of the best ballplayers I ever saw."

first inning. First three men got on, and Gibson hit a home run, and the score was 4–0 before Dean knew what happened. Then four more in the second inning. People were booing and everything. Dizzy wouldn't pitch anymore, and he went to play second base, which he couldn't do very well.

We wound up winning by a big score, and all we got was about $7 apiece, while Dean got his $350.

It was rough barnstorming. We traveled by bus, you see. You'd be surprised at the conditions we played under. We would frequently play two and three games a day. We'd play a twilight game, ride 40 miles, and play another game, under the lights. This was in the 1940's. On Sundays you'd play three games—a doubleheader in one town and a single night game in another. Or three single games in three different towns. One game would start about one o'clock, a second about four, and a third at about eight. Three different towns, mind you. Same uniform all day, too. We'd change socks and sweat shirts, but that's about all. When you got to the town, they'd be waiting for you, and all you'd have time to do would be to warm your pitcher up. Many a time I put on my uniform at eight o'clock in the morning and wouldn't take it off till three or four the next morning.

Every night they'd have to find us places to stay if we weren't in a big city up North. Some of the towns had hotels where they'd take us. Colored hotels. Never a mixed hotel. In New York we'd stay at the Theresa, in Harlem, or the Woodside. In the larger cities in the South we'd stay at colored hotels. In smaller towns we'd stay at rooming houses or with private families, some of us in each house.

You could stay better in small towns in the South than you could in the North, because in a small town in the North you most of the time don't find many colored people living there. And those that are there have no extra rooms. But in a small town in the South there are enough colored people living there so you can find room in their homes.

Once we were going from Monroe, Louisiana, to New Orleans. We had to cross the bridge over the river at Vicksburg, Mississippi. We were planning to eat lunch at a little town called Picayune. We stopped at a colored restaurant and asked if they had any food.

"Oh, not for all those men," they said. "It'll take us too long to fix food for all those men." It was spring training, and we had about twenty-five men.

When the restaurant people went outside and looked at our bus standing there, they said, "Say, whose bus is this? Any white boys in it?"

"No," we said.

"Who owns it?"

"We have an owner."

"Is he white or colored?"

"Colored."

"And all these boys on the bus are colored?"

"Yeah," we said.

"Well," they said, "you all better get out of the state of Mississippi quick as you can."

"Why?"

" 'Cause if you don't, they gonna take this bus and all you guys in it and put you all working on that farm out there. They need farm workers real bad. There's a lot of people now out there on the farm they caught passing through. They jail 'em for speeding and put 'em to serving their sentence out on that farm."

So we got back on the bus and drove straight through till we were out of the state of Mississippi.

When I was manager of the Kansas City Monarchs' farm team, we played a lot against the House of David. That was in 1948, '49, '50. They had a lot of ex-minor- and -major-league players on their teams. They had to wear a beard. We barnstormed with them through California, Colorado, Nebraska, Iowa, North and South Dakota, and Canada.

We met a lot of good people, but also a lot that weren't so good. Some of them wanted to be good. All the people that you see that say, "I don't want you to do this or that"—they aren't bad people, they're worried people a lot of time, worried about the public. When we traveled with the House of David, they had no trouble finding accommodations, so they had all their reservations made out before the season started. But we had to go to places where we never did know whether we could sleep. Most of the time we'd stay in these cabins on the edge of town. They call them motels today, but in those days they called them cabins.

We went into a lot of small towns where they'd never seen a colored person. In some of those places we couldn't find anyplace to sleep, so we slept on the bus. If we had to, we could convert the seats into beds. We'd just pull over to the side of the road, in a cornfield or someplace, and sleep until the break of day, and then we'd go on into the next town, hoping we'd find a restaurant that would be willing to serve colored people.

All those things we experienced, today people wouldn't believe it.

The conditions and the salaries, and what we had to go through. Lots of time for months and months I played on percentage—all of us did—and we'd be lucky to make $5 a game.

But I had a lot of fun in baseball. Saw a lot of great ballplayers. Guys you probably never heard of. Pitcher named Theodore Trent. He'd beat Paige an awful lot of the time. And he never lost a game to a big-league team barnstorming. When we played Max Carey's all-stars, Trent struck those guys out again and again, with that great curveball he had. One game he struck Bill Terry out four times.

Trent was a great pitcher, but he got TB and died young.

Satchel was the fastest, though. I never saw a pitcher throw harder; you could hardly time him. I've seen Walter Johnson, I've seen Dizzy Dean, Bob Feller, Lefty Grove, all of them. Also Dick

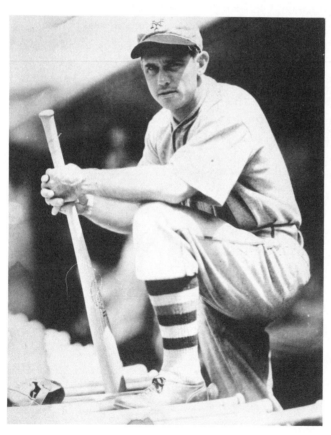

Bill Terry: "Trent struck those guys out again and again. . . . One game he struck Bill Terry out four times."

Redding and Smokey Joe Williams among our boys. *None* of them threw as hard as Paige at the time I saw them. All he threw for years was that fastball; it'd be by you so fast you could hardly turn. And he had control. He could throw that ball right by your knees all day.

Josh Gibson was a good catcher, but not outstanding. He didn't have good hands, and he wasn't the best receiver, though he had a strong arm. But he was a hitter, one of the greatest you ever saw. The most powerful. Never swung hard at the ball either. Just a short swing. Never swung all the way around. Pretty big man. About 190, 195 pounds. About 6'1". He died when he was only thirty-six.

Ruth used to hit them *high*. Not Gibson. He hit them *straight*. Line drives, but they kept going. His power was to center field, right over the pitcher's head. I played against Foxx, but Gibson hit harder and further more often than Foxx or any other player I ever saw.

But they rate Oscar Charleston the greatest Negro ballplayer of them all. He played outfield and first base. Then there was Buck Leonard, a very powerful hitter, and Judy Johnson, a wonderful third baseman, one of the best ever. So many of them, so many great players.

After I was through playing, I tried to get a coaching or scouting job in organized baseball, but nobody would hire me. The one man who might have given me a job was Bill Veeck, but I never could get to see him. Every time I went to see Mr. Veeck when he had the St. Louis Browns' franchise the people in the front office wouldn't let me in to see him. I'd been in baseball all my life and wanted to stay in it, but nobody wanted me.

But I'm not looking back at the past; I'm looking ahead to the future. I'm not angry at Mississippi or anyplace else. That's the way it was in those days. I pray that we can all live in peace together.

11

CLYDE SUKEFORTH

CLYDE LEROY SUKEFORTH
Born: November 30, 1901, Washington, Maine
Major-league career: 1926–34, 1945, Cincinnati Reds, Brooklyn
   Dodgers
Lifetime average: .264

Clyde Sukeforth came to the big leagues with the Cincinnati Reds in 1926, and his affiliation with baseball remains
intact to this day; he is currently the Atlanta Braves' chief
scout for the New England area. Sukeforth's finest season was
1929, when he hit .354.

Well, I've been in baseball for about fifty years now, and it's
never been dull. Disappointing sometimes, yes; frustrating
sometimes, certainly; and sometimes it's been downright infuriating.
But never dull. I've been a player, coach, manager, scout. So I've
seen the game from every possible angle.

Cincinnati brought me up from the Manchester club in the New
England League at the end of the 1926 season. Cincinnati was
pretty much a second-division club in those years. It wasn't the fault
of the pitchers, though; we had some good ones. There was Carl
Mays, Dolf Luque, Jakie May, Pete Donohue, Eppa Rixey.

Rixey was a great pitcher and a great character. He's in the Hall
of Fame today, of course. One of the fine left-handers. He was a
fierce competitor and a hard loser. When he pitched, you didn't
have to ask who won the game, all you had to do was look at the
clubhouse later. If he'd lost, the place would look like a tornado had
gone through it. Chairs would be broken up, tables knocked over,
equipment thrown around. The ball club didn't like that, needless to
say, but what were they going to say to Rixey? That fellow was an
institution in Cincinnati.

He was an old Southern boy, you know, and I guess he took his history as seriously as he did his baseball. Word got around that you could get his goat by whistling "Marching Through Georgia"—that was one of the songs the Union soldiers sang while they were ripping up the South during the Civil War. One time he was throwing batting practice and some fellow on the other bench started whistling that song at him. Rixey got the ball and fired it right into the dugout at him. Boy, did they scatter in there! Later we were sitting on the bench. Rixey was slouched down, his thumbs in his belt, scowling at the dugout floor.

"Eppa," I said, "why does that song make you so mad?"

He thought about it for a few moments.

"That song doesn't make me mad," he said. "The thing that makes me mad is that they *think* they're making me mad."

Hornsby was in his heyday when I broke in. The greatest hitter of all time, I'd say, or if not, then damn close to it. How did you pitch to him? You pitched and you prayed, was how. There was no way you could fool him. Just look at those averages. When Hornsby stepped into the cage to take batting practice before a game, everything on the field stopped. Everybody turned to watch him swing. And that included the old-timers, the tough old pros. Now that's an impressive tribute, I'd say. And he wasn't what you'd call a popular ballplayer either. Hornsby was a brutally frank man who always spoke his mind. But when he had a bat in his hand, he had nothing but admirers.

In the spring of 1932 I was traded over to the Dodgers. We didn't exactly burn up the league there either. But we had some live ones, like Van Mungo, Lefty O'Doul, Hack Wilson. Hack, you know, holds the National League record for home runs in a season—56, in 1930. Everybody knows that, right? Well, I'll tell you something that everybody doesn't know—he hit 57 that year, except that the record book doesn't show it. He hit one in Cincinnati one day, way up in the seats, hit it so hard that it bounced right back onto the field. The umpire had a bad angle on it and ruled that it had hit the screen and bounced back. I was sitting in the Cincinnati bullpen, and of course, *we* weren't going to say anything. But Hack really hit 57 that year.

Hack didn't look much like a ballplayer. He was stocky and muscular. Looked like a fire plug. Very strong. In fact, he was nicknamed

Rogers Hornsby: "The greatest hitter of all time, I'd say; or if not, then damn close to it."

after Hackenschmidt, the wrestler. Nice guy. Wonderful disposition. Easygoing. And I guess something of a playboy. He liked his beer, and occasionally he kept his own hours. He was involved in what I think is one of the best baseball stories ever. It happened in 1934, when Stengel was managing the Dodgers.

We had a pitcher, Boom-Boom Beck. Walter Beck. He was a pretty good pitcher. But he started to have his troubles. He got tattooed a few times, and it got to the point where his job was in jeopardy, and he realized it. Well, he gets what he thinks is probably his final start, in Philadelphia. And they start hitting him. They just kept knocking one after the other off of that right field fence in old Baker Bowl. It looked like a carousel, the way they were going around those bases.

Now, it was a real hot day. A scorcher. Hack was in right field, and maybe he didn't get all the sleep the night before that he should have had. And he's running down those balls one after the other. He'd no more than get into his position before somebody else would tattoo that fence and Hack would have to run it down and fire it into the infield.

Hack Wilson. Courtesy Chicago Cubs.

Finally Stengel goes out to get Beck. Walter, I guess, feels that he's blown his last chance, and naturally he isn't feeling too happy about it. So when he sees Stengel coming, he takes the ball and in disgust turns and just throws it out against the right field fence. And there's Hack, grateful for a moment's rest, bent over out there with his hands on his knees, staring at the grass, huffing and puffing. All of a sudden he hears that ball hit the fence and takes off after it, picks it up and fires it into second base.

Perfect peg, too.

I stayed with the Brooklyn organization after my playing days were over. I did some scouting, minor-league managing, coaching, even managed the Dodgers for a couple of games at the beginning of the 1947 season, after Durocher was suspended and before Burt Shotton came in. That was a job I was glad to get *out* of. That wasn't for me. You've got to have the right temperament to manage a big league ball club.

Branch Rickey took over as general manager during the war, and we got along fine. When he moved on to Pittsburgh in 1950, I went with him, to scout for the Pittsburgh organization.

Things were pretty rough in Pittsburgh in the early fifties. We were starving. Didn't have a dime. Couldn't win a ball game. One day during the 1954 season Mr. Rickey called me into his office.

"The Dodgers have just sent Joe Black to Montreal," he said. "Montreal is opening a five-game series with Richmond, in Richmond. I want you to go there and stay until Black pitches. Look him over. We might be able to make a deal for him."

So I went to Richmond. I got out to the ball park early the next evening, wanting to see everything I could. Montreal came out for fielding practice, and here's this baby-faced kid in right field with a real great arm. I mean, a rifle. Outstanding. Naturally you've got to notice that. Well, the game starts, and he isn't playing.

Around the seventh inning Montreal was behind, and who should go up to pinch-hit but this kid? He hits a routine ground ball to shortstop and turns it into a bang-bang play at first base. God, he could run. He could fly. Well, I said to myself, there's a boy who can do two things as well as any man who ever lived. Nobody could throw any better than that, and nobody could run any better than that.

They'd announced his name when he came up to pinch hit, and I made a note of it: Clemente.

The next night I'm out there bright and early, watching batting practice. Up comes Clemente. He's kind of an unorthodox hitter, but he's got the good wrists and the quick bat. Well, the same thing: He doesn't play, except to pinch-hit.

I stay around for five days, and Joe Black hasn't pitched yet. Max Macon was managing the Montreal club. Now I knew Max; he'd played for me when I was managing Montreal. I asked him about Black, and he told me Joe wasn't ready, that he had a little arm trouble, and it was uncertain when he would pitch. I was disappointed, naturally, but by that time I had something else on my mind. You see, Pittsburgh was going to be finishing last, and the National League had the first draft pick that year.

I said to Macon, "Max, I want to ask you a favor."

"What's that?" he asked.

"I want you to take care of our boy Clemente. He's just a young boy, away from home for the first time. Don't let him get into any trouble. Just look after him the same as you would your own boy. Protect him for us, Max," I said, "because he's just as good as on our own club."

Max laughed. "You mean you want *him?*"

I didn't know if he was trying to move me off the trail or not, but I just said, "Do me that favor, Max."

You see, I had found out in the meantime that the Dodgers had signed Clemente for a $10,000 bonus, and at that time there was a thing called the $4,000 bonus rule. Any boy that had signed for more than $4,000 had to go through the draft before he could be taken up to the big leagues—*if* he had been signed to a minor-league contract. The Dodgers had made a critical mistake here. They'd given Clemente the $10,000 and signed him to a Montreal contract instead of protecting him by signing him to a Brooklyn contract and optioning him down. I guess somewhere along the line they realized their mistake and were trying to cover it up by playing Clemente as little as possible.

So I sat down and wrote Mr. Rickey a letter. "You and I will never live long enough," I wrote, "to draft a boy with this kind of ability for $4,000 again. This is something that happens once in a lifetime. Now, if you don't take my word for it, see him for yourself. *But don't lose him.*"

Later in the season we held our draft meeting out at Mr. Rickey's farm just outside Pittsburgh. All the scouts from around the country were there.

"Well, boys," Mr. Rickey said, "we're finishing last, so we've got the first draft choice. Who is it going to be?"

Somebody suggested a pitcher out on the coast. Somebody else said an infielder out of the Southern League. Then he looked at me.

"Clyde, do you have a candidate?"

"Yes, sir," I said as emphatically as I could. "Clemente, with Montreal."

"Any of you other boys seen Clemente?" he asked, looking around.

One fellow spoke up.

"I have," he said. "I didn't like him."

"What didn't you like about him?" Mr. Rickey said.

"I didn't like his arm," the fellow said.

"Clyde," the old man said, "did you see this fellow Clemente throw?"

"I sure did," I said.

"What did you think of his arm?"

"Well," I said, "there's a question in my mind as to whether or not it's better than Furillo's." (Furillo had the best arm in the league at that time.) "It's right in the same class as Furillo's, and it may even be a little bit better."

"I see," Mr. Rickey said. "There seems to be some difference of opinion here. One man doesn't like the arm, while another says it's as good as the best. We'll have to sort this out."

So he sent George Sisler and another scout up to Montreal to see Clemente. I guess they decided he could throw, as well as do a few other things, because they recommended we draft him. That's how the Pirates got Clemente, for $4,000.

I never did get to see Joe Black pitch.

Mr. Rickey sent me out on another assignment which I guess you might describe as memorable. This was in August, 1945. We were still with Brooklyn. He called me into his office one day and told me to have a seat.

"The Kansas City Monarchs are playing the Lincoln Giants in

Clyde Sukeforth.

Chicago on Friday night," he said. "I want you to see that game. I want you to see that fellow Robinson on Kansas City. Talk to him before the game. Tell him who sent you. Tell him I want to know if he's got a shortstop's arm, if he can throw from the hole. Ask Robinson to have his coach hit him some balls in the hole."

Mr. Rickey had been talking about establishing a Negro club in New York called the Brooklyn Brown Bombers, and we had been scouting the Negro Leagues for more than a year. But you know, there was always something strange about it. He told us he didn't want this idea of his getting around, that nobody was supposed to know what we were doing. So instead of showing our credentials and walking into a ball park, as we normally would have done, we always bought a ticket and made ourselves as inconspicuous as possible.

"Now, Clyde," the old man went on, "if you like this fellow's arm, bring him in. And if his schedule won't permit it, if he can't come in, then make an appointment for me and I'll go out there."

Mr. Rickey go out there? To see if some guy named Robinson was good enough to play shortstop for the Brooklyn Brown Bombers? Well, I'm not the smartest guy in the world, but I said to myself, *This could be the real thing.*

So I went to Chicago and started calling every hotel I thought a Negro club might be staying at. But I couldn't contact him. Later I found out why—they'd come in from somewhere out in Iowa the night before by bus, saving themselves a hotel bill.

I went out to Comiskey Park the next day and bought myself a ticket. I sat down front and began studying my scorecard. This was in August, and those scorecards are so often inaccurate that late in the year; but I seemed to remember that this fellow Robinson's number was eight. A few fellows came out, and one of them had number eight on him. I stood up and said, "Hey, Robinson." He walked over. I introduced myself and told him just what I was supposed to tell him.

He listened carefully and when I was through, he spoke right up—Jackie was never shy, you know.

"Why is Mr. Rickey interested in my arm?" he asked. "Why is he interested in me?"

And I said, "That is a good question. And I wish I had the answer for you. But I don't have it."

"Well," he said, "I'd be happy to show you what arm I have, but I'm not playing. I've got a bad shoulder, and I can't throw the ball across the infield."

I talked to the guy for a while, and I thought to myself: Mr. Rickey has had this fellow scouted. The only thing he's concerned about is his arm. Is it a shortstop's arm? Well, I had heard reports that he was outstanding in every way. A great athlete. So I thought: Supposing he doesn't have a shortstop's arm? There's always second base, third base, outfield. I liked this fellow.

"Look," I said, "you're not in the lineup. If you could get away for two or three days, it won't arouse anybody's suspicions. Tell your manager that you'll be back in a few days. We'll go into New York; I think the old man would like to talk to you."

Now this is Friday night, and Sunday I have to see a second baseman in Toledo. So I asked Robinson to meet me down at the Stevens Hotel after the game, and we would talk some more. He said all right.

Later it occurred to me that they might not let him in. This was 1945, remember. So when I got to the hotel, I saw the bellman out front, and I gave him a couple of bucks and I said, "There's going to be a colored fellow coming along here, and I want you to show him to the elevator." He said he would do that.

Evidently Jackie had no trouble getting in, because he came up to the room later on. And he starts right off.

"Why is Mr. Rickey interested in my arm? Why does he want to see me?"

"Jack," I said, "I can't answer that. I don't know."

"You can't blame me for being curious, can you?"

"I can't blame you," I said, "because I'm just as curious as you are."

You could feel it boiling inside of him: *Why is Mr. Rickey interested in my arm?*

"Look, Jack," I said, "you know that the old man has originated a lot of things, he's revolutionized a lot of things, and I'm hopeful it's something along those lines . . . but I just don't know."

Jackie Robinson in 1946: "Why is Mr. Rickey interested in me?" he asked.
New York Daily News *Photo.*

But he wouldn't let up. He kept pressing me.

"Tell me what he said."

"I told you," I said.

"Tell me again."

"He told me to come out and see if you've got a shortstop's arm. He *also* said that if you couldn't come to Brooklyn to see him, he would come to see you."

The significance of that last part wasn't lost on him. I could see that. He was no fool, this fellow. Don't ever sell Robinson cheap. No, sir!

The more we talked, the better I liked him. There was something about that man that just gripped you. He was tough, he was intelligent, and he was *proud.*

"Mr. Sukeforth," he said, "what do *you* think?"

I was honest. I'd learned in a short time that that was the way you had to deal with Robinson.

"Jack," I said, "this could be the real thing."

It evidently sat well with him. It pleased him. Was he afraid of the idea? He was never afraid of anything, that fellow.

Then I told him I had to be in Toledo on Sunday. I asked him if he would meet me in the Toledo ball park, and in the meantime I would make transportation arrangements to New York.

"I'll meet you in Toledo," he said.

"You got money?" I asked.

"I've got money," he said.

So I'm in Toledo on Sunday. I look up between games of the doubleheader, and there's Robinson, sitting back up in the stands, watching me. I don't know how long he'd been sitting there, his eyes on me. I waved to him to come down and join me.

"I'm glad you made it," I said when he sat down.

He didn't say much; he was pretty quiet. Evidently this thing had been going around in his mind.

We boarded the sleeper for New York that night. I got up the next morning, somewhere in New York State, and he's already up.

"Jack," I said, "let's go get some breakfast."

"No," he said, "I'll eat with the boys." He meant the porters.

I didn't make an issue of it. I went and got breakfast and came back, and we sat and talked on the way in. When we got to New York, I took him straight out to the Brooklyn Dodgers' office, at 215 Montague Street.

I brought him into Mr. Rickey's office and made the introductions. Then I said, "Mr. Rickey, I haven't seen this fellow's arm. I just brought him in for you to interview."

But the old man was so engrossed in Robinson by that time he didn't hear a damn word I said. When he met somebody he was interested in, he studied them in the most profound way. He just stared and stared. And that's what he did with Robinson—stared at him as if he were trying to get inside the man. And Jack stared right back at him. Oh, they were a pair, those two! I tell you, the air in that office was electric.

Listen, Mr. Rickey was under a lot of pressure too for signing Robinson. He was criticized by a lot of people, including some of the big wheels in the Brooklyn organization. They thought it was a bad move. But he was always that much ahead of everybody else. He knew this thing was coming. He knew that with the war over, things were going to change, that they were going to *have* to change. When you look back on it, it's almost unbelievable, isn't it? I mean, here you've had fellows going overseas to fight for their country, putting their lives on the line, and when they come back home again, there are places they're not allowed to go, things they're not allowed to do. It was going to change all right, but not by itself, not by itself. Somewhere along the line you needed a coming together.

Do you know for how long the idea was in Mr. Rickey's head? More than forty years. For more than forty years he was waiting for the right moment, the right man. And that's what he told Robinson.

"For a great many years," he said, "I have been looking for a great colored ballplayer. I have reason to believe that you're that man. But what I'm looking for is *more* than a great player. I'm looking for a man that will take insults, take abuse—and have the guts *not to fight back!* If some guy slides into second base and calls you a black son of a bitch, you're coming up swinging. And I wouldn't blame you. You're justified. But," Mr. Rickey said, "that would set the cause back twenty years."

He went on along those lines, talking about turning the other cheek and things like that. He told Jack that he wanted to sign him for the Brooklyn organization, to play at Montreal. He described some of the things Robinson would have to face—the abuse, the insults, from fans, newspapermen, from other players, including some of his own teammates.

When the old man was through, Robinson just sat there, pondering it, thinking about it. I'd say he sat there for the better part of five minutes. He didn't give a quick answer. This impressed Mr. Rickey.

Jackie Robinson and Branch Rickey: "Oh, they were a pair, those two!"

Finally Jackie said, "Mr. Rickey, I think I can play ball in Montreal, I think I can play ball in Brooklyn. But you're a better judge of that than I am. If you want to take this gamble, I will promise you there will be no incident."

Well, I thought the old man was going to kiss him.

Yes, that's about thirty years ago now, since those two came together. I guess you could say that history was made that day.

What was I doing while it was going on? Listen, I was pretty uneasy—remember, I hadn't seen the guy's arm!

Doc Cramer.

12

DOC CRAMER

ROGER MAXWELL CRAMER
Born: July 22, 1905, Beach Haven, New Jersey
Major-league career: 1929–48, Philadelphia Athletics, Boston
    Red Sox, Washington Senators, Detroit Tigers
Lifetime average: .296

If consistency is indeed the hobgoblin of little minds, as
Emerson contends, it nevertheless is the hallmark of substan-
tial ballplayers. Few were ever more consistent, and efficiently
so, than Roger "Doc" Cramer. Posting a .296 batting average
for 20 big-league seasons, Cramer also set a major-league
record by seven times leading the league in at bats. In his 20
years Cramer accumulated a modest 345 strikeouts, a figure
approached by some of today's finest hitters every two years.

I think I'm one of the few guys in the whole history of baseball
who's ever gone six for six twice. Did it once against Chicago—
got a few of those hits off of Ted Lyons, I believe—and once against
Detroit. Actually, the first time I did it I didn't even know it. I knew
I had a lot of hits, but I didn't realize I was going for number six.
Second time I knew every hit.

I don't know if it was the first time or the second time, but one
more hitter and I'd have been up again, for a seventh try. Maxie
Bishop hit a line drive, and somebody made a good play on it;
otherwise I'd been up for the seventh time. We scored 19 runs that
day, I think. Why, I had five hits in five innings. That's a record.

I played twenty years in the big leagues. Two decades. I worked
winters as a carpenter all the time I was playing ball. Built my
house with my own hands. Two years before I went with the A's,
Brooklyn wanted me to go with them. But I turned them down. You
see, I had two years' in carpentry and I wanted to finish my appren-
ticeship. Once I did that I was ready for anything.

I was playing semipro ball in Beach Haven, here in New Jersey, around 1928. Cy Perkins and Jimmy Dykes came over from Philadelphia one Sunday (Philadelphia didn't play Sunday ball at that time). I fancied myself a pitcher in those days, and I always could hit pretty good. Anyway, I must have done something to impress them because they came up to me after the game.

"What about coming to Philadelphia for a tryout?" they asked.

"When?" I asked.

"Wednesday."

"Can't make it," I said. "Got to work."

I never will forget that. I couldn't believe what I was hearing myself saying. Anyway, I went, and never came back to stay until twenty years later.

My dad didn't think much of my playing ball. See, I was a carpenter and had steady work. He'd say, "Look, you've got a good job and baseball don't amount to nothing"—that's the way he put it. But he got over it. They didn't want me to go away, that was the thing; they just didn't want me to leave because I'd never been anywhere.

Did I want to play ball? Well, the A's gave me a contract for I think about $3,500, and I'd have paid *them* that much to let me play. I stayed the rest of that year with the A's, working out—I wasn't into any games.

In '29 they sent me to Martinsburg, West Virginia. Blue Ridge League. They considered me a pitcher at first. But I hit so well every time I pitched that Mr. Mack heard about it and sent word for them to change me to an outfielder. So they sent me to center field, and that's where I stayed; never played any other place.

I liked it in Martinsburg. But you know, if you're having a good year, it doesn't much matter where you're playing. Did I have a good year? I guess I did. I hit .404. I won the batting championship, but not until the last day. I was being chased by Joe Vosmik— remember Joe? Good hitter. He was with Frederick. Well, we played Frederick the last game of the season, so it came down to Joe and me swinging against each other for the batting championship. Just before the game the manager came up to me and said, "Well, Doc, you pitched on opening day, so you might as well pitch on closing day."

I'll tell you what happened that day. I got four or five hits, and at the same time I walked Vosmik four times. So he didn't get a chance to swing, and I beat him out. Oh, was he steaming! Years later, when we were on the Red Sox together and were good friends, he'd still bring it up. He'd really tell me about it. "Remember that day in Frederick?" he'd say. Did I walk him on purpose? Well, maybe only three times.

In 1928, the year I sat on the bench with the A's, they had a pretty good outfield. They had Al Simmons, Mule Haas, and Bing Miller, plus a couple of other guys who were just finishing up—Ty Cobb and Tris Speaker.

A lot of people didn't like Cobb, but that never seemed to bother him. Anyway, he was very nice to me. I liked him.

Joe Vosmik.

I don't think Cobb ever wanted to quit. He hit over .320 his last year, but he was forty-two years old and couldn't move in the outfield anymore. He had slowed up so much he'd lose a game for you. Ty Cobb. Yes, sir. In fact, he lost a series in New York late in 1928 that cost the A's a pennant. Mr. Mack had those other guys to put in there, but he played Cobb and Speaker for drawing cards. It cost them. Mr. Mack admitted it later, said it was a big mistake.

Speaker was a great guy, both on and off the field. I learned a lot just from watching him. He was a good teacher. He'd take you out there and show you how to do it. Cobb wouldn't do that. He'd talk to you, tell you all about it, but he wouldn't take you out there.

But Eddie Collins was my man. To me he was the real baseball man. He just about ran the Philadelphia Athletics at that time. Mr. Mack didn't do too much without talking to Collins first. Eddie Collins was the greatest second baseman I ever saw and one of the best ballplayers. He could hit, he could run, throw, field, and he had it upstairs, too. Smartest baseball man I ever met. Eddie could stand at third coaching, and I don't care who was pitching, in two innings he'd have their signs; he'd know what that pitcher was going to throw and call them.

How was I treated as a rookie with the A's? Well . . . it could've been a lot better. It wasn't like it is today. You couldn't even go up and have batting practice. The regulars would crowd you out; you couldn't mix in with them until you'd shown them you could play. That's the way it was in those days.

One day up in Boston Mr. Mack called me in and said, "You're my center fielder from now on, until you show me that you're not my center fielder."

That's the way he told me. He said I was going to hit second, in Haas' place. So I went out to hit with the regulars, and the next thing I knew they were jumping all over me, wanting to know what I was doing out there. One in particular got pretty hot about it.

"What are you doing out here?" he wanted to know. "You're supposed to hit in the morning." That's when the subs took batting practice, in the morning.

"Mr. Mack told me to hit here," I said. "I'm playing today."

"You are, huh? Well, nobody told me anything about it."

"Why should they?" I said. "You're just another ballplayer around here."

"Is that so?" he said.

"As far as I'm concerned."

Just another ballplayer! I've got to laugh now when I look back on it. I was talking to Al Simmons.

I really don't know how to tell you about Connie Mack. He was as good a man as ever lived, any way you take him. And he knew baseball. I'd say he was the best outfielder that ever lived. We played by his scorecard; that's all we played by. He'd move us into position by waving that scorecard of his, you see. Of course after you'd played a year or so for him you knew where to position yourself.

We were playing in St. Louis one time, right after I'd broken in. We had a one run lead in the ninth inning, two out, and Goose Goslin was the hitter. Eddie Rommel was pitching for us. Now, Eddie was a good pitcher, but they could pull him. So I played Goslin back about where I thought we always did play him. But Mr. Mack kept waving me in with his scorecard, until I swear I wasn't more than fifty feet in back of second base—for *Goslin.*

Well, Rommel threw the ball, Goslin swung, and I just stood right there and caught the ball. Never moved an inch. Right where he put me.

I asked Mr. Mack about it later, and he said, "That was just a hunch, boy, that was all. Just a hunch."

First time I met him, tell you the truth I was scared to death. Plumb afraid, that's all. I'd never been out of Manahawkin or Beach Haven; going to Philadelphia was like going to Europe, for me. I went up on the train in the morning, at six o'clock. Went to Camden, crossed over on the ferry, and then took the trolley car out to the ball park. That's the way you got there in those days.

I'll tell you, after I'd talked with him for five minutes, why, he was just like a father to me. He was a good man. He'd never bawl you out for a mistake till the next day. Then you'd go up to that little office up there, and he'd be waiting for you. Boy, he could tell it to you when he had to. That's if you'd made some sort of mistake that he thought you shouldn't have. I don't mean errors. He'd never

get on a man for making an error. "You're supposed to make them," he'd say. "I know you're trying when you make an error."

In my first year, in '29, he put me up to pinch-hit. It was in Washington, against Fred Marberry. I had the count three and one. I looked down to Collins, who was coaching at third, and I thought I got the sign to hit. Well, it was "take." I swung and popped up. Collins jumped me about it, said I'd missed it. I didn't think anymore about it after that.

Then we got on the train that night, going back to Philadelphia. I was walking through the car and there he was, Mr. Mack. He crooked his finger toward me, and I went over and sat with him.

Shibe Park in 1929.

"Young man," he said, "you're going to Portland, Oregon, tomorrow morning."

I said, "How come?"

He said, "You're going out there to learn the signs. And you might as well learn how to field too while you're out there."

"By God," I said, "I'm not goin'."

"Yes, you are," he said.

I thought about it for a while. Then I said, "Portland, *Oregon*?"

"That's right," he said.

I told him, "Well, you kept me in the United States, didn't you?"

"Just about," he said.

1928 A's outfield: Simmons, Speaker, and Cobb.

Then, after he'd won the three pennants in '29, '30, '31, Mr. Mack went broke. Lost all his money in the stock market, like a lot of other people at that time. So he had to start selling everybody. Attendance had started to fall off, too. See, the fans knew we were going to win, so they stopped coming out. Nobody could beat us in those days. God, we had Grove, Earnshaw, Walberg, Quinn, Rommel pitching. We'd pitch Grove, Earnshaw, and Walberg the first three games, and we didn't care who they pitched—we had 'em wore out.

Grove was quick. I'll say he was. Whew! You haven't got anything today as quick. Koufax? No, sir. I've seen him pitch. Nobody was any quicker than Grove, that I ever saw. Well, just one instance. We were in New York one time, and Jack Quinn was pitching. We had them beat by a run. They got the bases full in the ninth with nobody out. Mr. Mack brought Lefty in to relieve. Ten pitches and we were in the clubhouse. He struck out Ruth, Gehrig, and Lazzeri on ten pitches—Lazzeri fouled a ball. And Grove threw only fast balls. Didn't have much of a curve until he was near finished. That's what I mean by him being so fast. Everybody in the league knew what he was going to throw, and they still couldn't hit it.

Lefty Grove. Mr. Mack always called him Robert.

But he was a tough loser, Grove was. Nicest guy you'd ever want to meet, but a tough loser. He hated to get beat—and they didn't beat him often. Why, when he was just pitching batting practice—you hit one through the box, and you'd go down on the next pitch. In *batting practice*. On the last swing we'd try to hit one back through him, just to rile him up. Once I hit a home run off of him in a game in Fort Myers, Florida. It was just a scrimmage between the team. I was on the scrubs. Next time I come up Cochrane says to me, "Hey, kid, be ready—he's gonna throw at you."

Well, I was young, I didn't hardly know what it meant. But I found out in a hurry! Boy, he hit me in the ribs, I thought it was going to come out the other side. Knocked me right down. But he wouldn't ever throw at anybody's head. He'd hit 'em in the pockets—that was the way he said it.

I was always on Grove's team. I never hit at him, except for one year, because I went to Boston a year after he did. Ted Lyons was one of the toughest I ever hit at. Great stuff, great control. I hit at Bob Feller a lot, but I had awful good luck with him. In fact, he walked me one time to pitch to Cecil Travis; I never did forget it. I could hit Bob pretty good. But he had great stuff, a really good curve. Johnny Allen was a good pitcher, and Wes Ferrell, when he was with Cleveland. Wes was like Grove—he wanted to win. I saw him stomp a brand-new wristwatch one day in the clubhouse after he'd got beat. He was putting the watch on, it slipped and fell, and he stomped it right there.

"Well, I won't drop you anymore!" he said.

I mentioned Cochrane before. You've got to talk about him. God, he was a great catcher, that fellow. He could do it all. I used to have a lot of assists, you know. I could throw pretty good. But you didn't have to make a perfect throw to Cochrane. If it was out a little ways, he'd go and get it and come back and get that guy. I'll tell you, there were few things as exciting as watching somebody trying to get in there on a close play with Cochrane. Home plate was *his*, you see. You had to take it away from him. Tough? Just the same as a piece of flint.

He was a tough loser, too. That whole gang were tough losers. You have Grove pitching and Cochrane catching, and you lose 1–0, you're a little timid about going into that clubhouse. I've seen it happen.

Lefty Grove and Mickey Cochrane: "You have Grove pitching and Cochrane catching, and you lose 1–0, you're a little timid about going into that clubhouse."

There was the time when Grove had won 16 straight games—which tied him for the league record with Walter Johnson and Smoky Joe Wood—and was going after number seventeen. Well, Dick Coffman of the St. Louis Browns beat him, 1–0, on a misjudged fly ball no less. Well, it's hard to believe what happened in the clubhouse after that game unless you were there to see it.

I was in center field in that game, and Jim Moore was in left field—he was the boy who misjudged the ball. Simmons should have been out there, but he'd told Mr. Mack he was going to Milwaukee for a couple of days for one reason or another, and he did. Back then they'd let you take off some time once in a while if you needed it. Well, to this day, if you talk to Grove about that game, he doesn't blame Jim Moore for losing it, he blames Simmons, because Simmons went to Milwaukee. That's the one he blames. He'll tell you that if Al had been in left field that day where he belonged, it never would have happened.

It was Oscar Mellilo who hit the ball. Moore ran under it, and it got away. There was a man on base when it happened. I retrieved the ball and threw it in, but the run scored. Coffman had good stuff and he beat us. Before you start blaming anybody for anything, you've got to remember that the man shut us out.

So we went into the clubhouse. The sparks were flying off Grove. Oh, I mean to tell you. I knew it. I knew it was going to happen. Well, he was about three lockers down from me. I saw him stand up and take hold of the top of his shirt with both hands—we had buttons on our shirts in those days—stand like that for a second, and then *rrrip*! He tore that shirt apart so fast and so hard that I saw the buttons go flying past me, three lockers away. Then everything went flying—bats, balls, gloves, shoes, benches. He broke up a couple of chairs. He kicked in a couple of lockers. Nobody said a word. There was no point. You had to wait till the steam went out of him. Next day he was all right. But I never will forget those buttons flying past me.

Grove was a tough customer all right. Wasn't afraid of anybody—Babe Ruth included. I'll tell you something about Ruth. You might have fellows today hitting more home runs than Babe Ruth, but you still don't have Babe Ruth. To me it was remarkable what a drawing card that man was. The fans—grown-ups as well as kids—would ache just to touch him.

One time we lost six or seven straight, coming off a Western trip. We didn't expect much of a crowd. We were playing the Yankees. Twelve o'clock they put up a sign, Standing Room Only. That was Ruth, that's all it was. He could fill any ball park, no matter where he went.

He was a great outfielder, too. You couldn't just go from first to third on him; you wanted to be sure because he could throw you out. That's all there was to it. He could fire that ball, and most of the time not on a hop either—it would come whistling in there on a line.

He was a great guy personally, too. I've been out to dinner with him, gone over to his house. I knew his wife and daughter. You just had to admire him, any way you take him. If you had a kid sick, he'd come visit and leave the kid a $100 bill and think nothing of it.

I went barnstorming out West with him one year. We played a game in Billings, Montana. The fences were way back. They told Ruth that nobody had ever hit one out of there. He laughed, and said, "The Baby'll hit one out"—he called himself the Baby.

First time up, right on out of the ball park it went. Tommy Thomas was the pitcher, from the White Sox. Ball parks didn't make any difference to Ruth; when he got a-hold of the ball, it was gone. I don't care what park—and some cornfields, it would go out of them, too.

He could hit a ball so hard it was tough to handle in the outfield. Sometimes it would come out to you and then sink, like a spitball or a knuckler. I never saw anybody else hit a ball like that.

Foxx was the same kind of hitter as Ruth, only right-handed. Once I saw him hit a ball in Chicago, a line drive against the center field fence, he had to slide to get into second base. The ball was hit so hard that when Appling went out to get the relay, it bounced right back into his glove; he turned and threw, and Foxx just made

Jimmie Foxx in 1924, with Easton, Maryland, in the Eastern Shore League.

it—and Jimmie could run. That's how hard Foxx could hit them. He was strong.

Now Gehrig, he had plenty of ability, too. We respected Lou pretty much as we did Ruth up at the plate, I'll tell you that. You could fool Gehrig a little more than you could Ruth, but you weren't fooling him much.

Gehrig put on the biggest one-man show I ever saw in a ball game—four home runs, in Shibe Park. That was in 1932. He hit the first three off of Earnshaw, who was one of the best, and the fourth one off of Lee Roy Mahaffey. And I'll tell you—he pretty near hit five, because Simmons made a spectacular play on him in center field. One of the greatest plays you ever saw. Lou would've had five home runs that game. Still, four ain't a bad day's work, is it? They beat us, 20–13. Lost by a touchdown.

Grove never threw much at Gehrig. Didn't want to wake him up, he said. Lou was a quiet, good-natured sort of guy, and you didn't want to get him mad. "Let him sleep," Grove always said. Ruth, too; though once in a while he'd put one under Babe's chin, just for luck. Ruth just laughed. You expected that sort of thing in those days. If you hit a home run, you'd expect to be knocked down the next time up. That's the way it was. Or if you beat a guy a ball game, you wanted to be ready next time that fellow pitched against you. He'd let you have it.

Johnny Allen was the worst I ever saw for that. I said to him one day, "I believe you'd throw at your own mother."

"Oh, no," he said. "I wouldn't throw at her. But I might brush her back a little."

I was with the Red Sox when Williams broke in. First time I saw Teddy it was just like DiMaggio—you knew this fellow was going to be a ballplayer. And he wasn't shy, that boy. First day he walked into the clubhouse he called Cronin Skip. Ted was a great boy. I liked him.

That first spring he was with the team, we were coming up from the South, heading for Boston. We stopped off in Atlanta to play a game with the Atlanta Crackers. Ted was playing right field. Somebody hit the ball out to him, and it went between his legs, all the way to the wall. He chased it down, mad as the dickens at himself for missing it, and when he got to it, he picked it up and just threw that ball over the right field fence—right through Sears, Roebuck's plate glass window, we learned later on.

I was there alongside him when he threw it. I had to hold my hand over my mouth to keep from laughing. Then I looked around and sure enough, he was coming—Cronin. Walking out from short-stop, ver-r-r-y slow.

So I said, "Ted, here comes Cronin. Now keep your mouth shut. Don't say anything. 'Yes' him. That's all there is to it."

Cronin didn't say much. Wasn't much he could say. He just took Ted right out of there and sat him on the bench. It didn't bother Ted too much, except he wanted to stay in and hit. That boy loved to hit. With good reason.

George Earnshaw in 1930:
". . . one of the best. . . ."

Cronin said to me a few days later, "I want you to take Ted out and teach him how to field."

I said all right. So I had him out there with somebody hitting them to him. He'd miss one, catch one, then miss a couple more. Finally he said, "Ah, Doc, the hell with this. They don't pay off on me catching these balls. They're gonna pay me to hit. That's what they're gonna do."

And I said, "Well, I can see that, Ted. They're gonna pay you to hit."

There was no trouble seeing that. He had that swing.

Now, you know during the war the caliber of play went down somewhat, but hell, it was still baseball, and in 1945 we won the pennant. I was with Detroit then. Hank Greenberg had come out of the service in midseason. Hank won it for us with a grand slammer on the last day of the season, in the ninth inning. That was doing it with style—which was generally the way Hank Greenberg did things.

I always kid Greenberg about that. I was hitting third and he was hitting fourth that game. Nelson Potter was the pitcher. We had men on second and third, and they walked me to get to Greenberg, loading the bases. They were looking for the double play. But I swear, before I got to first base, Greenberg hit one into the bleachers and we won the pennant.

So anytime I go anywhere and Hank is there, I always say, "You know, once they walked me to get to Greenberg"—and never tell 'em what happened, and then Hank always jumps in and says, "Hey, tell 'em what happened."

But I never do; I just let it go at that.

We played the Cubs in the Series and beat them in seven games. Claude Passeau beat us one game with a one-hitter, and Hank Borowy beat us twice. Then he came back for the seventh game, and we clobbered him. Five runs in the first inning. Newhouser went all the way for us and we beat them.

In twenty years in the big leagues, that was my only world's championship. It's a great feeling. You know you've done it all then. We drank champagne on the train all the way back to Detroit.

13

MAX LANIER

HUBERT MAX LANIER
Born: August 18, 1915, Denton, North Carolina
Major-league career: 1938–46, 1949–53, St. Louis Cardinals,
  New York Giants, St. Louis Browns
Lifetime record: 108 wins, 82 losses

Although many fans today associate Max Lanier's name primarily with his "jump" to the Mexican League in 1946, Lanier was at the time of his departure one of the best left-handers in the National League. From 1941 through 1944 his highest earned run average was 2.98, his lowest 1.90 in 1943. With Army service, his time in Mexico, and his subsequent suspension, Lanier lost the greater part of five prime big league seasons.

Looking back on it all, I can tell you that it happened too quick. It doesn't seem like it could be that long ago. Time really flies. I know when I signed that first contract, it looked as big as this room.

I was pitching a high school game, down home in North Carolina. I won it, 2–0. When I came out of the ball park later, this guy was standing there waiting for me.

"Hi, Max," he said.

"Hi yourself," I said. I didn't know who he was.

"Can I give you a ride back to the school?" he asked.

"Well, I don't know you," I said.

He pulled out his identification and showed it to me. Frank Rickey, Branch's brother. Representing the St. Louis Cardinals.

"You interested in playing pro ball?" he asked.

"Yes indeed," I said. That was one of my dreams. I was already playing semipro ball while I was still in high school. We had a pretty good semipro club there in Denton, North Carolina. This was around 1934.

Frank Rickey signed me to a contract when I was sixteen years old. My family wasn't too enthused about the idea. You see, I'd been offered a scholarship by Duke University, and my parents wanted me to accept it, but I turned it down to play pro ball.

I signed right out of high school, with a class B club. I stayed there a week and then they wanted to send me to a D club, Huntington, West Virginia, for $70 a month. I didn't go for that, and I quit and came home. That was my first money dispute with the Cardinals. It didn't take long, did it? One week.

I started playing semipro ball again, in Ashbury, North Carolina. In 1936 I won 16 straight games. That's against no losses. One day I walk out of the ball park, and there's Frank Rickey standing there.

"Back again, are you?" I asked.

"How would you like to go to Columbus in the American Association?" he asked.

"Why should I?" I asked.

"It would be a great opportunity for you," he said. "That's Triple-A ball."

"I might consider it," I said. "Under one condition—that you guarantee I'll be on the ball club the whole year."

I guess you talk that way when you've got a 16-0 record, no matter who you've won them against.

"How do you know you can pitch in Triple-A?" he asked.

"I think I can," I said, "because we've got a lot of ballplayers right here who are that good, and I'm doing all right against them."

He went along with it. I was talking tough, but to tell you the truth, you couldn't afford to bargain too much with the Cardinals back then, because they had so many ballplayers. They were way ahead of everybody else in that respect. At one time they had about thirty farm clubs. And they kept us hungry. That was Branch Rickey's philosophy: a hungry ballplayer was a better ballplayer. I'll tell you one thing about him: he could tell you how much he paid you for each pitch, not how many games you won or lost.

The competition was murder. When I was coming up, they had, just in left-hand pitchers, fellows like Howie Pollet, Al Brazle, Harry

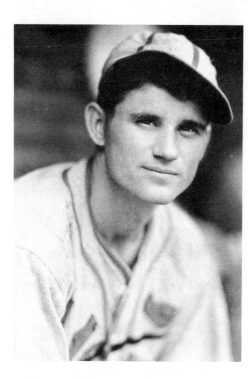

Preacher Roe.

Brecheen, Ernie White, Preacher Roe. That was pretty stiff competition. Why, Preacher Roe couldn't even make the club!

I got lucky at Columbus and won 10 and lost 4. The next year I went up to the Cardinals. Frisch was managing then. He was tough on young ballplayers. I didn't appreciate it then, but I did later. He'd find faults no matter what you did, but if you paid attention to him, you'd find yourself learning something. He was a good baseball man and a full-fledged character at the same time. I remember one time Paul Waner was wearing us out with line drives. Finally Frisch stood up in disgust and yelled, "Who on this ball club can get that Waner out?" Max Macon was sitting on the bench—this was before he went to the Dodgers. Well, Max liked to pop off a little anyway, and he said, "I can get him out." Frisch was delighted to hear that. He clapped his hands and said, "Atta boy. Get down there and warm up." Waner comes up again. Frisch brings in Macon. The first pitch Waner hits a line drive and breaks Macon's little finger. Frisch couldn't help but lie down on the bench and laugh himself silly.

Pepper Martin was on that ball club. I'd say he was the most colorful ballplayer I ever saw. He was a real fun lover. He'd come into the clubhouse and tie your uniform into knots or nail your shoes to the floor. Sometimes during a game you'd be out there pitching, and he'd walk over from third base to talk to you and slap a wad of chewing gum onto your wrist.

One day, I think it was in Chicago, he pulled a beauty. He was great at throwing paper sacks full of water out the window. Well, there was a mezzanine in the lobby of this hotel, with a staircase leading up to it from the ground floor. Pepper got himself a paper sack full of water and hung around by the mezzanine window, with a newspaper in his hand. He was waiting for Frisch. When Frisch came along, Pepper dropped his water bomb right on Frank's head, then tore back down the stairs, threw himself into a big chair, crossed his legs and opened the newspaper and looked as though he'd been sitting there all day.

Frisch came storming in, wringing wet. He ran up to Pepper and said, "Damn you, if I wasn't seeing you sitting there, I'd swear it was you that did it!"

Pepper Martin: "He was a real fun lover."

Pepper brought his paper down, looked at him as innocent as a baby, and said, "Did what, Frank?"

Another time, we lost a doubleheader in the Polo Grounds. That's pretty rough going, when you lose two. You don't hear a voice in the clubhouse, much less see anybody smile. So we trudged into the clubhouse, and it's like a tomb. Buzzy Wares, our first-base coach, goes to light up a cigar. Well, Pepper had switched matches on him, and the matches were loaded. Buzzy strikes a match, and it explodes. Buzzy exploded right along with it.

"Damn you guys!" he yells. "Lose a doubleheader and you're still pulling pranks."

He went and got another book of matches. But Pepper had loaded the cigar, too. Everybody's sitting there watching Buzzy light it. When twenty-five guys are sitting stone still watching you light your cigar, you ought to suspect something. But I guess Buzzy was too mad to take notice. Boy, he took notice a second later. The damn thing blew up in his face, and he had tobacco in his eyes, his ears, his nose. Twenty-five guys turned around and looked into their lockers, their shoulders shaking. You wouldn't want to be caught laughing then, would you?

Pepper kept you loose all right.

Joe Medwick was in his heyday when I joined the ball club. So was Johnny Mize, one of the greater left-hand hitters. He and Medwick were as good a pair of hitters as I've seen. Of course, after Joe took that beaning, he seemed to lose some of his edge. That was in 1940, at Ebbets Field, soon after he'd been traded over to the Dodgers. I've heard stories that there was some bad blood, that we were throwing at him, but I never believed it.

I was rooming with the fellow that hit him, Bob Bowman, and I didn't know of any reason for Bob to be throwing at him. Here's what I think happened. Charley Dressen was coaching third for Brooklyn, and he always tried to call the pitches. He was skilled at that, but sometimes he called them wrong. Bowman was wrapping his curveball, and then he wrapped a fastball the same way, and it faked Dressen. Medwick stepped right into it, thinking it was going to be the curve. I think that's what happened. And Joe got hit hard.

Bowman was upset about it, I know. He never showed up in the room that night. He was supposed to be in at twelve, and he didn't come in. I thought, gosh, maybe something's happened to him. I didn't want to call the manager, because there was the chance Bob might be out having a couple of drinks, and I didn't want to get him in dutch. So I called Pepper, and he told me that they'd sent Bowman on to Boston. They wanted to get him out of town because they were afraid some of those very rabid Dodger fans might try something the next day. But I wished somebody had told me about it.

We had some pretty good throwing contests with the Dodgers in '41 and '42. Guys like Whitlow Wyatt and Mort Cooper would come close to you when they wanted. Of course, we never threw to hit anybody, but we'd brush them back. We had some great battles with the Dodgers.

Somebody would start throwing close, or there would be some jockeying from the dugout, and that would start it off. Durocher was

Joe Medwick.

a great one for that. You could hear him in the dugout: "Stick it in his ear. Knock him down." Stuff like that. You never knew when he meant it. You take that kind of thing, some mean pitchers, a great rivalry, and put it in the middle of a tense pennant race, and you're going to have some fun out there.

I remember this one time Marty Marion was taking a throw at second and Medwick slid into him pretty high. I guess Marty didn't like spikes up in his face, so he just flipped Joe. The next thing you knew the whole gang was out there. I was pitching that day. Dixie Walker ran right by me and made a diving tackle into Kurowski, and then Jimmy Brown and me went after Walker. Oh, it was a great one. Players rolling and scrambling and wrestling all over the grass. Nobody got hurt. Nobody ever gets hurt in those things. Safest place to be in a baseball fight is right in the middle of it.

Another time, in St. Louis, in 1942, I saw Stan Musial get mad. It was the only time I ever saw Musial really get mad. Les Webber was pitching for the Dodgers, and he threw four pitches behind Musial's head. That's the worst place to throw, because a guy's instinct is to jerk back from a close pitch.

Musial was steaming. The whole ball club was steaming. You just knew something was going to happen. Walker Cooper was the next hitter. He hit a ground ball, and when he went across first, he jarred Augie Galan. Augie was playing first that game. Mickey Owen was backing up the play, and he didn't like what Cooper had done. What does Mickey do but jump right up on Cooper's back. Mickey was a scrapper, but he wasn't too big, and Cooper was like an ox. I remember looking at that sight and thinking, What in the world is he doing up on Cooper's back, how's he going to get off, and what's going to happen when he does get off?

Well, Cooper, he was so strong, he just threw Mickey right over on the ground and held him there. Next thing you knew, we were all out there again.

I had particularly good luck against the Dodgers. One of the reasons, I think, was Durocher. He'd sit in that dugout and holler at me and get me mad. He thought he was going to upset me, but the madder I got, the better I could pitch.

I believe there was more pressure in '42 than in '41. We were 10½ games behind the Dodgers in August. Then we went on the road and won something like twenty-three out of twenty-six ball games. Finally we got within two games of the Dodgers and went into Ebbets Field. Mort Cooper pitched the opener, and he beat Whitlow Wyatt a close game. That put us just one back.

I was scheduled for the next day, but I'd been having a little trouble with my elbow. Billy Southworth came up to me in the clubhouse.

"Max," he said, "I believe I'll pitch Beazley today and let you rest that elbow."

"No, sir," I said. "I've beaten them four times already, and I think I can beat them once more."

He thought about it for a moment, then handed me the ball.

I beat Max Macon 2–1 that day. Kurowski hit a home run in the second inning with one on, and then they got one run in the second inning. And that was it.

I can tell you who was the last hitter I faced. Billy Herman. One of the best. I threw him a fastball and he took it. Well, I knew Billy—when he takes a pitch, he's looking for something else. So I wasted my curve and threw him another fastball for a strike. He was a guess hitter, and I figured he was guessing on the curve. So I threw him another fastball, right down the middle, and he took it for strike three. And we were tied with the Dodgers for first place.

We went on from there to Boston. Naturally you're not supposed to look at the scoreboard, and naturally you do. We were behind late in the game, and when we saw the Dodgers had lost, we went and came up with a big inning and won the game. We took over first place, and from then on they never caught us.

We played the Yankees in the Series that year. The Yankees had been in a lot of World Series and they were a little bit cocky, though any ball club that had won as many pennants as they had had a right to be. I think we were kind of nervous in the first game. They beat us, 7–4, but something happened in that game that took away our nervousness and gave us confidence. We were behind 7–0 going into the last of the ninth. We scored four runs and had the tying run at the plate. Musial was the hitter, and he flied out to deep right.

Well, that rally made us feel better, even though we lost the game. It showed we could throw a scare into the Yankees. And then we did more than scare them. We beat them four straight. I think that was one of the biggest World Series upsets ever.

I'll tell you, beating the Yankees in '42 will always be the highlight for me, more so than winning in '44 against the Browns, even though I beat them in the sixth game for the championship.

I went into the service in 1945 and missed most of that year. I came back in '46. I reported to the club in St. Pete. I was rarin' to go, but I hadn't signed my contract yet, so they wouldn't let me work out. The reason I hadn't signed was that old bugaboo, money. I'd won 17 in 1944, plus the big game in the Series. I was making $10,000 and was holding out for more.

Walter Alston, Cardinal rookie, 1936.

Eddie Dyer was the manager then, and he was anxious for me to start working out. I was hanging around the clubhouse, waiting to get the thing settled. Eddie saw me there.

"Come into my office," he said.

I followed him into the office, and he closed the door.

"I'm going to call Mr. Breadon in St. Louis," he said.

"Think it'll do any good?" I asked.

"I don't know," he said. "We can try. You get on the other phone."

So I listened to the conversation.

"Mr. Breadon," Eddie said, "this boy is worth more money than what you've offered him."

"Do you think so?" Breadon asked.

"Yes, I do think so," Eddie said.

"Well," Breadon said, "I'll give him five hundred more. He can take it or go home."

So I had to take it. I wasn't satisfied, but I took it. I felt I'd been dealt with unfairly, but there wasn't much I could do about it.

When the season started, it seemed I couldn't do anything wrong. In the first month I had six starts, six complete games, six wins. I was pitching great ball, but I still wasn't entirely happy, because of the way I'd been treated by Breadon.

One night I was leaving the ball park in Philadelphia, and a couple of guys approached me. One of them was Bernardo Pasquel. He was the brother of Jorge Pasquel, a multimillionaire Mexican who owned a league in Mexico. They were offering a lot of money to big leaguers who were willing to jump. Some guys, like Mickey Owen and Sal Maglie, had already gone.

That first conversation didn't amount to much, but he said he would contact me in New York, which was our next stop. I didn't say much to him one way or the other at that time.

When we got into New York, I found out that Lou Klein, our second baseman, and Fred Martin, a pitcher, had already agreed to go to Mexico. They started talking to me about going with them. Then Pasquel contacted me, and we all met at the Roosevelt Hotel. I was a little hesitant; after all, it was quite a big move to be contemplating. But I'll tell you something. I'd had some trouble with my elbow the last few games. Nobody knew about it but me. I wasn't letting on to anybody, but I was getting concerned. I knew if that elbow went, I'd be in trouble. I'd be nowhere then. You know what a pitcher with a bad elbow is worth.

So I began to get receptive. Pasquel's first offer wasn't good enough, but finally he made me the right offer. I got a bonus of $25,000 to sign and $20,000 a year for five years. I couldn't turn it down. I said, shucks, I'll pitch the rest of my life for the Cardinals and come out with nothing. I think the highest-paid guy on the ball club at that time was $14,000, and I'm talking about a ball club that had won three out of the last four pennants and had a lot of top stars on it.

After the meeting I went back with Klein and Martin to the Hotel New Yorker, where the Cardinals were staying. After thinking it over, I let Pasquel know the next day. We didn't tell anybody, not the Cardinals, not anybody. We went to St. Louis and from there drove to Mexico City.

I thought I was making the right move at the time. Remember, I'd just received this shabby treatment from Breadon. In the long run, though, I think that whole business probably didn't help us as much as it did some of the rest of the players because I do know the Cardinals started paying more money.

When I got down there, Jorge Pasquel told me just to run and work out for a couple of days to get used to the high altitude. But my third day there I got into a ball game. It was the damnedest thing. I was sitting on the bench, watching the game. In the ninth inning the other team got the bases loaded with nobody out. All of a sudden the game stops. I look around to see what's happening, and Jorge Pasquel is coming out of his box. He walks across the field and comes to our dugout and says to Mickey Owen, who was managing the team, "I want Max to go in." Mickey didn't say anything; he just looked over at me and shrugged, as if to say, "It's his money."

So they stopped the game long enough for me to warm up. And I went out there and threw nine pitches and struck the side out. Pasquel came into the clubhouse after the game and patted me on the back and said, "Max, I won this game, didn't I?"

Pasquel owned the whole league, you see. They said he was worth something like $70,000,000. He used to sit up in his box during the game and eat off silver trays.

Conditions down there weren't too good. Half the time you couldn't play, you were so sick. You know, problems with the water. Mexico City was the only place where you didn't have to boil the drinking water; they had artesian wells there. And I got to where I was eating out of cans most of the time; I was afraid to eat the food.

I couldn't believe there was that much difference between two countries that were so close together. The conditions in the smaller cities were terrible. Tampico. San Luis Potosí. Puebla. Gosh, that Tampico was hot. I'd be so tired after pitching a game there that I couldn't talk above a whisper. There was no air conditioning, for one thing. Didn't even have screens in the windows. They had these overhead fans with the big black blades that used to go around and around very slowly and not do a damn thing.

Sometimes we traveled by plane, sometimes by bus. Those bus rides through the mountains were hell. They'd drive on either side of the road, didn't make any difference. The one that had the loudest horn had the right-of-way, I'll tell you.

The whole thing didn't last very long. I stayed in Mexico about a year and a half. We found out later why the Pasquel brothers were after the big leaguers to come down there. At that time Alemán was running for President, and I think there was some family relationship between him and Jorge Pasquel. Now the people in Mexico loved baseball. It was worked out so Alemán got the credit for us coming down there. They figured he'd get some votes out of it. And he did get elected. So I think the whole thing was strictly a political deal. After the election Pasquel started cutting everybody. He cut me from $20,000 a year to $10,000. That's when we started jumping back to the States.

Of course, everybody who went to Mexico was suspended from the big leagues for five years. I thought that was a little stiff. Heck, we didn't go down there to hurt anybody. We just didn't think we were making enough money.

After I got back, this was in '48, I formed an all-star team, and we

Max Lanier.

went on the road and played about eighty ball games against college and semi-pro teams. We played all over, Kansas, Iowa, Nebraska, Wisconsin, Indiana, Louisiana. But do you know, we got to where we couldn't get a ball game. I'm not especially against Happy Chandler—I suppose he had his job to do—but he tried to stop us from playing. We knew we couldn't play in professional ball parks against professional ballplayers, but he shouldn't have tried to stop us from playing against colleges and semipro clubs. But he did.

We were supposed to be suspended for five years, but in '48 we started a lawsuit against baseball, and that's how we got back. We had them by the tail then because the suspension was illegal.

I went up to Drummondville, Canada, in '49 and was playing ball there. Around the end of June I got a phone call from Fred Saigh, who now owned the Cardinals.

"You've been reinstated," he said. "You ready to come back?"

"Sure," I said. "If the price is right."

"Look," he said, "you did the club an injustice when you went to Mexico, and we can't give you any more money."

"You don't have any reason to say that," I told him, "because you didn't even own the ball club then. You can forget about it if you think I'm going to come back for the same amount of money I was getting before I left. I'm making more money here in Drummondville than you're offering me."

Eddie Dyer got on the phone then.

"Max," he said, "we sure would like to have you back. We think we can win the pennant, and the fellows would like to have you back."

"Eddie," I said, "if you were managing in the minor leagues making more money than the major leagues offered, what would you do?"

"I'd probably stay where I was," he said.

"Well," I said, "those are exactly my circumstances right now."

Saigh called me back the next day.

"We'll double your salary," he said. "And we'll give you expense money if you can get to St. Louis by the Fourth of July."

Well, that sounded just great to me. As a matter of fact, I was there on the second of July.

I pitched for the Cardinals for a few more years and then in '52 was traded to the Giants. The next year I went back to St. Louis, but this time it was with the Browns. Bill Veeck owned the ball club, and what a great guy he was. Veeck was a generous and good-natured man and a real hell raiser when he wanted to be. Of course, we didn't have a very good ball club, but that didn't seem to dampen his spirits any. One time we'd lost eight straight, and he decided to give a party, to loosen us up.

This was in Cleveland, at the Aviation Room in the Carter Hotel. It was a pretty fancy place, decorated with a lot of airplane stuff, and had a big, glass-framed picture of Eddie Rickenbacker on the wall. Veeck told the whole ball club to be there, every man. He hired a piano player, and he had plenty of food and drink laid out. It was a great time; we were singing songs and laughing and telling stories. You'd have thought we had just won the World Series instead of riding an eight-game losing streak.

Around one o'clock in the morning a few of us started getting ready to leave. But Veeck got by the door and said, "Nobody can leave until I say they can leave." Then he started opening champagne and squirting it at everybody. Vic Wertz and myself, we caught him and poured a bottle of it right down his back. He was laughing so hard we could hardly hold him. Then there was one bottle of scotch left and Veeck grabbed it and threw it at Eddie Rickenbacker's picture and smashed the glass frame into a thousand pieces.

It was a great party. Cost him $1,850, Veeck said. We went out the next day, nice and loose, and lost our ninth straight.

14

SPUD CHANDLER

SPURGEON FERDINAND CHANDLER
Born: September 12, 1907, Commerce, Georgia
Major-league career: 1937–47, New York Yankees
Lifetime record: 109 wins, 43 losses

Spud Chandler stands as the hardest-to-defeat pitcher in baseball history, with a lifetime won-lost percentage of .717. His earned run average of 1.64 in 1943 is the third lowest recorded in the era of the lively ball—since 1919. In 1947, at the age of 40, Chandler led the American League in earned run average for a second time.

When Joe McCarthy was asked who were the greatest pitchers he ever managed, he named Lefty Gomez, Red Ruffing—and Spud Chandler.

I used to have this reputation for keying myself up before a game to the point where I was so angry people couldn't talk to me. They said I used to sit in the clubhouse and scowl and glower, and that not until I was full of rancor was I ready to go out and pitch.

Well, that just wasn't true. I was just so determined to win that it might have looked that way. But I never got what you would call mad, or disgruntled, or overbearing. But that's the idea people got. Milton Gross, who used to cover the Yankees, wrote a story one time, "The Yankees' Angry Ace," and it was on the cover of the *Saturday Evening Post*. My father-in-law read it and began wondering what kind of monster his daughter was married to!

Angry? No. No reason to be. Determined, that's all I was. Jee-minney, without determination how are you going to be a winner?

Well, maybe I should qualify it a little. I was kind of sore once before a game. It was my first start in the big leagues, in the spring of 1937, against the White Sox. I had the butterflies about as bad as you can get them. Joe McCarthy noticed that, and he called me into his office. He had a very stern look on his face.

"Chandler," he said, "what are you playing baseball for?"

"I'm playing baseball because I love it," I said, "and because it's my livelihood." I didn't know what in the world he was driving at.

"Do you think you're any good?" he asked.

"Yes, sir," I said. "I think I'm pretty good."

"You do, huh?"

"Yes, sir." I was getting irritated now.

"Do you think you're going to win today?"

"There's only one way to tell," I said. "Get your uniform on and come on out and we'll see."

Well, I pitched a four-hitter and got beat, 1–0. Zeke Bonura hit a home run.

McCarthy had seen how nervous I was, you see, and what he was trying to do was get my mind off that by getting me irritated. A little of the old psychology. He had a way of sticking the ice pick in you when it was real cold. But he had a reason for it. He always had a reason for everything he did.

I never heard McCarthy second-guess a pitcher the whole time I was with the Yankees. He was a terrific manager. You couldn't help but respect him, and he demanded respect, and he received it from every player on the club.

I was going along fine in 1937 until I hurt my arm. I had seven wins and two losses, and then I was pitching in Cleveland and hurt my arm. It became very doubtful whether I would pitch anymore that season. The Yankees wanted to strengthen their pitching staff a little bit, so they got Ivy Andrews from Cleveland and sent me to Newark for the rest of the season.

The Newark Bears in 1937 were unbelievable. You know, that was a big league ball club. They were tremendous. If my memory serves me correctly, just about every man on that club went to the major leagues except one, and he was an older pitcher that had pitched in the major leagues and came back down there as a relief guy. His name was Phil Page. But every one of the pitchers, the two catchers, the entire infield and outfield went to the major leagues. That had to be the greatest assemblage of minor-league players in the history of baseball.

The catchers were Willard Hershberger and Buddy Rosar. We

Spud Chandler.

had George McQuinn at first base, Joe Gordon at second, Nolan Richardson at shortstop, and Babe Dahlgren at third. The regular outfield was Charlie Keller, Bob Seeds, and Jimmy Gleason. The pitching staff was Atley Donald, Steve Sundra, Vito Tamulis, Joe Beggs, Phil Page, Marius Russo, and myself. Frank Kelleher was a utility man. There were others, too, but I can't remember them all now.

We won the pennant by 25½ games. Funny thing about the way the Little World Series turned out. We played Columbus, the Cardinals' Triple-A farm club. They came into Newark and beat us three straight. So a lot of people thought it was a long train ride from Newark, New Jersey, to Columbus, Ohio, just to play one game. But we went out and beat them four times and won the Little World Series. That was the 1937 Newark Bears. There's never been anything quite like them in baseball before or since. Who else but the Yankees of that era were good enough to have a major-league farm club in the minors?

In those years every kid wanted to play for the Yankees. That was the magic name. You didn't have to offer a kid a bonus to sign; that Yankee contract was bonus enough. But things have changed drastically since then. It changed when the other clubs began pouring out those big bonuses.

When I was finished as a player, I became a scout for the Yankees. I tried to sign Herb Score, and I begged and cried and pleaded for the money to get him with. Score wanted to go to the Yankees, too. Mr. Weiss used to tell me, "Now, don't just get a major-league prospect, get a Yankee type." What was a Yankee type? Well, I guess what he meant by that was a guy who really wanted to go with the Yankees and was willing to take whatever he was offered. Score had the greatest arm I ever saw on a young pitcher. Cleveland got him. I missed Frank Lary by $2,000. I missed Lary, I missed Score, and when you miss those kind, you're about ready to quit. That's what I did.

I guess it was that Yankee magic that got me. They were always the number one club in my mind. I'll tell you something, and a lot of people might think this is farfetched. But I made a statement one time in Yankee Stadium in a football uniform. I was with the University of Georgia football team, and we were in New York for a game with New York University. This was in 1929 or '30. It was on a Friday afternoon, the day before the game. During the preliminary workouts I was standing on the pitching mound, with a football in my hand, and I made the statement to two or three of the guys: "Right here is where I'm going to be."

I graduated from high school in 1928, in a little town in northeast Georgia by the name of Carnesville. It's the county seat of Franklin County. Then I went to the University of Georgia and played baseball there for four years, along with football and track. But baseball was always my first love. In the summers I worked all week on a construction job, from Monday morning till Saturday noon, then jumped in a Model T Ford and rode 20 miles and pitched one game and played outfield in the other.

The Cardinals tried to sign me in the summer of 1929 and the Cubs in the spring of 1932, but I continued in school and then signed with the Yankees after I graduated. You know, I received a much greater offer to go with the Cubs than I did with the Yankees —but there you are, that Yankee magic.

I ran into some trouble along the way in the minor leagues and was four and a half years getting to the majors. Even after I was with the Yankees for a few years, it still took a while before I became what I considered firmly established. That was in 1941. I came up with an extra pitch, a slider, and that turned everything around for me. I lost very few games after that. For the rest of my career my winning percentage was something like .750 or thereabouts.

I started the second game of the World Series that year, against Brooklyn. I thought I had real good stuff, but Whitlow Wyatt beat me, 3–2. People said at the time that I got tired running the bases and lost some of my effectiveness after that.

You see, we had instructions to take the extra base on Pete Reiser. We were told that he had a sore arm and couldn't throw too well. Well, we were ahead 2–0 in the fourth inning, and Joe Gordon opened with a single. I forced him at second. Then Johnny Sturm dropped a single into short center, and I elected to try for third. I shouldn't have gone over, but I did. I could run pretty good and thought I had a chance. But I was thrown out on a close play.

After that I ran into trouble, and they blamed it on the running I had done, but I don't think it was that. I wasn't hit all that hard. Joe Gordon made a bad throw in the sixth to let a man on, and then Billy Herman got a single, and I was out of there. We lost the game, 3–2.

That was the Series where Mickey Owen let that third strike get away and turned the ball game around. It was all the opening we needed. All hell broke loose after that. Base hits like thunder. One of those freak games. Like the one Bevens pitched in Ebbets Field in the '47 Series. It always happens in Brooklyn, doesn't it? Sure seems that way. Everything is going along fine, and then boom! it explodes in your face and it's over. The no-hitter is gone, the game is gone, everything is gone, and you're in the clubhouse scratching yourself and wondering where it all went.

Bevens had good stuff in that game but he was wild. Walking men all over the place. What did I think when I saw Lavagetto's shot heading out toward right field? I was wishing the park was just a little bit bigger, so Henrich could catch it. But it wasn't, and he didn't, and that's the way those things happen. Nothing you can do about them. You have to take the bitter with the sweet, don't you? Like the day Deacon Jones, the umpire, cleaned off the Athletics' bench. Wally Moses was sitting down there in the corner, and Wally, you know, never said an unkind word to anybody in his life. So when Deacon Jones started to run them all, Wally just sat there.

"Wally," Deacon says, "you've got to go, too."

Wally jumped up and said, "You know I didn't say anything."

"Well, that's true," Deacon says. "But you know, when the law raids a house of prostitution, the innocent have got to go with the guilty. So get going!"

You know, you always hear about the Yankee power. We had it, of course. But we had to pitch just as hard as anybody to win because everybody was always out to beat us. The other clubs always had their best pitchers stacked up for us; often they would take them out of rotation to have them ready for us. You go to Detroit, and you know you're going to get Bridges, Rowe, Newsom. Same thing with the White Sox—you're going to get Thornton Lee, Ted Lyons. Cleveland always had Bob Feller and Mel Harder waiting. Those fellows didn't give up many runs, and you had to work hard to beat them. And we did beat them. Don't underestimate that Yankee pitching staff. It was *strong*.

Of course we had Joe DiMaggio, and that was a ball club in itself. For all-around ability and everyday play, DiMaggio was the greatest player I ever saw. Williams might have been a little better hitter, but he could only beat you one way, where DiMaggio could beat you about four. The most complete ballplayer I ever saw. And he was a great team man, very loyal to the ball club; he gave his best, he never caused any trouble, he never got into any arguments.

I want to tell you a story that happened to me. I'm in Maryville,

Tennessee, three or four years after I retired as an active player. I'm sitting in the ball park with a scout from the Milwaukee Braves. We're looking at Tennessee State Teachers and Kentucky State Teachers playing a baseball game. Three college kids come in and sit down right beside us. A few minutes later somebody hits a long clout to center field. It was over the center fielder's head, and he turned and ran and made a leaping catch with his back to the playing field. It was a terrific play as far as I'm concerned, as good as you'll ever see.

One of the collegians jumped up and started giving the center fielder a cheer, but one of the other boys said, "What's all the excitement?"

"Well, that's the greatest play I ever saw."

And the other one said, "That was nothing. You should have seen the one I saw one time."

Of course I can't help but to be overhearing all this.

"I hate to interfere with your conversation," I said. "But you mean you've seen a better play than that?"

"You bet I have," he says.

And I say, "Well, if you have, I bet you I can tell you where it was, who hit it, who caught it, who pitched it, and what the pitch was."

The fellow looks at me as if I'm a real wise guy.

"Was it in Yankee Stadium?" I ask him.

"Yes, sir," he says.

"Did DiMaggio catch it?"

"Yes."

"Well, Greenberg hit it, didn't he?"

"Yes," he says.

"Well," I said, "I'm the guy that threw it, and it was a fastball."

Talk about things coming back to you. Here I am, in the hills of Tennessee, and a kid is talking about the greatest play he ever saw.

It was probably the greatest play a lot of people ever saw. It's hard to believe that a fellow could hit a ball as high and as far as Greenberg did and have it caught. When the ball was caught, Greenberg was at second base—that's how far he'd run before it came down. It was hit all the way to what we used to call the graveyard out there in center field by those monuments. About 460

Hank Greenberg: "Well, Greenberg hit it, didn't he?"

feet. DiMaggio—who played a comparatively short center field— took off with the crack of the bat, on a dead run, going at kind of an angle toward the fence. I don't think he ever looked back; he just seemed to have it in his head where that ball was going to come down. Right at the fence, at the 460 mark, he just flicked out his glove and caught the ball.

That occurred late in the season in 1939. We were way behind in the game at the time, and nothing was at stake. But that's the way Joe played ball—everything was at stake for him, all the time.

Another fellow I have nothing but praise for is Bill Dickey. He was a great guy to work with. He was real patient with a young pitcher, he'd always encourage you, and he seemed to know what to call for. I never questioned Bill but one time in a ball game. We were playing in New York, and I was pitching against Washington. Through the first seven innings I hadn't thrown anything but fast balls. As we went into the dugout at the bottom of the seventh, I said, "Bill, when are you gonna call for a curve ball?"

He sat down on the bench and began to undo his chest protector. Without looking at me, he said, "When they start hitting your fast-ball."

"Well," I said, "I don't think they're gonna start hitting it this late in the ball game, but I'm getting tired of throwing it. My arm is getting bored."

He called for one curve in the eighth and one in the ninth.

Then Detroit came in, and he called for but three curveballs in that game. I guess he saw that my fastball was running and sinking so good he'd stick with it. But I threw only five curveballs in two games and won them both easily. You didn't argue with Bill Dickey.

Ted Williams? He got me in his book the first game I pitched against him. Didn't take him long. He hit a ball way back in right field in the Stadium. I saw right then that there was no way I could pitch him with fastballs without him hitting those home runs. So I didn't throw him any fastballs; not for strikes anyway. He was the only hitter that I was ever a defensive pitcher against. I usually went after every hitter from the first pitch right on down. But with Wil-liams it had to be different. I'd always set him up for the fastball and never give it to him. I'd make him hit the curves, the sliders, the changes, and I had great luck with him doing that. You always had to maneuver the ball around with Ted, no matter what the count was. He was such a great hitter. You just couldn't throw him a fast ball. He'd hit it. Feller's, anybody's. A tremendous hitter.

He said to me once, "You son of a gun, I always thought you'd eventually try to slip that fastball by me, and I was always ready for it. I was going to hit it out of the park. But I never got it."

He made a statement once that the three toughest pitchers he ever hit against were Bob Lemon, Hal Newhouser, and myself.

The Yankees always had this reputation for being all business, and on the field I guess we were. But off the field, well, we had our moments, just like anybody else. I'll tell you one that Atley Donald and I pulled on George Stirnweiss and Bud Metheny, when they were rookies on the club.

We were in Detroit, and we had a rainy day. Donald and me are sitting in our room watching the raindrops strike the windows.

"Hey," Donald says, "what do you say we get old Metheny and Stirnweiss on the phone and sell them some Huskies?"

"What are you talking about?" I ask him.

"We'll tell them we're coming up with a new breakfast product, and its name is gonna be Huskies, and we want their endorsements."

So he gets on the phone, with his hand sort of over the mouthpiece to disguise his voice, and he gives them a real sales pitch. Stirnweiss, you know, had set a record in the International League the year before for stealing bases. So we were going to give him $500. Then he gets Metheny on the line.

"Well, Mr. Metheny," he says, "it's true you led your league in runs batted in, but somebody does that every year; you didn't set any records. So we can't give you but three hundred."

You should have heard Metheny. He really put up a battle, telling how important runs batted in were. But Atley finally got him to agree to $300.

"We'll pick you up in the lobby at four o'clock," he says.

At four o'clock we go down to the lobby. We get off the elevator, and there's Stirnweiss and Metheny, looking at everybody, waiting for the Huskies people. We pretended we had some business at the desk, sat around awhile, then went outside. We came back about thirty minutes later, and they're still sitting there.

That night we're going over to Cleveland, by boat. We get down to the dock and I say to Atley, "We ought to send them a night letter, explaining why we didn't make it."

"That's a great idea," he says.

So we sent them a night letter, and the address we gave was a bar that was right down the street from the Cleveland ball park. We were staying at the Cleveland Hotel, and from the end of one of the

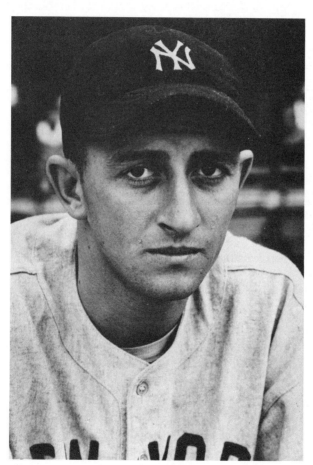

Atley Donald: originator of the new breakfast product.

hallways there you could see down the street to the ball park. You also could see that bar. We told them in the night letter we were going to meet them there at ten o'clock in the morning.

We got into Cleveland at about eight o'clock in the morning and went straight to the hotel. At ten o'clock Donald and I go out into the hallway to that window. We're watching for a few minutes and then here they come, walking across the street. They walk down a block to the bar. And the bar is closed. Doesn't open till one o'clock. So they stand there and start shaking the doorknob and beating on the door. Then they backed up and started talking. I think they were beginning to get the idea that somebody was pulling their leg.

They came to the clubhouse that day, and they were looking at everybody with a big grin, wondering who had been selling them the Huskies. We never did 'fess up, though.

That little escapade took place in 1943, which also happens to be the year I like best to remember. That was my peak. I was 20-4 and with any luck could've been 24-0. The most they scored off of me in any one ball game was four runs. I had 19 wins and 2 losses, and I lost an extra-inning ball game to Cleveland, and then after that I lost 3–2 in extra innings to Washington. My last start was in the stadium against Detroit, and it went fourteen innings before I won it, 2–1. After that game some photographer wanted a picture of Dickey and me, and while we were getting ready for that, Bill said, "This game got you the Most Valuable Player Award. You just won it, I guarantee you that." Well, I hadn't been thinking about that, but it turned out he was right.

I won the opening game of the World Series against the Cardinals in New York. And then I shut them out in the fifth game to win the Series. I wasn't what you'd call brilliant that game, even though I shut them out. I gave up ten base hits and a couple of walks. They left eleven men on base.

To my mind, the turning point in the ball game came in the fourth inning. There was still no score. Whitey Kurowski got on with a hit, and I walked Ray Sanders on four pitches. The next batter was Johnny Hopp. My first three pitches to him were wide of the mark. I'm in pretty deep trouble right here.

Bill Dickey.

Dickey came out at that point to talk to me.

"What's the matter?" he asked.

"Nothing," I said.

"Then get the ball over the plate," he said, and went back.

Well, I got the next two over, and he took them for strikes. So now it's three and two. And I'll tell you what was in the back of my mind as much as anything else. Mort Cooper was looking great for the Cardinals. He'd struck out the first five men he faced and was throwing hard. The only way we were going to beat him was to hold the Cardinals down and wait for something to happen.

I made that three-and-two pitch to Hopp and I never will forget it as long as I live. It was a fastball, and it had to be at least eight to ten inches outside—and he swung at it and missed. I got the next two men on ground balls and was out of the inning. When I went back to the bench, I was so elated I said, "Fellows, there's no way I can lose today."

Cooper continued to be tough. But then in the sixth inning we broke through. With two out Keller got a single and Dickey hit one over the right-field roof. And that was it. That wound up 1943. That beautiful year.

15

FRANK McCORMICK

FRANK ANDREW McCORMICK
Born: June 9, 1911, New York, New York
Major-league career: 1934, 1937–48, Cincinnati Reds, Phila-
  delphia Phillies, Boston Braves
Lifetime average: .299

Frank McCormick entered the National League as a spectacular rookie and remained to become one of its most warmly
regarded veterans. In his first full year, 1938, he hit .327 and
led the league in hits; in his second year he hit .332 and led
the league in hits and runs batted in; in his third year he hit
.309 and led the league in hits and doubles. In 1941 McCormick struck out just 13 times in 603 at bats, a remarkable sta-
tistic for a power hitter.

I can remember, when I was about seventeen years old, I was
talking with my father, and he said to me, "What are you planning to do with your life, Frank?"

Well, out of a clear blue sky, I said, "I'm going to be a baseball
player."

Believe me, a few seconds after I said that, I was scared to death,
wondering why I had ever said such a thing. My father didn't say
anything; I think he was as surprised as I was. But he understood
my love for the game and sympathized with my determination to
make good at it, and he went along with me. Later, as things began
to materialize for me, he was delighted. But I don't think he ever
quite got over that first shock of hearing about it.

It wasn't that I didn't have baseball on my mind; I'd been thinking about it an awful lot and, of course, playing. At that time I was
playing ball on Sundays for a man named George Halpern, who had
a team that traveled out of the Bronx.

When I first joined that team, they had only so many uniforms. I came out there week after week and had to sit on the bench, because they couldn't suit me up. Halpern kept giving the uniform he promised me to a guy named Harry. Finally one day we were playing up in Mosholu Field in the Bronx—it's called Frankie Frisch Field now—near the New York Central Railroad tracks, and my family and my friends all came out to see the game. So I went to Halpern.

"George," I said, "I've got to play today."

"Gee, Frank," he said, "I'm sorry, but Harry's going to have the uniform."

"Listen," I said, "I've been with you four or five weeks now, sitting on the bench, and I've never complained. But now my family's here, my friends are here, and I want to play."

He thought about it for a couple of moments.

"Okay, Frank," he said. "You can get in there today."

So I put the uniform on and played that day. I got two home runs and a double. After that, the uniform was waiting for me every Sunday. That's how I got started in high-caliber sandlot ball.

Frank McCormick in 1935.

It was around that time that the Athletics brought me up to Yankee Stadium for a tryout. I met Connie Mack in the dugout, and we shook hands.

"Fine pair of hands, young man," he said to me. "Now get out there and let's see if you can hit."

So I went out on the field and stepped into the batting cage. Ed Rommel, the old pitcher, was on the mound. Now, I don't know what kind of mood he was in, playful, mischievous, nasty, or what, but he started throwing knuckleballs. And I mean big-league knuckleballs. I could hardly believe what I was seeing, much less hit them. So I went flat on my face in that tryout. I got to know Rommel well later on, and we used to chuckle over that. He'd just been having his fun, that's all. And who knows—if Rommel had thrown me fast balls that day, I might have wound up with the A's.

You know, I worked out with the Giants, too, for a whole week once. That was about in 1932; Bill Terry had just taken over. I'd been working in the shipping room of an art gallery in New York. One day I was holding some Early American glass, a cream pitcher and a sugar bowl. They were worth about $450. Well, somebody attracted my attention, and I sort of bumped them together and broke them. Some pair of hands! So I got fired. It was soon after that that I went up to the Polo Grounds to try out.

I thought I did all right, but they said to me, "Son, if you have a good job, keep it."

And that was right after I'd lost the job. This was during the Depression, remember, and jobs weren't easy to come by. So I was feeling pretty low when I took the subway home that day.

At that time some friends suggested to me that I take the test for the police department. I was sure I could pass, and it was for that very reason that I *didn't* take the test, because I knew if I passed, I probably would have taken the bird in hand and never known whether I could make the big leagues or not. And I'd made up my mind that I was going to be a baseball player. At least, I was going to give it my best shot, give myself every chance, and not ever have to be one of these frustrated athletes who goes through life wondering what might have been.

Six years later I was a unanimous choice as the National League's all-star first baseman, and Bill Terry—who'd turned me down at the Polo Grounds—was one of the men who picked me. I guess it would have been nice to play for the Giants, being a New York boy, but to tell the truth, I just wanted to get to the big leagues, and it didn't much matter who it was with.

Anyway, Larry MacPhail was running the Cincinnati Reds in those days, and George Halpern eventually inveigled MacPhail to send me a bus ticket to a tryout camp in Beckley, West Virginia. This was in 1934. I was an outfielder then, and just before I left, Halpern came up with a suggestion.

"Look, Frank," he said, "there's going to be about a hundred and fifty kids down there at that camp, and a lot of them are going to be outfielders. Why don't you buy yourself a first baseman's mitt? You'll have a better shot if you do."

I took his advice, and it turned out to have been a pretty good idea.

So my uncle loaned me fifty bucks—which didn't last very long— and I took a bus down to Beckley. It was up in the mountains of West Virginia, and it was cold. Sure enough, the field was flooded with kids trying out. But I'd made up my mind that I was going to make it. Anytime somebody hit a long ball, I'd tell myself that I was going to hit one further, and I did. One thing I could do was hit, and I was determined to show them that. I guess after a few days I was feeling pretty good about myself, because Bobby Wallace, an old-time shortstop who was one of the scouts running the camp, came up to me and said, "You've got a good bat, kid, but how are you with that glove?"

"Try me," I said.

"I'm going to hit one through your legs," he said.

"No, you're not," I told him. Now that was pretty fresh, wasn't it? Bobby Wallace had played in the big leagues for *twenty-five* years!

So he took me out there, and for about a half hour he slashed them down to me. He marked up my shins, my knees, my arms, my chest, but he didn't get one through my legs. When it was over, I said to him, "Let's try it again tomorrow."

He laughed. "No, thanks. You've worn me out."

When I saw that I was going to make the team, I really began to feel my oats. I had a letter that said I'd get $100 a month if I made the team. But the contract they offered me called for only $90. I wouldn't sign.

"The letter says a hundred," I told them, and thought to myself, *Holy mackerel, McCormick, you're a holdout.*

"We can't change the contract," they said.

"So what are you going to do about it?" I asked.

They thought it over, then said, "Okay. We'll give you ten bucks under the table every month."

And that's what they did.

Life in the minors can be rough, there's no question about that. But I'll tell you, you can like it an awful lot if you know you have a chance to make the big leagues. I felt I had a good chance, so I

Frank McCormick: Flying high in spring training.

enjoyed it. And you know, when some of us get together today, the reminiscing we do more often than not is not about the major leagues and the good times, the good money, the good food; it's about the days when we traveled by car and by bus. You talk about the days when you had to eat hot dogs by the roadside and slept all night on the bus, and the times when the bus broke down and you had to get out in the middle of the night and push the darn thing along a country road until you found a garage. You remember the clubhouses that didn't have showers and the ball parks without dugouts, where you had to sit out in the broiling sun throughout a Sunday doubleheader. Those days seem like the great days, when things were tough, when you were young, when you had all that drive and desire and ambition going for you, when you had that lovely goal at the end of the rainbow—the big leagues.

I had a good year at Beckley. Hit around .350. Our season closed in Charleston, West Virginia, and I was told then that the Reds were bringing me up for the last three weeks of the major-league season.

I got on the train and rode all night in the coach car. Didn't sleep a wink. I just sat there stiff as a board, staring out the window. Couldn't sleep, couldn't eat, couldn't even think. The Reds were in Brooklyn then, and that's where I was heading.

My first time at bat in the major leagues was at Brooklyn, in old Ebbets Field. Charley Dressen, who was managing Cincinnati then, sent me up to pinch-hit. Dutch Leonard was the pitcher. I was so nervous that if you had put a brick between my knees, I'd have ground it into dust—that's how bad I was shaking.

I guess you never forget that first big league at bat. I hit a scorcher that handcuffed the second baseman, but they scored it an error. Later on, when I got to know Dutch Leonard, he said to me, "You know, Frank, they should have scored that a hit."

But you know the old story—if the guy gets his glove on it, it's an error.

Then we went into the Polo Grounds. I was sitting in the dugout when Carl Hubbell went out to warm up for the Giants. You should have heard the moaning on our bench: "Oh, it's that guy again." "Here's where I get the collar." Talk like that. Gee whiz, I thought, these guys are whipped even before they walk out on the field. I made up my mind that wasn't going to happen to me.

In the middle of the game I was sent up to pinch-hit against Hubbell. I walked up there thinking: Hubbell or no Hubbell, the guy has to throw the ball over the plate, and it's up to me to swing or not to swing. Well, I hit one right past him into center field. Dressen let me stay in the game, and the next time up I got myself another single to center. Two hits off of Carl Hubbell. Boy, my chest was all swelled up. I was half expecting a ticker-tape parade.

You know, a funny thing. I always had pretty good luck against Carl Hubbell—until he lost his stuff. That's right. Seems I just couldn't get it into my head that he didn't have that real great stuff anymore, and I'd go up there looking for it and keep getting fooled.

Later on, in St. Louis, I pinch-hit against Dizzy Dean. I hit a ball to deep short to Durocher. If there hadn't been a runner on first, who got forced out, I would have had a hit to deep short. The things you remember, huh? Well, why not? It's only forty years ago.

I guess I'd have to say that Dean and Feller were the fastest I ever saw. Flip a coin between them. They threw aspirin tablets up there. Now, I know you've heard that expression a thousand times—but it's still the best description.

I was farmed out the next few years and came back for good in 1938. Bill McKechnie was the Reds' manager then. He was the real fatherly type. You liked to play for him. He was very understanding, sympathetic. And yet I'll tell you one thing—when he put his hand across his chest and looked at you over his bifocals, he was mad. And as fine a gentleman as he was, he could be rough as a corncob when he thought you hadn't done the right thing.

We knew in 1938 that we had a good team in Cincinnati. We could feel it happening. We went to spring training the next year, in 1939, in a confident mood. After about the first six weeks of the season we became conscious of the fact that we could win the pennant. And we did win it. Bucky Walters and Paul Derringer won 52 games between them that year. Those guys were just remarkable.

Then of course there was the World Series that year. I should say, "What Series?" The Yankees took us four straight. I'll tell you though, it was the way that we lost the first game in Yankee Stadium that I think took the heart out of us. A fly ball in the ninth inning that might have been caught was the crucial play. Paul Derringer pitched brilliantly, but we lost, 2–1. If we had won that game we would have made, at least, a more presentable Series out of it.

We won the pennant again in 1940 and this time went against the Detroit Tigers in the Series. That 1940 World Series was an exciting one; it went the full seven games. They had us three games to two,

Paul Derringer.

but we still had Walters and Derringer. Bucky shut them out in the sixth game to even it up, and Derringer started the seventh game against Bobo Newsom.

Bobo was a tough character in that game. In fact, he was tough every game we saw him. He'd already beaten us twice and had us down 1–0 going into the bottom of the seventh of the last game. I came up and led off with a double. Then Jimmy Ripple hit one out to right field that Bruce Campbell just missed catching, and I scored the tying run. Jimmie Wilson sacrificed Ripple to third, and then Billy Myers hit a long fly ball to score Ripple. They couldn't score off Derringer the last two innings, and we won it, 2–1.

I'll tell you, winning that championship is quite something. It isn't just the money; it's the honor and the prestige, the pride you take in being called champion. You can't imagine what that means and how it feels until you've done it.

There was some icing on the cake for me that winter. I was voted the National League's Most Valuable Player. Well, coming on top of the World Series victory, that was quite a dividend. That's the ultimate, of course. There are a lot of honors in baseball, like being in the opening-day lineup, playing in the All-Star game, the World Series. But getting that MVP award is a special thing. That's in a class by itself.

I look back on 1940 as being a great season for the team and for me personally, but unfortunately it was marred by a very sad and tragic incident. In August, one of our catchers, Willard Hershberger, took his own life. There seemed to be no apparent reason for it; I suppose it was just one of those things that builds up inside a man until it reaches a point where he can't fight it off anymore.

It happened while we were in Boston. Most of the time Willard was a nice, easygoing fellow, but he could be moody; sometimes his spirits would be way up, other times way down. The night before it happened, he was way down. We were all in the lobby, and we saw him come out of the elevator with McKechnie. Willard obviously was in some emotional distress; his eyes were all welled up with tears. We saw that and turned away. Nobody said anything. He and McKechnie went into the dining room and had dinner, just the two of them.

Willard Hershberger.

The following day, no Hershberger at the ball park. Then some-body came hollering for McKechnie, and we knew something had happened. We learned later that Willard had taken a razor and cut his throat behind a locked door in his hotel room.

Why things like that happen is not for me to say. I couldn't tell you. The only one who could have shed some light on it was Mc-Kechnie. "I know what the story is," he said later. "I know what happened, but I'm going to my grave with it." And he did. Whatever it was that Willard confided in him, McKechnie would never tell it. That's the kind of man he was.

Rip Sewell.

16

RIP SEWELL

Truett Banks Sewell
Born: May 11, 1907, Decatur, Alabama
Major-league career: 1932, 1938–49, Detroit Tigers, Pittsburgh
  Pirates
Lifetime record: 143 wins, 97 losses

Inventor and sole owner and proprietor of the famous blooper pitch, Rip Sewell has won himself a place in baseball folklore for his mastery of this baffling and effective delivery. Lest the blooper overshadow his other achievements, however, it should be remembered that Sewell was an ace pitcher for the Pirates for a decade, twice winning 21 games in a season and in 1943 leading all National League pitchers in complete games.

In 1931 I was attending Vanderbilt University, in Nashville, Tennessee. I was there on a football scholarship, even though baseball was still my favorite sport. I always had my eye on a career in professional baseball, ever since I was a kid growing up in Decatur, Alabama.

I was studying mechanical engineering at Vanderbilt, but I soon came to realize I wasn't going to make it as a mechanical engineer. Tell you the truth, a degree didn't seem so attractive in those days. This was during the Depression. You saw quite a few fellows with degrees under each arm trying to get a job, any job.

So I left school and went to work for Dupont, in Old Hickory, Tennessee, right across the river from Nashville. Got a job in the plant. I also started playing semipro ball in Old Hickory. Still had that baseball bug. The baseball virus.

The sports editor of the Nashville *Banner*, Freddie Russell, was a fraternity brother of mine. I went to him and said, "Freddie, I know I can play ball. I just want an opportunity to prove it to somebody."

He took me down to see the owner of the Nashville Vols. I worked out there, and they signed me to a contract for $400 a month. That was the most money I'd ever seen in my life. When I signed the contract, they told me, "If we sell you before the year is over, you'll get ten percent of the selling price." It was a verbal agreement, nothing in writing. Sure enough, Detroit bought me. They paid $10,000 and three ballplayers for me, Detroit did. But I still haven't seen any part of that $10,000 or of the three ballplayers either for that matter.

I was up with the Tigers for a while in 1932. They used me in relief, though I didn't see too much action. I can tell you about the game that knocked me out of the big leagues at that time. It was one pitch that did it. I went in to relieve against the Athletics. There were a couple of men on base, and Jimmie Foxx was up. To this day I can see him standing there, his big-muscled arms looking like piano legs hanging out of a churn. I threw him one of my best pitches—I thought—and he hit it over the left field wall. The next day I was on my way to Toronto.

The Tigers recalled me in 1934, and I went to spring training with them in Lakeland, Florida. I had high hopes of sticking this time, but something happened down there that put a damper on my chances. About a week before camp broke, I had a fight with Hank Greenberg, who at that time was one of their up-and-coming young players. It was just one of those things that happens for no good reason and that you're real sorry about later. Hank and I had played together at Beaumont, and we'd been good friends, so this thing just came out of nowhere.

It started on a bus ride, coming back from Bradenton, after a game with the Cardinals. Tex Carleton had shut us out, 3–0. He'd struck Greenberg out two or three times. Sidearm fastballs, you know, and Hank didn't like it one bit. He was brooding on it.

After the ball game we got on the bus to go back to Lakeland. Greenberg gets on and sits down next to an open window, some-where around the middle of the bus. Denny Carroll, the trainer, and Gerald Walker got on and went to the back of the bus together. When Gerald went by Hank—Gerald was a character anyway—he rubbed his hand over Hank's face and said, "Why don't you get that sour look off your puss?" Something like that. That didn't help Hank's disposition, I'm sure.

I was sitting two seats behind Greenberg, and in front of me was a kid pitcher. You know, the kind you call bush. Once the bus got going, the wind started blowing and it was getting cool. Denny Carroll called out to Greenberg, "Henry"—he called him Henry—"pull that window down. You'll give everybody back here a cold."

Greenberg didn't do anything. Just sat there.

The bus kept going, and the wind kept blowing in, and it was getting real chilly.

"Henry," Denny Carroll called out again, "pull that window down. Everybody back here's getting a chill."

Greenberg didn't say nuts. He just sat there.

So the kid pitcher is sitting behind him, and I'm sitting behind the kid pitcher. The kid could have reached forward and pulled the window down. I tapped him on the shoulder and said, "Hey, bush, pull the window down."

Well, Greenberg evidently thought I was talking to him. So he turned around and said to me, "Who you calling a bush, you Southern son of a bitch?"

Well, you know that's fightin' words in my part of the country. Son of a bitch is bad enough, but *Southern* son of a bitch, that was the kicker. So I said, "You, you big Jew son of a bitch, if it fits you." So I got right back. I didn't back off from anybody.

He said, "I'm gonna take your ass on when we get to Lakeland."

I said, "You can stop the damn bus right now if you want to do that."

There wasn't another word said until we got to Lakeland. We pulled up right in front of the hotel. Mickey Cochrane, who was the manager, and Frank Navin, who owned the club, were sitting there —they'd taken a car back. They were sitting in wicker chairs in the big front window, their feet up on the windowsill.

We started getting off the bus. Greenberg was ahead of me. When I stepped off, he hit me right upside the damn head. He must've had a ring on or something, because he just took the skin right off.

Well, we fought; hell, it must've been a half hour. And Cochrane and Navin sat there in that big window and watched. We just fought and fought and fought. Off the curb and into the street, out of the street and across the grass and through the hedges. He was a big guy, and so was I. Nobody tried to stop it. Finally a plainclothes cop came walking across the street and pulled out a blackjack. "Y'all stop this damn fight," he said, "or I'm gonna bop both of you." So he was the one who finally stopped it, this plainclothes cop. Then Cochrane told us to get up to our rooms and he'd see us in the morning. Why didn't Cochrane break it up? Well, I guess he figured he didn't start it. Only thing I can think of. Mickey was from the old school.

But after that I knew I was gone. I knew it. The next day Cochrane called me in and said, "Rip, don't think I feel any the less about you

Hank Greenberg: "We fought and fought and fought. He was a big guy, and so was I."

for it; in fact, I think more of you. But we've got thirty pitchers and only one first baseman. What do you think I'm going to do?"

"Well," I said, "I know what you're going to do."

I spent that summer in Toledo.

You know, just to jump ahead, in 1947 Greenberg joined the Pirates when I was still there, and we became good friends. He didn't stay with the Pirates but one year, but we were real close friends then, I'm happy to say.

The Pirates bought me from Buffalo at the end of the 1937 season. I went to spring training with them in '38 and made the club. Pie Traynor was managing then, but I didn't really get a chance to pitch until Frankie Frisch took over a year or so later. Frisch gave me my chance, and I owe everything to him.

Arky Vaughan was in his heyday at shortstop for the Pirates when I got there. I'd say that he was as good a man at short as I ever saw. He could do it all. And he was a good hitter. He could hit for power, and he could hit for average. And could he ever fly around those bases! I never saw anybody who could go from first to third or from second to home faster than Vaughan. Like we used to say, when he went around second his hip pocket was dipping sand. That's how sharp he cut those corners.

Paul and Lloyd Waner were still in the outfield for the Pirates. You liked to see those fellows out there when you were pitching. And they could still wheel those bats. You know, they came from back on the farm in Oklahoma. They used to raise corn there, and they always used to have a great big stack of corncobs after shelling the corn and getting rid of it for the grain feed. Lloyd told me that's where he and Paul learned how to be good batters. They'd throw wet corncobs all day and try to hit them. You take a wet corncob and break it in half and throw it, and it'll go like a rocket. He said that was their pastime out there when they were kids growing up. For a bat they'd use an old pick handle or anything else they could come by.

You say you want to know the story of the blooper pitch? Well, that started with a shotgun blast in the Ocala National Forest on December 7, 1941. So that's a date I'll remember for more than one reason. I was out deer hunting that day. I was walking through the woods when another hunter spotted something moving. What he spotted was me, but he didn't realize that until he had turned suddenly and discharged two loads of buckshot out of a twelve-gauge shotgun at about thirty feet. Caught me in both legs. That shot tore holes in me as big as marbles. One of them smashed up the big toe which I pitched off of.

I had to learn to walk all over again, keeping that big toe up when I moved. Naturally my whole pitching motion had to be changed. I had to pitch just like I walked, like I was taking a step forward, all the while keeping that big toe up.

That's how the blooper ball came about, from having to learn to pitch with that motion, like I was walking toward you. I was the only pitcher to pitch off of the tip of his toes, and that's the only way you can throw the blooper. It's got to be thrown straight overhand. I was able to get a terrific backspin on the ball by holding onto the seam and flipping it off of three fingers. The backspin held it on its line of flight to the plate. So that ball was going slow but spinning fast. Fun to watch, easy to catch, but tough to hit. It helped me win 21 games in '43 and again in '44.

I was fooling around with Al Lopez in the bullpen one time and started looping the ball and dropping it into his glove. All of a sudden Lopez said, "Why don't you throw that in a game?"

I laughed. "Man, no," I said. "Frisch would get after me, and so would everybody else if I threw it in a game."

Then we were in Muncie, Indiana, playing an exhibition game against the Detroit Tigers. Dick Wakefield was at bat, with two out. Out of a clear blue sky I decided I was going to throw him that blooper ball. So I wound up and let it go. The thing went way up in the air, and coming down, it looked like it was going to be a perfect strike. He started to swing, he stopped, he started again, he stopped, and then he swung and missed it by a mile. I thought everybody was going to fall off the bench, they were laughing so hard.

Later I was sitting in the clubhouse, and all the newspaper boys came around to ask me what in the hell that was. Maurice Van Robays was sitting next to me. Maurice says, "That's an eephus ball."

Somebody said, "What's an eephus ball?"

Maurice says, "Eephus ain't nothin', and that's what that ball is."

So then they started calling it the eephus pitch. That's the way it got started. I got more funny reactions from that than you can imagine. The fans loved it. And a lot of times some of the players on the opposing team would whistle out to me, when one of their own players was at bat, and make their fingers dive up and down through the air, telling me to throw it. You see, most guys usually swung at it no matter where it was. It was like waving a red flag in front of a bull. Made them mad as hell. It looked like anybody could knock it out, and they always tried.

I had as good control of it as I did of my fastball and curve. I'd spot it around here and there, when they were least expecting it. It reached an arc of about 25 feet.

When I first started throwing that thing, I had more trouble from the umpires with it than I did from the batters. Some of the umpires said they wouldn't call it a strike, no way. I heard about that and told Frisch. He became concerned because that damned pitch was becoming a drawing card. We had people coming in from West Virginia and Ohio and everywhere else just to see it.

The Pirate management got hold of Bill Klem. He was the supervisor of National League umpires at that time. And of course you know Klem's reputation—the greatest umpire of them all. So he came to Pittsburgh and came into the clubhouse to see me. He told me to get a catcher and a batter and to go out to the mound. We did that, and he got behind the plate to see if it was true the blooper was a strike. I began demonstrating it. He watched me throw it in for a while, and then he said, "Okay. It's a strike, and I'll see that they call it." From then on they called it.

I guess the most famous blooper pitch was the one I threw to Ted Williams in the '46 All-Star game in Fenway Park. Before the game, Ted said to me, "Hey, Rip, you wouldn't throw that damned crazy pitch in a game like this, would you?"

"Sure," I said. "I'm gonna throw it to you."

"Man," he said, "don't throw that ball in a game like this."

"I'm gonna throw it to you, Ted," I said. "So look out."

Ted Williams: "Hey, Rip, you wouldn't throw that damned crazy pitch in a game like this, would you?"

Well, if you remember that game, they had us beat 8–0 going into the last of the eighth. It was a lousy game, and the fans were bored. I was pitching that inning, and Ted came to bat. You know how Ted used to be up there at the plate, all business. I smiled at him. He must've recalled our conversation because he shook his head from side to side in quick little movements, telling me not to throw it. I nodded to him: You're gonna get it, buddy. He shook his head again. And I nodded to him again. He was gonna get it. So I wound up like I was going to throw a fastball, and here comes the blooper. He swung from Port Arthur and just fouled it on the tip of his bat.

He stepped back in, staring out at me, and I nodded to him again: You're gonna get another one. I threw him another one, but it was outside and he let it go. Now he was looking for it. Well, I threw him a fastball, and he didn't like that. Surprised him. Now I had him one ball, two strikes. I wound up and threw him another blooper. It was a good one. Dropping right down the chute for a strike. He took a couple of steps up on it—which was the right way to attack that pitch, incidentally—and he hit it right out of there. And I mean he *hit* it.

Well, the fans stood up, and they went crazy. I walked around the base lines with Ted, talking to him. "Yeah," I told him, "the only reason you hit it is because I told you it was coming." He was laughing all the way around. I got a standing ovation when I walked off the mound after that inning. We'd turned a dead turkey of a ball game into a real crowd pleaser.

And he was the only man ever to hit a home run off the blooper. Ted Williams, in the '46 All-Star game.

Bob Feller.

17

BOB FELLER

ROBERT WILLIAM ANDREW FELLER
Born: November 3, 1918, Van Meter, Iowa
Major-league career: 1936–56, Cleveland Indians
Lifetime record: 266 wins, 162 losses

In a sport not noted for its prodigies, Bob Feller stands supreme. Achieving star status at seventeen with a suddenness that was as dramatic as it was remarkable, Feller became baseball's most electrifying performer since Babe Ruth. In all of sport, there are few names that match the magic and glamor of Bob Feller's. Among the most eye-catching of his many achievements, in addition to his three no-hitters and record-breaking strikeout performances, were the 12 one-hitters he pitched.

Feller was elected to the Hall of Fame in 1962.

How fast? Well, it so happens I can give you a precise answer, because they tested it once. This was in Washington, D.C., in 1946. When we got into town, I read in the paper that Clark Griffith was going to set up a speed meter at home plate and that I was going to throw the ball through it to measure my velocity.

Griffith's attendance was down at the time. He had a terrible ball club that year—they'd cinched last place by about Mother's Day. So, to help draw a crowd, he got this photoelectric-cell device from the ordnance plant in Aberdeen, Maryland. Aberdeen was a proving ground where the government tested the speed of projectiles, of ammunition, and so forth. He had it set up over home plate and loud and clear announced that I was going to throw through it. Without asking me. Nobody had ever asked me about it. Griffith hadn't told me or the Cleveland ball club a thing about it.

Well, all I had going for me at the time was I was tied with Hal Newhouser in wins, I was trying to break the strikeout record for a season, and I was leading the league in earned run average. So I was in no way going to go out there and throw through that Mickey Mouse-Rube Goldberg device without being *asked*. And I never was asked, until Griffith came into the clubhouse before the game.

"Bob," he said, "the fans are waiting out there now. We've got the device set up over the plate. So why don't you get out there and take your warm-up pitches and throw through the meter before you start the ball game?"

"How many times do I have to throw through it?" I asked.

"Oh, about thirty or so," he said.

"And then go out and pitch my ball game. Well, I'll tell you, Mr. Griffith, I have a contract based upon my number of wins, so I have a lot going for me every time I pitch. You're asking me to throw a lot of pitches that could jeopardize my game. So it'll take a thousand bucks for me to go out there and throw through that bunch of wires."

When I said that, his head and his feet changed places.

"Bob," he said, "this kind of promotion is good for baseball. The fans really appreciate this sort of thing."

"That's all well and good," I said. "But you've got thousands and thousands of people out there who've come to watch it. You're not losing anything on it, are you?"

"That's not the point," he said.

I don't know if we ever decided what the point was, but he finally talked me down to $700 to go out there and do it.

I lost the ball game that night. I don't know if I wore myself out on that damned machine, but I lost the game something like 2–1 in ten or eleven innings. Griffith probably made over $20,000 on the deal, if you want to count the concessions. And I got my $700. But all he had to do was ask me first, and I probably would have done it for nothing.

What did the ball clock in at? 98.6 miles an hour as it crossed the plate. I threw thirty or forty times. I guess I was as fast as I ever was that night. I was as fast in '46 and the early part of '47 as I ever was.

At that rate of speed it took about a third of a second for the ball to leave my fingers and get up to the plate. Which means the hitter had that much time to make up his mind whether it was a curve or a fastball or a slider, a ball or a strike, whether to take it or to swing at it, and where he wanted to hit it. I think it takes more ability to be a complete ballplayer than it does to play any major sport that I know of. Good reflexes, good eye, good coordination. You'd better have them.

Where did it all start? Van Meter, Iowa. I grew up there on a farm, about three miles outside town. It was a corn and hog farm. I did the usual chores that any kid does on a farm—milk the cows, feed the pigs, clean out the barn on Saturdays, put up fences.

In the early thirties the dust storms, the grasshoppers, the lack of rain played havoc with us. The cattle were starving and dying of thirst. Perhaps it wasn't so bad in that part of Iowa as it was further out in Nebraska and Kansas and the Dakotas. But we had to carry water out of the river, when the river had water in it, and put it in the wagon and dump it into a tank and haul it for the livestock. The streams were very low. Nothing would grow. The dust would pile up along the fence lines like snow.

Things were pretty rough, but we always managed to have a garden, and we had enough water to water it, so we had fruit and vegetables. And we did have the livestock, and we did have corn and grain in storage, which we fed them. Farmers, at least in that part of the country, usually had enough to eat, one way or the other. It may not have been enough, but it was something.

But whatever we didn't have, we always had baseball. I guess I could always throw hard, even when I was eight or nine years old. I used to play catch with my father in the house. I'd throw from the kitchen into the living room and he'd sit there on the davenport and catch me with a pillow. It wasn't long after that that he got a mitt for himself and a glove for me, and bats and balls.

Then he made a home plate in the yard, and I'd throw to him over it. He even built me a pitching rubber. When I was twelve, we built a ball field on our farm. We fenced off the pasture, put up the chicken wire and the benches and even a little grandstand behind first base. We formed our own team and played other teams from around the community on weekends. We had tournaments. The field was up on a little hill and we called it Oak View because you looked

Bob Feller, age ten: "But whatever we didn't have, we always had baseball."

"Where did it all start? Van Meter, Iowa." Main Street, Van Meter, circa 1937.

right down over the Raccoon River and saw a lot of oaks in the forest there. The crops and the trees and the river made a very pretty view. Artistically speaking, it was rather an interesting ball park.

Obviously my father loved baseball, and he cultivated my talent for the game. I don't think he ever had any doubt in his mind that I would play professional baseball someday. There was no question about it being his ambition for me.

We practiced together constantly. In the wintertime we'd throw in the barn. In 1924 we got a Delco plant to electrify the property— this was about fifteen years before the power lines came in. We had a windcharger, and on a windy day that would charge the batteries, and we would use the lights in the barn to play night baseball—if you want to call it that—two or three nights a week to keep my arm in condition.

Dad would have me pitching under game conditions. We would simulate an entire game. I'd pitch with men on base, and we had a standard which he moved from side to side in the batters box so I'd have to pitch to both right- and left-hand hitters.

One summer's night we were in the barn, and I was pitching a "game." My father crouched down to give me the sign. He put out two fingers to call for a curveball and got set for it. Well, it was kind of late in the evening, around nine or nine thirty, and getting dark in there, and I thought he'd called for a fastball. So instead of the ball breaking down and away, as he expected, it came in straight, with a hop, and hit him in the side and broke a couple of ribs. They had to tape him up from his waist to under his armpits, and for a farmer to have to work under those conditions was miserable.

I played four years of American Legion ball, beginning when I was twelve. In 1934 some of the umpires in Legion ball started telling Cy Slapnicka of the Cleveland Indians about me. At first he didn't pay much attention to them—scouts are always getting these rave reports on kids from one source or another. But they kept after him. You know how people can be—the less attention you pay them, the more enthusiastic they're apt to become. So they kept bombarding Slapnicka about me. "Greatest thing since sliced bread," etc. etc.

He didn't get out to see me until 1935, and even then I think it was just to humor those umpires and get them off his back. He came out there, figuring he'd have a look at the farmboy and then go on and attend to some serious business—he was planning to scout Claude Passeau, who was pitching for Des Moines, in the Western League.

Well, he never did see Passeau. He didn't buy Passeau. He bought me. Gave me a big bonus, too—an autographed ball and $1—to sign a contract for $75 a month. I was glad to get it, and my relationship with the Cleveland ball club, and Cy Slapnicka in particular, and the fans in Cleveland in general, and the writers, was a very happy one. I'm glad I didn't get a bonus. I think you're supposed to get paid after you do your job. I was well paid in Cleveland and have no complaints whatsoever.

This was in June, 1935. I was sixteen years old then. I was supposed to go to Fargo, North Dakota, when high school was out. But then I pitched five games in eight days in the state high school tournament, and I strained my arm. I couldn't throw. I informed the Cleveland ball club, and they brought me to Cleveland for the trainer to fix my arm up. All I needed really was some rest. I worked out with the club, played pepper, did some running. I had no broken bones or torn cartilages, so for what was bothering me, rest was the great healer.

In 1936 I stayed with the Cleveland ball club. Slapnicka was general manager then. What he did, in order to make me eligible to pitch for Cleveland, was put through a series of phony transfers of my contract through different minor league clubs until it was switched to Cleveland. This was clearly in violation of the rules, and Judge Landis caught up to him later on it.

I spent the spring of '36 with Cleveland trying to learn my business. And I had a lot to learn. Pitching in the big leagues is more than just throwing a fastball. Then, on July 6, during the All-Star game break, the St. Louis Cardinals came to town for an exhibition game. Slapnicka suggested I pitch a few innings, kind of as a lark, to save the pitching staff. Of course, he knew me better than anyone else did and figured, kid or no kid, I probably wouldn't embarrass myself.

The Cardinals had a pretty good lineup—Joe Medwick, Frankie Frisch, Pepper Martin, Rip Collins, Leo Durocher. No, I wasn't nervous. I never had any concern about the hitters as long as I could get that ball over the plate. My only concern that day was the crowd. I'd never seen so many people before in my life.

If anybody was nervous that day, it was the Cardinals. I was very wild and had them scared half to death. The first big league batter I ever pitched to was Leo Durocher. The first pitch was over his head and into the screen. The next one was behind him. And of course those pitches were pretty fast. The next two pitches were strikes. Then Steve O'Neill, who was catching, said, "You'd better be careful, Leo. He's liable to stick this next one right in your ear." So Leo, who'd been pretty loose up there, dropped the bat and ran back to the dugout and hid behind the water cooler, pretending he was scared. Cal Hubbard, who was umpiring, told him to come back up to the plate, that he had another strike coming. Leo leaned out from behind the water cooler and cupped his hands around his mouth and yelled, "The hell with you, Hubbard. You take it for me." Dizzy Dean was sitting there laughing his head off. Leo was the first big-league hitter I ever struck out.

I pitched three innings and fanned eight out of nine. There's a story that went around at the time, that after the game some photographer asked Dean if he would pose for a picture with me, and Dean is supposed to have said, "You'd better ask *him* if he'll pose with *me*."

Right after that I joined the Cleveland pitching staff, getting into games that were lost, mopping up, that sort of thing. Then they started me, against the St. Louis Browns. This was in August. I had very good stuff and felt confident. I went out there and struck out 15. That hit the newspapers pretty hard. It wasn't that 15 strikeouts was so great, it was because I was so young. I was only seventeen. But also you have to remember that generally there were fewer strikeouts in those days. You had more choke hitters, they weren't swinging so hard.

I threw the fastball primarily in that game, but I had a curve then, too. I always had a good curve, even when I was a kid back in Iowa. I think if you talk to the guys who hit against me, they'll tell you, "Fastball hell, look at the curve he had." I struck out as many with the curve as I did with the fastball.

Three weeks later I struck out 17 Philadelphia Athletics, and that broke the American League record. I was pretty excited over that. I knew I was approaching the record. I was counting those whiffs. There's no way you can duck it. And the closer I got to that record, the more I wanted to break it. I just kept pouring them in, trying to keep the ball over, hoping the guys wouldn't start choking up on the bat and start pushing the ball around.

That hit the newspapers like thunder and lightning, and I guess that's when people began to realize I was for real.

Was I the most famous kid in America in 1936? Come on now. You're forgetting about Shirley Temple, aren't you? And what about those kids in the *Our Gang* comedies? Anyway, I was seventeen years old. You want to call that a kid? Okay, maybe by baseball standards.

I tried not to let it all bother me too much. I went back to the farm, went hunting with my friends, went to basketball games. Sure, people would gawk at me and point me out like I was some sort of circus freak, and it took awhile to get accustomed to. I didn't pay that much attention to it. My father had a lot of common sense, and he saw to it that I didn't get swell-headed about it. He told me that people would be nitpicking and asking silly questions and trying to use me, that people always wanted to bask in reflected notoriety, good, bad, or indifferent. Sometimes your best friends are your worst enemies, wanting to keep you out late at night so they can be seen with you. These things happen in all walks of life, not only baseball.

So my life didn't change as much as it might have, given all the circumstances. I knew where the stakes were set, due to the fact my parents told me where they were set. They gave me a pretty good idea of values. My mother was a schoolteacher, and it was important to her that I get that high school diploma, and it was important to me too. I didn't exactly crack the books until three o'clock in the morning, but I did graduate.

In the winter of '36 Slapnicka's manipulating of my contract came to the attention of Judge Landis. You see, in those days major-league clubs couldn't sign free agents. Minor-league clubs would sign all the players and then sell them to the major-league clubs to make ends meet financially. This was by agreement. Well, the major-league clubs were all cheating. They were signing players off the sandlots, and Judge Landis knew it. I was one of them. So it became within his authority to make me a free agent. If he had done that, I could've picked up $100,000 or more in bonus money. There were

"I didn't exactly crack the books until three o'clock in the morning, but I did graduate."

scouts sitting in the Chamberlain Hotel in Des Moines with blank checks in their hands, just waiting.

But I was loyal to the Cleveland club, and so were my parents. The ball club had done a great deal for us and had been very friendly. When my arm was bad, they took care of it, brought me along with compassion and understanding, instead of shooting me up to Fargo, where I might have injured it permanently and wound up milking cows the rest of my life—nothing wrong with that, but it wasn't my life's ambition to be a dairy farmer. I wanted to be a baseball player.

Well, my father and I met several times with Judge Landis. The judge said he was going to declare me a free agent. My father didn't like that one bit.

"The Cleveland ball club has treated us fair," he told the judge. "It's our intention for him to play for Cleveland, if they want him, and they want him. And if you won't permit that, then we're going to sue you in civil court, because we have a civil law contract and we want to test it to see if baseball law supersedes civil law."

Well, the judge wanted no part of that. He didn't want to hear anything about it, and this is why I was able to stay with Cleveland.

How did I feel about it? Well, sure I could have gotten $100,000. But I didn't care about that. I wanted to stay where I was. I was happy. I was pitching major-league baseball and was quite successful. I figured if I was worth that kind of money, I'd make it later, after I'd proved I was worth it. And if I wasn't worth it, then I had no business having it.

It took me about three years to learn how to pitch in the big leagues. Like I said, it's more than just a fastball. You have to learn how to hold runners on, how to field your position, how to *think* out on the mound. By the end of 1938 I'd absorbed a lot of that. That was my first really big year, 1938. Coming down to the last day of the season, I was running close with Bobo Newsom for the lead in strikeouts. I was anxious to lead the league, and so was Bobo. Well, I pitched my game and went into the clubhouse. I no sooner get in there than I get a phone call. It's from Bobo. Long distance. I forget where he was, St. Louis or someplace.

"Hey, Bob," he says, "how are you?"

"Pretty good, Bobo," I said. "How are you?"

"Okay," he says. "Listen, it's been a hell of a race for strikeouts, hasn't it?"

"Sure has."

"I think I beat you out," he says. "I struck out twelve today. What kind of a game did you have?"

"Well, I lost four to one, Bobo."

"That's too bad."

"But I struck out eighteen."

There was a long silence, which was unusual with Bobo, and then he said, "Congratulations."

Yeah, that was the day I broke the record. October 2, 1938. That's a day I'll always remember. It was the last day of the season, and we

Bobo Newsom: "Listen, it's been a hell of a race for strikeouts, hasn't it?"

were playing the Tigers a doubleheader in Municipal Stadium in Cleveland. There must've been about 30,000 people in the stands. But they weren't there to see me; they were there to see Hank Greenberg try and break Ruth's record. Hank had 58 home runs, and this was going to be his last whack at that record.

In anticipation of Hank's breaking that record, there were newsreel cameras in from New York and elsewhere to document it. Well, instead of getting Hank breaking a home run record, they got me breaking the major-league strikeout record for one game, which was nice for me, because it's all recorded on film.

I was fast that day and had a very good curve. If I remember correctly, I struck out the side in the second, third, and fourth. I know that by the end of five innings I had 12 strikeouts. At the end of seven I had 15. I got one more in the eighth and went into the ninth inning needing one to tie the record—which I held jointly with Dizzy Dean—and two to set a new record.

I tied the record by fanning the leadoff man, Pete Fox. Then Greenberg came up. I'd already fanned Hank twice, and this time he hit a long fly ball to center. The next batter was Chet Laabs. I'd been feasting on him all afternoon—striking him out four times. So he was as determined as he could be not to strike out again. I ran the count to one and two. Then I threw him a fastball around the knees, close to the corner. He made a move as if he was going to swing, but he didn't swing. He took it. It could have been called either way. Cal Hubbard called it a strike. Number 18.

It was a nice way to end the season, and I basked in that one all winter long, even though I lost the game.

The 1940 season started off on a high note for me. We opened in Chicago against the White Sox. It was a cool day, I remember, the temperature in the 40's. My parents were there, and my sister, and some friends and relatives from Iowa.

We got a run in the fourth inning. Jeff Heath singled, and Rollie Hemsley tripled. That was the only run of the game. I don't think I had particularly good stuff that day, but when it came down to two out in the ninth, I had a no-hitter going. Taft Wright was the hitter. He was always tough for me. Sure enough, he hit a hard shot between first and second that Ray Mack, the second baseman, made a tremendous play on. He speared the ball about five feet back on the grass, did a complete 360-degree turn, and threw Taft Wright out by a step at first base. It was a tough play; the ball was well hit.

I got a big kick out of that. It was my first no-hitter and still the only one ever pitched on opening day.

We were running well in 1940; in fact, we were about 5½ games ahead in August. But we were having a problem with our manager, Oscar Vitt. It went back to when he first came to the team in 1938. Some of the players didn't like him for one reason or another. They thought his strategy was bad, his selection of pitchers was bad, his batting order was bad. Oscar Vitt is dead now, so I won't go into the details completely. But a lot of the players felt that tactically he just was not an able manager and that we wouldn't win the pennant unless he changed his approach.

So some of us went to the club president, Alva Bradley, and told him what we thought. We told him we felt we should have a change in field management. Mr. Bradley always said that Oscar Vitt talked too much, and he happened to be right. In fact, he told Oscar that when he hired him. If you talk too much, inevitably you're going to say the wrong thing. That goes for anybody, myself included.

But Vitt stayed till the end of the year, and we blew the pennant. I don't think our rebellion—if you want to call it that—had anything to do with it because that happened in June and we blew the pennant in September. Naturally the situation with Vitt wasn't conducive to a happy summer. It got into the papers, and the fans picked it up. One of the players had squealed to a friend in the press about the meeting with Bradley. I know who it was, but never mind. It shouldn't have been in the paper—it was a family squabble, you might say—but this guy wanted to get himself in good with one of the writers and told him about the meeting, and the thing ignited. So we got the name "crybabies," but that was a lot of nonsense. We felt we were justified in what we were doing.

At the very end of the season the Tigers came in for a three-game series needing only one win to clinch it. We really had our backs to the wall. I started the first game on a Friday afternoon. I'd been pitching real fine ball against the Tigers and was hoping to get us started off on the right foot.

The Tigers had a great pitching staff. They had Bobo Newsom, Tommy Bridges, Schoolboy Rowe. Each man was a fine pitcher, and experienced. Whichever one went out that day would give us a battle. But the damnedest thing happened. Detroit didn't start any of them. They started a fellow named Floyd Giebell, who they'd brought in from Buffalo a few weeks earlier. I don't think anybody had ever heard of him before. I blinked when I saw him come out to warm up. I had no idea who he was.

You see what they were doing. They didn't want to start any of their big pitchers against me; they were going to save them for the last two games. So they threw Giebell in as a give-up. Some give-up! All he did was shut us out. We got some hits off of him, a few walks, but we left a lot of men on base. Floyd Giebell pitched the game of his life and shut us out.

I gave up just three hits, but one of them came after a walk to Charlie Gehringer. Rudy York hit one that was in on his fists and lifted it down the left field line, and it went just far enough to carry

Floyd Giebell: "I blinked when I saw him come out to warm up. I had no idea who he was."

over the barrier for a home run. That was the ball game, right there. And the pennant.

Floyd Giebell never won another game in the big leagues, but I guess he made a place for himself in baseball history that day.

Joe DiMaggio? Sure, Joe gave me a lot of trouble—listen, he gave everybody a lot of trouble. He was a very fine hitter, with great power. He could do everything. He was a tremendous base runner; he could go from first to third, break up the double play. Wonderful arm; always threw to the right base. And he could cover the territory. He was an inspirational ballplayer, a real pro.

I started getting him out later on, after I'd learned how to pitch to him, but that was about the time he hung up his spikes. I started throwing him fastballs in tight, around his fists and his belt, crowding him, pushing him back. If I'd have done that earlier, I would have been all right. But I didn't do that. I was afraid I'd hit him, and I didn't want to hit him, any more than I wanted to hit anybody else, but particularly Joe and Ted Williams, because they were such great hitters and great competitors and drew a lot of people into the ball park. I didn't want to be boring in on them any more than they wanted to hit line drives through the box.

Did I ever throw intentionally at anybody? No, heavens no. It's only a game, you know. Now, when I say that, I don't mean anything derogatory about conditioning yourself, about preparing yourself to win and trying to win and doing all you can to win. But none of that gives you a license to go out there and maim somebody.

Williams hit me well at times and not so well at other times. Nobody had his number. I never could get him out consistently, and he could never hit me consistently. But if it was one way or the other, he hit me more times than I got him out. He was the best hitter I ever pitched to. Ted didn't hit me as well as Tommy Henrich, who was the toughest hitter for me, but he hit me pretty good. There wasn't a pitch he couldn't hit. He had no weakness.

One of my favorite catchers was Rollie Hemsley. A great catcher and a good friend of mine. He had a drinking problem—that's no big secret—but he could catch drunk better than most guys could sober. He loved to kid around. He set a train afire one time by throwing matches into the upper berths. We were traveling north

Joe DiMaggio in 1938.

with the Giants and were going from Richmond to Washington. Hemsley was walking through the car with too many drinks in him and just for the hell of it started throwing lighted matches into the upper berths where the equipment was kept. He started a couple of small fires, but they were put out in time. Yeah, Rollie was quite a Rollie. Slapnicka finally talked him into joining Alcoholics Anonymous. Hemsley did that and went on the wagon and never drank again.

Johnny Allen was another guy who was not exactly a teetotaler either. He was a rough, tough character. Good pitcher, a real competitor. Hot-tempered. He hated to lose. Sometimes when he lost, he'd take it out on inanimate objects. He lost a tough game one time in Washington and went back and tore up his room at the Wardman Park Hotel. He threw a few chairs and lamps out a window. Then he took a fire extinguisher and went down to the lobby with it and drenched the room clerk and whoever else was down there. That was at three o'clock in the morning. A few hours later the whole ball club was thrown out of the hotel. We all had to go to another hotel. Tough losers are a lot of fun to have on your club.

Fun and games. You always had a few guys around to liven it up. One night in Griffith Stadium we had a rookie sitting on the bench. Just up. Kind of nervous, looking around, not saying anything. One of the guys said, "I see that clock out there is a little fast." Everybody agreed. The clock was fast. And that was that. Well, there was no clock out there, but there were so many signs and so many different colors on those outfield walls that it was hard to be certain. Of course, a rookie is not going to ask too many questions, and for the rest of the game we'd catch him frowning out at the fences, looking for that clock.

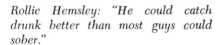

Rollie Hemsley: "He could catch drunk better than most guys could sober."

In December, 1941, I was on my way from Iowa to Chicago to go to the major league meetings, just to be doing something. It was on a Sunday. About the time I was crossing the Mississippi River at Moline the broadcast came over the car radio about Pearl Harbor. I kept going and checked into the Palmer House in Chicago and called Gene Tunney in California. He was the head of the armed services athletic program, and he'd been hounding me to get in. So he flew out to Chicago, and I signed up at eight o'clock the next morning at the courthouse.

My dad was dying of cancer, and I wouldn't have had to go in. I was what they called 2-C. Farmer. I couldn't have played ball, though; I would have had to stay on the farm. Otherwise there was no way I could have stayed out. But I figured, too, that it was the right thing to do, and so I went in.

I went to war college in Newport, took a gunnery course in Norfolk, went to PT boat school. I was pretty good at antiaircraft gunnery. I ended up in the South Pacific, on the *Alabama*. Battleship. I requested combat duty. I probably could have sat in Honolulu drinking beer, but the hell with that. I figured if I was in, I might as well be in all the way.

The *Alabama* was with the Third Fleet and we got into quite a few of those scrapes. Tarawa, Kwajelein, the Marshalls and Gilberts, Iwo Jima, the Philippines. Our job was to protect the carriers. We'd have those air battles, and the Japanese planes would try to get at the carriers. And sometimes they'd come after us. Torpedo bombers. They'd come in low, to get underneath our shells, sometimes so low they would fly right into a wave or a big swell. I'd be up there on the main deck with a bunch of kids, banging away with Bofors. The one that gets you you never see; that's the scary thing. You can never be sure about anything one minute to the next. Was it as scary as pitching to Jimmie Foxx? I'll say. That's for keeps, that racket. (And anyway, Jimmie couldn't hit me with a paddle.)

I came out of the Navy late in the season in '45 and pitched in a few games, but that didn't amount to much in my mind. I didn't feel like I was really back until spring training in 1946. I got myself into great shape and was looking forward to having a good year.

Right early in the year, in April, I pitched a no-hitter against the

Being sworn into the United States Navy by Gene Tunney.

Yankees in New York. That's a game that will always stand out in my mind.

We had quite a large crowd that day, almost 40,000. In fact, it was the largest crowd ever to see a no-hitter up to that time. The Yankees weren't going anywhere that year, but it was still a tough lineup. They had Stirnweiss, Henrich, DiMaggio, Keller, Gordon, Dickey, Rizzuto. That was a pretty fair ball club.

In the first inning Boudreau made a great play behind the pitcher's mound on a high hopper by Stirnweiss which was the only tough chance of the ball game. You don't start paying attention to a no-hitter until about the seventh or eighth inning. I knew I had pretty good stuff that day and figured I might go all the way with it. The only problem was we didn't have any runs. You get to thinking about that. Hell, I figured, here goes a whole day's work. I'll probably walk somebody, wild pitch him to second, then watch him come around on an error, and I'll lose a no-hitter. I'd had a lot of oddball things happen to me late in games in Yankee Stadium.

But then in the ninth inning, my catcher, Frankie Hayes, hit one into the left-field seats, and I had a run to work with.

A hell of a lot of tension had built up for that last of the ninth. Stirnweiss led off, and he got on through an error. So there was a man on first, nobody out, and Henrich, DiMaggio, and Keller coming up. Talk about earning your money.

Henrich laid down a bunt and sacrificed Stirnweiss over to second. DiMaggio came up, and I got two strikes on him and then he started fouling them off. Finally I threw him a slider, and he ground out to Boudreau. Keller was next. The tying run was on third now, so I had other things to worry about besides the no-hitter. I threw him a big overhand curve, and he beat it into the ground to second. Ray Mack charged the ball, picked it up, and then slipped and went down to one knee. There wasn't a damn thing I could do but stand there and watch him. He recovered in time and threw to first base for the out. I've got to say that was one of the sweetest moments I ever had on a ball field.

The best stuff I ever had in my life, though, was in 1947, in a game against the Athletics in Philadelphia. I'd struck out nine of the first eleven, and I hadn't thrown a curveball all night. Then I threw a curve to the next hitter, Barney McCoskey. When I threw my curve, I stepped a little differently from when I threw my fastball. Well, I had raveled up a lot of dirt, and I hadn't knocked it off to get the loose dirt out of the way so my left pivot foot could go into the clay. So, when I threw the curve, I stepped on top of this loose dirt and slipped. My leg went straight out, and I fell hard. When I got up, they were throwing the ball around the infield—I'd struck McCoskey out. But I'd pulled my shoulder and my knee. I was in pretty bad shape. I missed a month of the season at least. I thought I could have struck out 20 that night. They had a lot of hard-swinging right-hand hitters, and I was very fast and had pretty good control. But I had to leave the ball game, so I'll never know how many I could have struck out that game.

I missed the All-Star game that year because of that injury. Some people made a big stink out of my not going. But I didn't want to go because I couldn't throw. Any better reason? But it made a better story for the papers to say I wasn't going because I didn't want to go.

Then in '48 I was having a lousy year. I couldn't get anybody out. But they put me on the All-Star team anyway, probably for sentimental reasons. I didn't belong on the All-Star team that year any more than you did. No way. Bill Veeck, who owned the Indians then, told me, "You need some rest. Don't go. Go fishing."

"Hell," I said, "I can't get out of this. I had a legitimate reason not to go last year, and I got hell. What are they going to say this year?"

"If I tell you not to go, don't go," he said. "Tell them you cut your finger on a razor blade."

"Oh, horseshit," I said. "That's not gonna work."

"Well," he said, "I'll figure out something. I'll tell them you got an injury."

"It's not gonna work," I said.

"We'll see," he said.

Well, he was absolutely right, but he shouldn't have done it. I should have gone, told them that I had a bad arm, that I would throw a little batting practice, run around, smile at people, sign autographs, but not pitch. I know a lot of guys that do it. They get on the team, they get the gift, they get the prestige, they have a little fun, a few drinks with the guys, a few laughs. Hell, I know a lot of guys who do that.

Anyway, the Cleveland ball club's publicity department came out with a statement: "Feller has withdrawn from the All-Star game. Reasons unknown." Something along those lines. Made me look great.

When I saw that in the paper, I started trying to track Veeck down. I finally got him on the phone at some nightclub, at about three o'clock in the morning.

"Goddamn," I said, "what in the hell is this anyway?"

"Don't worry about it," he said.

"Look," I said, "I want you to come out with the whole story. You tell them the truth."

Which he did. He released a statement which said, in effect:

"Veeck takes blame for keeping Feller out of All-Star game. Veeck says it was his mistake, that Feller was willing and wanted to go but was not permitted." But nobody ever saw it in the paper. Did you? Neither did I.

Fastest pitcher I ever saw? Koufax was fast. So was Ryne Duren. Rex Barney. Barney could throw as hard as anybody, but he couldn't get the ball near the plate. Anyway, speed alone isn't enough. It's what the ball does that counts, if it hops or sinks or

Walter Johnson: "I would say he had to be a harder thrower than I was."

sails. My ball had a hop, and it would rise. When I threw it sidearm to right-hand hitters, it would run in on them.

Walter Johnson? I knew if we talked long enough, you'd mention him. In my opinion Walter Johnson has to be the fastest pitcher of all time, for the simple reason that he didn't have a curveball and he struck out so many hitters. I would say he had to be a harder thrower than I was. People who saw us both in our prime generally say that. I heard somebody say one time that Johnson, after seeing me pitch, said I threw pretty hard but that he thought he threw harder. Well, of course he's going to say that, but I'm sure he was absolutely honest and sincere about it and probably 99 percent correct.

What would my record have looked like if I hadn't lost those years in the service? I think I would have hung around a few more years to see if I couldn't have won 400. I ended up with 266 and could have won 100 easy during those four years. Might have pitched another no-hitter or two, struck out another 1,000 or 1,200 guys. Hell, I was averaging before and after the war 250 a season. So I could've been up to around 3,700 or 3,800 strikeouts lifetime, which would have put me at the top of the list, ahead of Walter Johnson.

But we'll never know, will we?

A Sense of
Something Lost...

Another season underway. And again the lies, the damnable lies . . .

I tell you, he never hurtled headlong into those outfield walls, never ripped loose his viscera or sundered his brains. He played on. God, did he play on! Forget Cooperstown. There's another Hall of Fame, the real one where the game's true dreams are lodged, and where his plaque is the one at which we pause in wonderment, where we muse in awe upon the glory of his times . . .

HAROLD PATRICK REISER

"Pistol Pete"

Dodgers 1940–1963

ELEVEN TIMES NATIONAL LEAGUE BATTING
CHAMPION, HAD .364 LIFETIME AVERAGE
INCLUDING THREE SEASONS OVER .400.
INCOMPARABLE DEFENSIVE CENTER FIELDER,
VOTED PLAYER OF THE DECADE, 1940–1950,
AGAIN 1950–1960. RETIRED WITH 4197
BASE HITS AND MORE DOUBLES, TOTAL BASES,
AND RUNS SCORED THAN ANY PLAYER IN
HISTORY.

Fools there be, who will claim you cannot look it up. Trust them not, for their souls are dark. There is no Smoky Joe Wood at Cooperstown either, no Addie Joss and no Shoeless Joe. Herb Score, they say, took that line drive in the eye, and Ted lost five years to two separate wars. Is the *Iliad* true, was there an Achilles?

Reiser lives!

—DAVID MARKSON

18

PETE REISER

Over the winter of '47 I was invited to talk—for the *fifth* time—to the Missouri School for the Blind, in St. Louis. I was beginning to wonder about it. Every year they were getting me. So I said to the director, "Look, I don't mind coming here, but why do you keep asking me?"

"You're our favorite player," he said.

"But I'm from Brooklyn."

"That makes no difference," he said. "Our children here always have problems with walls, and they hear that you have the same problem. They figure you're one of them."

Actually, you know, I only ran into the wall twice that I *really* hurt myself: in '42 and '47. Hell, any ballplayer worth his salt has run into a wall. More than once. I'm the guy who got hurt doing it, that's all. I remember somebody asking me one time how long I think I would have played and what my averages might have been if I hadn't played as hard as I did. If I hadn't played that way, I told him, I may never have got there to begin with. It was my style of playing; I didn't know any other way to play ball.

Remember, when I was twelve years old, I was playing ball with guys five years older. My brother Mike used to bring me around to play on his team. The other guys would say, "What's this kid doing here?" My brother said, "He'll show you." So maybe it started there, having to try hard, hard, and harder, to prove to them, to live up to the expectations of somebody you admired the hell out of, and to keep on proving it. And I always felt I could do better than I was doing, that there was no limit. I couldn't wait from one day to the next to get out there and prove it.

Late in July in 1942 we went into St. Louis to play a series. In our two series prior to that, in Chicago and Cincinnati, I'd gotten 19 hits in twenty-one at bats. I came into St. Louis hitting .380, and just starting to get warm. Just starting to get the bead on everybody. I could've hit .400 that year. No doubt in my mind about that. And to make it all the sweeter, we had a 13½-game lead.

Whitlow Wyatt, who for a few years there was the finest right-hand pitcher I ever saw, was hooked up in one of his famous pitching duels with Mort Cooper, who was also a tremendous pitcher. We were playing the second game of a doubleheader, and in those days they didn't turn the lights on to finish a ball game. It was getting dark, and this was probably going to be the last inning. We were in extra innings—the thirteenth, I think—and there was no score, and Wyatt is out there pitching his heart out. I know this sounds melodramatic, like I'm making it up, but those were the kinds of ball games we had with St. Louis in '41 and '42.

Mort Cooper.

Enos Slaughter leads off the inning, and he ties into one. It's a line drive directly over my head, and my first thought was that it can be caught. Which is pretty much the way I felt about *any* ball that was hit. I'm a firm believer in positive thinking. I used to stand out there in center field and say to myself, *Hit it to me, hit it to me*. Every pitch. I wanted that ball.

Well, if this ball isn't caught, it's a cinch triple, and Wyatt can get beat, and above all the Dodgers. I caught it, going at top speed. I just missed the flagpole in center field but I hit the wall, hard. I dropped the ball, picked it up, relayed it to Pee Wee—how I did that I'll never know—but we just missed getting Slaughter at the plate. Inside the park home run. Wyatt's beat, 1–0. And I'm out cold in center field. It was like a hand grenade had gone off inside my head.

Was I being foolhardy in going after that ball the way I did? After all, we had a 13½-game lead, didn't we? You can slow up in those circumstances, can't you? No, you can't. You slow up a half step, and it's the beginning of your last ball game. It might take a few years, but you're on your way out. That's how I look at it. You can't turn it on and off anytime you want to. Not if you take pride in yourself.

What kind of a kid was I? Ornery. Mean. Nice. A nice mean kid. I had a bad temper. My grandfather, who I never knew, was a professional soldier; he fought in the Civil War. He was a cavalry officer, and we had his sword in the house. I'd get mad once in a while and chase my sisters and anybody else who was in the way with that sword. Just to scare 'em.

Sure, I wanted to be a ballplayer when I was a kid, but it wasn't my first love. Football was. My ambition was to be the greatest football player Notre Dame ever had. When I was ten, I was competing in football against fifteen-year-old kids. Running right over them. Knute Rockne was one of my idols. I heard him talk once on the radio, one of his inspirational talks. I'll never forget it. I'm very emotional. I cry at the movies. I still get the chills when I hear "The Star-Spangled Banner."

I was a hell of a soccer player, too; in fact, I was declared a professional soccer player when I was fourteen years old. I was playing for the Catholic school in St. Louis when some guy came along and offered me $50 to kick soccer one Sunday. He was trying to compete against the pros in St. Louis, and he was signing all the kids from the Catholic schools who could kick soccer and who could run. And he was giving us $50, which was a lot of money. Hell, my dad was making $25 a week and supporting twelve children.

My dad made everybody in the family play ball, boys and girls alike. As soon as you were old enough, he put a ball in your hand. He'd played ball in St. Louis, in the old Trolley League. You ever hear of the Trolley League? That was quite a league in those days around St. Louis and part of Illinois. He was a pitcher. A printing company saw him pitch. They were part of an industrial league, and they offered him a job, work five days and pitch for them on the weekend. He was married then, already had two kids, so he took the job. He always regretted not taking a crack at professional baseball. He always thought he could have pitched in the big leagues. You know how it is, the older you get, the better you were. But he was a good ballplayer.

I was a nut for the Cardinals, but when I was a kid, my favorite major league ballplayer wasn't a Cardinal, he was a New York Giant —Mel Ott. I don't know why; you just get attached to a guy I guess. Then of course, later on I got to play against him. But idol or no idol, he came into me one time at third base with his spikes kind of high, and I dumped him on his ass.

I was always a pretty good ballplayer, but the real ballplayer in the family was my older brother, Mike. He was five years older than I was, and he was my hero. Mike could do everything, and then some. But it wasn't meant to be. He died when he was seventeen— just after he'd signed with the Yankees.

That was around the winter of 1931. Mike got scarlet fever. And I caught it from him. I wasn't supposed to go into his room, but I did, and I caught it. We ended up with throat infections, and the doctor lanced our throats. Operated on both of us right in the house. The doctor was more concerned about my condition than Mike's, and he told my parents to watch me, that I could have a rough night. So I was the one everybody was worried about. About two o'clock in the morning my brother asked me how I was. I told him all right.

"Well," he said, "I've got something in my throat. I've got to get a drink." And then he coughed, and the blood just came rushing out. I screamed for my mother, and she came running in. It was terrible. She yelled for somebody to get a priest. I ran out of the house, in my bare feet. It was snowing out. I ran for twelve blocks. I got to the door of the rectory and pounded on it. When they opened the door, I said, "My brother is dying." Then I collapsed.

I woke up the next morning in the hospital—not a damn thing wrong with me. My throat was almost healed. Perfect health. It was a miracle. It had to be. I was the one who was supposed to have the hemorrhage, not him. That's what the doctor said. We both should have been in the hospital, but there was no money for that. He was some kind of ballplayer, my brother Mike. But I guess it just wasn't meant to be.

When I was fifteen, I went to a Cardinal tryout camp. It was held at Public School Stadium on Kings Highway Boulevard, off of St.

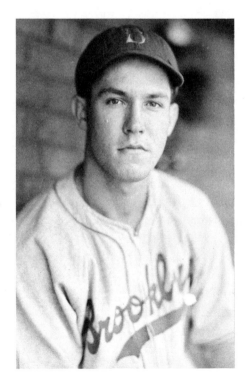

Pete Reiser.

Louis Avenue. About 800 kids showed up for it. It was supposed to be for sixteen-year-olds and up, but I lied about my age and went out there. I wanted to see how good the competition was.

It was a Cardinal camp, but scouts from other clubs were there too. Just because the Cardinals had organized the tryout didn't give them exclusive rights.

With so many kids on hand, you didn't get much chance to show your stuff. You ran a 100-yard dash, threw from center field to home plate, and got three swings. That was it. Then they weeded the kids out, asking the ones they liked to come back the next day. I was one of the ones cut the first day. I went home, really feeling bad. I told my father, "Well, Dad, I guess I'm not as good as I thought I was."

"Don't worry about it," he said. "You're only fifteen years old."

A couple of days later this big Buick pulls up in front of the house, and out comes Charley Barrett, the Cardinals' head scout. He knocks on the door and my father answers.

"Reiser residence?" Charley asks. My father says yes. Charley introduces himself and says, "I want to talk to you about your son."

"Well, I want to talk to you too," Dad says. "Why'd you cut him?"

"We didn't want anybody else to see him," Charley says. "That's why we didn't ask him to come back. We know who he is."

It turned out they'd been watching me play ball since grade school. They never said anything because they didn't want anybody else to know they were interested in me until they could sign me. You see, in those days if the Cardinals showed any interest in a kid, the other clubs would rush in to try and sign him, simply on the basis of the Cardinals' interest. That's the kind of reputation the Cardinals had in those days.

So Charley Barrett signed me. My Dad was the happiest guy in the world, since he always wanted me to play ball, and especially with the Cardinals. He had to sign for me, of course, because I was underage. But contract or no contract, I still couldn't play for a while because you had to be at least sixteen years old, and I wasn't quite that yet.

What they did was pay me $50 a month to go around with Charley Barrett that summer. Whenever he went out to scout different places, I went along. I was officially listed as his chauffeur, and every once in a while on an open road he'd let me take the wheel. We went all over the map, wherever the Cardinals had a club—and they had tons of them in those days. We went to Georgia, Alabama, Louisiana, Kentucky, Tennessee, Arkansas.

Whenever we went into a town, I'd work out with the club, take infield, batting practice. Then, when the game started, I'd have to get out of uniform. When Charley was ready to leave, the manager would say to him, "Say, Charley, leave the kid here." "Can't," Charley would say. "He's only fifteen." "So what? We'll change his name." "Unh-unh," Charley'd say, and off we'd go again.

I'll tell you how green I was in those days. Our first stop when we left St. Louis was Mayfield, Kentucky. We went into a restaurant, had a nice meal, and left. We were about 25 miles down the road, and I was feeling pretty proud of myself because I thought I'd done Charley a favor. Finally I told him about it. "You know what you did, Mr. Barrett?" I asked. "What?" he asked. "You left some money on the table back at the restaurant. But I picked it up for you." "You did *what?*" he yelled. "I picked up the money you left," I said. "By God, boy," he yelled, "that was a tip!"

Hell, I'd never eaten in a restaurant in my life. How was I supposed to know any different?

Well, you know the story. I never got to play for the Cardinals. You see what happened, in those years the Cardinals were signing every young ballplayer who showed any promise. No bonuses. Just sign 'em. Then let the good ones prove who they were. In doing that, in having so many ballplayers, they had to do a lot of manipulating of contracts, and they broke a lot of organized baseball's rules. Sooner or later that bubble had to burst. The old judge was commissioner then, Landis; he was a sharp guy, and he had a pretty good idea of what the Cardinals were doing.

In the spring of 1938 Landis turned loose about 100 of us. The "slaves" from the Cardinal "chain gang," the papers called us. When that happened, the Dodgers signed me to a contract, for $100 bonus.

The Dodgers sent me to Superior, Wisconsin. I was a shortstop at the time and a strictly right-handed hitter. Well, I could always run real good, but often I was just getting nipped at first base, and it would aggravate me. I said to myself, "Hell, if I was on the left side of the plate, those would be base hits." So, with the manager's permission, I started hitting left-handed. It took a little time, but gradually I began making contact, and I was beating out some of those grounders. I was the happiest guy in the world, believe me. It cost me some points on my batting average, but I didn't care about that—I'd learned how to hit left-handed.

Charley Barrett lived in St. Louis, and so did I. Over that winter I went to him and said, "Charley, if I could just get down to spring training in Florida early, I could get a jump on some of these guys." He said, "Well, a very good friend of mine has just been named manager of the Dodgers. Leo Durocher. I'll talk Leo into bringing you down."

Pete Reiser.

So I went to Clearwater in the spring of '39, just to shag and run and get the feel of a big-league camp, as a favor to Charley Barrett from Leo Durocher. I was like any young kid. I was eager. Every time somebody was slow getting into the batting cage I jumped in, which I wasn't supposed to do. Made some of the regulars pretty sore. When I wasn't hanging around trying to sneak into the cage, I'd be out in the field someplace, doing something, keeping busy all the time.

Leo took a liking to me. Even though I was just a kid nobody, Leo saw me out there. I'll tell you something: Leo Durocher sees *everything* that's going on on a ball field. He may not be looking, but he sees it.

They had a guy down there, I think his name was Cesar. He was supposed to be the fastest man in the Dodger organization. One day Leo says to MacPhail, "I got a kid that'll beat Cesar by ten yards."

"Bullshit," MacPhail says.

"I've also got," Leo says, "a hundred dollars to back it up."

They would bet on anything in those days.

Next thing I know Leo is calling me over. "I want you to do a little running, kid," he says.

So here all of a sudden I'm running against the fastest guy in the Dodger organization, and the manager and the general manager are betting $100 on it. And all I'd wanted to do was come down there and work out in a big-league camp and mind my business.

Well, I did beat the guy. Yeah, by 10 yards.

So Leo really had his eye on me after that. He liked me. But there was one play that I think really cemented it for him. We were playing Detroit, and I was playing second base that day. I got on first, and somebody hit a ground ball. I took off for second with one thought in my mind: break up the double play. Billy Rogell was playing short for them. A veteran, and rough and tough. I knew damned well who he was and didn't care. I barreled into him and knocked him flying. "You bush son of a bitch," he said, "when I get on that base, I'm gonna cut you from ear to ear." "You've got to get on base first," I told him.

So then he does get on, and everybody knows he's coming. Leo was playing short, and he says to me, "I'll handle the throw."

I said, "*I* want the throw."

"No," Leo says.

"I'm taking it," I said. "So you stay clear." I'm talking to the manager like that.

First pitch, here comes Rogell. He's going to barrel into me. I went over, took the throw, laid it on him, and stepped aside. He threw up a ton of dirt but never touched me.

From that day on I think I became Leo's pet.

On St. Patrick's Day, which is my birthday, we had a game scheduled. I wasn't in the lineup, but just before the game started, Leo came up with a migraine headache.

"How'd you like to play short today?" he asked me.

"Hell, yes," I said.

Well, I played short that day, and I played the rest of the exhibition games after that. I hit something like .485 in about thirty exhibition games. My first twelve at bats I got on base—three home runs, five singles, four walks. I hit home runs off Gomez and Tommy Bridges. Was I surprised? Honestly, no. I'd been doing it all my life, in my mind, and I'd convinced myself I was going to do it for real when the time came. So I wasn't surprised. I expected it.

We barnstormed north with the Yankees from Florida, rode the same train, stayed at the same hotels. One day Joe McCarthy walks up to me and says, "You're going to be my third baseman this year." "How do you figure that?" I asked. "We're going to make a deal for you," he says. A few days later, the same thing. "It won't be too long now before you're a Yankee. The deal is almost made." And he emphasized it again: I was going to open at third for him. Red Rolfe or no Red Rolfe.

I don't know exactly what they were offering, but it was supposed to be a pretty big deal. The Dodgers needed ballplayers at that time, and the Yankees had those great farm clubs at Newark and Kansas City filled with first-rate players.

How did I feel about it? Well, in those days anybody who didn't want to play for the Yankees was crazy. Baseball was the Yankees, and the Yankees were baseball.

Leo heard about it and said, "No way." He threatened to quit if MacPhail made the deal.

So I was having a hell of a spring, wasn't I? Now I'm the boy wonder and what-not, and Leo has got me in the opening day lineup at shortstop for the Dodgers. I take infield, then batting practice with the starting lineup; then I go into the clubhouse to change my shirt. The telephone rings.

"It's for you, Pete," somebody says. "Mr. MacPhail wants to talk to you."

I took the phone and said hello. That's about all I got to say.

"I don't give a damn what Durocher says," he said. "You're going to go to Elmira." And he hung up.

I just sat there stunned. Jesus crimminy, I thought, he can't do that to me. I had a good spring, didn't I?

Leo comes in and sees me sitting there like that and says, "What's the matter, kid? You scared?"

"Hell, no," I said. "Mr. MacPhail just called and said I was going to Elmira."

Leo looked dumbfounded for a second, then said, "Like hell you are!"

So Leo called him, and they argued hot and heavy. Then Leo hung up.

"There's nothing I can do about it," he said. "He won't sign you to a major-league contract, and I can't play you until he does."

Leo Durocher: "If you didn't know him, you'd hate his guts; but if you knew him, you'd love him."

So I went to Elmira. Didn't like it, but I went. I had some injuries there—broken elbow, brain concussion—and didn't play a full season. But I did all right anyway. Hit .300.

The next spring, 1940, I go to spring training not with the Dodgers but with Montreal. Clyde Sukeforth was the manager. He kept telling me, "I don't give a damn what they say, you're my center fielder."

"But I don't want to play the outfield," I said. "I want to play the infield."

"Well," he said, "regardless of where you play, you're going to play on my ball club."

So he had me playing all over the place that spring, infield and outfield. Then right after the season opened the Dodgers cut their squad and sent a bunch of veteran players down to Montreal, and Sukeforth was told to play them. I had to sit down. Boy, I'm really mad now. Then, a few nights later, they really laid it on me. Clyde called me up to his room.

"I know you're not going to like this," he said. "I've got some real bad news."

"What?" I asked.

"MacPhail said to send you to Elmira."

"Bull*shit!*" I said. "No way you're going to send me to Elmira."

"Pete," he said, "my hands are tied. MacPhail promised the people in Montreal a winner, that he would not take one player away from the Montreal ball club. He's afraid that you're going to do so well that he'd have to break his promise and take you up to Brooklyn. He does not want to offend the people who are supporting a valuable franchise."

Then I get a telephone call from Elmira, from Bill Killefer, who was both the manager and general manager of the Elmira ball club. He gave me some soft soap, and then he said, "You come to Elmira and I'll make you a promise. If you're going good before July 1 and the Dodgers don't bring you up, I'll sell you to the highest bidder."

"How are you gonna do that?"

"You're being optioned outright, and I'm the general manager of this club, and I can do what I want. I don't have more than a year or two left in this game anyway, so the hell with them. You should have been on the Dodgers in '39."

I always liked the guy, trusted him, and so I believed him.

"All right," I said. "But, boy, if I'm not up there—"

"You'll be there, kid," he said. "Don't worry."

So I went to Elmira, and I'm having a great start. It's well into June and I'm hitting around .380. I'm really chomping. Then I hear the Dodgers have made a deal with the Cardinals for Joe Medwick. It was a pretty big deal, involving Medwick and Curt Davis and some other players and a lot of money and a player to be named later. So now they've got Medwick in Brooklyn. The outfield was filled out, and they had Pee Wee playing shortstop and having a hell of a year. Where did that leave me?

So I went to see Killefer.

"Bill," I said. "it's getting pretty damned close to July 1."

He smiled and said, "You're going to Brooklyn tonight. You've been called up." Then he told me, "Do you know why you didn't stay there in '39? Because you were property of the Cardinals."

You see, when I was declared a free agent, I was barred from playing in the Cardinal organization for three years. So there was a gentlemen's agreement between the Dodger and Cardinal scouts that I would play in the Dodger organization for three years, and then I was going to be returned to the Cardinals. Killefer was the one who really kicked up the fuss, when he threatened to sell me to the highest bidder. Well, I became the player to be named later in the Medwick deal; I was supposed to go back to St. Louis eventually. Instead, they gave the Cardinals some more money.

So there were two things that could have happened to me in those years. They could've sold me to the Yankees, and I probably would have been the Yankee third baseman for a long time. And if I played for the Cardinals, I probably still would have been an infielder, because they had guys like Slaughter and Terry Moore in their outfield. Plus the fact if I would have been declared a free agent in '39, there's no telling how much money I could have got to sign. So you see how your whole life changes.

Anyway, the Dodgers called me up on June 22, 1940. I felt great.

I rode the bus all night into New York. Couldn't sleep a wink, I was so excited. The first game was a night game, and afterward I'm leaving the ball park, and some big guy hits me on the shoulder.

"Hey, Pete," he says in this deep voice.

Here was the meanest-looking son of a bitch you ever saw. I asked myself, "What the hell does *he* want? "

"You don't know me, do you?" he says.

"No, I don't think so," I said.

"Well, I know you."

"From where?"

"Elmira," he says.

"Oh, you from Elmira?" I asked.

"No," he says. "I'm from Brooklyn. But you and the Elmira Pioneers came up there last year and played an exhibition game at the prison. Listen," he says, "I just got out. And I want to tell you I appreciate things like that from you athletes. Listen, anybody gives you any trouble in this town, I want you to know I'm gonna be out there every ball game. You just whistle up to me. Anybody gives you any trouble, they're dead."

Welcome to Brooklyn!

You know, I saw that guy out there as long as I played in Brooklyn. I'd walk out to center field, and he'd stand up and yell, "Everything all right, Pete?" "Great, buddy," I'd yell back.

You know, that Ebbets Field was a hell of a place to play ball. Some of those fans were unbelievable. And they were out there day after day. You got to know them. One who still stands out in my mind is Hilda Chester. She never missed a game, it seemed. She'd sit out in the bleachers yelling in a foghorn voice and ringing this big cowbell she always carried. I remember one time, it was in either '41 or '42, we were in the seventh inning of a game. I was going out to take my position in center field, and I hear that voice: "Hey, Reiser!" Hilda. There could be 30,000 people there yelling at once, but Hilda was the one you'd hear. I look up, and she's dropping something onto the grass. "Give this note to Leo," she yells. So I pick it up and put it in my pocket. At the end of the inning I start heading in.

Now MacPhail used to sit in a box right next to the dugout, and for some reason he waved to me as I came in, and I said, "Hi,

Larry," as I went into the dugout. I gave Hilda's note to Leo and sat down. Next thing I know he's getting somebody hot in the bullpen; I think it was Casey. Meanwhile, Wyatt's pitching a hell of a ball game for us. In the next inning the first guy hits the ball pretty good and goes out. The next guy gets a base hit. Here comes Leo. He takes Wyatt out and brings in Casey. Casey got rocked a few times, and we just did win the game, just did win it.

Leo had this rule that after a game you didn't take off your uniform until he said so. Usually he didn't invoke it unless we'd lost a tough one. But this day he goes into his office and slams the door without a word. We're all sitting there waiting for him to come out. Finally the door opens and out he comes. He points at me.

"Don't you *ever* give me another note from MacPhail as long as you play for me."

"I didn't give you any note from MacPhail," I said.

"Don't tell me!" he yells. "You handed me a note in the seventh inning."

"That was from Hilda," I said.

"From *Hilda?*" he screams. I thought he was going to turn purple. "You mean to say that wasn't from MacPhail?"

I'd never even looked at the note, just handed it to him. Leo had heard me say something to MacPhail when I came in and figured the note was from Larry. It seems what the note said was: "Get Casey hot, Wyatt's losing it." So what you had was somebody named Hilda Chester sitting in the center-field bleachers changing pitchers for you. You talk about oddball things happening in Ebbets Field, you're not exaggerating.

There was a guy named Eddie, used to come out to all the games. He owned some apartment houses in Brooklyn. He was a real rabid fan. He came up to Boston with us in '41 when we cinched the pennant, and naturally he came back on the train with the team. Well, there was a big mob to meet us at Grand Central that night and the reporters are interviewing everybody who comes off the train. Somebody asks Eddie how he feels about it. He says, "I'm so happy about this I'm going to put all new toilet seats in my apartment buildings."

There really was no place like Brooklyn.

Anyway, I'm finally there, in June, 1940. And I don't play. Finally I do a little filling in at second base. Then Pee Wee breaks his ankle, and Leo says, "Go to short." So I go to short. I'm there for a few days, and Lavagetto has a busted appendix in Cincinnati. So now Leo puts himself back on the list, and he plays short, and I play third till the end of the season. Bill McKechnie came up to me one day and said, "You're the best third baseman in this league. I think you've found your position." I loved third base.

I figured I could beat out Lavagetto for the job next spring. I went to spring training in '41 figuring I was the Dodger third baseman. One day MacPhail and Leo called me into the office.

"You want to play for the Dodgers this year?" MacPhail asked.

"Damn right I do," I said.

"Well, then you learn to play center field."

Hell, I thought, anybody can play center field. All you had to do was run a ball down. Nothing else to worry about. So, with help from Charley Dressen and Freddy Fitzsimmons, I spent that spring becoming a big-league center fielder. When the season opened in '41, I felt as if I'd never played anywhere else.

I made another big change that spring—I stopped hitting right-handed. The Dodgers almost blew their stacks. But I got hard-nosed about it. The guy who suggested it to me was Paul Waner. He was watching me in the cage one day, and when I got out, he said, "Why in the hell do you switch-hit?"

"Because I'm a natural right-hand hitter," I said.

"Maybe," he said. "But your stroke left-handed is perfect. I know you've got more power right-handed, but you're an entirely different hitter. You uppercut right-handed; left-handed you don't. With your speed, you stay left-handed, kid."

Well, Paul Waner knew something about hitting, to say the least. So, once in a while during an exhibition game, when there was a left-hander out there, I tried it. No problem. Left-handers didn't make a bit of difference. But still I had to convince Leo. We were playing the Yankees one day, and Gomez was pitching.

"I hit him pretty good right-handed," I told Leo, "but I'll hit him better left-handed." You know, I was just a kid, and a little cocky.

But I went out and did what I said I was going to do. I made Leo a
believer. Then MacPhail was going to fire him for letting me hit left-
handed. MacPhail was always firing Leo. But I stayed stubborn and
refused to hit right-handed, I didn't care how much dust MacPhail
kicked up. MacPhail got so goddamned mad that he came within an
ace of trading me to the Cubs in the Billy Herman deal. But I guess
by the end of the year MacPhail was a believer, too. What the hell, I
hit .343 and led the league. Batting left-handed.

That was some kind of year, '41. Everything happened. I got
myself beaned twice, each time pretty hard. Ike Pearson of the
Phillies zonked me in Brooklyn early in the year, and then later on
Paul Erickson hit me in Chicago. What provoked the Chicago beaning was something that had happened on our previous trip in. I was
on first and somebody doubled down the right-field line. I came all
the way around, and the catcher thought he had the plate blocked. I
knocked him on his ass and scored. Jimmie Wilson was the Cub
manager, and he didn't like what he saw. He came up to me and
said, "We'll get you for that, bush." I didn't give it another thought.

Next trip into Chicago this big Paul Erickson is pitching. He
could fire. I come up. You can hear it coming out of the dugout:
"Stick it in his ear."

The old judge is sitting in a box behind the dugout. Landis.

Erickson winds up, and the next thing I know Landis is visiting
me in the hospital.

"Do you think that Paul Erickson threw at you intentionally?" he
asks.

"No, sir."

"You didn't hear, 'Stick it in his ear'?"

"I heard something like that," I said.

"Then why don't you think he threw at you intentionally?"

"He doesn't have that kind of control," I said. "I lost the ball in
the shirts in center field."

"Then you won't accuse him of throwing at you?"

"No, sir," I said.

He was skeptical. He was no dummy, the judge. But he had to
accept it. Christ, in those days all you heard was "Stick it in his ear."

Beaned by Ike Pearson at Ebbets Field, April, 1941. The catcher is Mickey Livingston. New York Daily News Photo.

"Put him in a squat position." "Drill him." "Flip him." If you got hit, you got hit. And nobody ever said excuse me. You wanted to play ball, you played the way it was played.

You know, you wonder sometimes how much of this game is psychological. I'm not all that highly educated, and I can't explain

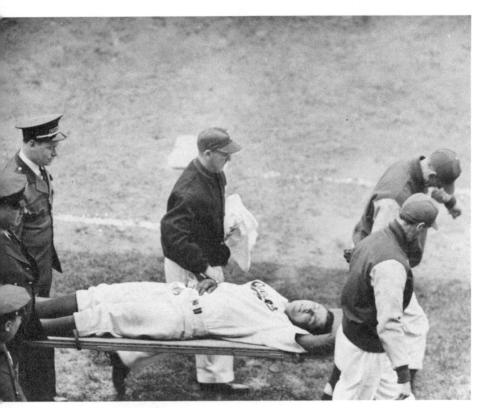

After the Pearson beaning. New York Daily News Photo.

why certain things happen, but I do know they happen. I remember one time, in '42, we came into Cincinnati for a series. A sportswriter named Grayson met me at the railroad station and asked me to have breakfast with him. I was going real good at the time, and he wanted to write a story about me.

Judge Kenesaw Mountain Landis: "You didn't hear, 'Stick it in his ear'?"

It was an enjoyable breakfast, and as he was leaving, he said, "By the way, what does Bucky Walters do to tip off his pitches?"

"I don't understand you," I said.

"Well, I talked to Bucky the other day about you. He says he throws you everything and you seem to know what's coming. I looked it up and you're hitting eight hundred against him."

"Against Walters?" I could hardly believe it. He was one of the best pitchers in the league. "You've got to be kidding."

"No, I'm not," he said. "Bucky can't figure it out. He says he's done everything to you—knocked you down, come close, thrown his best stuff, done everything he can think of. But you still hit him, like you know what's coming."

I never thought I was having such great luck with Walters. I knew I enjoyed hitting against him because he was a control pitcher, always around that plate, and I loved to swing. I was what they called a Bible hitter: They shall not pass.

"Incidentally," Grayson said, "Walters is pitching tonight."

Great, I say to myself. There's three for four. But you know what happened, don't you? I can hardly remember getting a hit off of Walters after that. The point is, I had great luck against him until it was pointed out to me and I started thinking about it. Maybe I became overconfident, and if you become overconfident with a pitcher as great as Walters, it's fatal. I stopped challenging him the way I had been doing, and from then on the advantage was his.

Well, we won the pennant in '41, and we figured to repeat the next year. And we would have, too, if it wasn't for me. I cost the Dodgers the pennant in '42. I told you about that injury when I hit the wall going after Slaughter's drive. Well, that was the start of it.

I woke up in St. John's Hospital in St. Louis. The Cardinal club doctor, Dr. Hyland, who was a very good friend of mine and of all ballplayers, said I had suffered a severe concussion and a fractured skull. He recommended I not play anymore that year.

When MacPhail heard about it, he went through the roof. He began screaming that Hyland was saying that just to keep me out of the lineup. Stuff like that. He said he was going to have his own doctor examine me.

The injury occurred on a Sunday, and on Tuesday I left the hospital. I wasn't supposed to, but I told Dr. Hyland that I had to get back to Brooklyn. I insisted on leaving, whether they liked it or not. I was kind of bullheaded. Probably still am. Instead of going to Brooklyn, I stopped off in Pittsburgh, where the Dodgers had gone to play their next series. What the hell, to get to Brooklyn you have to go through Pittsburgh, don't you?

I got there in about the seventh inning. I was sitting behind the dugout, and when the guys spotted me, they figured because I was out of the hospital I must be all right. Leo poked his head up out of the dugout.

"How you feeling?" he asked.

"I'm feeling all right," I said.

"Go put your uniform on."

"I can't play."

"Put it on," he said. "I'm not going to use you."

So I went in and put my uniform on and sat on the bench. We went into extra innings. By the fourteenth inning we don't have

anybody left to hit, and the winning run is on second base. Leo
looks at me.

"You want to hit?" he asks.

Now, he didn't ask me if I could. There's no way I could. But I
wanted to. There's a big difference.

I went up to hit. Kenny Heintzelman was the pitcher. I hit a line
drive over the second baseman's head and scored the run. I rounded
first base and fell flat on my face. Passed out. I woke up in a hospital
in Pittsburgh now.

They took me back to Brooklyn, to Peck Memorial Hospital, and
the doctors there suggested I not play anymore that season. Three
weeks go by. The club is losing now. MacPhail has blasted the team,
accusing them of complacency. He's willing to bet that we're going
to blow it. What he was trying to do, of course, was jack us up.

So I volunteer to play. I guess I didn't do that badly for a couple
of days, but gradually I kept getting weaker and weaker. I was
ducking away from pitches I couldn't see—that were right down the
pipe. Babe Pinelli, the umpire, finally told Leo one day, "You'd
better get him out of there because he's not seeing them. I know he's
not seeing them."

Leo kept me in there, but I probably shouldn't have played. Fly
balls I could stick in my hip pocket I didn't see them until they were
almost past me. I went from .380 down to .310. But the big thing
wasn't the batting average; it was the fly balls that I couldn't run
down. That's what hurt us. So we blow the pennant. I say blow—we
won 104 ball games! But there's no question in my mind that by
being stubborn, I cost the Dodgers the pennant in 1942.

Do I blame Leo for keeping me in there? Listen, if you'd ever
played for him, you wouldn't ask that. You have to have played for
him. He wanted to win so bad it hurt, and I wanted to win so bad it
hurt. I don't blame Leo; I blame myself. I've heard a lot of guys
knock Leo about a lot of things. But I've always said this about him:
If you didn't know him, you'd hate his guts, but if you knew him,
you'd love him. He was the best. He was aggressive, and he fought
for you. He always fought for you.

Leo kept things boiling out there on the field. He'd get the umpires riled up, the opposing players, the fans, everybody. There

were times I thought we should've got combat pay, playing for Leo. One time in Chicago, this was in 1940, he gets on Claude Passeau something terrible. Passeau was a big guy, and mean. He keeps looking over, trying to catch who's doing the yelling. Joe Gallagher was with us then. He's a big, good-natured guy, strong as hell. He's sitting on the bench, not paying attention to anything. Leo yells something particularly rough, and Passeau has had it. He throws down his glove and starts walking in, yelling, "The guy who made that last crack doesn't have guts enough to come out and back it up." Leo looks at Gallagher, who's still preoccupied with something else, and says, "Joe, get out there and hit." So Joe picks up a bat and comes out of the dugout. Passeau walks up to him. "You need a bat, you big son of a bitch?" he says, and hauls off and belts him. Gallagher doesn't know what the hell's going on. "Claude," he says, "what's wrong with you?" Passeau belts him again, hard, but that Gallagher is like a stone wall. "Claude," he says, "don't get me mad." Passeau winds up to hit him again, and Gallagher drops the bat and grabs him and starts to squeeze. "Claude," he says, "if you don't want to talk about this thing, I'm just gonna keep squeezin' and squeezin'." They both get kicked out of the game, and I'll bet to this day Gallagher doesn't know what the hell it was all about. Next trip into Brooklyn, Passeau finds out who was on him. He winds up from the mound and fires one into the dugout at Leo. Just missed him. Just.

Like I say, Leo kept you alive out there.

We had some great times and some great ballplayers in Brooklyn back in those days. Pitchers? Give me Whitlow Wyatt. He was always one of my heroes. He was nice to me when I was a rookie at Clearwater in '39. What did he do? He said hello to me. That was a rare thing for a rookie to hear from a veteran in those days. And he worked hard and was dedicated and felt the same way I did about baseball.

If I could sculpt a statue of what a pitcher should look like, for form and grace and style, it would look like Whitlow Wyatt. I said it before, for those few years there in the early '40's he was the best right-handed pitcher I ever saw. He could do just about anything he wanted. We'd hold a meeting before the game, going over the other

Whitlow Wyatt: "Pitchers? Give me Whitlow Wyatt."

team's batting order. He'd hold the list in his hand and say, "Well, there's twenty-seven outs here." He's telling you he's already won the ball game. "First two hitters, there's no way they're gonna touch me. Third, fourth, and fifth hitters, may get a hit. Sixth hitter, he'll bloop one maybe. The last three hitters, no contest. Get me a run." And that's the way it would be. It was a pleasure to play behind him. A real gentleman, too. A prince of a man. But a hell of a competitor out on the mound. All business, and, oh, he was tough.

He knocked DiMaggio down in the fifth game of the '41 Series, I'll never forget it. In fact, I was talking to DiMaggio not too long ago about that. We were talking about that Series.

"You know who was the meanest guy I ever saw in my life?" he said.

"Yeah," I said. "Whitlow Wyatt."

"You remember that?" Joe asked.

Joe liked to dig in, you know. Wyatt didn't like that. First pitch, Joe goes down. He didn't say anything. He gets up, digs in again. Second pitch—whiz!—down he goes again.

"What the hell are you trying to do?" DiMaggio yells.

"Joe," Wyatt yells, "you do that against me again, you'll be in a squat position the rest of your life. You can hit me, but don't dig it."

He hit Marty Marion once. Marion was in the box, smoothing out the dirt, taking his time. Wyatt's standing out there, watching him with those big green eyes. When Marion's finally set, Whit yells, "You ready?" Wyatt winds up, fires it in, and down Marion goes. I guess he was expecting it, because he got up laughing. Next pitch—wham!—right in the ribs. Marion arches his back; that hurt. "Jesus Christ, Whit!" he yells.

"Don't laugh when I'm on the mound," Wyatt says.

I'll tell you a story you probably never heard before. I believe it's true—I was told by somebody in good authority that it was true—but I've got no way of proving it. MacPhail was so mad at us after we'd lost the '41 Series that he had us all traded to the St. Louis Browns. We were waived out of the National League and sold to the Browns for $3,000,000 or $4,000,000 and the Brown ball club. How'd he get us out of the league? Master waiver. He put the whole club on waivers, and everybody laughed, thought it was a big joke. Time elapsed, and we were waived out of the league. The whole club, lock, stock, and barrel.

Don Barnes was the owner of the Browns. He started running around to the St. Louis banks to raise the $3,000,000 or $4,000,000. The banks thought he was off his rocker. "What do you need these millions for, Don?" "I'm buying the Dodger ball club for St. Louis." They thought he was crazy.

Now I don't know if MacPhail would have gone through with it. I doubt it. But can you imagine what would have happened in Brooklyn if the St. Louis Browns had turned up there one day all wearing Dodger uniforms? Give *that* some thought.

After the '42 season I got to thinking about things. The war was on full blast then. I decided I'd join the Navy. So I went and took a physical. But because of all the injuries I'd had playing ball, I turned up 4-F. They told me no induction center in the country would take me. Then I get a call from the Army. I go down to the induction center, go all the way through, and I'm told to sit with the rejects.

I waited around for about an hour while they were processing everybody's papers. Then some captain came out and said, "Is there a Harold Reiser here?"

"Yes, sir," I said. I figured he's got my papers all signed up.

"Goddamn, boy," he said, "why don't you use your right name when you come into this man's army?"

"What are you talking about?" I asked.

"Aren't you Pete Reiser, the ballplayer?"

"Yes, sir."

"Goddamn," he said, "your papers have Harold Patrick. Where's Pete?"

"Pete's my nickname," I said.

He gave me a fishy look.

"What are you going to do if we let you go?" he asked.

"Play ball," I said.

He turned around. "Sergeant," he said, "fingerprint this guy and induct him."

I'm in.

Dixie Walker.

January 13, 1943, I'm inducted. I go to Fort Riley, Kansas. First two days there we're put on a 50-mile forced march, full pack. It's 15 below zero. I catch pneumonia. I wake up in an Army hospital; don't know where I'm at and care less. A doctor comes over. He's been studying my case history.

"Feeling better?" he asks.

"Yeah."

"How long you been in the Army, son?"

"Three weeks."

"How'd you ever get in?"

"They told them to fingerprint me and induct me."

"You'll be out in two weeks," he says. Pats me on the shoulder and walks away.

So I'm in the casual outfit—guys who are waiting for their medical discharge. I'm hanging around for about ten days, and then this announcement comes booming over the bitch box: "Private Reiser report to camp headquarters."

I go to camp headquarters, and I'm told to go in to see some officer. He's sitting behind the desk.

"Private Reiser?"

"Yes, sir."

He tells me who he is. Colonel so-and-so. Graduate of West Point, etc., etc. I don't know why he's telling me all this. Then he says, "One of the greatest things in my life is that I'm a sports fan. I've followed all sports, but my love is baseball."

I say to myself: Oh-oh.

"You wouldn't happen to be related to Pete, would you?"

"Yes, sir."

"You're not Pete, are you?"

"Yes, sir. I'm Pete."

"You know," he says, "I've always wanted to meet you."

"Thank you, Colonel."

He looks down at the desk. "I've got your papers right here. They want to discharge you. It's up to me to sign them or not. Tell me, what happens if I sign?"

"I'll probably play center field for the Dodgers," I said.

"I was looking forward to having a hell of a ball club here in Fort

Riley," he said. "Now do you really want to go back to Brooklyn? The war's going bad, you know. I think it would be a shame if you left the Army. No, I'm not going to sign this." He picks up the papers and rrrip! Then he says, "You don't like that, do you?"

"I didn't say anything, did I? Just tell me what I'm supposed to do."

"You don't do anything," he says.

He writes out a pass for me, from 0600 to 0600 daily. I can go anyplace I want. I also get a private room in the barracks—which made my hard-assed sergeant turn blue in the face—and no duties. I stayed there for a couple of years, playing center field for Fort Riley, Kansas.

We ended up with a hell of a ball club. We had Joe Garagiola, Lonny Frey, Creepy Crespi, Harry Walker, Al Brazle, Murry Dickson, Rex Barney, Ken Heintzelman. We whomped everybody we played.

One day a Negro lieutenant came out for the ball team. An officer told him he couldn't play. "You have to play with the colored team," the officer said. That was a joke. There was no colored team. The lieutenant didn't say anything. He stood there for a while, watching us work out. Then he turned and walked away. I didn't know who he was then, but that was the first time I saw Jackie Robinson. I can still remember him walking away by himself.

When the war ends I'm in Camp Lee, Virginia. By this time I've got enough points to get out; I don't need a medical discharge. But then they start talking about sending guys over to Europe for a year to entertain the occupational forces. I'm selected as one of the entertainers. Before I could go overseas, though, I had to take a physical. I walk in, and there's a colonel sitting at a desk going over my papers. He's got a chestful of medals and ribbons and battle stars. He's been through it all. I look at that chest, and I figure I'm gone.

He looks at me and says, "How the goddamn hell. . . . For three years you've been putting up with this crap?"

I don't say anything.

"You come with me," he says.

I went with him and he signed some papers and said to a sergeant, "I want this man discharged in twenty-four hours."

Jackie Robinson: "I can still remember him walking away by himself."

I was out the next day. That was in January of '46.

So it was back to the Dodgers. I stole home seven times in 1946. That's still a record. It was really eight, but Magerkurth missed one. It was in Chicago. I had it stolen clean, against Johnny Schmitz. I come sliding in there, and Magerkurth throws his thumb up in the air and says, "You're out!" and then says, "Goddamn, did I blow that!" He looked at me and said, "Called you out, kid. Sorry." Nothing I could say about it.

I'll tell you a great story. Professionalism. Billy Herman. One of the greatest second basemen in National League history, right? Why he isn't in the Hall of Fame is beyond me. Brilliant career with the Cubs and the Dodgers. He comes back from the service in '46 still a great star but with mileage on him now. Rickey has all these young kids coming out of the service, so what's he going to do with this thirty-six-year-old outstanding star? He trades him. Herman gets a call at two o'clock in the morning, right at the trading deadline. "You have been sold to the Boston Braves." This is two o'clock on a Sunday morning. In Brooklyn. Now who do you think played a doubleheader for Boston *in* Boston that afternoon? You're damn right. Billy Herman. He left his hotel at two o'clock in the morning and got right up there. What did Billy Herman have to prove to the Braves? That he could still play? No, it was something else: I *want* to play. That's a pro.

I mentioned Jackie Robinson. I guess you heard the story where some of the Dodgers were getting up a petition against him that first year—'47—to get guys to say they wouldn't play with him. Well, I'd had an experience when I was in the Army. This was in Richmond, Virginia. I'd just been transferred there. My daughter got very sick. So I looked up a doctor in the phone book. He told me to bring my daughter to the office. The office was in a Negro neighborhood. The doctor was a Negro. I didn't think anything of it. What the hell was the difference? He gave her a shot, penicillin I think it was, and cured her.

I told that story to one of the players who wanted me to sign the petition against Robinson. I said, "What would you have done?" He said, "I would have turned around and walked away from that neighborhood." I told him I thought he was a goddamn fool, and then I told him what he could do with his petition. Here's a guy asking me not to play ball with a man because he's black—after I'd just told him that without any doubts or hesitations I'd entrusted my daughter's health to a black man!

In '46 we're fighting the Cardinals down to the wire for the pennant. Just like old times. With two days of the season to go, I was playing with a very bad hamstring pull. I told Leo, "I can play, but I can't run." In the first inning I get on base with a walk. Next thing I know the damn steal sign is on. Jesus Christ. So I get off to take my lead, and the pitcher makes a routine throw over, and I try to slide. My spike caught, and I could hear my ankle crack. Leo comes running out. "Get up," he says, "you're all right." "Not this time, Skip. It's broke." The bone was sticking out.

Then in '47 I had that bad accident in center field, in Ebbets

Field. I almost died. I was paralyzed for ten days. You see, Rickey
(he was general manager of the Dodgers then) had cut the fences;
he took about 40 feet out of center field. So there's this long fly ball
to center, and I tell myself, "Hell, this is an easy out." I'm going full
speed . . . and oh, my God. I'd completely forgotten about the 40
feet that wasn't there anymore. When I woke up, I couldn't move.

I joined the club after five weeks, in Pittsburgh. I was out in the
field during batting practice, and Clyde King ran into me. We
bumped heads. I was knocked out, but I didn't feel that bad. That
night I was sitting in the Schenley Hotel with Pee Wee. He looked
at me kind of funny. "You all right?" he asked. "Yeah. Why?" I said.
"What's that big knot on your head?" I touched it and it felt like a
big boil. "Maybe you'd better get the doctor," he said.

The doctor came, had one look at me and called Mr. Rickey in
Brooklyn. Next thing I know I'm being flown to Johns Hopkins in
Baltimore to be operated on. I had a blood clot. I'd had it from the
wall injury, and when King ran into me, that moved it. They told me
I'd never play again. But I went back. Played the last two months
and hit .309. But I could feel myself getting weaker and weaker and
weaker.

We won the pennant. We're in the Series against the Yankees. I
slide into second to break up a double play and feel something go in
my ankle. The doctor X-rayed it that night.

"You've got a broken ankle," he says. "A very slight fracture."

Boy, was I ticked off! Did it have to happen right in the middle of
a World Series?

"Listen," I told the doctor, "don't say anything. Just put a tight
bandage on it, say it's a bad sprain, and that I'm through for the rest
of the Series. That's all."

I was afraid that if he said it was broken, Rickey would give me a
dollar-a-year contract next year—meaning I would have to prove I
was physically fit to play before I could sign a regular contract.

Then we get into this game where Bevens is pitching a no-hitter.
It's the last of the ninth, two out, and Al Gionfriddo is on first.
Shotton sends me up to hit. Gionfriddo steals second, and why he
did that I'll never know, because it wasn't on. Then Bucky Harris,
who was managing the Yankees, told Bevens to put me on. The

winning run. Pretty unorthodox move. Because of the bad ankle, Eddie Miksis ran for me; and then Lavagetto hit that double down the right-field line, and Bevens lost his no-hitter and his ball game all at once.

DiMaggio told me years later that Harris knew I had a broken ankle, but that he still didn't want to pitch to me. "He'll still swing, ankle or no ankle," Harris said. That was a nice tribute to me, but it cost him.

In '48 Rickey didn't want me to play at all. He said he would pay me if I sat down all year. Being bullheaded, I said I wanted to play. But by that time all of those injuries were beginning to take their toll. My record after the war was all right, but nothing like it had been before. Something was gone. It had always been so easy for me, but now it became a struggle. I was only twenty-nine, but the fun and the pure joy of it were gone. When something that you like

"I stole home seven times in 1946." One of the times, August 14, 1946, against the Giants. The catcher is Walker Cooper. The pitch is being called a strike, but batter Bruce Edwards' attention is occupied elsewhere. New York Daily News *Photo.*

to do, and that you always did well, becomes hard to do, that's the time to get out of it. No way was I going to go out there and make an ass of myself.

But you know what really bothers me? I meet people today, and they say, "Oh, you're the nut that used to run into the walls." That's a hell of a way to be remembered.

But as I said before, it was my style of playing, the only way I knew how. You can't turn a thing like that off. Why should you? It's born in you, it's part of you. It *is* you.

No, I don't have any regrets. Not about one damned thing. I've had a lot of good experiences in my life, and they far outnumber the bad. Good memories are the greatest thing in the world, and I've got a lot of those. And one of the sweetest is of the kid standing out on the green grass in center field, with the winning runs on base, thinking, Hit it to me. *Hit it to me.*

INDEX